Unyielding

Out of the Box, Book 11

Robert J. Crane

Unyielding
Out of the Box #11
Robert J. Crane
Copyright © 2016 Revelen Press
All Rights Reserved.

1st Edition

Dedicated to the great Jo Evans, whose
incredible contributions to the *Sanctuary* series
ended up left out of the credits in *Legend*,
and who, honestly, deserves more than one book
dedicated to her. But if I had to pick only one,
I think *Unyielding* is the one that fits her best—
in the best possible way.

1.

I woke up alone, in a bed that wasn't my own, as I had for months. The smell of stale cigarette smoke had long ago settled into the furnishings around me, and into my nose, a subtle, constant irritation. I blinked, looking at the thin slits of light that made their way through the blinds into my room. It was a small room, though it was probably not any smaller than my last.

It felt smaller, though.

I drew a deep breath, sucking in the cool mid-morning air. The red clock on the dresser at the foot of my bed told me it was 10:56 a.m. I pushed my face back into the pillow. The rough, buzz-cut sides of my head scraped against the pillowcase. I still wasn't used to that feeling of having a mohawk. It wouldn't have been my first choice, but I'd been living in Cedar City, Utah, for months, and between the hair, the glasses and the new wardrobe, no one yet had realized that I was the top slot on the FBI's most wanted list.

I fumbled at the nightstand and grabbed my glasses. I'd stolen them from a hipster in Denver, Colorado, and popped the lenses out. I'd had the lenses replaced with non-prescription ones in Las Vegas, right before I picked Cedar City as the place I was going to hide out. It had been an easy decision, picking Cedar City. I'd just looked at a map, recalled all the places I'd been in my law enforcement career, and found one that I had zero ties to.

Et voila. Cedar City, Utah. Population: 29,162. Plus one.

It was a nice town, nestled against a series of brown

mountains that rose in the distance. Quiet, bordering on sleepy, really. I had no complaints on that score. Given how I'd left my last hometown, action was not something I was seeking. Quiet was.

I rolled out of bed, my feet touching the thinly carpeted floor. I smacked my lips together, my mouth dry like I'd gone for a flight low over the desert sands. It was like that every morning, the cottonmouth of a dry climate. My ears itched every day like someone had sucked all the moisture out of them, and when I scratched them, little flakes of skin came out like ear dandruff.

Still better than the fifteen inches of snow Minneapolis had probably had by now, though.

There was a calendar pegged to my wall, with the days crossed off. I didn't know why I was crossing off days. It's not like something important was coming up. I wasn't working a job or anything, just existing on a daily basis, sliding through life in Cedar City while trying not to draw any attention to myself. I woke up in the mornings, mentally groused about the dryness, watched TV, wandered out to the corner store for a little while, hit the Walmart if I was in the mood to, ate at Sushi Burrito, IHOP or Denny's, and watched cable news throughout the day.

If my old psychiatrist, Dr. Zollers, had known how I was filling my time, he probably would have put me on suicide watch. And it might not have been a bad idea.

I scratched at an itch on my forehead as I kneaded my toes against the pitiful carpeting beneath them. I grabbed a hair tie off the end table and put my mohawk in a ponytail. I stood up and wandered out of the bedroom and into the bathroom, staring at myself. What remained of my hair was pink, the color of Pepto-Bismol. My eyes were green now, the result of contacts I'd picked up in St. George or someplace; I couldn't recall where. I had other disguises at the ready, hidden here and elsewhere. Sooner or later, even as dumb as the people in charge of hunting me were, they were bound to find me, and I'd need to run.

Again.

That was all I was waiting for, really, for them to catch up to me, so I could start this whole process over again by rabbiting hard to my next bolt hole. I looked at myself in the mirror, and I looked ... thinner. I'd never been a Skinny Minnie, but I was getting closer now. I was eating less, sleeping less, and I might have considered taking up smoking if not for the gawdawful smell that already permeated my new residence. I needed something to soothe my nerves and fill my time, and booze wasn't the answer. At least not in Utah. They didn't make it easy here, and even with as much time as I had to fill, I'd gotten lazy about how many hoops I was willing to jump through.

I wandered out of my bathroom, adjusting the strap of my wife-beater-style shirt, scratching at myself beneath the cloth boxer briefs I'd bought at Walmart on the cheap. It wasn't a look I would have been sporting normally, but that's the first rule of changing one's identity—don't ever look like yourself.

I settled into my easy chair, one loose spring poking up into my right butt cheek, and I growled. The spring had been busted for a month, but I wasn't motivated enough to do anything about it, at least not yet. I turned on the TV with a click, setting the remote on the little table next to me, and fished down below into the magazine rack beneath the surface, coming up with a protein bar. I ripped it open, dropped the wrapper in the trash, and starting chewing on almonds and some sort of sweet peanut butter and honey flavor that was holding it together as I stared, eyes half-lidded, at the TV.

"... and it's day thirty-five of the manhunt for Sienna Nealon," a handsome young reporter was saying, microphone held in front of his chin, "with authorities in the FBI capture team still claiming to have abundant leads. They are, however, still encouraging anyone with any information to please contact them at the tip line—"

I snorted with bitter laughter. Yeah, the news was still covering me almost twenty-four seven. It wasn't even the least bit nice, either. Most days, I found at least five completely manufactured stories about me on the news—on average, two would involve sightings, never anywhere near Cedar City, two were about past misdeeds I'd done, at least seventy-five percent of them total bullshit, and the last was generally an update from FBI Director Andrew Phillips, whose standard-issue, "We have no further information at this time," was the entirety of the report six days out of seven.

Watching cable news report on how the world was doing with me missing? Well, it wasn't exactly *It's a Wonderful Life*. Watching this crap, you might think the entire planet was at peace except for the United States, which was clearly suffering from an advanced case of Sienna Nealon Being the Worst Thing in the World. All the other problems must have been solved, I guess, because they sure as shit weren't talking about them. It was all hunting me and human interest stories. A more cynical person might have thought the books were being cooked, the deck was being stacked—

Oh, wait. I was as cynical as it got.

But I still couldn't pry myself away from watching the self-hate fest that was every major news network. I glared at the reporter, who had stopped to take a question from in studio. "… Any idea," the anchor was asking, "… when we'll have an update from the FBI?"

The reporter on scene nodded. "The FBI is intending to have a full press conference later this afternoon." He smiled bleakly. "For those keeping score at home, this will be only the second press conference in the course of this investigation—"

That made me sit up. Phillips had been stonewalling for damned good reason; the FBI didn't tend to comment on ongoing investigations, and answering questions at a presser during an active investigation meant sending in someone to lie like a mofo to try and dodge the questions they didn't want answered. Questions like, "Do you actually have any idea where this fugitive is?" The answer to which was a soundbite that would be played for the next month on repeat loop and make Phillips look like an ass. Phillips didn't like to look like an ass, this much I knew about the bastard. (Okay, I knew a lot more than that about the bastard. He had been my boss, after all, before climbing the ladder to become FBI Director.)

If he was holding a press conference on this case, that probably meant something was happening.

Something big.

I swallowed, saliva barely present in my dry, desert-filled mouth as I sat forward in my chair, wondering what the hell it could be.

2.

Scott Byerly

"We need to do this fast," Scott whispered in the mid-morning quiet. There was a sleepy little mid-sized city around him that was clearly awake, just not terribly busy. He wondered when—or if—this place ever did get humming. A big tractor trailer rattled by, its cargo made up of logs, the engine rumbling as it down shifted on the main street. "She can't have a whisper of warning that we're coming, or this is going to turn messy fast."

"Whisper quiet, got it," Augustus Coleman said, snapping his M4 Carbine up in a ready position. He was garbed entirely in black tactical gear except for his head, which was exposed. It seemed like a good play; if Sienna Nealon had an ounce of mercy left in that ragged mess she called a soul, it'd be for someone she cared for, like Augustus. Or—

"Speed is the name of the game," Reed Treston said, nodding once, sharply. He, too, was wearing the black tactical gear of a man about to take part in a SWAT raid. He was carrying a submachine gun and checked the chamber before letting the slide click closed. The smell of gun oil wafted up into Scott's nostrils and he flared them, blowing a breath out to cleanse the scent before it stuck in his nose.

"She could run, you know," Friday said, his chest swelling as he Hulked-up for entry. He didn't have a rifle; he was slung with some unbelievably huge machine gun that looked like it belonged in a war zone rather than small-town

6

America. His chest expanded from normal size to something that would have looked bizarrely out of place even on a bodybuilder in the Mr. Universe contest. His biceps were cut, each one the size of a giant tortoise shell. His forearms looked bigger around than a hog's head—not that Scott had had much experience with hog's heads. He'd seen one in a specialty butcher shop one time.

"Yeah, she might rabbit if she sees it's us," Augustus said, straitlaced and serious.

"Don't bet your life on it," Reed said tightly. "She's 'round the bend, there's no predicting what she's going to do. She could kill us all, snap flame blasts that'll cook us in our tac gear and roast marshmallows over our corpses." He fidgeted with his weapon, checking the chamber again and accidentally ejecting a bullet in the process.

"Damn," Augustus said, showing the first sign of regret. "I didn't figure she'd lose her mind like this, but ... damn, y'know?"

"She's been going downhill for a while," Reed said tightly, adjusting the sling of his weapon.

"She's been at the bottom of the hill for a long damned time," Scott said, putting a glare on Reed that got returned with slightly less force. "I'm just glad you and your team finally realized that."

"Let's just get this over with," Reed said, and he pulled his hand back from the slide of his gun, stopping himself before he fiddled with it again.

"Right," Scott said, and he could feel the nervous energy churning in his belly. He spread out the blueprints on the table in the center of their panel van. They were parked on a side street, and had the back door open, letting the cool air filter in. The van had cameras hidden in the sides, and he glanced continuously at the angles of approach around them, making sure that she wasn't sneaking up to ambush them as they did the final planning. "We enter here, front door, breach and clear," he ran his finger through the map of the living room past the entry. "Reed is on point, face out—"

"The better for her to disintegrate it," Reed muttered.

"—Augustus, you're secondary," Scott went on. "Friday,

you're going around the back to intercept if she tries to flee out the rear window."

"Where are you gonna be?" Augustus asked. There was no hint of sarcasm, which was a welcome change from their first few weeks together. He'd settled down nicely, though, now that he was past the adjustment period and understood the horror of what they were up against.

"Right behind you," Scott said. "If she uses fire, I'll douse her as best I can." He fiddled with his vest; it had two tanks of compressed $H2O$ built into the back, as well as a canteen that was filled to the brim. He'd been prepping for this encounter for weeks, and all he needed to do was flick a switch built into his glove and he'd have enough water to drown the entire room with plenty left to spare. "I'm not going to lead because she's more likely to kill me than either of you, but I won't be but a step behind. Okay?" He looked around for concord, but settled for a lack of open antipathy.

Reed seemed sullen, but nodded once. "Let's get her."

"Yeah, let's," Friday said, and jumped down out the back doors. The entire frame of the van bounced. "I know you guys are hoping for some fun on your end, but I hope she runs right out into me." He fussed with his machine gun, adjusting it so he could look over the sights. It was a monstrous beast, but then, so was Friday. He was still hiding his face behind that weird black mask, though. Months of working together, and Scott still had no idea what he looked like beneath it.

"Go time," Scott said, and jumped out of the van after Friday. The suspension didn't protest nearly as much when he did it. He wasn't carrying a machine gun, though—or even a rifle. He had a standard Sig Sauer P226 in one hand, the same kind the Secret Service used—and kept his other free in case he needed to deploy the emergency water. At this elevation, and as dry as the air was, he'd need every drop.

"Let's make some noise," Augustus said as he hopped down out of the van. The local cops were about a hundred yards away, keeping a nice little cordon up around the street. Scott stared at their target in the distance; it was an old apartment building that looked rough, its planks of wood siding having long ago turned grey with age and hard weathering. Whoever was living here didn't exactly have a bundle of money, that was for sure. It was a small enough town to lack the ubiquitous cameras on every street corner that could be co-opted to scan with facial recognition software, and yet not so small that everybody knew everybody and any stranger would be immediately noticed. A college town, with lots of new arrivals every fall.

It was the perfect place for a young woman to hide.

Friday trotted off at a run. Scott led the way toward the front of the apartment complex, threading his way through the not-quite-empty parking lot. The police had cleared the complex quietly, and they'd surveilled the building for a couple hours and seen movement behind the blinds in their target, so ... someone was here.

"Go quiet," Scott whispered, so low that even meta hearing wouldn't pick him up unless it was close. He had a mic on his collar, and he could hear Friday puffing into it.

"Rounding the corner," Friday said. "Will be in position in ten seconds."

"Let's go, let's go!" Scott hissed, catching the railing to the external staircase with one hand and hurrying up on quiet footsteps. He was leading the way, though he would have to pull back and let Augustus and Reed take the fore when he got to the front door for the breach and clear. He wasn't excited about that, by any means, but he'd finally begun to trust the two of them after these last few weeks. That hadn't been easy, but he'd seen enough out of both now to know that whatever their personal feelings about Sienna, they were as convinced as he was that she was a menace.

A menace they were going to deal with together.

There was one question lingering in Scott's mind, though, and he paused at the top of the stairs, letting Augustus go by and catching Reed, stopping him short before they got too close to the door. "You sure you're ready to do this?" Scott asked, and caught a flash of angry brown eyes in response. "She's your sister. There's no shame in saying you don't have it in you to—"

"I'll do what it takes," Reed said, yanking his arm out of

Scott's grasp with a snap. His eyes were burning, his tanned cheeks a bright scarlet. Scott hadn't even meant it as a challenge; he'd kept his voice low, tone even so as not to provoke offense. Offense had been taken anyway, apparently. Reed moved past Augustus to rest by the door, taking a short, quiet draw of breath and motioning the two of them to get into position.

Scott nodded and stacked up behind Augustus. He felt the tension rise inside him, stomach twisting. This was it, the moment of truth. This was where his new deputies earned their spurs, where all the time he'd spent chasing the metaphorical—and occasionally literal—dragon that was Sienna Nealon would finally pay dividends. He caught Reed's gaze and saw it still burned. He'd do what it took, Scott was pretty sure. Scott held up three fingers and counted it down—*three ... two ... one ...*

Reed sprang off the door frame and kicked down the door, gun up and ready to shoot whatever was waiting for them on the other side.

3.

Sienna

I sat in my chair uneasily, that lone, annoying spring poking me in the butt, cable news anchors jabbering their stupidity incessantly, and I waited. Waited for something terrible to happen as I stole a look over my shoulder at the door to my apartment. Waiting. Interminable, boring, sitting in near-silence, listening for noise outside ... waiting.

Nothing but quiet, and the low-volume blathering of idiot cable news anchors.

Waiting.

Waiting for something to happen.

4.

Reed was in before the door was finished coming off its hinges, charging over the fallen wooden blockage and into the apartment, weapon up and ready. Augustus blew in right after him, his own carbine sights up as he looked left, then right, clearing the corners.

The smell of wood dust was heavy where Reed's entry had ripped the screws out of the frame. Scott inhaled the scent as he came off the wall and followed Augustus, his pistol up and sweeping. They were taking no chances in this case, their trigger discipline put on hold to make sure that if presented with a shot, they could take it in a second. His finger rested just on the trigger, making sure he didn't line the gun up with either of his compatriots.

The apartment was dark, light barely filtering in through the shades. Reed was already sweeping ahead, Augustus a few steps behind him, through a living room that sported a table covered in pizza boxes. There was a stale smell in the air, like someone hadn't flushed the toilet in a while.

Scott followed after them, his gaze sweeping the room. It was clear of people, that much he was sure of, and they moved forward as a unit, not quite running but not walking, either, boots thudding softly on the carpeting. Their steps were measured and Reed turned a corner to enter the lone bedroom, dipping out of sight for a mere second—

"CONTACT!" Reed shouted, and the sound of gunshots

followed, three loud, sharp, deafening staccato bursts. Augustus swept around the corner after him, out of Scott's view, weapon up and ready to assist.

Scott hit the panic button.

The caps blew off the compressed H2O containers on his back and he guided the water through the empty space in the living room. He swept a television off its stand with the bulb of water, and it crackled as it gained an electrical charge for a second before harmlessly dispersing it into a nearby wall with a fizzing pop that burned the drywall and started a small fire. Scott absently swept the water over the burgeoning flame as he came around the corner, ready to direct it toward Sienna with everything he had—

"She's down," Reed said, holding his weapon before him, smoke still sizzling out of the barrel. The smell of gunpowder reeked in the apartment's confined space, and Scott let his glance followed the barrel of Reed's—and Augustus's, now—guns.

A dark-haired woman lay sprawled on the floor, curled against the ground, her body arched like she was clutching her belly as she'd fallen. Scott stared into the semi-darkness, trying to penetrate it, to see the woman's face, but it was futile. Her head was turned so that she was facing away from the three of them, away from the door, and a slow pool of dark liquid was spreading from beneath her.

Scott started forward, but Augustus put a hand on his shoulder to halt him. "I doubt that would kill her."

"What would you sugg—" Scott started, but three more shots answered for him as Reed's gun fired again. Scott flinched; the noise was deafening in such a confined space, but even more than that was the unreserved lethality that Reed had employed. Scott looked back at the fallen woman; all three shots had caught her in the back of the head, and there was a commensurate splatter from the carpeting to the box springs and mattress beyond, which were laid directly on the floor with no bed frame. Blood dripped like paint spots spattered by a careless brush.

"What the hell?" Scott asked in quiet astonishment. Something had snapped in him to see this, the unrestrained violence unleashed on a fallen body. He looked at Reed, his mouth fallen open. "What … what did you …?"

Reed had a hard look, no hint of remorse. "She's dangerous, and she can heal from shots to center mass. You know that." He kept his weapon pointed at the fallen form. "She can't heal from that, though. I don't think." His finger still hovered over the trigger. "You want to check her while I cover you?"

Scott felt a sudden spring of nausea taking hold in his belly, and he wavered, afraid he might topple over where he stood. Augustus's hand was still on his wrist, and he managed to get control of himself, to remove his arm from the black man's grip. "I—yeah, okay." He composed himself, taking a breath, and stepped forward.

A small snuffling sound from beneath the woman made him jump back as soon as he had started forward. There was a faint motion, small, too small to be anything but nerves twitching, but it startled him nonetheless.

"You don't think that's …?" Augustus's voice trailed off.

"I'll just make sure—" Reed started.

"No!" The answer burst out of Scott with more violence than the last three shots. He gave a look that quelled Reed— that trigger-happy bastard. Scott pulled his water reserve forward, a bulbous lake drifting through the air, just in case Reed was right. He could imprison her in water, possibly, if she was truly injured. Finish her that way, if he had to.

Scott stepped forward, pausing to stand over the body. Her dark hair lay pooled on the ground, and hints of pale flesh peeked out at the temples. It certainly looked like her, at least from the back, with the wider hips, her body almost tented where it lay. "Did she fall on something?" he asked.

"A rifle, I think," Reed said. "I didn't get a clear look before I opened up, but I could tell she had something in both hands." His gaze was coldly inscrutable, but then, that was how he'd been throughout this entire process. The hardest converts to this mission were the truest believers, at least that was how it seemed to Scott. He'd been a pretty hard convert himself, until he realized exactly how badly Sienna Nealon had screwed him over.

He looked down at the body. There was no breath being drawn, which was a good sign that Reed had done as he'd hoped. Scott eased forward another step, trying to get a look at the face. He could see where the last three shots had torn through, and wondered if making a positive ID was even going to be possible. He hesitated, not wanting to touch her, his breath sticking in his throat. His hand shook a little, and he wondered if it was from the shock of the sudden, unexpected nature of those last shots—something about them had shaken him up in a way he couldn't recall feeling in a long time. There was an animal-like revulsion crawling around inside him now, tickling his skin. The whole place reeked, too, and he wished he could spare a hand to hold over his nose.

Scott had pictured this moment—standing over Sienna Nealon's downed corpse—a thousand times since he'd taken the job of bringing her down. It hadn't ever quite been like this in his head, though. It had been a glorious struggle, a fight to the finish in which she'd admitted her wrongs and surrendered, or screamed defiance to the end and gone down in a hail of bullets. Those were his fantasies, anyway, the things he imagined sitting at his desk after a long week. It had been a worthy goal toward which he'd been working all this while.

None of those fantasies had ended like this, though, in a two-bit town, in a run-down apartment, with the girl in question gunned down from behind and then shot through the skull without mercy while she lay there bleeding. By her own brother, no less.

He leaned over, trying to maintain his balance while stealing a look at her. She was slumped sideways, head against the floor, something keeping her belly from touching the ground. There were three definite red spots in her back, the blood oozing but no longer pumping from them. Reed's first bursts had taken her below the ribcage, around the spine. That would have paralyzed her, Scott supposed, trying to keep his calm by being analytical rather than reacting to the horror of what he was seeing as he leaned further over.

Because her face was—

15

He ignored the missing chunk in her forehead, and the hints that the cheekbone nearest the floor was gone, a mess of crimson spreading in the beige carpeting beneath her face. Likewise, her chin seemed to simply disappear along with the bottom portion of her mouth, her jaw ending inches shy of where it should have. He stared at the eye he could see. It stared down, glassy and dull, reminding him of one he'd seen in a dead deer that had been mounted on a friend's wall.

The eye was not blue.

"It could be contacts," Scott muttered to himself, breath catching in his throat. He stared at the forehead, or what remained of it, and at the nose, which was rounded. The skin was pale, though death surely had stolen some of the color. He stared again at the nose, trying to reconcile it with the eye color, with the shape of the eye, and all the while he took another breath, sharper this time, and another, going from breathing deep to a sharp panting, his breaths running away with him—

"Dude, settle," Augustus said, "you're gonna hyperventilate."

"It isn't her," Scott said, cold horror rushing over his skin, causing it to tingle. He felt suddenly clammy, flushed and feverish, the world around him hot and sticky, though he knew it wasn't really—

Because they were in Cheyenne, Wyoming, on a November morning, the temperature was close to forty degrees, and there was not a reason in the world why his body should have reacted like it was a Georgia swamp in the summertime.

Scott's legs wobbled and he collapsed, fell right on his backside, landing beside the dead woman, feeling the numbness creep up his legs. His tailbone cried in protest, but he ignored it until the body gave another faint lurch, and he turned his eyes away, across the room, where he saw—

A crib, all done in white, blankets rumpled, no sign of its occupant.

"Oh … oh …" Scott's voice failed, him falling to quiet, and now his skin froze, the clutch of fear grabbing him. "Oh, God … no …"

"What are you on about now—" Augustus stepped into the room, followed his gaze, and all the starch went out of him. "Awww ... awww ... no ..."

Scott's hands felt as though they were no longer his own. Shaking, he put them on the girl, the woman, the one who was dead and was most definitely not Sienna Nealon. He tugged at her. She moved with his pressure, rolling with little effort as he pulled her toward him, onto her back. He caught a glimpse of her remaining eye, rolling with her body, and of the face that was not Sienna's, like a jigsaw puzzle with pieces missing—

The moment she was moved, the small, snuffling noise became a cry that almost drowned out the screaming somewhere in the back of Scott's head. It was sharp, and pained, and the tiny, pink-fleshed bundle that had lain beneath the woman's body drew screaming, shuddering breaths, its lungs turned out in fear, fury, and confusion.

It was an infant beneath the body, and Scott watched as blood oozed out of a bullet hole in the child's leg, watched in horror, and shoved his hand down urgently. "Oh—oh—oh, God—" he said, and his brain connected for a moment with his mouth, and nonsense stopped falling out and sense emerged. "Augustus—get the—get the paramedics in here now! Get the—get—get HELP!"

The baby screamed in pain, and Augustus's feet pounded the floor as he ran out of the apartment. Scott picked up the baby gingerly, sparing a last, horrorstruck gaze at the dead mother as he cradled the child in his arms, desperately trying to staunch the bleeding. There wasn't much, fortunately; it looked like the bullet might have just nicked the leg. Scott tried to catch his breath, hands still shaking, and then reached out with his mind as he stood, raising the child with him. Blood was mostly water, after all—

The paramedics rushed in moments later, moments that felt like an eternity. The entire apartment was soaked from where Scott had let go of the water that he'd brought into the battle. He hadn't even noticed. Shoes squished against wet carpet; the body had been washed up against the bed by the force of the flood when it had become uncontained.

17

The child was still crying, though it was less sharp now, less pained, and Scott handed over the baby to the paramedics with numb hands. His mind stayed where it was needed, though; no hint of red . He heard no words spoken, though he knew dimly the paramedics were speaking, were putting the child on a gurney, were restraining it as it flailed in protest at being taken from Scott's chest, its cries nearly exhausted now. He could hear them, but barely, like a voice screaming in the back of his own head.

He kept his mind on that wound. He could feel it at a distance even as the paramedics raced out of the apartment with the child, could feel the little plug of liquid he held in place like a dam against the rush of blood trying to escape the child's wound. Scott's breaths came raggedly, his brow was coated in sweat, and he mopped at his forehead as he stood up straight. He almost didn't feel like he had the power to impel his legs to walk.

But I have to, he thought, his mind still on holding in the blood in the infant's body. *I have to.*

He started forward uneasily, toward the bedroom door. Reed was still standing there where he'd left him, his expression hard as stone, resolute. His gun was still in hand, still raised, eye still fixed on the sight. Scott halted, then stepped aside.

The gun was still pointed at the girl's corpse, barrel lined up with the back of her head.

"... Reed?" Scott asked, keeping his mind on holding in that blood from the tiny body that was receding into the distance. He didn't care how far away it went; if they'd airlifted the child from Cheyenne to Maine, he would have given everything he had to keep that blood in place. It would go nowhere while he was still breathing, just to the heart, to the little lungs, and back again in that infinite loop. He could feel it in the baby, the natural flow, and he refused to let it go, even as the question stirred to mind.

Reed did not move, just kept his gun fixed on the corpse. He blinked, staring at it. "We didn't get her," he said simply, not coming off the sights, not lowering the weapon.

"No," Scott said, casting a look back at the dead woman.

"No, we … we didn't." He eased toward Reed, gently putting a hand on the barrel of the submachine gun. He pushed it down, so that it was no longer aiming at the body.

Reed blinked, then looked up at him, letting the weapon go. It rested in the sling against his chest. Reed took a breath of his own, then another, and it sounded like the tension was leaving him. "I was so sure it was her." His voice had a dreamlike quality.

Scott just stared at him. "But … it wasn't."

"I know." Reed blinked once more, then seemed to relax. "Next time. We'll get her next time."

And he walked out without another word, without a look back, and without a hint of remorse.

5.

Gerry Harmon

Being the president of the United States is a funny thing. Everyone seems to think you have much more power than you actually do. Your most loyal supporters seem to believe you're God, able to do no wrong, regardless of how you work the levers of power. Your most loyal detractors will never believe you do anything right, ever, even if you were sign a bill into law granting them every single thing they've ever hoped for. Most of the electorate seems to fall somewhere between the ranks of the loving and the loathing, and into what I call the largely indifferent.

Actually ... quite an enormous number fall into that realm.

Meanwhile, it's really like any other job, in its way. Except the hours are beyond terrible. You're on call all the time. I was once woken at three-thirty in the morning after getting to bed at one-thirty following a long day of campaigning and fundraising, because some idiot in Russia had decided to blow up a train station. True story. Given the hour, I naturally didn't care much about a train station in Russia, but the president of the United States has to care about every event on the world stage, no matter how small.

And for the most part ... I do care. When I'm fully awake. Which is most days.

But this ... was not one of those days.

"Mr. President?" Serena Abernathy asked me. She was a tall, willowy brunette, classically pretty, dressed in a nice little skirt that extended to mid-calf, and a pink t-shirt that said, "I Heart My Class." I blinked as I stared at her, unaware that I'd gotten lost in thought. Lost in thought*s*, to be more precise.

"Yes, I'm sorry, Ms. Abernathy," I said, putting on my most charming smile. It was the one I used for campaigning. "What were you saying?"

"That we're understaffed," she said, not really reproachful. She was being blunt, but she wasn't unpleasant about it, as some tended to be.

I looked away from Ms. Abernathy and out at her charges. We were standing on a playground, a small one, in the middle of a city—Chicago, that was it. I forget sometimes, because I go to so many cities. I'd slept on Air Force One on the flight in, and sometimes I get a little muddled. I looked around, trying to orient myself, but I was in one of the suburbs, and downtown wasn't immediately visible. "You've been understaffed for a while, haven't you?" I asked, trying to keep the conversation going without giving it my full attention. Every school in the world was understaffed.

"Yes, sir," she said softly. "And your education bill ... it doesn't really do anything about that." The cries of the children at play were loud, disruptive. They made following the conversation even more difficult. Ms. Abernathy waited in silence for a moment, her question unanswered and then changed the subject on me rather abruptly. "You don't have any children of your own, do you?" It was just as well she changed the subject, because my response to her first comment wouldn't have been likely to please her.

"Hm?" I asked, to give myself a moment to respond without profanity. Her intent was mostly innocent, but there was a hint of an edge beneath it: *Oh, you don't have children, so how can you possibly understand what we parents go through?* I measured my response carefully. "No, unfortunately not," I said with an edge of sadness. "My wife died at age thirty, while we were still ... contemplating ... having a family." I let my gaze drift over the playground, a modern knot of metal and plastic, with green slides and blue steel barriers around the top platform to keep children from falling off in fits of ecstatic joy. There were twelve up on the platform by my count, and only two slides.

"I'm so sorry," Ms. Abernathy said, and there was genuine sincerity in her voice.

"It was a long time ago," I said. She'd already known that my wife had died young, of course. She was just fishing for my reaction, to see that I was human. I gave her what she was looking for. "Of course … not a day goes by that I don't miss Elizabeth." I added the appropriate amount of staring, slightly sad-eyed, into the distance.

It hit the mark. "I'm so sorry, I shouldn't have …"

"You're fine," I said, with just a tinge of faint, faint recrimination to warn her away from picking at that particular scab. One of the kids had caught my attention, trying to squeeze through the bars of the top platform. I pointed at him. "Uhh, I think he—um—" I stopped just short of shouting at him to knock it off before he hurt himself.

"Jonah!" Ms. Abernathy called, catching the little bandit as he wriggled through. Honestly, who manufactures these things where kids can wriggle through? It's as though they don't know what their equipment is used for. "We don't use the playground inappropriately."

Jonah, showing less remorse for his transgression than Ms. Abernathy had for her invasive questioning of the president, pulled his head back through the bars and ran toward the slide. There, he pushed three children out of the way and forced himself down the chute.

"No, wait—" I started to chastise him, but it was fruitless, he was down before anyone realized what I was even saying.

Little Jonah collided with a child at the bottom of the slide who was still in the process of extricating herself and her pretty little pink dress from the opening at the bottom. There was a solid SMACK! as two heads collided, and I cringed at the sound, audible even where I was standing. The tears started immediately, of course, and that made me cringe further, though I desperately tried to hide it. Ms. Abernathy darted off without so much as a farewell, off to soothe her troubled charges.

It was just as well. She was insufferable.

"Mr. President," Jana Gordon slipped up next to me. Her official title was something like "Personal Aide to the President"; she was essentially the person who kept my life and schedule running on time wherever I went. Jana was young and vivacious, but also serious and professional. She didn't smile much in public, which was a good call on her part. Too unserious and you get a reputation for being frivolous when you're a young woman of her age. It's a prejudice of the old against the young.

"Jana," I said. She'd been with me for several years, and I'd become quite accustomed to her steadfast way of doing things.

"Your call with the premier of Revelen has been delayed to eleven o'clock," Jana said, spouting out the next few details of my schedule.

"I hope it's due to severe intestinal malady on her part."

"She didn't specify," Jana said, glazing over my unkind words. There were a few flashes as the cameras here for photo ops caught me talking to her, smiling as I always did. "The Joint Chiefs have a briefing for you on the escalating situation in the Middle East—"

"Is there ever not an escalating situation in the Middle East?"

"Sometimes they de-escalate," Jana deadpanned. "Because if all they did was escalate, they would have—"

"Reached the sun by now, yes," I said, catching the thrust of her joke before she could punchline it. "What about the progress on the education bill?" I gave her all my attention now, and registered her unease.

"Speaker Thurston is working on it, sir," she said, and I knew she wasn't telling me the whole truth.

"You're far too edgy for that to be all."

"She says …" Jana hesitated, "… that we're going to miss it by three votes."

"Three?" My eyebrows went up involuntarily.

"That's what the majority whip says."

"Who are the three most on the fence?"

"I don't know for sure, sir—"

"Don't give me that," I said, turning to look at where Ms. Abernathy was trying to console poor Jonah, victim of his own stupidity and intemperance. "You either have a very clear idea yourself or you know someone who does."

"Probably McSorley, McCluskey, and Shane." Jana spat out the three names without hesitation once I prodded her. She didn't like the politics part of this job. She thought it was indelicate, so she played coy instead, trying to avoid giving me bad news.

"Set up a meeting," I said. "With them."

"You're going to try and coerce them?" She sounded surprised. She shouldn't have.

"They call me the Persuader-in-Chief, you know."

"I know, sir, but—"

"You think they're too entrenched in their position," I said, finally getting to the nub of it. "That when you say that they're mostly on the fence, it doesn't mean they're actually on the fence at all." I turned my head from the playground spectacle to give her my full attention. "They're firmly against it, they're just less firmly against it than anyone else because they're members of my party rather than the opposition."

Jana stared at me for a second, then shrugged. "They're unlikely to move. The bill lacks the carve-outs they're seeking on—"

"Yes, I am aware," I said. "Listen … we need this victory. Just a little thing to whet the appetite of the public."

"The base hates it."

"Yes, well, you can't please all the people all the time."

"Abe Lincoln said that, sir, and it wasn't 'please,' it was 'fool.' He was talking about—"

"The electorate. That's what he was talking about." I looked back at little Jonah, now on his feet. His victim, the little girl who'd suffered for his stupidity, was still sniffling, leaning hard against Ms. Abernathy, who was very, very concerned about them both. About their feelings. It was touching, really.

Of course, if Jonah had just been willing to follow the rules, it never would have happened. But that's what people don't see, because they lack perspective. Jonah couldn't see the girl at the bottom of the slide, because he wasn't far enough away from the situation—like I was—to know what would happen if he came down in a hurry. He didn't know.

But I knew. I had the gift and the torment of seeing, of knowing things that others didn't. I had perspective, could see the game unfolding, could see the problems, and I knew I could solve them. All of them. I'd been working toward it for the last seven years.

The education bill wouldn't solve all the problems. Slapping around three congressmen who were not that interested in putting their names down in the "yea" column was unlikely to do much to aid the future of the world. In the long run, no one would even remember this small thing, done to try and streamline the American education system.

But it was important for now. It was a gesture, symbolic to some extent, but with a few decent intentions written into it.

"Set up the meeting," I said, coming back to my conversation with Jana before she could try and direct my attention to the next thing. "When are we back in Washington?"

"This afternoon, sir," Jana said. "Three o'clock."

"Set up the meeting for four," I said. "I'll have a talk with them."

Jana paused, and I could tell she was racking her brain, trying to decide if she should ask. "Why, sir?" she asked, curiosity winning out.

"Because the American people elected me to make their lives better," I said, glancing at the Secret Service agents dotted around the playground. Beyond them lay the press, trying to take it all in and mercifully far enough away that I didn't have to worry about being recorded. "And I'd be a lousy human being if I shirked that duty." I smiled and waved to the press corps, the scum of the earth, while I waited for Ms. Abernathy to come back and lecture me some more on what needed to be done in the education system.

6.

Sienna

The morning passed without incident, nothing reported on cable. I was just waiting around for stupid Phillips's press conference, but when it actually happened, it was a pretty subdued thing, almost entirely bereft of substance.

Almost.

He got to about the middle and looked up from his statement, which had been pretty boring procedural stuff. He looked right at the camera and said, "In order for our system of justice to survive, wrongdoers have to be punished. Those who flout our laws, who make themselves enemies of the state, cannot, and will not, be suffered to live in their state of insurrection against lawful authority. Failure to yield to the laws of the people is not acceptable. They, by example and deed, are a threat to us all."

There was a snowball's chance in a Texas summer of him actually having written any of that himself. He may have agreed with the sentiments, which were basically, "Sienna Nealon is a bad person who has thumbed her nose at all our supercool efforts to bring her to a cell, and we need to find her and kick her ass so other people don't get the idea that this shit is okay," but he didn't write the words himself, mainly because Phillips didn't speak like that. He wasn't capable. He was a moron.

And he was in charge of catching me. I felt relief, remembering that.

Of course, he wasn't the only one in charge of catching me. The fact that my brother had joined up with the cause, along with Augustus and J.J. and presumably everyone else … that stung. I hadn't heard a peep about them since the press conference where President Turgid Penis Harmon (he should change his first name from Gerry to that; it flows better and it's more accurate) announced the task force for my capture. I knew they were still out there, though, because they were still showing up in the background pictures on websites that were actually reporting what was going on in the Sienna manhunt. Unlike the news, which seemed basically to be taking everything at face value and not bothering with its own reporting.

Speaking of which, it was about time for my daily sweep of the web.

I was incognito in Cedar City, but part of maintaining my cover meant that I had to look and seem normal. I'd seriously considered not even bothering with getting a phone, but someone of my age group who didn't have a cell phone would be absolutely inconceivable. It would go beyond hipster, cool-because-no-one-else-is-doing-it, and into the realm of weird-beyond-all-reckoning. So I had a smart phone—several, in fact—and I used them regularly.

But I used them carefully.

The GPS was switched off, for one. Location services were disabled; I checked in the menu, just to make sure the OS hadn't somehow turned them back on in the night. Secondly, it was not registered in my name. I had a full boat of fake IDs, some very excellent ones, in fact, put together by one of the finest cobblers—that's someone who makes fake documents—in Europe. So this phone was registered to Matilda McCoy. I didn't know who Matilda McCoy was, or if she was even real, but it was unlikely that the FBI was looking for her. So there was that. Thirdly, I didn't take or make calls on the phone. No one had the number.

And fourth, when I went on the internet, I used a Virtual Private Network or VPN to hide where I was browsing from. To anyone watching, they couldn't see what I was looking at nor could they tell where I was looking from. I always had it set for Canada, so my IP address looked like I was in Toronto. Just another Canadian browsing fringe sites, NSA. Nothing to see here. Finally, when I wasn't using the internet, I both shut down the internet and turned off the phone. I had six different phones to browse from, and used them each randomly throughout Cedar City. Every one of them was the same model, with the same look, so that if anyone did take notice of me, it would seem like I was using the exact same phone. Five out of the six, I never used in the apartment. I was tempted not to use the last here, either, but checking my websites was a thing that kept me calm, helped me feel ... not totally disconnected from the world.

It let me feel like there were a few people in the world that didn't hate me.

There were a few sites that I checked daily, because they only added content once a day or less. There was one site, though, that seemed to have enough contributors that they were updating constantly. It was called SiennaWatch, though the web address was something totally random. They actually had photos from scenes where Scott and Reed and the hunting party had run raids on places where they'd suspected I was. They had a pretty big network of people crowdsourcing these photos and story details. Some of them sounded like bullshit ravings of nuts, but ... the ones with pictures attached tended to be somewhat credible based on how I knew the FBI and Scott operated.

Also, there was one photo two weeks ago where Guy Friday had gotten squirted—presumably by Scott—right in the crotch. So naturally, everyone in the comments section made fun of the big guy for peeing himself. Or worse. I don't normally go in for internet comments, but in this case, I basked in the warmth. Like Guy Friday in his own pee.

I pulled up SiennaWatch, waiting for my 3G super-slow service to load the damned web page. I hoped for a solid update, something like Scott and Co. raiding a women's clothing store and getting tangled up in the lingerie section. Those sort of photos would make my day.

What I got was something else. Not the sort of thing that would make my day at all.

I looked over the image, the headline, and I didn't quite comprehend what I was seeing. I flicked my gaze to the TV screen with Phillips's face still hogging the majority of the real estate, his faded, thin blond hair and wide jaw still irritating me, begging me across the thousands of miles between us to punch him. It was a distinct contrast from what I was reading on my phone. There was no mention of the website headline in the chyrons scrolling beneath his fat, stupid face, not a hint of the horror that I'd just taken in.

FBI TASK FORCE LAUNCHES WARRANTLESS, NO-KNOCK RAID IN CHEYENNE, WYOMING, THAT KILLS LOCAL MOTHER, WOUNDS INFANT.

I could scarcely imagine a more horrifying headline. The sheer gut-wrenching disgust I felt for what my pursuers had done in their overzealous haste to kill me almost caused me to drop my phone. My fingers felt numb, and I set it down on the table, internet still active, before my grip could fail me.

I'd done a few no-knock raids in my time. When you're up against an implacable foe, a really nasty meta with deadly powers, kicking down the door and bum rushing them seems like a far better alternative to someone blasting away at you in a civilian neighborhood with a pistol or rifle or energy-projecting powers.

But this … whatever had happened in Cheyenne this morning, was, without a doubt, a full-scale disaster that should have gone down in history as a textbook example of the worst consequences of a no-knock raid gone terribly, terribly wrong.

I looked up at the screen, though, and I had a feeling that it wasn't going to make it to any textbooks. If the traditional media hadn't publicized this little incident yet, it meant either it was untrue or they were ignoring it. I knew which one I was betting on, but I couldn't say for a total certainty if I was right or just assuming the worst of the press because I hated their guts—and the rest of their smarmy, elitist, ass-kissing selves, too.

I ran a hand over my forehead. It was greasy, the result of my failure to shower in the last twenty-four hours, if not more. It was funny how I had all this time and couldn't seem to find any to take care of basic hygiene. Then again, I was trying to keep people at a distance, so this sort of helped.

"… and again, I think the strongest part of Director Phillips's statement," I looked up to find some overpaid jackass talking out his rectum, "is that line where he went directly after Sienna Nealon and her actions—that we can't suffer this kind of indifference to our rule of law as a society from any metahuman, especially not one as powerful as Ms. Nealon."

"But don't you think, Greg," a condescending anchor came up, some douche with more clothing budget than brains, "that Ms. Nealon is effectively stealing the narrative right now? I mean, she hasn't been officially sighted in weeks, and the FBI and the DHS are turning every single rock over looking for her. I mean, doesn't this speak to the inefficiency of our federal agencies?"

"No," Greg said. I wished I was in studio so I could slap the pensive look off his face. (Violent much, Sienna?) "I think it a lot more likely that some external state actor has given shelter to Ms. Nealon, someone like North Korea, or maybe a non-extradition country that would use her for her talents—someone with a grudge against the Harmon administration or the USA who wants to humiliate us. Her continued status as a fugitive is a thumb in the eye to the Justice Department—"

"Screw you," I said, and hit the mute button. Of course, Greg's stupidity kept flowing in text form in the black closed-caption bubble, but I didn't turn off the TV because removing the knife from my belly was asking for more from me than I was capable of giving. I just couldn't keep from salting the wounds, from looking at the nasty things people said about me. It wasn't like I had anything else to do with my life.

I snatched up the phone from the table and scrolled down, deciding to read the article now that I'd gotten myself thoroughly enraged. It was a short read, sounded like it came from a first responder, although the bloggers took some pains trying to disguise it to make it sound like maybe it didn't. It was all laid out, with the name of the victim, Shannon Christensen, and her baby, who was in the local hospital in critical but stable condition. They didn't have a picture of Shannon Christensen when she was alive, but they had one of her from the scene that looked like it had been sneakily taken on a camera phone, and it ...

Well, it was grisly.

Whoever had killed her hadn't been merciful about it, which sent my stomach in another loop-de-loop. She was dark haired, wide-hipped, and looked pretty much like I used to, at least from behind. It was hard to say what she might have looked like from in front, because, after I scrolled past the "****WARNING! GRAPHIC CONTENT!****" flag, I was presented with photos of a woman who'd been shot through the back of the head three times with hollow-point bullets, and those had left their mark.

I gagged, and it wasn't because I hadn't seen more grisly crime scene photos—and crime scenes—than this one. It was because if Shannon Christensen hadn't been a few pounds overweight and had the same hair color as I did, she wouldn't be dead.

I reached down and grabbed my trash can, emptying the contents of my stomach into it. It was like someone had turned my belly inside out, reached down in and just ripped it up and propelled it clear of my mouth with meta force.

Shannon Christensen was dead because she'd committed the crime of looking like me.

That's not true, Zack whispered in my head.

"Oh, yes it is," I said, and retched hard into the trash can again. It smelled dank and disgusting, that sour tinge of stomach acid reeking in my nostrils, the contents slushing in the plastic can.

She's dead because they didn't care *if they had the right door,* Bastian said. *That's not on you.*

"I'm dangerous," I said. "They'd be idiots to knock on my door and wait for a response."

There's a line, Zack said. *Between preparing yourself for danger and storming into someone's house. They probably didn't even announce they were FBI.*

I had to grudgingly concede that could be the case. She might have thought it was a home invasion.

You're being stalked by predators, Wolfe said. *You didn't ask for this.*

"No," I said, "I didn't." And I hadn't. I hadn't asked for Gavrikov to come to the fore and blow up all my enemies in the second before they murdered me.

But I wasn't sorry he'd done it either, in spite of the collateral damage to my life and already-tarnished reputation that had ensued.

This is not how it is supposed to be in this country, Gavrikov said, slipping into the conversation a little more cautiously than he might have before he'd caused umpteen deaths and millions in property damage about a month earlier. He wasn't sorry he'd saved my life either, but he was treading lightly because I'd let him have it a few times since without a lot of reason. I didn't entirely blame him for my predicament, but since I had no one else to unleash on, the voices in my head tended to get the brunt of my ire. Them and the stupid news. *There is procedure and this is not it.*

"Stop channeling Reed," I snapped, not even because I was angry at him, but because the thought of him arguing along the line that my brother would have taken had he been here made me raw. It stung that he'd betrayed me. Reed, of all people.

None of these betrayals are natural, Eve Kappler said darkly. *Your friends, as much as I loathed them, were not the kind to throw you to the wolves so easily.*

"I don't think it's that unnatural for them to see me blow up a part of Eden Prairie and think that maybe I've lost my ever-loving mind?" I said. "I mean, I did send them all away ostensibly for the purpose of drawing out and killing the people who were trying to kill me. It's not out of the question that they could have seen that and thought, 'Oh, hell, she's lost it.'"

Without the benefit of the doubt? Zack had pursued the skeptical tack on this as well, but I didn't want to hear it. It was easy for me to believe that everyone would just wash their hands of me and walk away given sufficient provocation.

It had happened before.

"It doesn't matter," I said and put down the trash can, the nausea having passed. I picked up the phone again, staring at the bright screen and the photos of the woman who'd been murdered. She didn't even really look that much like me, I didn't think, except maybe from behind. But someone—Scott, I was pretty positive—had tagged her with three rounds in the back, then another three in the back of the head to make sure she didn't get up. That was the whole ball game for Shannon Christensen, and now her baby was going to grow up without a mother—if the child even survived being shot.

God, what a cockup.

Not your fault, Zack said.

"It's at least a little—"

Were you there? Wolfe asked, roused to anger again. He'd been getting madder and madder since we'd gone into exile. Of course, his solution to the current crisis was murderousness visited upon all who defiled my name. *Did you pull the trigger yourself? See the rivulets of gore spray from the girl's face?* I cringed; Wolfe was good with violent imagery. He should have been, though, because he'd certainly painted with that brush enough. He was the Bob Ross of mass murder, a different picture every day.

"The responsibility has to rest somewhere," I said. "Maybe if I'd—"

Turned yourself in? Bjorn asked. *Subjected yourself to imprisonment for fighting for your own life?*

Yes, Gavrikov said, *how dare you have the gall to defend yourself against attack? Against being murdered?*

You should have just lain there, defenseless, Eve mocked, *and let them kill you. Let your brains be spread across the pavement. Then this girl would still be alive. All you would have had to do was trade your unjust death for hers.*

But it'd still be unjust, Zack said, taking up the point nicely. They were an annoying choir at this point, working in tandem.

"Is it—" I started to say.

Yes, it's unjust, Wolfe said, rushing in again. *When they leave it to murderers and criminals to execute you outside this precious system of justice you seem to venerate—yes, it's unjust. And if you'd leave the maudlin, childish self-pity behind, you'd see it, too.*

"Wow," I said, "Strong words from the ethereal asshole gallery."

True words, though, Bastian said grudgingly. *You've been sitting around feeling sorry for yourself for a month now. Yeah, the world's against you. Yeah, it's worse than it was last time. Yeah, you can't have two beers on the table in front of yourself in this state at the same time—wait, where was I going with this?*

The world spins on around you, in spite of you, Eve said, taking up Bastian's lost thread. I got the feeling this little team of mine might have rehearsed this while I wasn't paying attention to them. *You heard your former boss, dog-shit-for-brains, empty-air-for-testicles, ire-for-all-emotions—*

He speaks of justice, Gavrikov said, *but calls for your summary execution as a threat—an enemy of the state. That is the sort of thing I saw in my own country. Here it was supposed to be different.*

That's not justice, Zack said. *Not my conception of it, anyway. No trial by jury, no talk of capture, and then they go and slaughter a woman, holding a baby in her arms, probably on an anonymous tip.*

'Wrongdoers must be punished,' Wolfe said. *You heard him. Your old boss said it. Who did the wrong here?*

I ground out my answer through gritted teeth. "Not me."

Did you turn loose the Bastille of the Cube? Eve asked. *Did you ask for them to come kill you?*

"No."

Were you the one with the gun in her hand, trying to murder someone? Zack asked. *Were you lurking around any of those criminals' homes without cause, pursuing any of them?*

Were you wrong when you arrested any of them? Bastian asked. *Were any of those people innocent of the crimes you accused them of, locked them up for?*

"Hell, no," I said. "They were scum, pretty much all of them. They preyed on people who didn't have a tenth of their strength, bullying them, using force, hurting anyone who tried to stand against them."

Sounds like Phillips, Bastian said, with all the moral authority he had, which was more than anyone else in my head except Zack. *Sounds like your old squad, with what they're doing now.*

'*Wrongdoers ... have to be punished,*' Wolfe said again.

"I'm actually not the wrongdoer here, am I?" I whispered it, barely daring to believe it was true. It was hard for me to believe, because I'd done bad things in the past, no doubt. I had a crushing sense of being in the wrong quite often, all the way back to childhood. I wasn't always repentant about it, but I was keenly aware of the feeling lurking in the back of my mind at all times, guilt so thick you could spread it on a sandwich. It wouldn't taste very good, probably, but there was certainly enough of it.

No, Zack said. *You're not in the wrong. Not this time.*

"I've been hiding," I said, staring down at my phone, "and this—this is the price of that. They just ... run me down everywhere. Lie about me."

They wanted you to lie down and die, Bjorn said. *It offends them that you didn't.*

"Well, I'm done with that, now," I said, looking down at the trash bin by my side, feeling a sense of sick guilt fueled by anger as a fresh resolution took root inside. "You're right, they've been getting away with all this—this press campaign against me, a manhunt for a crime I didn't commit, and now this ... murder. And they'll get away with it, too." I wiped my chin on my shirt. "I'm not going to sit here anymore and let them lie about me, about what they're doing." I set my jaw. "I'm not going to let my friends think I'm a killer and a nut anymore, without a word spoken in opposition. I'm going to get out there, and I'm going to—I'm going to—well, I'm going to do something."

Here, here, Bastian said.

Yes, Gavrikov agreed, *I don't think we could have taken another week of this hiding shit.*

Wolfe is bored, Wolfe said.

"You won't be bored for long," I said. "We're going to get out there. We're going to find something to do, something that will make a difference, some ... first step to digging out of this gigantic hole I'm in—and we're going to do it." I clenched my fist. "And nothing is going to stop me—"

And at exactly that moment, the screen on my TV changed, and the words "BREAKING NEWS" splashed across it, showing me a picture of something terrible going on … something I could actually do something about.

7.

Harmon

I was still waiting for the day when they'd install an escalator into the steps of Air Force One, but had a feeling I'd be waiting a long time. I'd had a friend who was a mechanical engineering genius, and he'd promised to take a look at making that happen, but unfortunately he'd gotten distracted with other, more important projects, and then died before completing any of my requests.

A shame, indeed, but such is life.

"Good morning, Mr. President," said the Air Force officer who flew my plane. I had no idea what his rank was, nor did I care, really. The pilots were a slate of constantly changing faces, and I paid as little attention to them as I did the furniture or the Secret Service agents. It didn't pay to pull my brainpower away from more important things, like how I was going to snap McSorley, McCluskey, and Shane into line for the education bill vote. Honestly, this was what a party whip was for, yet somehow I had gotten saddled with it. I gave the Air Force officer a nod, dismissing him, and headed to my cabin. The air in the plane was slightly stale, as though they hadn't turned on the air conditioning yet. "Wheels up in ten minutes, sir!" the Air Force officer called back to me as I walked away.

"Mr. President!" someone called. I looked up to see Jana; she caught me just as I was about to enter my cabin and shut the door. I needed recharge time before I did what I had to do this afternoon, and the breaks were never as long as I needed. The flight from Chicago to DC would be quick, with no lines before takeoff, no waiting in a queue. "Director Phillips is on the line for you—"

"Oh, for God's sakes—" The press wasn't around, so I didn't bother to control the roll of my eyes. "Fine. I'll take it in my cabin." I ducked inside before anyone else could harangue me and picked up the phone off its base, then flipped the button that was blinking. "Yes?"

"Mr. President," Andrew Phillips's dull voice sounded slightly more urgent than it usually did. Phillips was a big man, physically imposing in a way I had never been. He didn't intimidate me, but I'd seen him tower over underlings, his bulk straining. Phillips had gained all his middle-aged weight around the belly, and he'd been gaining steadily since I'd first made his acquaintance a few years earlier. It was predictable; working for me didn't tend to produce abundant amounts of time off for visits to the gym. "There's been an incident."

His alarm was obvious. "Make it quick," I said, trying not to betray my lack of patience. I'd spent the morning with children, after all, and it tired me mentally to be around them.

"Two things, actually," Phillips said, still dull as plain chalk. "Scott Byerly and his team executed a raid in Cheyenne, Wyoming, this morning based on a credible tip—"

"The elusive Ms. Nealon, then?" I sighed. She'd been a pain in my ass for entirely too long, having outlived her usefulness the day after I was re-elected.

"It wasn't her," Phillips said. "The woman matched her description, but unfortunately—"

"You killed the wrong person," I said, closing my eyes. My anger flared, but I kept it on a tight leash. "Does the press know?"

"They're not poking," Phillips said. "But it's on the web. The usual suspects are sniffing."

"Someday soon, I'm going to deal with these conspiracy theorists," I said, opening my eyes as I slid down to rest in my very comfortable leather chair. I had a desk and office on

Air Force One, and while it wasn't my favorite place to work, it wasn't bad. "Someday very soon, I hope."

"Well, they're not wrong in this case, sir," Phillips said, as though I didn't already know that.

"They're right about as often as they're wrong," I said, "but that doesn't matter, does it? I'm not annoyed with them for their lack of accuracy, I'm annoyed with them because they're like a plague of locusts that has settled on my fields. I'm trying to accomplish things and they're a drag on my very being." I took a long breath. "Keep the press away from this. Just deny, and it'll divide nicely. None of the credible outlets will touch it because it'll sound like backchannel whining from the opposition to them."

"Yes, sir," Phillips said, still tense. "And—"

"The other thing, yes," I said, pre-empting him. It was so much easier when he was standing in front of me. He took forever on the phone to come to a point. "Get on with it." In the background, I heard Air Force One's engines start up, and the lights flickered for just a second. I didn't lose him, unfortunately.

"There's a metahuman incident in progress in Las Vegas," Phillips said. "Casino heist gone very wrong. Local PD is engaging three of them on the Strip right now."

"The press won't stay out of that, for certain." I brought my thumb and forefinger up to the bridge of my nose. I could feel the beginnings of a headache forming. This was what always happened when I overtaxed myself. "What do we have available?"

"The governor of Nevada is calling out the National Guard," Phillips said. "We're throwing everything we have at them, but it's getting ugly, sir. They're not taking the money and running. It's turning into a battle. We've got three casinos on fire, cars wrecked—"

"Where's your response team?" I asked, clenching my eyelids closed.

"Still in Wyoming," Phillips said, with no more emotion than if he'd been informing me he'd come in under budget for the year. No, actually, he would have been considerably more lively had he been delivering that news. "I'm scrambling them, but it'll be at least two hours before they're on the ground."

I sighed a long and ragged breath, as Air Force One started to taxi. "This will be interesting to deal with," I said, feeling utterly drained. "I suppose there's not much else you can do. Suggest to the governor that he stop engaging with these idiots and let them flee—"

"He's tried that, sir," Phillips said. "The police attempted to pull out twenty minutes ago." I heard shuffling behind him, muffled voices as someone delivered Phillips an update. "They've realized that no one can stop them, so …"

"So why stop?" I leaned my head back against the padded chair.

There was a noise in the background behind Phillips. "Stand by, sir," he said, and the bastard put me on hold. A Muzak version of Andy Williams's "Moon River" drifted through the earpiece at me, and the beauty of the song momentarily quashed my annoyance at being placed on hold. Not for long, though, because this was not the sort of thing you did to the president of the United States.

I hung up and grasped for my TV remote. I clicked it on, and the flatscreen mounted into the wall flared to life, immediately resolving into a picture of chaos in the streets of Las Vegas. I'd never been that fond of the town myself, but I had no particular desire to see it leveled to the ground. Especially not when I could conceivably take any kind of blame for it.

The chyron at the bottom of the screen declared chaos in a slow sprawl, but there was something else, words emblazoned that gave me chills:

"SIENNA NEALON ARRIVES AT VEGAS METAHUMAN INCIDENT; MOTIVES UNKNOWN."

"You all really are a bunch of idiots if you don't know her motives," I said, sagging back in my seat. Another sigh, long and irritated, escaped. I knew, beyond doubt, that this Vegas incident was about to be settled more surely than if Phillips's team had been deploying right now.

But I would rather have seen the whole damned city burn than let Sienna Nealon get credit for saving the day.

8.

I had to be very careful escaping Cedar City in the middle of the day. I'd flown low and quick over fences and flat desert until the city was out of sight, then I'd streaked skyward and hit top speed somewhere over endless scrub and sands. I headed southwest, hewing close to the freeway, until I'd see it popping up on the horizon, an oasis in the middle of the desert.

Las Vegas.

Black smoke was billowing out of the strip, clouds stretching skyward like someone had installed a coal-burning plant in the middle of the casino mecca. I had my hoodie on, had in fact stapled the damned thing to my forehead along with a dark-haired wig to hide my new hairdo, and I'd left my glasses behind in the desert, like I was Kara Danvers or something. I wasn't wearing a unitard, though, or high red boots and a cape. It was just me and my hoodie, and some baggy jeans as usual, with steel-toed boots for the ball-kicking power they provided.

Vacation was over. Now I had my suit on and it was time to get back to work.

I flew in hot, near the speed of sound, not entirely sure what I was dealing with. The news had offered me an alert of the sort I used to live by. I knew there were metas down there, I knew they were causing havoc and ripping stuff up. I liked Vegas, and had always meant to come back here for a vacation. These clowns tearing up the Strip were probably the least of the reasons I wouldn't be back anytime soon, but they were the ones I could most easily deal with.

I didn't know exactly what I was waltzing into as I flew past the massive Ferris wheel that aped the London Eye, but I knew fire was at least part of it, because one of the Aria towers—the taller one—was burning, blazing orange flames shooting out the windows. A siren howled in front of me and I saw a Las Vegas Fire Department engine heading toward the chaos as an explosion sounded over the strip. Two cop cars were screaming along behind them, and all I could see ahead was black clouds, fire blossoming up in the middle of the street. Faint blue flashes that looked like they might have been lights from a cop car lit the clouds of black.

In spite of the chaos and the screaming pedestrians running down the sidewalks and across Las Vegas Boulevard, the first responders, the police, the ambulances were still heading into the chaos rather than away from it.

I did the same.

I slowed as I flew blind through the billows of black smoke. A cop car in flames added to the sooty mess, and I drew out the fire and snuffed it as I came in. I darted down a side street, figuring first things first—I needed to put out the Aria tower, because it was unlikely the fire department was going to be able to do much about it given how bad things were looking on the boulevard.

I came up the side of the tower and landed on the roof. I could kindasorta feel the flames within, Aleksandr Gavrikov close to the front of my mind, his powers at my fingertips. The back of the tower wasn't burning yet, which meant someone had started the fire out front, as though they'd pitched it in through the front windows.

That I could deal with.

I took a running start and jumped off the roof, letting gravity carry me down the front of the tower. I stopped in place about fifty feet down and started to draw the flames to me. Screams carried on the wind, and I cringed as another explosion went off below. I pulled the fire out of the front segment of the tower, absorbing it into my hands, my mouth, the skin on my face. It was hot, like swallowing a flaming torch, but I did it, the smoky residue tasting like someone was having a barbecue on the tip of my tongue.

I drifted slowly downward, pulling the fire to me as I went. It probably looked funny, if I was even visible to anyone through the cloud of smoke. I hoped I wasn't, because I wanted the element of surprise on my side when I went to deal with these assclowns who were destroying the city. I prioritized saving lives because as long as they didn't light another hotel on fire, keeping the Aria tower from collapsing was almost certainly my best bet for immediate impact.

Besides, I was still chewing over a pretty big decision, and it tormented me, bouncing around in my head, all the way down as I drifted my way to the ground. I usually make my decisions swiftly, but in this instance ...

In this instance, I was pretty torn.

I drifted out of the bottom of the cloud, every single bit of fire pulled into my skin, which felt flushed and hot. I'd broken into a sweat, and not just because of the hoodie, the wig, and the desert heat. All that fire didn't just dissipate inside me, after all. It took time, like I was ingesting a big meal, and by the time my feet touched ground, I was tired and wanted to go home to sleep it off. Preferably after a shower to get the smoky smell off me. It no longer resembled the scent of barbecue, because all the insulation and drywall and plastic and bedding had all lit off in the blaze, which meant I was coated in about a million and a half chemicals, none of them exactly Febreeze fresh.

Someone cackled maniacally about a hundred yards ahead of me, and I peered down the hazy street. I caught a glimpse of motion, and I wasn't quite sure what I'd seen at first. It took a minute for my brain to chug along, to decipher exactly what I was looking at.

It was a man in armor.

It wasn't cool armor, either, like the newer iterations of Iron Man. No, it was Tony-Stark-in-the-cave-with-hammer-and-anvil type stuff, rough plates of metal bound tightly around a big frame. I couldn't see the guy hidden beneath, but I'd certainly seen this MO before. I'd fought a man named David Henderschott early in my career who'd used his metahuman ability to bind to any surface to armor up with giant plates of metal and cause various and sundry problems. Some of my early exploits had surfaced since the manhunt had begun, and I had to guess that whoever this guy was, he'd taken some notes from Henderschott, probably figuring that wearing armor was a smarter, more efficient use of his skin-anchoring powers than trying to play like Spider-Man without the webbing.

And so far, it looked like he'd been right. He stomped up to a police cruiser that was already on fire and smashed a metal fist into it, sending it skidding back down the street. A crashing noise informed me it had found some target, probably not a good one, and an explosion followed a moment later.

"Well, all right, then," I said, decision made. I'd been contemplating how hard to go after these guys, and this had settled it for me. They were murderers, for certain, and they weren't just here to hit and run, grab some cash and leave.

This guy was having fun.

Only a month ago, he probably wouldn't have had the brass to try something this big because there'd always been a nuclear deterrent waiting in the wings if a meta got too out of hand. I knew the criminals whispered in the dark, keeping their little schemes quiet, hidden. Most of the idiots I caught were first-time offenders or offenders who'd flown under the radar for a while before I came after them. No one did chaos like this unless they were blindingly stupid or had a death wish, because ...

Because if you did something like this in the United States of America, criminals knew that Sienna Nealon was gonna get your ass. Your ass and the whole rest of you, too, and if you were lucky, she'd just put you in jail after a hard beating.

But now Sienna Nealon was one of the wanted, so chaos? It was fair game.

Except it damned sure wasn't.

Not in my country. Not anywhere I could easily reach.

Not ever.

I launched at the armored ass, fury driving me forward at a

speed just below the speed of sound. I angled myself so as not to cause too much collateral damage, but I couldn't help some. I kicked him, tendons in my foot protesting that I'd just brought steel boot backed by bone and flesh to metal armor, but a quick thought of *Wolfe!* shut my crying nerves up.

My steel toe caught metal man right in the ribs and sent him into the air with a perfect punt. He launched headfirst into the side of the Cosmopolitan, the sound of tinkling glass and crunching metal carrying through the smoke to let me know he was going to be busy picking himself up for a few minutes. I didn't care if he lived or died, though I hoped that the Cosmopolitan was evacuated by now. I suspected it was.

I set down for a second, limping on my right leg as Wolfe finished stitching the bones and tendons and muscles back together. I peered into the smoke-induced darkness, and heard the unmistakable sound of something heavy and metal thumping to the concrete on the other side of the Cosmopolitan. "And the field goal is *good*," I noted, and came around to figure out where the rest of the idiots who'd dared were hiding.

I caught a bolt of lightning in the face as I whirled, and I thumped to the street on Las Vegas Boulevard, shaking in agony as the black smoke seemed to reach down and envelop me in its darkness.

9.

Scott

Scott's hand was shaking like the plane as it bucked through the turbulence, fighting against headwinds as it lanced through the sky toward Las Vegas. He didn't like the feel of it, this rattling sound as the FBI Gulfstream jet fought against the skies around them. His mind was still on the baby in the Cheyenne hospital. He could feel still that plug of liquid he'd created. He'd started to dissolve it now that the wound was sealed, but it was still there, diminishing bit by bit as he carefully let the liquid disperse now that there was stitching to bind the wound together and clotting to fill the spaces between the stitches.

"Yo, can you do something about this already?" Augustus Coleman asked with thinly masked irritation. The plane jumped again, as though it had crested a wave and then dropped five feet. Augustus's eyes were firmly anchored on Reed, who was staring straight ahead, lips in a flat, expressionless line.

"Hm?" Reed came out of it, his trancelike expression dispelled by Augustus's question. He blinked a few times. "Oh. Yes." He lifted a hand, and instantly, the ride smoothed.

"You all right?" Augustus asked over Friday's low, rumbling snores. The big man was sleeping through it all.

"Fine," Reed answered stiffly. Scott watched him, but Reed's face didn't register much other than tight focus, that same determination that had been driving him since he'd joined up with the FBI Task Force. "I'd be a lot better if that had been her that ate the bullets this morning."

Scott blinked. Something about it was bothering him, something that had been tickling at his mind since he'd helped pull the squirming, bleeding baby out from beneath the woman's corpse. Reed had pulled that trigger without question, hadn't he? *Pop, pop, pop,* and the woman was down. No remorse, no hesitation.

Since when has Reed ever been like that? The question simmered in his mind. "This is serious business," Scott said, the words bursting out like a shot from Reed's gun.

"Damned straight," Augustus said with a sharp nod.

"It requires the most definitive measures," Scott went on, and his resolve sounded firm, at odds with what was going on in his head.

"Without doubt," Reed said. "No mercy."

"No hesitation," Augustus said.

"No ..." Scott's voice trailed off, and the other two looked at him, both questioningly. "No mercy," he echoed, the thought he might have voiced faded. He got twin nods of agreement as Augustus and Reed turned back to the front of the cabin.

Scott stared back and down at the carpet, though, as though he could see through it, through the belly of the plane, and back to Cheyenne, where somewhere behind them a baby lay in a hospital with stitches in his leg and no mother. Scott felt a squirm, and somehow he knew the child was crying, and perhaps wondering where his mother was. Something about that made those questions bubble up even more quickly, like lava from a vent at the bottom of the deepest ocean.

10.

Sienna

Turning your back on an uncleared street in the middle of a fight is not wise, Wolfe growled as he restored me to consciousness with a shock, my eyes snapping open. It didn't help as much as you might think; Las Vegas Boulevard was an obstacle course of police cars, civilian vehicles, ambulances and fire engines in flames. Smoke threatened to overwhelm me, as though inhaling half the Aria tower hadn't been bad enough for my health. I pinched my eyes tightly closed again, knowing that someone out there had lightning to toss if I presented myself as a target.

"… Didn't think she'd show up," a low voice said about twenty feet away.

"No one thought she'd show. Did you get her?" another voice asked. Both male, both tentative, which meant they had more brains than I wanted them to have. I'd prefer they'd been lobotomized destruction machines rather than thinking, aggravating, sucker-punching-me-with-lightning humans.

"Right in the face," the first voice crowed. Lightning man. I knew a few of those, but none that sounded like him. He had a little trill of excitement now, thinking he'd dropped Sienna Nealon. "She's gotta be dead."

"Well, so is Charlie, I'm guessing," the second voice said. I mentally tagged him as Secondi, like the second course in an Italian meal, because I was gonna eat him up, and soon.

48

Charlie must have been the Iron Monkey I sent flying. "Did you see him go?"

"Yeah ... he could make it," Lightning Man said. "He's tough, y'know?"

"He went through a building, dude," Secondi said. "We should get the money and get out of here. We heisted two casinos and ripped up the Strip, that's enough for me."

"We can't leave without Charlie," Lightning Man said. He was barely going to be Antipasti; I had a hand ready, flames prepared to fling at his head. I was through messing around with these turds. "He'll lead right back to us if they ID his body."

"You want to go crawl out there and fetch him?" Secondi asked. "Because it's outside the smoke, which means they can see—"

"So go light some fires for cover and get him," Lightning/Antipasti said. I'd found the brains of the operation, and also figured out that Secondi was a damned Gavrikov. I was about tired of Gavrikovs by now, because they kept popping up. Lightning throwers did too, those Zeus/Thor types, but all the ones I knew that were still alive were on my side, save for Antipasti. I intended to change that.

I opened my eyes a crack, pleased that they'd lost focus on me in their internal debate. I rolled my palm, aimed it at Lightning's head, and shot a burst of fire right for his face to repay him for the bolt he'd run through my brain—

The flame burst arced through the air like gravity had changed its course, and swirled into Secondi's palm as he dispelled it as easily as I'd taken care of the Aria fires. "Shit! She's still ali—"

The street exploded into chaos as I summoned my inner Idina, defied gravity, and shot thirty feet into the air. A bolt of lightning lanced past me and connected with a hanging traffic light, twisting blue coruscations running over its surface as the red, yellow and green lights all lit brightly for a second and then blew out in a shower of sparks. The pole worked as a lightning rod, of sorts, but apparently Antipasti's strength was pretty intense, because I caught some stray voltage. I felt my heart skip a hundred beats as I staggered in the air like I was flying drunk.

"Gyaaaaaaah!" I cried as I went sideways into a palm tree's upper fronds. I wished I still had Kat on my side; she could have used them to yank me out of the way before Antipasti's next bolt of lightning came squirting at me. I flipped backward behind the tree, and the blast grounded out as the palm tree absorbed the electricity then burst into flames.

I stuck out a hand, absorbing the fire from the tree and also from a ball of flame that Secondi threw at me. It swerved around the tree, preserving my cover and dispelled harmlessly into my hand. "I don't suppose you idiots want to make this easy and just surrender now?" I asked, my heart still stammering as Wolfe tried to it get back to normal cardiac rhythm. My head hurt like someone had used it as the titular prop for a particularly talentless episode of *The Gong Show*.

"Why would we?" Mr. Lightning J. (for jerkoff) Antipasti called back. "We're winning!"

"You're winning? You're down a guy already," I said. "Either give up now or I'm not even gonna make it nice when I beat you, like I would have when I was working for the law. I'm lawless now, so I'm going to strip the flesh from your bones with a finger like a blowtorch after I cut your hands off. When I'm done with you, you're gonna wish Predator or Hannibal had caught you rather than me."

That was mostly a bluff, but it hung in the air as Secondi and Lightning chewed it over. Predictably, Secondi was the one who responded first. "Well ... if we do give up, are you going to turn us over to—"

"Shut up!" Lightning Antipasti slapped him. "We're going to be the death of you, bitch. Just you wait and see." He shot at me again, and the tree once more took the juice.

"Heard that one before. Just remember," I called back as the bolt finished sizzling, "you had a chance to do this painlessly, and you chose the pain instead."

"Oh, for f—I want to surrender!" Secondi Fireball called.

"You chickenshit!" Lightning Antipasti screeched at him.

"Are you out of your mind?" Secondi asked. "The only

reason we did this was because she was supposed to be out of the picture. She's clearly not!"

"She's nothing!" Lightning screamed.

"I'll remember you said that," I muttered under my breath, and then shot into the sky while they were arguing among themselves. I used a cloud of soot for cover, twisted as I reached the top of the hotel towers, and then centered myself on my targets and started back down. "Eve?"

Ready, Eve Kappler's steady voice said. *Let us make them our bitches instead.*

"My sentiments exactly," I said and shot toward the ground.

It didn't take me long to come back below the black clouds clogging the air above the strip. I pierced the veil in seconds and found Secondi and Lightning still bickering. Lightning shot off a stream of electricity at the palm tree where he must have thought I was still hiding, his eyes firmly fixed on Secondi.

I fired a hundred nets at him before the first one hit. They were all small, little webbings of light. They ripped him to the ground, hard enough to crack the pavement, pelting him like paintballs that exploded on impact and interlaced with bright light fibers. They sewed him to the street, and I came down to deliver the coup de grace, my knuckles to his jaw. Bones broke on both sides of that impact, but he got the worst of it, his head crashing into the pavement as the threads of my webbing pulled tight. He was bound to the road, eyes rolled back in his head, still alive but nursing a head wound that wasn't going to be right for a day or two, even with meta-healing.

I let the webbing pull him tight and then stayed there, hovering above his downed carcass as Secondi's eyes widened at the display. "I hope you haven't changed your mind about that surrender thing," I said casually, "because it'd be a real shame if I had to—"

He didn't wait for me to respond, flame bursting out of his pores like he'd gone Dark Phoenix. It projected out like he had flamethrower valves under both arms, blossoming out in all directions; at me, at the street, at the world around us, like he had rage to throw and he wanted it to go everywhere at once. I watched it flare, like a bomb going off, and felt the heat rise around me, and I didn't know if I had enough left in me to stop him.

11.

The heat was intense, even for me, fire bursting out of Secondi's hands and body like a star going nova. Waves of heat washed over me like I'd thrown myself into the flaming torrent rising off a nuclear bomb blast. Sweat rolled down my forehead, my arms, and I channeled it away from the thin disguise of my hoodie and into my fingers, into my toes, melting my damned boots into slag and scorching the cuffs of my jeans.

I had a feeling that preserving my hidden disguise was going to be a full time job if I was going to try and continue fighting evil and stupidity and metas. Mostly evil and metas. It was possible to fight stupidity with pure snark, which likely wouldn't result in my hoodie and wig getting burned off. Hopefully. You never knew with me.

My hands shook as I absorbed the fire. I didn't know exactly how much flame I'd taken in, but it had to be, like, a quarter-star's worth. I also didn't know exactly how they measured flame, because, let's face it, no one absorbed fire except me and apparently this guy.

"You should have given up when I gave you the chance," I said, sweating and floating closer to him. He was really pouring it on, blasting at me with full heat, and I just kept channeling it away from my clothes. The zipper on my hoodie felt like I'd left it on the front seat of a car parked in a Vegas parking lot all day. I could feel it eating through my shirt and into my skin, but I didn't dare take it off.

Secondi was screaming in fury and determination as he

threw everything he had at me and I took it all in. His flame started to sputter and die, choking off out of his left hand first, then guttering out from his right as his shoulders slumped and he started to sweat. He looked about two steps away from passing out, and I took the last flare of heat into my palm, absorbing it and letting a little puff of smoke escape from between my lips, as though I were about to blow a ring out to impress Bilbo Baggins.

"How …?" Secondi croaked, and he looked pitiful. "How did you—?"

I hit him with a shoulder tackle at high speed and carried him up into the air, the staple in my hood tugging at my forehead as the wind tried to rip it loose. I carried Secondi up, his eyes as big as roulette wheels (come on—thematically, it fits, people), and I brought him down at ludicrous speed into the Bellagio fountain just down the block. They were spraying, mid-show, strains of Celine Dion's *My Heart Will Go On* tickling my ears before I slammed into the water, Secondi-first (heh heh. I kill myself. Mostly others, but occasionally myself, only in the laughing way. Not the others, though. I kill them fer realz).

The air left him in a burst of bubbles. I used his solar plexus, that spot in the center of his belly where the wind gets knocked out of you, to cushion my own landing. I could see him choking for air, sucking in great gasps of water, as I pushed him to the bottom of the fountain.

Believe it or not, I wasn't even being vengeful as I drowned him. I shoved his face into the rocky bottom of the fountain as hard as I could, scraping his cheek off and turning the water around us red. I was about as cool and dispassionate as could be, and if he hadn't possessed the power to turn thousands of people into scorched piles of organic matter with a single burst of anger, I probably would have left him unconscious and let the Vegas PD work out what to do with him.

Some people, though … were just too dangerous to live. At least the government seemed to think so when it came to me, so I had no moral difficulty taking the same position when it came to a man who'd just (stupidly) tried to nuke me into oblivion.

He sputtered a few times, blood churning out as he thrashed ineffectually against my claw-like grip. I was holding my breath with everything I had, and fortunately I could do that for a decent space of time (I'd practiced, since a guy who controlled water was presently hunting me to the death), and certainly longer than a guy who I'd just knocked the breath out of.

It took less than a minute for Secondi to drown, but it was a painful minute. He finally stopped moving, and I waited another thirty seconds after that to come back up, checking to make sure my hoodie was still stapled to my head before surfacing (it was, and also, still oww). Just to be safe, once he was limp, I broke his neck and pushed him away. His body got caught in a jet and hurled to the surface.

I broke the surface and took a long, sweet breath of smoky, hellish air. Secondi's corpse bobbed like an apple, in time with Celine as the fountain jets pushed his carcass away from the center of the show.

I looked around. The Strip wasn't burning anymore, but neither was it in peak condition. Cop car lights were blinking just outside the perimeter of the fountain, and I was expecting a hail of gunfire to greet me, but it didn't. What greeted me was a hell of a lot worse.

Screams were coming from the side of the Bellagio closest to the carnage. Something stomped hard against the ground, and I heard something go SPLAT! with authority. I came out of the water like one of the fountain jets had caught me in the ass and launched me out, streaking toward the disturbance. I had a feeling I knew what I'd find, and as I came to the far edge of the fountains, rising above the bushes and trees that lent the desert landscape the touch of the Italian greenery they were looking for when they built this resort, I caught sight of that damned asshole in armor hammering his way down the Bellagio's driveway, smashing the cars that had gotten trapped in the chaos.

People were fleeing on foot in all directions. A few even jumped over the edge of the walkway and into the fountain. Maybe they figured it'd be safer than running back up to the hotel, given that the Cosmopolitan next door had a massive, gaping hole in it, and the taller Aria tower was still smoking down the street. It didn't matter to me, because my job was to stop this mess before it got any worse.

A helicopter made a choppering sound overhead, the whoosh of its rotors turning out a steady cadence as I came in fast. People had cleared away from Iron Moron, and he was rearing back to kick another cab. I saw movement inside, and knew I couldn't hesitate.

I sent a hot rush of concentrated flame at him in a tongue of fire no bigger around than a dowel rod. It caught him just below the neck and surged between the plates of his armor. He stiffened as though I'd poked him, then shuddered.

Then he screamed.

It was a horrifying sound. The fire I poured into him was hot enough to liquefy flesh and light muscle on fire. He jerked and danced like I had him on a string, but smoke poured out of the joints of his metal coverings. His legs failed him first, and he dropped, his blood boiling inside his suit and superheating his body.

The metal plates he'd adhered to his skin all released at once as his power failed, dropping to the pavement in a series of THUNKs! What lay beneath the metal encasements ...

Well, it wasn't pretty anymore, assuming it had ever been.

Iron Not-so-much-a-man-now had melted from the inside out, his skin bubbling off, blood boiling, squirting out and searing the pavement beneath him as he fell. He wasn't even recognizable as a human being any longer, just a biomass of indeterminate origin, pretty much how I always imagined a transporter accident going in *Star Trek*, though I didn't think they'd ever shown one on screen.

His scream lingered in my mind long after it cut off in reality, fading behind the sirens out on the Strip. I hovered over the field of battle, stuck in place as surely as if he'd somehow anchored me to my spot in the air.

"Wh ... why did you do that?" someone called from below, and I looked down to see a woman with blood running out of her dark hair speaking up to me. She blinked at me, as if surprised I would deign to look at her. "You're bleeding," she said.

"So are you," I said, pointing at her. I felt for my nose, and realized that Secondi must have headbutted me while he was thrashing about. I hadn't even noticed, and it didn't matter. "You should go over there to the ambulances, get it checked out. Scalp lacerations can be a sign of concussion."

She blinked at me, as though she hadn't understood what I'd said, and asked me, "Why are you here? With everything you have going on ... there's no way anyone would have expected you here."

I looked at the ambulances, the cop cars, the fire engines. Some of them were destroyed, their crews probably dead. "These guys ... these women ... they had to know what they were riding into after the first of them got attacked. They kept coming anyway."

She stared at me blankly. "That's their job. You're ... wanted. Hunted. You've got no reason to come out here ... no reason to play ... hero."

I stared at the ruin and felt a paralyzing sense of regret. The helicopter whipped overhead, and I realized it was a news copter, not a police chopper. They were probably filming me. "I had no reason not to," I said to the lady. "I don't care what they say about me—I know who I am." I stared at the new chopper in defiance, looking right at the cameraman inside the door, as if daring him and anyone else watching to hate me. "Get that wound looked at," I said to the lady, and then, with a last look at the chopper, I shot the news the bird, then shot off, straight up into the sky.

12.

I watched the live feed from Vegas with rising irritation. It wasn't as though I expected a bunch of half-baked hoodlums with a casino robbing scheme to kill Sienna Nealon.

But still, it would have been nice.

Air Force One rattled as the pilot banked, bringing us around gently. Final approach had to be coming up soon. I hadn't had much time to rest, even isolated as I was from people. "Dammit," I said under my breath. I didn't typically talk to myself out loud, but this was undoubtedly a problem. The camera followed her as she stared back at it evenly; they'd captured almost the entire battle.

Her entire *victory*.

"Dammit," I said again, clicking off the TV as she escaped into the sky. "She's back in the game."

13.

"We've got a reasonable estimation of how far she had to travel," Reed said with muted enthusiasm. He was still wearing that furious intensity like a mask, staring at the TV screen at the front of the Gulfstream's cabin, the live feed from the cable news net showing the devastation of one of the most famous streets in America. "Based on when the news broke on the net and the networks, and how long it took her to get there. If we match her top speed and draw a circle—"

"We get an idea of how long it took her to get there," Augustus said, joining in with a quiet intensity. "Then, if she shows up somewhere else soon, nearby—"

"We triangulate," Reed said. "The search field narrows, and we have a narrower search field to look for unusual events." He leaned back in his seat, folding his arms before him. "I know Sienna. Wherever she is, she's never totally quiet. She's incapable of it."

Scott stirred, thoughts slow like they'd congealed together over the course of the flight. The plane was banking, turning back to Washington. They were hardly necessary in Vegas now that the incident was settled, so Phillips had probably called them back. It wasn't the first time he'd issued orders to the pilots without bothering to have them relayed to Scott and the others.

"She's smarter than you think," Friday said. Scott had been

59

sure he was still sleeping. He wasn't normally so small, but apparently on the flight he felt safe enough to shrink down to a surprisingly skinny size. His arms were about as big around now as a water bottle, giving him an almost frail appearance. "I bet she's doing something to throw us off her trail."

"She's got an ego problem when it comes to helping with emergencies like this," Reed said. "Give her another meta emergency in a place where she can get to it, and I bet you she comes running."

"Oh yeah, bait the trap," Augustus said with a vigorous nod. He was fiercely on board with this idea, that much was obvious. "No more of this waiting stuff. If she's going to be out and playing the game, let's outplay her."

"If we're going to make her come to us," Friday said, "we better make sure we're stacked up and ready. Because if you think it gets bad trying to kick down a door in hopes she's not waiting on the other side, wait 'til you see what happens when she comes flying into danger. You saw what she did to that guy in the metal suit." He shook his masked face. "She's got nothing holding her back anymore."

"She didn't scorch the Zeus, though," Augustus said, pensive. "You think she might hold back on us?"

Friday snickered, his sunken chest heaving up and down comically. "Want to bet your life on it?"

"No," Augustus said sharply.

"I wouldn't, either," Reed said with a shake of the head. "But these are the choices—lay a trap, or track her to her den. I'd rather corner her in her den."

"You would," Scott said quietly.

Every head swiveled to him. "You say something, boss?" Friday was probably half joking by calling him boss. He was never serious about that.

"I don't want to go into her den, whatever it is," Scott said, blinking away his surprise at speaking. What the hell was wrong with him? There was something lacking today, a clarity, a focus. Maybe it was fatigue. "But I don't know how we bait a trap and ensure she comes to it without putting civilians in harm's way."

"It's a reasonable sacrifice," Reed said coldly. "Maybe we could arrange for this lightning meta to get cut loose in the middle of transport, but not too far from here. Say … in Denver. If she shows up right away, even if things go wrong with our trap, we know she's somewhere in Mountain Time. If it takes her a little longer, we know she's on the West Coast."

"Well, we'd be able to narrow it down, at least," Augustus said. "But I'd rather flat out kill her, maybe put a sniper nearby and pop her skull off when she comes in for a landing." He rubbed his hands together. "Save ourselves some trouble."

"You'd need more than one sniper," Friday said, sounding like he was coming alive, then his skinny frame shook. "Maybe a whole division."

The phone in the bulkhead in front of Scott rang, and he picked it up. "Call from Washington, sir," one of the pilots said, and there was a fizzing sound followed by a click.

"Hello?" Scott asked, his mouth feeling suddenly dry.

"Byerly," Andrew Phillips's dull voice sounded urgent. "I've turned you around. You're coming back to Washington immediately."

"Yes, sir, I figured," Scott said, with a nod that Phillips obviously couldn't see. It was a habit.

"You'll be briefing the president this afternoon," Phillips went on. "He's cancelling other meetings so he can talk with you."

"Ah, yes sir," Scott said, momentarily taken aback. He hadn't seen President Harmon in almost a month, since the press conference announcing the task force formation. "I—uh—what does he want to know?"

"He wants an update on the hunt," Phillips said. The word 'hunt' caused Scott's stomach to rumble strangely. "You're to provide one, and make it to his satisfaction."

"Well, we have a plan," Scott said, still feeling desperately unsettled.

"Good," Phillips said, "make sure it's ready for prime time." And he hung up without another word.

Scott hung up the handset and swallowed hard. The saliva

in his throat seemed like it had suddenly dammed up. A meeting with the president? Why should he feel so nervous about that? It wasn't as though he didn't have something somewhat good to tell the man.

Still, though, that feeling lingered as Scott settled back in his seat and shut his eyes, even though he knew sleep would be a long time in coming.

14.

Sienna

My phone rang as I walked up the stairs to the upper level of my apartment building in Cedar City. I stared at the display blankly. It said unknown caller. I almost answered it, but hesitated, then flipped it to the voicemail I hadn't set up yet. No one had this number, so it must have been a stupid autodialer. Probably trying to sell me something I had no use for, like life insurance. As if there was an insurance company around that would have taken on a risk like me.

I had my hoodie and wig all balled up under my arm, my glasses firmly back on my nose (they annoyed me even after a month of wearing them) and had my head down as someone approached. I saw it was a guy, totally bald, the shaved-head look, with nothing but a goatee of reddish-blond hair to stand out on his pale face. I didn't know him, and even though I felt his eyes sliding over me, I studiously avoided eye contact, because I wasn't Sienna Nealon right now. I was ...

Uhh ...

Shit, what was my cover name again?

He slowed as we drew closer together on the upstairs walk. It was a sunny day, and that sun was leaking down beneath the overhang that covered the exterior walkway we were on. My bare feet scuffed on the concrete, and I moved aside to give him plenty of room to pass.

"Holeeeee crap," he said, apparently taking me all in. "You

got blood on you." I looked up to find him studying me with interest.

"It's been a rough day," I said, and moved almost against the wall, trying to pass him without further scrutiny.

"Are those burn marks?" He pointed at my t-shirt, where the hoodie's zipper had seared through my shirt. I looked down. Yep, those were burn marks, little tiny ones like tracks exposing my bare, pale skin beneath. It didn't help I wasn't wearing a bra, because it left a nice little swath of between-boob exposed under the little teeth-mark holes. I was just lucky it hadn't burned harder, or I might have been wearing an open shirt.

"It's a new style I'm trying out," I said, covering. I looked up at him, and flipped my ponytailed mohawk.

His gaze fixated on the small, exposed track prints of my cleavage. "It's a good look," he said appraisingly. There was nothing dirty about how he said it, fortunately, or I would have been tempted to put his nose through the back of his head. He said it with a kind of sly self-assurance. "That blood, though ..."

"That's, uhm ..." I looked down, trying to figure out a way to cover for that. It might have come from when I'd gotten hit in the fight, it might have come from when I pulled the staple out of my head in the desert to take off the hoodie. Scalp lacs bleed a lot. "I kinda got in a scuffle."

"Man, even Cedar City isn't safe anymore." He shook his head, then extended his hand. "I'm Bilson. I, uh ..." He chucked a thumb over his shoulder to indicate the doors behind him. "I live a door down from you."

"I'm April," I said, remembering my cover ID. "Wait, you know where I live?"

"Nothing stalkerish, I swear," Bilson said, bald head bobbing up and down. "It's a small community here. Don't get me wrong, people come and go all the time, but still ... tough not to notice new arrivals."

Shit, was what I was thinking? The whole point of being here was not to be noticed. I didn't say anything.

"Um, so you're new in Cedar City? April?" He proceeded right past the nice little point where we could have politely let the conversation die and plunged forward into conversational CPR instead.

"Yes," I said, feeling pinned in place, as though Iron Moron had transferred his power to my feet, and they now clung to the cement.

"That's cool," he said. His gaze swept left, to the mountains that rose above the city. "I, uh, teach self-defense classes in town." He pointed at the blood on my shirt again. "You know, in case you ... need that sort of thing."

I looked at my shirt and started to immediately shut him down. Buuuuuuut ... I was a stickler for training, and it had been a month since I'd had a sparring partner. "Where do you hold these classes?" I asked, trying to tamp down on my interest. I was feeling very slack, and that was a problem since I'd just declared my return to the field of battle with a somewhat explosive kicking of ass. The idea of being out of fighting shape—so to speak—while preparing to go head to head with both the government and the nastiest metas in the country did not appeal. Even a Band-Aid might help patch this metaphorical wound, and sparring with a human or twelve was a Band-Aid, no doubt.

"Every night," he said, and fumbled, bringing up a card out of his black and grey gym shorts. "Some daytime classes, too, in case you're on evening shift or something. Address is on here. Easy ten minute or so walk." He made a *brrr* sound. "Though you might want to drive." It was chilly, but not exactly Minnesota-cold yet.

"I'll ... think about it," I said, pretty sure I was going to land on the side of checking it out. He smiled at me, and I got the sense he knew I'd already come to a decision.

Something made me shiver slightly, and I looked over the rail toward the parking lot. There was a woman standing there, dirty-blond hair piled on top of her head. She was wearing one of those yellow construction vests with the reflective tape, jeans that looked like they'd been given a dirt bath in an old quarry, and sunglasses that were dark enough to hide her gaze. She seemed to be looking right at me, though it was impossible to be sure without ripping them off her face. Which was tempting, because if she wasn't giving me daggers, she clearly had a lot of anger for the entire rest of the apartment complex. "Uh oh," I muttered.

"Hm?" Bilson followed my gaze and drew a sharp breath. "Oh."

"You got a jealous wife or something?" I asked.

"Sandra is not my anything," he said firmly, giving her a sour look right back. He stepped protectively in front of me, and I almost snickered. Gallant. She broke off her hate-watch of me and disappeared into the parking lot. A big truck started up a minute later, and I caught sight of her through tinted windows as she drove off, throwing one last glare at me as she passed.

"She seems nice," I said.

"She's a nightmare," he pronounced, then shook it off. "We had a thing, but it lasted about ten seconds and ended months ago. She has … issues."

"I don't doubt it," I said. I could smell the crazy on her from across the mountain. "Ten seconds, huh? Most guys wouldn't cop to that."

"What?" Bilson blushed across those pale cheeks. "Well, it lasted longer than that …"

"Sure it did," I said, playfully. Even ten seconds was sounding pretty good to me right now. I wasn't a nun, and he wasn't bad looking, though between hitting on me and dating Crazypants McDirty-looks, he did seem to have some suspect taste in women.

"I'll see you later, I hope." The way Bilson said it, I did detect genuine hope.

"Maybe," I said and started to drift past him. I wanted to get back to my apartment; I felt exposed standing out in the hall, like a drone was going to catch sight of me and launch a missile to wipe me off the planet.

"Nice to meet you, April," Bilson called, his voice following me as I made my retreat. "Didn't catch your last name, though?"

"I try not to go throwing it around," I said, playful in spite of the obvious crazy waiting for me in the form of Sandra. "Breakage charges are a real bitch, you know. And so is your ex-who's-not-your-ex, by my reckoning."

"I kinda figured that out for myself," Bilson said. "Later."

"Maybe," I said again, as my phone started to buzz again. I fished it out only to find the same damned unknown caller. "Ugh," I said, once Bilson was safely back on his course to the stairs and out of earshot. I debated once more answering the call, but hit ignore. I was going to have to depower and destroy this phone, just to be safe. I hadn't carried it to Vegas, but still, no one should have had this number. I fumbled and unlocked the door to my apartment, stepping into the dark, listening for any sound. After a few moments there was none, so I breathed a silent sigh of relief and got about the work of ridding myself of the phone and then cleaning up from my morning battle.

15.

Harmon

I breezed through the White House, ignoring the Secret Service agents as I always did. They might have been potted plants for how well they blended into the background of servants and secretaries and other unimportant support personnel. They did their job, I did mine, and we tried not to cross each others' paths.

"Mr. President," Ida Krall said as I stepped into the Secretary's office just outside the Oval one. "I've made the adjustments to your schedule that Jana sent me—"

"Good," I said, not letting this detail slow me down.

"Sir," Ms. Krall said, trying to get my attention. Ida Krall was probably in her late sixties, though I'd never cared enough to figure it out. She was a widow, had lived in DC for most of her life, and had a soft-spoken demeanor until someone crossed her. Then I'd seen her channel a dragon, nearly breathing fire in her defense of my schedule. She didn't let anyone in without an appointment, not the National Security Advisor, not the SecState, not the Joint Chiefs, not even the DCI or any of those other infinite acronyms. "Director Phillips of the FBI is on his way over with—"

"Is there a Director Phillips of another agency?" I asked breezily. Ms. Krall was a perfect foil for my brand of sly, dry humor.

"Yes, sir," Ms. Krall said without hesitation. "There's a

Director Yvonne Phillips of the Office of Community Services over at the Administration for Children and Families in the Department of Health and Human Services."

"Mercy," I said in mild surprise. "Who knew? Other than you, obviously."

"FBI Director Phillips and Agent Byerly are going to be here shortly," Ms. Krall said without missing a beat.

I sighed. "Very well, Ms. Krall. I trust you'll give me warning before they barge in. A chance to pull my pants up, you know."

"Yes, sir," she said with a perceptible tightening of her voice. She didn't like my humor, let alone when I progressed into the territory of the rude, but what was she going to say?

"And you," I said, wheeling to acknowledge the two Secret Service agents in my wake. "Stay, dogs." I smiled, they didn't. They never did, oddly, when I used this wonderful joke. It was obvious they couldn't stand me. I didn't much care, though. I didn't hate them; I just didn't deign to notice them.

I swept into the Oval Office and shut the doors behind me. I normally would have left that to someone else, but I didn't have the patience for Ms. Krall or a Secret Service agent to do it for me. "This was a terrible morning," I pronounced to the not-quite-empty room. "We're heading toward a wasted day, in fact, so I hope you have brighter news for me."

"I don't know that I have much to share at this point," Cassidy Ellis said, her pale skin so white it practically glowed against the creamy backdrop of the walls. "It's not as though it's been long since last we spoke."

"Cassidy, I need you nearby," I said, striding behind the Resolute desk and taking my comfortable seat. There were chairs in the middle of the room designed for more intimate meetings, ones that took place without the forbidding obstacle of a boat of a desk—or rather, a desk made out of a boat—between the participants and the president, but those chairs were terribly uncomfortable, and I avoided intimate meetings wherever possible. Keeping people at a distance was infinitely preferable, even if it was a distance of mere feet. "In case you missed it this morning—" I knew she hadn't missed anything. Cassidy didn't miss information. Feelings she missed, and quite often, but raw data? News? Impossible. She absorbed that sort of thing in her sleep, which she did in a coffin-like device designed to isolate her from the world so as to avoid overstimulation.

"I saw," she said simply. She knew I was just poking at her. Cassidy might have been a somewhat attractive girl if she gained about twenty pounds and spent some time in the sun. As it was, she looked like she would combust in the daylight, if the mere act of laying a hand on her shoulder didn't break her first. It was deceptive, really; she still had metahuman strength, but she looked almost like a skeleton with long, dark hair. "She'll be a problem."

"Of course she is," I said, thinking irritably of Sienna Nealon once more. "She excels at that. It's why I wanted her gone months ago." I didn't say it out loud, but I was regretting not having had someone actually kill her instead of merely destroying her reputation and kicking the pins from beneath her support system. I thought it would keep her out of the way for longer than thirty days, though admittedly I had hoped my other plans would have come to fruition by now. Now I was feeling the double pinch of my side of the equation not being ready and her side coming ready too early. I sighed again. "I suspect you'll know what I mean when I say this, but—I only wish the whole world could see things the way I do, and do them the way I do. Competence is at such a premium, and everyone goes rushing around like fools." I chuckled to cover my mild exasperation. "Take, for example, this morning. I was at a playground—" I stiffened. I could hear activity in the secretary's office a moment before my phone buzzed.

"Mr. President," Ms. Krall's voice sounded shrill over the speaker, "Director Phillips of the FBI is here."

"Yes, I guessed that Ms. Phillips of the Administration for Children and Families wasn't showing up out of nowhere," I said, and nodded to Cassidy. "Go run along into the hallway to my study, will you? Keep the door cracked if need be, but I want you to hear this."

"I'm … giving everything I have to the project you've got

me on," she said, low and a little worried. "I—"

"I need you to multitask," I said. "My wife always used to tell me that women were good at that." I smiled at her smarmily. "Prove her right. Do your job, and also help me come up with a way that we can keep Sienna Nealon's nose out of the business until such time as you've completed priority one."

"I've tried to kill Sienna Nealon," Cassidy said, flushing bright red. "Over and over—"

"You're afraid of her," I said, not terribly surprised. "My goodness. She's thwarted you often enough that you're actually intimidated by this simpleton. Fascinating."

She flushed even redder, looking like I'd smeared tomato on her lily-white face. "I'm not ... afraid—"

"You know, I talked to Eric Simmons the other day," standing up and casually throwing out the name of her love. I hadn't actually talked to him, because he was a worthless piece of surfer trash. I looked right at Cassidy to see that the flush had faded as she'd paled back to her original shade. She knew I was lying—or rather, employing a rhetorical device designed to not-subtly remind her of what I had over her head. "He seems well."

"Is he?" Her voice was pitifully scratchy, almost non-existent.

"I know you'd like to see him again," I said, "and I'd take it as nothing less than my duty in life to reunite you two love birds." I poured regret into my words, even knowing that Cassidy, with her failure to understand emotion, probably wouldn't notice it. "It'd be a real shame if you didn't hold up your end of our bargain." I gave her the expectant look, the sort that only a father or perhaps the president of the United States can properly pull off. Not that I was her father. I would have eaten her like a hamster eats its young if my genes had produced her.

"I'll ... I'll ..." She stood, wobbly on her legs which were thin as apple tree shoots. "I'll listen and—and—" she stammered, "—I'll get right back to work on both projects."

"Excellent," I said with enthusiasm. "I knew I could count on you." I made a shooing motion with my hand, and she wobbled into the hallway to my study and pulled the door to. I could have let her stay in the room, but that would have required an exercise of power to smooth things over with my next guests, and I didn't really want to go to any extra effort. I strode back around the carved monstrosity that comprised the remains of the HMS *Resolute* and pushed the button on my phone to call Ms. Krall. "Send them in," I said, and settled back in my chair to await my next meeting.

16.

Scott

Scott had been in the Oval Office a few times, but he still wasn't used to it yet. A Secret Service agent in a black suit opened the door for Phillips and Scott to walk in, then shut it behind them almost noiselessly. There was a peephole, and Scott could sense the agent against the door, looking in. That was creepy, he decided, and it made him wonder what other rooms in the White House might have peepholes.

"Yes, they're watching us," President Harmon said from behind his desk, not rising to greet them. "And yes ... they watch me everywhere. The bathroom. The bedroom. I can't wipe my ass in this house without a Secret Service agent looking in on me." He smiled bitterly. "The price of power, I'm afraid, but also the answer to the age old question of 'who watches the watchmen?' Well. Sort of, I suppose. I guess I'm not exactly a watchman, though I am always on watch here."

"Uhm, Mr. President," Director Phillips said, as dully as always. Scott stared at the big man; Phillips's emotions seemed to be on perpetual mute. He hadn't worked with him for very long, but Scott was left wondering if the man ever cracked a smile. He had his doubts.

"Yes, I know, Director," Harmon said. The president seemed less charming, less amused than the last times Scott had met him. "She's back. Like a loaded dice, she keeps giving us snake eyes." He turned his attention to Scott.

"Anything to say for your misstep in Wyoming this morning?"

"That was Reed, sir," Scott said, feeling strangely possessed to unburden himself. "He shot first without confirming the target."

"Let's not kid ourselves," Harmon said. "He shot first, second, third—all the way to sixth, as I understand it, without confirming his target." The president did not sound amused.

"You wanted us to take her out, sir," Phillips said, and Scott had a vision of him trying to cover his ass ineffectually with both hands, "she's not easy to take out without lethal measures."

"Without shooting first, you mean," Harmon said.

Scott felt that dull scratching in the back of his mind again, that feeling like he was overwhelmed, a sick sensation in his stomach trying to claw out. He bent slightly forward and sucked in a breath of air. It was cool and fresh, and it helped not at all.

"Is there something wrong with you, Mr. Byerly?" President Harmon asked, fixing him with a strong gaze.

"I just, uhm ..." Scott said, not daring to look away from the president. "It was a tough day."

Harmon's eyes narrowed. "You're thinking about that child, aren't you? The one that was shot?"

Scott felt his breath catch in his throat. He could still feel the last traces of the plug of blood, nearly dissolved, now. He was holding on to that last little bit, even at this distance. Stirring it enough to keep it from coagulating, from clotting too heavily. His hand shook at his side. "That was our screwup, sir—"

"That was Mr. Treston's screwup," Harmon corrected. "He got a little aggressive. His heart was in the right place—"

"His heart was in the place where he thought killing his sister was the best course of action," Scott said, mouth suddenly dry. The world was too bright around him, daylight filtering in through the white sheers that covered the windows of the Oval Office.

Harmon stared at him, assessing. "That bothers you?"

"Of course not, sir—" Phillips started.

"I don't recall asking you, Director," Harmon said evenly, and Phillips shut up.

"I don't know," Scott said, and looked away. He couldn't stand looking into those eyes anymore. He felt like a rat staring into the eyes of a snake, like Harmon was chasing him around the office even though the president was still seated. "It just doesn't seem ... right."

"You told me when we first met that you were on board," Harmon said. "That you were looking forward to clashing with Sienna Nealon—"

"I was," Scott said, staring at the rug beneath his feet. It was the presidential seal, the eagle with wings spread, arrows clutched in one hand and an olive branch in the other.

"But you're not anymore?"

"That baby ..." Scott said, not even consciously trying to answer Harmon. "I mean, he ..."

"Listen," Harmon said, soothingly, "I understand. You saw something terrible this morning. I wish law enforcement was a simple business where nothing bad ever happened, but you are tasked with chasing down the worst people in the country. People who challenge the very fabric of our society. They push at the rules, break them at will, and it seems so simple to say that with all the crime out there, letting one or two slip without pursuing them to all ends is a small matter. But it's not a small matter at all. No, we can't catch every criminal. But when one comes along as brazen and terrible as Sienna Nealon, one that thumbs her nose at established order, we owe it to ourselves to pursue her with everything we have. Yes, a terrible price was paid this morning, but I'm asking you to pay it—to live with those consequences— knowing if you don't continue on the path, a worse price will be exacted later. Do you understand me?"

Scott looked up. Harmon's eyes were on him, slitted and angry. "I ... I ..."

"All right," Harmon said, standing up abruptly. "Director ... pull your man together."

"But, sir," Phillips said, "I haven't briefed you on—"

"I've seen everything I need to," Harmon said. He glared down at Scott. "I trust your associates, Mr. Coleman, Mr. Treston and Mr … J.J.? I trust they're not flagging in their enthusiasm for this mission?"

"No, sir," Phillips answered.

"Good," Harmon said, never taking his eyes off Scott. Scott watched him, or at least his tie. No, the others weren't doubting like he was. They were still as firm in their belief as he'd been when he'd first sat across this desk and taken the job. He'd felt so damned certain he was doing the right thing, then.

What the hell was wrong with him now?

"Get him out of here," Harmon said, waving, and Phillips grabbed Scott by the arm and tugged him toward the door, which was opened by a Secret Service agent who had apparently been peering in through the peephole. "I'll see if I can get you some additional help."

"Much appreciated, Mr. President," Phillips said. Scott couldn't see his lips reach all the way to Harmon's ass, but the sentiment was plainly there. The doors closed behind them. "Get yourself together, dammit!"

Scott drew a hard, ragged breath. All he could think about was that baby, the sound of its plaintive cries, waking up without a mother … it was squirming even now, trying to settle but unable. "He knows," Scott whispered. *He knows his mother is gone.* Something about that tore at the corners of his eyes.

"If Sienna Nealon hadn't run," Phillips said in a rough voice, more full of emotion than Scott had ever heard him, "that baby's mother would still be alive right now. She's a menace, and more people will die if you don't do your damned job and bring her to justice."

A cold feeling trickled down Scott's skin, like someone had poured cold water over him and it was tracing lines over his flesh. "You're …" He straightened. "… You're right."

"Of course I'm right," Phillips said, back to dreadfully dull. He slapped Scott on the arm. The secretary was looking at him cautiously, as if afraid he might start blubbering right there on the carpet. Scott looked back. The Secret Service agent at the door was watching him, too, but not obviously. "Get it together."

"I'm ... together," Scott said, standing fully upright, spine straight. "I'm ... fine." How had he gotten so lost? Phillips was right, this was all down to Sienna. Her fault, not his, not Reed's. She was the most dangerous person on the planet, and she'd run. They had to catch her, or else more people would die. More babies would lose mothers. His resolved tightened, he nodded once at Phillips. "I'm sorry. Won't happen again."

"Good." Phillips didn't seem put out by his struggles. "Let's get back to it."

17.

Harmon

I've always hated watching people work through excess emotion. Don't get me wrong, I'm good at feigning empathy, especially for a live studio audience or a political rally. I didn't get re-elected twice to the highest office in the land without being able to project some humility and to feel the pain of others in a way that seems normal rather than the response of a sociopath. I'm not a sociopath, by the way. I really do feel the pain of others, and quite acutely; I just don't enjoy wallowing in it the way some do. Useless people, getting paralyzed by emotion. Emotion gets nothing done, it only gets in the way of getting things done.

"He was a mess," Cassidy said, slipping quietly back into the Oval Office.

"He'll pull it together," I said, rolling my eyes. Innocent babies and their mothers died every day, and for considerably less reason than because someone thought they were Sienna Nealon. Car accidents, cancer, disease, random acts of violence. "It's a cold world, and Mr. Byerly is young. He lacks experience in pragmatism. He'll get there."

"You seem certain of that."

"Just as certain as I am that you'll accomplish what I've set out for you to do," I said, turning my attention to her. I rubbed my forehead lightly; a headache was coming on. It had been a long day, and I still had to browbeat some congressional idiots into embracing my education bill.

Cassidy almost gulped in reply to my statement of faith in her. Not quite the reaction I was looking for, but not a stupid one.

"I don't have enough to work with," Cassidy said.

I didn't blink at her. I knew what she was talking about. "I can get you some help, too," I said. "Access to ... outside resources. Ones that haven't been folded into the main project yet." I sighed. Decentralization was so annoying. I liked to have control over everything, to have it all at hand, but some of my associates hadn't cared for that approach, at least not in this matter.

"I could use it."

I walked over to my phone and dialed Ms. Krall. "Get me the premier of Revelen." I hung up; she'd connect the call once it went through. "As to the other thing ... I'll make some enquiries. There are certain other avenues we've attempted to pursue, though they've come up dry, as far as I know."

"You would know," she said, her gaze flitting around the room. "Why didn't you turn it all over to me sooner?"

"It's a big project," I said. "I gave you the majority. There are problems associated with trying to get the rest." I sighed for the thousandth time that day. "I left this in the hands of a capable man, but one who decided that decentralizing everything was for the best. He was usually very careful about covering his tracks, but unfortunately ..." I shrugged. "Time catches up with us all."

"Or Sienna Nealon, in this case." I didn't even bother to scowl at her. It was true, after all. "Throwing a bunch more trouble her way doesn't seem like it's going to do much more than slow her down."

"All I need is her slowed until you can finish the main job." The phone rang, and I answered it. "Madam Premier! Sorry to bother you this evening, I know it's late in Eastern Europe, but ... I'm calling about that diplomatic partnership you proposed ... Specifically, I'd like to take you up on that offer you made regarding the loan of certain ... military assets ... or metahuman resources, I guess you called them ..."

18.

Sienna

Once I was safely back in my apartment, behind the bolted door, I felt like the rush of adrenaline the fight in Vegas had given me was making everything that had seemed so hazy as I sat in the dark this last month suddenly clear. Where before I'd been stewing, not even reactive, now I felt like I was ready to step up and go on the offense. Or whatever football people call it.

They're all after you, Zack said worriedly.

They've been after her all along, Wolfe said with something approaching excitement.

"But now I've shown them I'm still out here," I said, silencing the voices in my head as I strode forward. I'd showered, I'd cleaned up, and now I was pacing in shorts and a t-shirt, my mohawk still wet and strung over my shoulder. "This problem ... it's one of scale."

What? Zack asked.

"It feels like the world is against me," I clarified. "Because I'm in the US and every cop and federal agent is looking for me."

Which is why you ran, duh, Bastian said.

"It's why I hid," I said, not quite liking the word *run* to describe my actions. "Figured I'd let the world spin on for a while without me. Well, it's still the same, still against me, and it's not going anywhere. And neither am I."

Unless they kill you, Zack said.

"What's a girl to do?" I murmured, ignoring the useless pessimism.

Tear them apart, Wolfe suggested.

"Kindasorta not really," I said, striding back and forth in front of my TV. The guts of the phone I'd taken apart were still sitting on the table. I'd vaporized the SIM card and the rest of the phone would be torched later, where it was less likely to set off all the smoke detectors. I'd probably have to go to the desert for that. All the rest of the phones were off, all lined up nicely on the end table. I didn't need any news alerts from them right now, the cable outlets were scrolling silently in the background. It was all Vegas coverage, breathless as usual and stupid as always. "I'm going to take my foes on—the real ones—one at a time, not by shredding them into ribbons like you might hope."

What pieces are you talking about? Eve asked.

"I'm talking about threads," I said. "Unsolved mysteries." My eyes narrowed, and I looked at the north wall of my apartment. "Timothy Logan. Palleton Labs, in Portland. There's a vault in that building, some secret that's hiding out there."

What does that have to do with you? Bjorn asked.

"Maybe nothing. Maybe something. Logan brought it to me for a reason."

So what are you going to do about it? Gavrikov asked.

"I'm going to find the secret, obvs," I said, not even slowing my pace. "That's first."

And then? Bjorn asked, a little hungrily. He was clearly warming up to this.

"There's a task force after me," I said. "Likely as not, they're going to be setting a trap soon. They're not stupid, and they do know me, so they're probably aware that I can't help but rush in where angels fear to tread."

You're a real fool that way, Eve snarked.

"Seems like that'd be a good chance for me to figure out what the hell is up my brother and Augustus's asses."

And Scott's? Zack asked tentatively. He was one ex asking about another ex, after all.

"I know what's up his ass," I said. "A bug the size of El

Capitan because I stole his memories of our relationship." That was an annoying truth. If we make our own demons, I certainly had my fair share of blame for this one. "Can't entirely fault him for that."

But he's hunting you, Zack said. *He let your house burn down, FFS.*

"Shit happens," I said, ignoring that. The house-burning-down thing had stung, I couldn't deny it. Some of the other things he'd done had hurt, too, and I knew I was going to have to deal with him at some point. I had an idea for it, too, but it involved whooping his ass in ways he wouldn't find favorable. Not that he'd ever found pain enjoyable. Probably why we were such a bad pair.

"Palleton Labs," I said, making my list, "then the FBI task force."

You think they'll just come out and face you? Easy as that? Eve asked.

"Not a chance," I said. "It'll be an ambush. They'll throw the kitchen sink at me, along with the countertops, the dishwasher, and probably the can opener. But I'll be ready."

Oh, good, Eve said, *and here I thought you were just going to fly stupidly into it like every other time.*

"Oh ye of little faith," I said, still pacing. "I wonder if I can find Timothy Logan?"

I wonder why you'd want to? Zack asked. *He betrayed you.*

"Everybody has betrayed me, dude," I snapped back, lightly. "I'm a little short on allies, and last time I saw ol' Timmy, he was standing like a whipped dog in my office door offering to spill some secrets." I slightly regretted not taking him up on that offer, but at the time I'd been so furious, I was trying to avoid ripping his spine out and beating him into oblivion with it. "Suddenly, his betrayal doesn't seem quite so terrible as it did when it happened. You know, compared to what followed." Compared to my entire team siding with the government against me after I'd blown up a street in Eden Prairie. It was self-defense, honest. Or Gavrikov defense of self. Something like that. I doubted lawyers had a category for it, really, but that was okay, because I hated lawyers these days almost as much as I hated reporters.

You think you can find him, though? Zack asked.

"Maybe," I said. "We won't know until we look, but I've got other things to do first."

Such as ...? Wolfe asked.

"I told you," I said, pulling a pair of secondhand, holey jeans out of my dresser drawer, and following them with a pair of socks. "Palleton Labs. The giant safe on the upper floor."

Gavrikov answered, with rising alarm. *That is locked. And thick. One of my kind attempted to burn her way through and failed even with hours to work.*

"I know this," I said, pulling on my socks.

But you are going to succeed where they failed? Gavrikov sounded befuddled, and I could sense the vague worry among the rest of the souls in my head. They didn't get what I had planned. That was okay. Few understood me, even in my own head.

"I am."

But how? Gavrikov asked.

"Because I'm me."

That's not an answer, Eve said. The light was starting to fade beyond the horizon. I estimated it was a few hours yet until sundown, but I was already chomping at the bit. It'd take me a little while to make the trek to Portland anyway.

"You'll see," I singsonged, in a much better mood than I'd started the morning. The air seemed fresher, cooler, more full of life.

Uh oh, Zack said, and the sentiment was echoed in my head by the others.

"*You* don't need to say 'uh oh,'" I said, unlocking the front door as I slipped my shoes on and pocketed my keys. I grabbed the hoodie and wig bundle, and readied myself. "Everyone who's facing off *against* me should be saying that right now. Though I kinda doubt they are." I ticked a few items off in my head, debating. There was a common thread to my problems, and while I wasn't quite sure how to handle him just yet, I was ready to add his damned name to my list of things to deal with.

Uh oh, Zack said again as that thought became obvious to

83

him.

"Yep," I said. "Number one—Palleton Labs. Number two—the task force. And number three —" I paused, because in truth, I had only the vaguest idea of what to do about this one, but now that I had it on my list ... I'd work the problem. I'd come up with a solution.

You can't do that ... Bastian said, uneasily.

"Oh yes, I can," I said, clicking the lock as I opened the door. "Number three ... President Gerry Harmon."

19.

It took me a few hours of slow flight to reach the outskirts of Portland, Oregon. I had walked out into the desert a ways and hung out there for a little while, waiting until the darkness started to fall before I really launched off. I didn't want to chance some real-time downlooking satellite getting a clear picture of my flight path, after all. They were going to come after me, but I didn't have to make it easy for them.

I kept the speed relatively low, tried not to race the sunset. That strained my patience, my hoodie stapled again to my damned head (seriously, you guys, ow) and wig hair whipping in the wind, but it was better safe than sorry, I figured.

I found Palleton Labs out in the Portland suburbs after night had fully fallen. It was a strangely pyramidal building, the sides sloping closer together with every floor as it rose. It was only four stories tall, which was fortunate, I guess, because a couple more and the top of the building might have come to a razor-sharp point. Thankfully it was distinctive enough that I knew it from the sky, and it took very little searching to pick it out.

I overflew the building twice trying to get a clear idea of what was waiting for me. Palleton Labs had been attacked by Timothy Logan and his buddies about a month ago, after all, and whoever was in charge of this establishment would surely have tightened security. We humans are really good at making sure to close that barn door after the horse has cantered off, after all.

Sure enough, I caught sight of security guards on the roof,

walking the perimeter, and even inside when I swooped low enough to take a look inside the well-lit hallways. Apparently whoever was running this show had decided a display of manpower was the best deterrent against another burglary.

Unfortunately for them, they were planning for the last burglars and not the one that was about to rob their asses blind.

I bound every one of the rooftop guards to the gravel on my next pass, then dropped onto the roof between their insensate bodies (I had put a little extra *oomph!* into the light webs I used. Not enough to crack skulls, but enough to cause significant bruising and loss of consciousness). Gravel crunched beneath my feet as I settled down, and I stalked over to where I'd burned through the roof the last time I'd been here.

The rooftop had been repaired, which was good for them, I guess. It would have been easier on me if all I'd had to do was lift up a sheet of unsecured plywood, but that was probably a little too much to ask for. I wondered if they'd taken my entry point as a critique of another of their security flaws and used it as a chance to improve. I suspected they had if they'd gone to the trouble of hiring a metric ton of security guards.

I sighed. "Fine, make my life difficult," I muttered. I stripped the pistol out of the holster of one of the guards, then helped myself to his ammo and several mags from two of the other guards. It was a full-sized Glock, looked like a 17, though I couldn't tell for sure in the dark. I checked the spare mags and they fit, so apparently the security guards had gone with a standard-issue weapon. I didn't know whether that was unusual for security guards, but it made me worry just a little bit that these were more than garden-variety rent-a-cops.

Rather than trying to carve through the ceiling like last time and finding out immediately how they'd improved their security system, I stuck my head over the side of the building. Two guards were pacing on the sidewalks below, but they weren't looking at me. I wrapped them to the concrete walking path with light webs, then flew up and did the same to the guys walking the beat on the other side of the building. I watched for signs of any other patrolling guards, and when all was clear after five minutes, I drifted over the side of the building in hover mode and wafted up to the big glass windows of the fourth floor. Offices were lined up inside, and I could see roving guards moving around in the hallways beyond. I waited until they were past, then cut my way carefully through the glass window, carving a circular section out using my finger as a blowtorch. I caught the glass before it fell into the office and crashed on the floor, then flung it like a Frisbee into the night. I heard it break in the distance, and after a few seconds in which nobody hurried to investigate, I sighed in relief and flew into the office.

Palleton Labs was pretty much as I remembered it; offices on the fourth floor ringed the exterior of the building, and inside was a windowless wall that hid a secure vault. I looked up at the tiles above me and decided at some point I was going to need to test whether they'd put alarms in the ceiling. But not yet, probably.

I dropped down to my chest like I was going to do a pushup, hiding behind the waist-high solid walls that separated the offices from the corridor. There were windows above that, but I was so close to the wall that the passing guards probably wouldn't be able to see me as they completed their circuit. Their footsteps were a steady clicking, a cadence, almost, which suggested they might be ex-military. That wasn't usual for security guards, especially not multiple security guards at the same location. More and more, I got the feeling that Palleton Labs was hiding something really valuable in that vault.

I just hoped, since I was going to the trouble of becoming an *actual* criminal, that it was going to be something worthwhile and germane to my mission to unravel the mysteries surrounding me. Ten thousand tons of diamonds would also have been acceptable.

I waited until the guards passed again and then bound them to the solid corridor wall with light webs. They thumped against it hard, damaging the drywall. Once they were out, I used the cracked drywall that one of them had so helpfully busted with his head and peeled back a layer. I found steel beams inside, as I'd expected. Last time I'd been here, I'd found the entry door to the interior of the fourth floor where they kept the vault sealed with a door that Timothy Logan's party had to burn through with their resident Gavrikov.

I looked around. The smoke alarms were glaringly obvious and seemed to be newly placed, the outline of old ones visible in the places where the ceiling tiles hadn't been replaced. There was a weathered, circular outline of paler coloring visible around the edges of the new smoke alarms. I suspected they'd gotten the full upgrade, including more sensitivity and maybe even heat sensors.

There were also cameras, which meant I probably didn't have a ton of time.

"As the great 21st-century philosopher Deadpool once said," I muttered under my breath, "maximum effort!" And I triggered a blast of pure Gavrikov-based heat.

The inferno leapt out of me as though I'd been carrying the Aria fire with me all this time, just waiting for a chance to let it out. It seared through the wall in front of me, turning the metal reinforcement behind the layer of drywall to molten slag. When I finished, there was an ovoid hole big enough for me to step through, and I did just that, finding myself once more in the presence of the Palleton Labs vault.

The vault itself was probably thirty feet by ten feet, a rectangular room in the middle of the floor, with biometric locks and keypads built into the steel door. I didn't even bother to try burning through, because I knew it had been attempted before.

What's the big plan now? Zack asked. I still hadn't shared it with him yet, because I felt like being mysterious.

"Stuff," I said casually. I'd had very little socialization over the last month, and it might have been making me more ornery than usual, if such a thing was possible. I looked down and cracked my knuckles. "Gavrikov?"

Huh? Gavrikov wondered, but he put his power at my disposal nonetheless.

Fire alarm klaxons were already wailing in the halls, and when I triggered off another quick burst of flame to burn through the floor, they started in the entry as well. I took a step forward and dropped down to the third floor before the sprinklers kicked in. There wasn't a vault on the third floor, but it was pretty obvious where the massive support columns had been placed to hold that monstrosity up. Water started to trickle down through the hole a second later, dripping like an indoor rainstorm onto the carpeting.

I was in a cubicle farm, no guards in sight. Why would there be? There was nothing on the third floor worth protecting, after all.

I took a few long strides into the middle of the room, mentally calculating where the vault would be above me. It didn't take a lot to eyeball it.

Are you going to drop the vault down? Eve asked, filled with curiosity. *Because I doubt that will open it.*

"You'd better wait and see," I singsonged, enjoying myself tremendously. I stared at the ceiling, finishing my calculations as the sound of booted footsteps hammered in the corner stairway. They passed right by the third floor without slowing down. Predictable, but a sign I needed to hurry.

I lifted off the ground and put my hands up when I reached the ceiling, placing my shoulders squarely against the underside of the vault. I pressed, crunching my way through the ceiling tiles and into the concrete subfloor. The pressure on my shoulders got intense in a hell of a hurry; I was against the bottom of the vault now, flush with the concrete supports holding it up.

Oh, man, Zack said, finally getting it. *Really?*

"Just like saving Chicago from a meteor," I said, far more cheerfully than I should have been considering I was about to lift several tons. "This should be good, because I haven't really worked my upper body in a month or so."

Yes, your deadlift has suffered, Bastian said dryly. *I bet you can only juggle six or seven garbage trucks at this point.*

"Thanks for the sweet workout idea," I said, grunting as I started to fly up. "If we ... make it through this shit ... I am totally ... using *THAT!*"

The last word came out in a grunt as the concrete subfloor separated from the steel beams that were holding up the vault. Most of the concrete peeled away; apparently the contractor hadn't bothered bolting the vault down, so when I broke through the slab, it busted all to pieces, aggregate material shattering into pebble-sized chunks and raining down around me.

I was pushing hard, and my shoulders slammed against the unbending steel barrier of the vault bottom. It was surprisingly lighter than I would have guessed, much, much lighter than the meteor I'd stopped with my shoulders only a year or so earlier. I rose and the vault rose with me, horrendous sounds of metal bending in the walls and drywall cracking and crumbling filling the air around me.

I felt the roof cave in around me as I lifted the vault out of its place on the fourth floor. Security guards nearly shit themselves before my eyes as I passed through the fourth floor. It crumbled after me, sending those dudes scrambling for safer ground rather than giving them a chance to shoot at me or something. If fortune favored the bold, then the lady stealing a multi-ton vault out of a suburban lab should probably have put some money on the lottery later tonight, cuz this? This was some serious chutzpah.

The last pieces of the roof came crumbling down around me, and I shook the vault slightly, careful to maintain my grip as I rose a hundred feet into the air. I wanted to get some of the debris off, but I also didn't want to get too high. If I stayed low, even with the metallic mass of the vault, I could avoid being seen on radar. That was important to my current plan.

Well, shit, Eve said in rough admiration, *you really did it.*

"Suck it, doubters," I said as I turned north and west. I propelled myself forward, and the vault, resting on my shoulders, came with me. "I bet this gives someone an ulcer."

The question is, Zack asked, *who?*

"I was wondering that myself," I said, as I flew off into the night, following the contours of the earth with care and dodging trees so as to avoid impaling myself on a pine. "I guess we'll just have to find a way to open this puppy up and figure it out."

20.

Harmon

I was half-asleep in my chair in the residence when the call came in. It was a chair I'd brought here instead of one that belonged, and it was—to use my wife's opinion—ugly. It was overstuffed, something approaching three decades old, probably the sort of thing you'd find in an old man's house, but I didn't care. It had been cradling my ass since long before it was a presidential ass, and as far as I was concerned, it could keep cradling my ass now that it was presidential.

The trilling of the phone was a familiar albeit unwelcome disruption. I answered it immediately, and barely got out a, "This is Harmon," before Cassidy's voice burst onto the line.

"Sienna Nealon just hit a place called Palleton Labs," Cassidy said, in that high-pitched, near-whining voice of hers. It was not my favorite part of her. (My favorite part of her was her brain. It was the only part of her I had any use for.)

I usually process news quite quickly. For some reason, that didn't happen this time. "Excuse me?" I asked, probably sounding like I was chastising her for the rudeness with which she was delivering this information. I wasn't; I didn't care for formality, at least in this. "She broke in?"

"Yes," Cassidy said, voice straining in a way that told me that a mere break in, it was not. There was more.

"And?"

Cassidy hesitated in the same manner that Jana had when

she'd failed to name McSorley, McCluskey and Shane just that morning. "I don't know for sure—"

"Yes, you do."

"I think she stole some kind of ... vault?" I knew it wasn't mere speculation; she knew it for a fact.

My eyes flicked back and forth over the private sitting room, but I maintained a steely calm. "Let me know when you're sure," I said, letting her verbal obfuscation be my excuse for ending the conversation. I hung up without a further word, my jaw clenching inadvertently. My hand closed into a fist, something that never happened; I detested physical violence, and had never stooped to it myself.

I sat in the silence, in the semi-darkness, and eyed the door, where the Secret Service were probably watching me through the peephole. I didn't care.

"That little bitch," I said, and barely kept myself from bringing a hand hammering down on the arm of my chair. I'd already lost one valuable thing that night, after all. She wasn't worth losing another.

21.

Scott

He was awakened in the middle of the night by a hard knock on the door to the small office in FBI HQ. Scott was half out of it, dreaming of wide waters, of the time he'd held back the MacArthur Park Lake from raining down on Sienna. Something about the memory was choking him, but the sound of the knock jarred him back to alertness, though he almost wished it hadn't.

"Got company, boss," J.J.'s voice came through the wood-paneled door. Scott felt the rough fabric of the couch against his sweaty palms. He reabsorbed the moisture and dabbed at his forehead. It came away wet, too.

"Who is it?" Scott croaked. His mouth was dry, at least. He forced himself to his feet and grabbed his jacket from where he'd left it, draped across the back of one of the visitor chairs in his office. He put it on as he opened the door and found J.J. standing outside, face more neutral than it had ever been in all the time they'd worked together. Most of that time had been during the war against Sovereign. *With Sienna on our side,* Scott thought dimly.

And now she's the new Sovereign.

Something about that prickled at him. *But is she, really?*

Yes, a small voice insisted within.

"Contractors, according to Director Phillips," J.J. said. "I guess the president called them in from overseas? Metas, you know."

"We don't have metas of our own to deploy?" Scott asked, feeling like he was walking hunchbacked, the weight of the world or the ocean or something on his shoulders.

"Not in civilian service, I guess?" J.J. didn't seem very sure. "I honestly don't know. He called, they came. Whistled 'em up and now they're here. They're waiting for a meet and greet with the man in charge, which, uh, is you, technically."

"Right," Scott said, and followed J.J. down the hall.

When he got to the small meta-division bullpen, he found a strange spectacle awaiting him. Six unfamiliar guys, most in black tactical garb, were waiting, clustered in a small knot in front of him. They were pretty standoffish, eyes directed at Scott's team, which was waiting silently and still across a chasm of desks. Reed and Augustus were just sitting there, staring at the newcomers as though they were going to attack at any moment.

"Oh, good, you're here," Friday said, hopping to his feet and drawing every eye in the room to him through the motion. *Hunters,* Scott thought. They watched for movement. Augustus and Reed were included in this assessment, too, though they had already gone back to staring down the new arrivals. Friday drifted over to Scott and inclined his head, whispering, as though everyone in the room couldn't hear him. "Lot of tension here."

"I noticed," Scott said tightly. He took a quick look at the new folks and stepped up, figuring he needed to introduce himself. "My name's Scott Byerly and I'm—"

"We know who you are," a guy in the front of the line said. He was Eastern European, with jet-black hair and had the accent, though Scott couldn't have placed it any more specifically than that if he'd had a gun to his head. The man looked to each of them in turn: "Reed Treston. Augustus Coleman." His eyes narrowed when he reached Friday. "You, we do not know, but our files label you as 'The Gimp.'"

"The hell?" Friday asked, swelling slightly. He'd already been partially hulked, as though anticipating a rumble.

"We did not pick it," the leader said with a shrug. His manner was brusque, and it was clear he didn't care much about endearing himself to anyone. "Apparently it was Sienna Nealon who tagged you that."

"Gahhhhhh," Friday said with a low grunt. "She called me Guy Friday, too, why couldn't you have tagged me as that?"

"Gimp fits better," the leader said, and didn't even bother to shrug this time. "My name is Rudi Fazekas. This is my team." Scott mentally tagged him as Rude-y, the better to remember him. Rudey nodded to each of his teammates in succession, starting with a pale-skinned fellow to his right. "This is MacDonald."

"Call me Mac," the man said with an accent that was as Aussie as a kangaroo. Mac pulled a knife and twirled it, one of the big bladed ones. Crocodile Dundee, Scott decided.

"This is Joaquín," Rudey went on, nodding at a man who had a distinctly South American feel to him; he was dressed in gaucho-lite, the only exception to the black tactical garb in their group. His jacket was still ostentatious but slightly toned down, a red bandana tied around his neck.

"Olá," Joaquín said. His eyes glowed for a second— actually glowed, then hissed, as though he'd started to fire a laser out of them and snuffed it before they burned. It was hard to miss, and Scott got the feeling he'd done it to make an impression.

"This is Ambrus," Rudey pointed to a man just behind him. Ambrus smiled, a wide, toothy grin with much less cool hostility than the last two. He looked like he might actually be a human being. "You can call him Booster. We all do."

"Like … Booster Gold?" Scott asked, that name sounding familiar for some reason. He looked to Reed. "Isn't Booster Gold a comic book character?"

Reed just glanced at him, staring blankly, then turned back to watching Rudey and his team. "I don't know."

Scott's brain itched, a small ache sprouting out like a vein within it had pulsated. "Okay." He looked at Rudey. "Sorry. Didn't mean to interrupt."

"But you did anyway," Rudey said with an impressive amount of pissyness. "We have a medic," he pointed at a blondish man with olive skin. "Gothric. And this is my second in command, Ferko." He pointed to another Eastern

European fellow who looked like he had slightly more humor than Rudey. Ferko, though, had long, dark hair, with barrettes in it. Scott stared for a second, then averted his eyes. He didn't need these guys taking his staring as a challenge.

"Okay, let me see if I got this," Scott said with a nod. "Rudi," he pointed at the leader, "Mac," the Aussie with the big knife, "Joaquín," the South American gaucho, "Booster," the grinning man, "uh, medic," the blondish fellow, "and Ferko," the man with barrettes.

"Yes," Rudey said, with a quick nod, almost like satisfaction, but an utterly humorless look.

"Great," Scott said, rubbing his fingers through his own dusky blond hair, trying to massage the scalp. "Well, you caught us at a good time. We were about to plan an ambush for Sienna." Ferko with the barrettes snorted, and a few of the others shared a guffaw. Scott stared at him. "Something funny about that?"

Rudey answered, and in his own inimitable style. "You have been hunting her for a month. Been trying to trip her for months before that. Always failing." He shared a look with his team. "We will plan this ambush for you, instead."

Reed was on the balls of his feet in an instant, like he was bucking forward for a confrontation. "This is *our mission.*"

"You've failed *your* mission how many times?" Rudey asked, no emotion in his voice. "This is why we're here. We hunt metas for a living, and you—you're no match for her." He stuck out his chest like he was going to cruise forward and ram Reed with it. "This is what we do. You had one job, as they say. You have failed."

"Oh, it's gonna be funny the first time she kicks all y'all's asses," Augustus said without a trace of humor.

"Will not happen," Ferko with the barrettes—Scott was still not over those—said. His hair moved over his shoulders, without so much as a touch from the man himself. It slithered, like a snake, and Scott's skin crawled. *He's a Medusa.* "We will choke her."

"I hope you do," Scott said tightly. "But let's be clear about something—you may be here to give us some firepower aid, but this isn't your job. It's ours. You can help us, or you can turn around and go home."

Scott could almost feel electricity moving between the members of this new team. Rudey answered. "You think you're man enough to send us back home to Revelen?"

They're from Revelen? Scott's brow creased. "I think if you cause an international incident by making a mess of a metahuman incident on US soil, I won't have to. The president will send in everything we have—Army, Navy, Air Force, drone strikes—and you'll go back to your country in coffins." That caused more bristling. "If you're here to help, then help us. You want to plan an ambush? Great, I could really use your help. You want final say on the role your men take during the fight? I have no problem with that. But if you want to whip out your piece and piss all over us, just go home now. We don't need a bunch of guys who think they're the kings of the world—"

"Am not no Leonardo DiCaprio," Booster's grin disappeared.

"Poor choice of ... whatever, I'm not looking for trouble for you or from you," Scott said. "Can we just please ... put aside this old school-new school rivalry and work together?"

Rudey looked hard at him for a moment, but to his credit, didn't take the temperature of his team by looking back. He was plainly in charge. "Yeah," Rudey said coolly, after a minute. "We can work together." He didn't smile, though.

"Good," Scott said and stepped up, offering a hand. He made sure to reabsorb the moisture from the sweat he'd started to generate while they were all standing off. Rudey stepped forward and took his proffered hand, but his grim expression made Scott nervous. "Let's get to work, then," Scott said, trying to bury that feeling. After all, the enemy they were facing was already dangerous enough without having to worry about their so-called allies.

22.

Sienna

I brought the vault down in Montana, in as isolated a spot as I could find, miles and miles from a single ground-based light source. I figured if there was no electricity for a good long ways, it was unlikely someone would come stumbling over the vault by accident. Still, I brought it down in a clearing and then pushed it into a small ravine, making sure the trees above it covered it well. I circled the area after, trying to gauge the approaches. Anyone who came looking for it would have a hell of a time getting to it; there were no roads close by, and the level of underbrush I had to push it into suggested no one had passed this way in a long time.

"All right, then," I muttered as I landed in a bare spot of ground that had been covered over with ferns and such before I'd slid the vault across the ground beneath it. I doubted a satellite photo would show the slide marks, though, because I'd waited until I was under cover of trees to set it down. I looked at the exterior and then took a quick walk around the entire thing. None of the sides looked weaker than any other. The top looked as thick as the walls, and the bottom, from what I'd seen as I flew it out here, was also just as apparently impenetrable. "Time to see if Logan's crew just sucked."

I lit my fingers like a blowtorch and cranked them up to full heat. Despite it being a cool autumn night in Montana, I immediately started to sweat. Being this close to a blazing heat source was worse than standing out in the desert on a summer's day. I pushed my hand forward to touch the vault, hoping I could burn through that as well.

I left my hand there for at least ten minutes, probing, pushing my joints against it, even pulling back and giving it a full-strength, superheated Wolfe-punch. They all did nothing. I stripped naked, threw my clothes far, far away, and then turned into dragon-form. I made my teeth superhot and bit down on the vault after sinking my jaws around it.

Nothing. It didn't even bend.

"What the hell?" I whispered as I hurriedly dressed, my body shivering against the chill of the night. Whoever had built this vault wasn't messing around. I'd never met anything that could stand up to my powers before. "What is going on with this?"

Even Wolfe was baffled. *This metal ... it is impossibly hard ... stands up to anything,* he said.

I've seen this before, Bjorn said with haughty self-importance.

I sighed internally, deep, below where my souls could hear it. I tried not to play favorites—okay, I didn't try that hard; Zack was my favorite, easy—but of all of them, Bjorn was, without doubt, my least favorite. I liked him less than Wolfe, and that took real doing.

"Where have you seen it before, Bjorn?" I asked, trying not to let it sound petulant. "And so help me, if this ends in a joke about your penis—"

Bjorn rumbled with laughter in my head. *No, though that would be a good one—*

"Not so much," I said, "since you don't have one anymore, eunuch."

Eve disagrees with you, Bjorn crowed.

Uck, it was one time, because I was bored, Eve said. *And never again, I might add.*

"Wait, what?" I almost heaved. "You people can—what are you doing in my head when I'm not looking?"

Some of us? Nothing, Gavrikov said, almost sadly.

Quite happily nothing, Zack added.

That's because you don't know what you're missing, Eve said, creeping me out.

"Eve, I thought you were—I mean, you were with Ariadne—"

Well, she's not here, Eve said tersely, *and in case you haven't noticed, this is a—what do you call it? A sausage party?*

"Ugh," I said, closing my eyes in revulsion, "and here I thought they didn't have sausages anymore. A thousand times, ugh. It's like you're all in prison together."

The vault, Sienna, Bastian said, a little too quickly, as though he was trying to change the subject.

"Et tu, Bastian?" I asked, sighing. I hadn't want to know this, but like passing a car crash, now that it was there, I almost had to look. Look, and perhaps dry heave at the bloody mess I was seeing.

You sleep a lot and we don't, Bastian said, sounding somewhat embarrassed.

"This explains some of my recurring nightmares."

The vault, Sienna, please, Zack said.

"You could have told me, Zack."

I don't want to think about it any more than you do, Zack said. *Anyway ... the vault?*

"Right," I said, trying to get back to some semblance of an even keel. "Bjorn ... where have you seen this kind of unbreakable metal before?"

Mjolnir, he said smugly, then waited a second, apparently for comic timing. *And my penis.*

"Damn you," I said, sighing in the distant corner of the Montana wilderness. "And ..." I didn't know how to process that other news, the non-genital related one. "... Shit."

23.

Scott

"Your operational concept is not ... terrible," Rude Rudi admitted after studying the very basic ideas that Scott and his crew had come up with. The Revelen squad leader stood over the planning table in silence, his teammates leaning over him, save for Gothric the Medic, who was spinning slowly in a desk chair next to a row of unclaimed cubicles. "I agree with the premise that Denver is the location for this."

"I was considering doing it in a less populated area," Scott admitted, feeling the reluctant tug of something in the back of his mind. What was it? Worry?

"Your news media will be slower to pick it up if it takes place outside a population center," Rudey said, shaking his head slowly. "It needs to be public to guarantee she's drawn in."

"She's got a hero complex," Mac said in that hard Aussie accent, stroking the side of his massive knife blade lovingly. "She gets wind of this, she'll come runnin' right into the punch."

"I agree," Reed said with subdued, almost grudging, intensity. "She comes charging in like a bull—"

"And we gut her, right?" Mac asked, grinning with his knife up against his cheek.

"Before she can so much as blink in surprise," Reed agreed. Mac held out a fist and Reed hesitated before bumping it awkwardly.

"Mark this point on the map," Rudey said, pointing to the Denver airport.

Scott started to reach for a pen, but Joaquín the gaucho's eyes glowed green, then a small, fluorescent green beam zipped down and made a pin-sized burn in the middle of the runways. "What the ...?" Scott stared up at Joaquín, who didn't smile, but the glow in his eyes subsided swiftly, leaving them a natural green.

"We want to keep the fight contained on the airport," Rudey said, as casually as if his man hadn't just burned a hole in the map with pinprick eye beams.

"Metahumans fighting at an airport ..." Reed's voice trailed off, and he stared at the ceiling. "Why does that feel ... familiar?"

"Yeah," J.J. said from behind Scott, nosing his way up to the map. "I feel like I've seen that before ... somewhere."

"Airports are a nice place to fight," Rudey said, tapping the map. "Lots of open space to operate."

"Should we ... clear the runways first?" Scott asked. There was a slight hitch in the back of his mind, as though his thoughts were chained to something heavy, and he was having to push to get them out.

"Too risky," Ferko of the Medusa hair said. He actually used his hair as a pointing device, running a strand up and down the runways. "If it's all clear when it shows on the news, she might see the trap coming. She's brave, not stupid."

"And sure of her own near-immortality, it would seem," Booster said from his usual position in Rudey's shadow.

"Because she is near-immortal," Augustus growled. "She can channel fire through her skin, fly, blow up like a bomb, hit hard enough to make an MMA fighter's guts blow out his back, net you up with ribbons of light, and turn into a dragon if she gets real pissed."

"Let's not forget the ability to hit you with a mind blast hard enough to stunt your growth for a few years," Reed said.

"Or heal from any wound," Rudey said. "We've seen the footage, read the dossiers. We know what we're up against."

ROBERT J. CRANE

He brought his finger back to the map. "When can you have this plan ready to execute?"

"Our prisoner is awaiting transport in Las Vegas," Scott said. There was something akin to a faint scream in the back of his head that made him hesitate, cocking his head, wondering if he'd imagined it. "He's ready to move, so we could send him to Denver tonight, get on a plane ourselves. We make sure his dose of suppressant is missed tomorrow morning, and by midday we've got ourselves a mess on aisle four that's crying out for cleanup." He paused, deciding whether he should throw the barb that was on his mind. "Unless you'd prefer to take a night, get some good sleep—"

"My men are ready," Rudey said, taking the insult exactly as Scott had intended. Scott doubted that Rudey's powers were a duplicate of Joaquín's or he might have worried he was about to get burned by eye blasts. "Let's not waste any more time. We go out there, we bait the trap, and we bring Sienna Nealon's head back to your bosses here in Washington—in a bag."

24.

Sienna

"So that's how Mjolnir got so damned legendary," I muttered as I started up the steps to my apartment. I was talking to myself—well, mostly—because I was still turning over Bjorn's revelation in my head. "Still, knowing about that doesn't really help unless I can—"

I froze at the top of the steps. It was a cool night in Cedar City, just like Montana but with a few degrees difference. The air had been a little more moist in Montana, and that made it feel colder. I looked down the open walkway of the second floor, and realized pretty quickly there was someone lurking in the shadows.

"I see you," I said, readying myself. I summoned Wolfe, Bjorn, Gavrikov and Eve right to the fore of my mind. I thought about employing flight, but the fight instinct was hard. *Bastian, stand by,* I thought.

Roger that, Bastian said.

"I'm not surprised," came a high voice as a slim figure detached from the darkness. The words were slurred, and I peered at the shadow, trying to discern a face. Whoever it was, they'd been drinking. It was a she, I could tell by the build. When my neighbor's front door light caught her, I sighed in relief, then annoyance. "With that hair color, you can probably see in the dark."

It was Sandra, the construction worker who'd been giving me evil looks earlier when I was talking to Bilson.

Local drama. Ugh.

"Something I can help you with, stranger?" I asked, halting before taking the last few steps up to the second floor walk. I didn't like the idea of getting in a screaming match with a weirdo right in front of my apartment.

"Yeah, I got a bone to pick with you," Sandra said, shuffling toward me.

"Is it a chicken bone?" I asked, easing back down the stairs. "With some meat on it? Cuz I'm hungry."

Sandra was acting like she smelled blood in the water, speeding up to intercept me before I got away. "I saw you talking to him earlier, eyeball-screwing him like he was yours or something."

"Uhmmm …" I continued to back off, making it down the stairs and to the corner of the nearest underpass that led out back of the apartment complex. I was trying to put up an inoffensive, non-aggressive front, but Sandra kept picking up the pace to match my retreat. "Yeah, I'm not interested in him. He just started talking to me—"

"You liar," Sandra pronounced, breaking into a drunken, lilting run as I turned the corner. I thought about waiting in ambush for her, but the idea of cold-cocking a normal human was bad, albeit satisfying. I was trying to avoid drawing attention to myself or my safe house, after all. She was also getting louder as her frustration with me grew.

I escaped the apartment complex and debated breaking into flight. I might have gotten away, too, but there was a chance she could have seen me, and that wouldn't do me much good, either. The last thing I needed was stupid Sandra shouting that some girl had flown away from her last night. It wasn't like the US was replete with flying girls, after all. It was pretty much just me, and so that would throw up a flag for law enforcement agencies that would tumble them to my hideyhole here in a flash.

"Shit," I said, making it about halfway through the rear parking lot before I stopped, resigned. I had a lot of options, but most of them I deemed pretty bad: beat the shit out of Sandra—bad. Fly away from Sandra—bad. Cause an extreme ruckus—bad. Burn her body to ash before she could so much as scream—*probably* bad. It was hard to say on that one.

I looked at the windows of the apartment complex. No lights were on, which meant hopefully Sandra and I hadn't woken anyone yet with our little confrontation. I took a few more steps backward, toward where the complex's dumpsters waited, open, bugs buzzing under the light poles.

I sighed. I'd come up with a lot of bad options, and had settled on what I deemed the least bad one. It was definitely the most humiliating, though, especially for me, but also the path of least resistance.

"Hey, I didn't mean to ... step on your Kool-Aid or whatever," I said, holding up both hands in surrender. "He's all yours—"

Sandra was drunk, and she telegraphed her punch. I could have dodged it even if I'd been blind drunk, or just blind. But I didn't. I took it right to the cheek, the unsatisfying sound of her knuckles slapping against my bone causing my head to whip around. I put a little extra gusto into it, playing it like it was worse than it actually was. I took a knee, too, and rolled my eyes in the darkness when I knew she couldn't see it.

"Haha, I'll show you!" Sandra crowed. She followed with a slap-punch, the kind of thing that would have made me yawn if I wasn't playing dead. One of her rings dug into my scalp as her knuckles cracked against the bone at the top of my head. She grunted in pain because the hit had been terrible— probably worse for her than for me, not that I cared.

I put on a frightened face and looked up at her. I teared up a little, too, but not from pain. My pride was stinging like someone had dumped this freshly opened wound into a vat of alcohol. "Please," I said, trying to make it sound like I was begging.

"You ain't nothing but trash," Sandra said and grabbed me by the hair. She yanked me halfway to my feet and I went along with it, trying to remember that murdering stupid people was naughty and not entirely satisfying. She punched me again, though it was more of a poke, in the side, and I folded a little, but kept walking as she tried to drag me toward the dumpsters. I rolled my eyes again, seething inside, and decided that no one would go entirely willingly and without a fight into this, so I gave her a little tap to the face with my open palm.

Her eyes blazed from the hit, anger rolling off her in equal measure with the drunk and the crazy, and she breathed whiskey breath right in my face as she jerked my hair hard. I was suddenly not so happy I had the mohawk, because it was a real tight pull, all her strength concentrated on the ponytail line across my scalp rather than spreading the force out over the entire thing. "You hit like a bitch," she slurred. "Hell, you are one. Trashy little bitch."

I kept my insults—and there were oh so many—to myself, controlling my tongue as I took this humiliation. I made mewling noises to cover the rage-filled words I wanted to sputter instead. "Please ..." I said again.

"In you go, trash!" And she half-shoved, half-pushed me, trying to get me into the dumpster. It didn't go so well because I was not light, and she was really drunk. I sighed at this indignity, and heaved myself into the dumpster, figuring it would be easier than punching her skull into Jello and reaping whatever consequences followed.

I landed in a pile of trash bags that were not entirely filled with soft things and lay there, staring up at the bugs buzzing in the light overhead, like tiny stars with wings swarming around the sky.

"You just stay in there and ... think about what you've done," Sandra said, shaking a finger at me like an angry parent. I noticed she'd cracked a nail in the scuffle. "Yeah. You just ... do that." And she shut the lid.

It reeked like diapers, like rotten food, like something had died in here decades ago and had never been properly expunged. I could hear Sandra's footsteps across the parking lot as she stalked away in satisfaction, muttering to herself. "Showed ... her ..."

I blew air out of my lips and almost choked on the rancid smell as I counted backwards from a hundred, hoping I'd hear Sandra's footsteps fade out of earshot quickly. I was determined not to start another brawl with her, especially not tonight. So I lay there, in the trash, thinking about how that had happened. "Best. Month. Ever," I said with all due sarcasm, and hoped I'd finally hit rock bottom.

25.

Harmon

I studied the grainy security camera footage that Cassidy had brought up to the residence. She was standing in silence with me in the Treaty Room over a beautiful, cherry-stained desk. I could tell she was worried about my reaction as we watched Palleton Labs of Portland, Oregon, covered in a haze of dust from various angles. She zoomed in on a frame of Sienna Nealon flying off with the burden of a metal vault on her shoulders, captured from a skyline camera miles away, and I just stared.

"Do you want any other angles?" Cassidy asked, voice quivering.

"I think I get the point," I said. "She stole the vault, and with it ... well ... you know."

"I didn't know, actually," Cassidy said quietly. "So Palleton Labs was one of the—"

I walked past a painting of Ulysses S. Grant that hung over a leather-covered bench and sat down. "You're a smart girl. Put it all together."

"I don't ... know nearly all of—"

"Come on," I coaxed her. "Draw conclusions. This is what you're best at."

"You had an idea," Cassidy said, starting tentatively. "But it was beyond your ability to execute."

"Right on one," I said, and eyed the phone. I was tempted to summon a butler to bring me a drink. I didn't drink much, but tonight felt like the sort of night when I might just choose to get hammered. Then again, we'd probably end up in a nuclear crisis with Russia or China, or the Middle East would end up going further to hell, and I'd be blitzed. Being president was not an easy job in that regard. I wouldn't have relied on my VP, Richard Gondry, to drive a bread truck, let along manage a crisis. He'd been a senator from Michigan before he'd been tapped for the VP role, mostly for the sixteen electoral votes he could deliver. If he was in charge, we'd end up in a nuclear war for certain, if only because he'd use the hotline phone to Moscow to order a pizza. I sighed at not getting my drink. Forbearance. The price of leadership.

"It required ... skill you didn't have," Cassidy said, again speaking the obvious. "But you knew a guy—"

"To use the parlance of our times."

"—a guy who could ... make it happen." She swallowed heavily. "Except he didn't."

"He tried," I said, leaning my head against the back of my seat. "He tried very hard. He had an incredible mind, too, probably one of the most genius ones on the planet, with a track record in industry to match it. The Howard Hughes of our day, but with slightly fewer strange predilections." I sagged against the back of my familiar chair. Days in the presidency were long, and this one had been longer than most. I had been exhausted in Chicago this morning, and now I was almost ready to sag to sleep in my chair.

"But Sienna Nealon caught him experimenting on human beings," Cassidy said.

"She caught him doing more than that," I said. "Bribery, corruption, murder, cover-ups, human experimentation ... Edward Cavanagh was a genius. It's a measure of how effectively he covered his tracks that his crimes didn't catch up to him earlier. The whole city of Atlanta was in love with him—hell, the whole nation." I thought of the million photos I'd taken with the man, the millions in donations he'd provided my campaigns over the years. "Until that all came out and he became toxic. I was worried I might have to answer some uncomfortable questions, but fortunately the press didn't dig too deep."

"Okay," Cassidy said. She was speaking like she was expecting an axe to drop on her head at any moment. "But Cavanagh—"

"Yes, Cavanagh," I said, rubbing my forehead. "He tried. He farmed it out to others, attempting something of a cellular approach to making a breakthrough. Some of the groups came … close, I suppose. Palleton Labs had some success. There were findings, obviously, like the one in Chicago earlier this year—"

"The one Sienna Nealon stopped?"

"She stops everything, haven't you figure that out yet?" I smiled weakly. "That professor in Chicago, though … he wasn't doing the research that Cavanagh set him to. He discovered something revolutionary, true, but …"

"Not exactly what you were looking for," Cassidy said. "It was a plague, wasn't it? Designed to kill every metahuman on the planet?"

"Yes. And now Cavanagh is dead," I said, staring at the far wall of the residence. "He was likely to break, anyway, if he hadn't died in jail."

"Did you … have anything to do with that?" Cassidy asked, probing carefully.

"You're a smart girl," I said, not daring answer that. I'd long ago disabled the recording devices in the White House used by the Secret Service to monitor my activities for safety purposes, but I didn't feel any need to answer that honestly.

Cassidy stewed in the silence for a moment. "So you think whatever Sienna took from Palleton Labs … might have held the answer we were looking for?"

"I don't think it was *the* answer, per se," I said. "But it was a promising avenue that I would have liked you to explore." I glared up at her. "I want it back. I want Sienna Nealon dead, too, for real this time."

"The Revelen squad you brought in is working on—"

"Work with them," I said. "I'll give you Scott Byerly's phone number. Whisper some suggestions in his ear. He's pliable. He'll listen. Make her death happen and find that vault." I stared at her evenly. "Yes?" I gave it the force of command.

"Yes, sir," she whispered meekly and gathered her computer, still paused and zoomed in on Sienna Nealon, flying away with the vault on her shoulders. "I'll do what I can."

"Do better than that," I said, trying to make it a threat as she left me alone with my churning, miserable thoughts – all of them focused on how best I could crush Sienna Nealon.

26.

It took a while to get the smell of garbage out of my hair, and the whole time I was washing it, I was cursing Bilson for ever opening his trap to speak to me. As interesting as the possibility of sparring with a real person or persons was, I was pretty sure it wasn't worth the admission price of being tossed in a dumpster.

I sat wringing the water out of my hair for a while before switching to my threadbare towels, because I hadn't bought a hair dryer yet. (Give me a break. Wal-Mart was across town and I had to walk everywhere in Cedar City. They don't exactly have Uber Anonymous—Wanted Fugitives Edition, y'know?) As I sat there, staring at myself and twisting my dyed locks, my eyes narrowed. Not at myself in the mirror—though I did see the look, and it worked nicely for my expert-level RBF game—but at the thoughts of Sandra. That woman was a hazard, dangerous, and I was clearly sworn to destroy such things.

Of course, if I destroyed her, it was probably going to blow up in my face in the form of raising questions for local law enforcement, but still ... she could have "disappeared" into the mountains. Maybe go for a late night flight and drop mysteriously into an isolated gorge. From two thousand feet up. Something like that. Could happen to anyone. Especially if they pissed me off.

I sighed. Tempting as it was, I wouldn't have killed her

even if I wasn't trying to hide. I generally matched the punishment to the threat level, and as annoying and shitty as she was, murder was an excessive punishment for her bullying. Well, it was at least a mildly outsized punishment.

I got impatient with getting my hair dry and threw it up on top of my head in a ponytail, then put my glasses on. I picked out an ensemble that just about showed my ass cheeks out the bottom of my shorts. Not because it was weather appropriate, but because Sienna Nealon wouldn't have been caught dead in it. I also put on something that reminded me of a German beer waitress's top, and added a pair of suspenders just for kicks. The local Mormon girls were easy to pick out in their uniform dresses, and I'd caught more than a few of them staring at me and whispering to each other in the grocery store. I couldn't blame them, I thought, as I stared at myself in the non-full-length mirror, then floated a few feet above the ground to consider the whole look. It wasn't my speed, but there wasn't a hope in hell that anyone would guess it was me.

As I was showering the trash out of my hair, I'd thought of a plan, but I couldn't really implement it until nightfall this evening. It didn't have anything to do with the vault, or Harmon, or the task force, but rather with an untied loose end that was wiggling out there, somewhere. It might have been related to the others, but I couldn't see the direct connection.

And that loose end's name was Cassidy Ellis.

I had a plan of attack, but with hours to spare before I could implement it, I was reduced to menial tasks. I checked the internet as I played with my wet ponytail, then decided that yes, today would be the day I'd go to Wal-mart and get a hair dryer, among a dozen other things the nearby grocery store didn't stock. There was really no news to speak of, so I turned off the phone and headed out the door.

I regretted my decision to dress like I had the moment I caught the frigid-ass chill that sent goosebumps up my newly-shaven and definitely exposed legs. Apparently a cold front had moved in some time after I'd come in from the dumpster but before I'd finished scrubbing myself clean.

"The weather turned on you, huh?" Bilson's clear voice sounded behind me, causing me to whirl. His bald head was gleaming like a billiard ball in the crisp, cold sunlit day. "Surprise. Welcome to Utah."

I stared at him as he ambled toward me, wearing a windbreaker. I was feeling a little envious since I hadn't bought a coat yet. "How do you know I'm new here?"

"Don't get me wrong," he said with a smile, "your complexion—it's nice—"

"You a big fan of milk white?"

"—but it's not quite what you end up with after a summer at this high altitude," he said. "You know, with the desert and all. You tend to get a little more swarthy, even if you're one-hundred-percent Irish redhead."

"Oh, I'm totally a redhead under all this dye," I said, twisting my ponytail. Wait. Why was I talking to this guy again? Dammit.

"I believe you," he said, playing impassive. "By chance," he said, pausing hopefully, "were you heading to my class? I know giving you the card was kinda weird and all, but ... seriously ... would love to give you a ride if you're heading that way."

I stood there with my mouth slightly open, struck dumb. "Uhm ... maybe?"

He grinned, apparently taking that as a yes. "Awesome. Come with me." He swept past with a spring in his step.

I stood there for just a second as my brain tried to get on board with what had just happened. I bypassed the obvious retort, "I didn't say yes!" because ... I really did want to spar with someone, even if I had to do it at human speed. I missed it. And also, in spite of his psycho ex assaulting me, Bilson was not a bad looking guy. Quite the opposite. The shiny bald head and goatee combo was working for me. His lean, muscular figure didn't hurt his chances, either.

And ... it had kinda been a while. Like, a month, at least. I'd been busy, but still. I was acutely aware of how much time had elapsed. I suppose I also should have been acutely aware that I'd left a boyfriend behind when I'd fled Minnesota, but I'd been indicted since then and had shoved him away, and he was probably being watched for contact with me, so that felt like an appropriate amount of closure. He probably wasn't waiting for me or anything. Hell, given all the crap I'd had happen lately, he could have been helping to hunt me.

I followed Bilson wordlessly as he led me out to the parking lot and to his car, at which point I stopped and stared. "Really?" I asked as he stood next to the driver's seat of a grey El Camino and unlocked it manually with jangling keys.

"You like?" He smiled again.

"It's like a Ford Ranger and an AMC Gremlin had sex, and nine months later this somehow got delivered unto the world," I said, my eyes rolling over the one-row cab and short bed of the monstrosity.

Bilson feigned wounding. Probably feigned. He smiled again a few seconds later. "See, I like the combo—I can haul stuff if need be, but I'm never forced to play taxi for my friends. It's all win."

"Not sure how you call this win, but okay." I'd seen the El Camino in the parking lot and just written it off to small town charm. You see a lot of weird things out in the country, after all. Like a girl in hipster glasses with a dyed mohawk wearing short shorts and a German beer wench's blouse with suspenders. And ankle-high boots. Can't forget those.

I got in the El Camino, remembering the warning about not getting in cars with strangers about six years too late to do me any good. I fought with the seat belt, which did not want to release so I could buckle it, and finally got the damned thing to work.

"These old cars get finicky," Bilson said, almost an apology.

"I need to go to Wal-Mart later," I said. "Any chance after—"

"No problem," he said, waving me off as he started the car and put it into gear. "We'll learn, we'll have some fun, and then we'll go partake of soulless commerce."

I stared at him, not really sure if he was joking or preparing to spring Marxist philosophy on me. Instead he drove the El

Camino out of the parking lot while humming lightly to himself.

"I had a little encounter with your ex last night," I said, and he hit the brakes hard enough that if the old car had possessed airbags, they would have deployed right into our faces.

"Oh, shit," he said under his breath, like I couldn't hear him. He turned to face me, eyes wide. "What happened?"

I stared at him, trying to decide how to answer that. "She drunkenly accosted me."

"I'm so sorry," Bilson said, getting us underway again with a creaky start. "She's not my ex, by the way. I'm very careful not to date anyone as crazy as Sandra."

"Well, you need to be a little more careful about what you stick your dick into."

He almost slammed on the brakes again, and looked a little guilty. "Uh ..."

"Yeah," I said, "no need for an answer. Just exercise caution next time. For everyone's sake, really."

He didn't say anything else, just gulped as we headed into a road construction zone. I saw him turn his head studiously away, and it took me a minute to realize he was actively looking away from the person holding up the Stop/Slow sign that was moderating the flow of traffic.

I stared at the sign holder, and it only took me a second to realize it was Sandra. In sunglasses. She was watching us with her lips tight. "You sonofa—" I started to say.

"She works here, it's not like I picked it on purpose," Bilson said, shoulders tense. "I didn't realize when I set out in this direction that she'd be on duty this way, or watching, or that you two had beef—"

"Oh, no, see, she had the beef—your beef—and now I'm stuck dealing with this psycho even though I haven't had any damned beef—actually, after this I'm thinking of swearing off beef entirely—"

"Because you'd prefer—"

"Don't say fish."

"—Her?" Bilson nodded toward Sandra, who was staring through her dark glasses at us. I couldn't see through them, but I imagined her bloodshot eyes expressive and hate-filled.

I looked out the window at Sandra as we passed, not breaking eye contact, and did the princess wave, side to side, as though I were going by on a parade float.

"Are you trying to get her to snap so you can get her fired?" Bilson asked, slightly nonplussed.

"Nah, just antagonizing her for my own entertainment," I said, having not really thought it through. We passed her, and somehow she kept a lid on the crazy, which surprised me. I figured she would have lost it and Bilson would have had to speed away in a cloud of dust and thrown gravel.

I mean, if I was going to be stuck in local drama anyway, I was resolved to at least make a proper mess of it.

"My studio is just up ahead," Bilson said, nodding down the street beyond the ditch diggers, pylons, and the requisite Porta-Potty that comes with every construction site.

"How likely is it that psycho hose beast is going to come stalking over on her break?" I asked, ignoring his effort to change the subject.

Bilson stiffened. "It's, uh, happened before. But she's usually smart enough not to start something in a self-defense class, you know."

"That surprises me almost as much as her keeping her cool when I pissed her off just now," I said. When Bilson looked at me questioningly, I explained, "Because nutbags usually lack the restraint that would take."

"She seemed normal enough when we first started talking," Bilson said, and I could tell he was uncomfortable being on this subject. He probably had other plans, plans that involved macking on me and being suave, plans that were right out the window because of his poor choice in previous prospects. "She didn't, uh, go all overly-attached-girlfriend on me until later."

"So she *was* your girlfriend."

"No, it's just an expression," he said. "Err, well, an internet meme, actually."

We pulled up to a building on Main Street, brick with two big glass windows on either side of the door. It looked like a pretty typical main street shop, except it wasn't. It had a few flyers tacked up on either side indicating that it was a self-defense studio, and I gave it a hard look.

"It's a work in progress," Bilson said, alternating between looking at me and his store front. "Only been open a couple months."

I got out of the El Camino and shivered again. I hadn't even realized it, but he'd been running the heat in the car. That was decent of him. He hurried up to the door and unlocked it, holding it open for me so I could slip inside.

The studio was a pretty big space, probably a hundred feet by a hundred feet, with mirrors on two sides and green carpeting covering the floor. I stared at the carpeting, which seemed out of place until Bilson said, "It was a retail shop until a couple months ago. I just picked up the lease and started putting some classes together, y'know?"

"Sure," I said. I supposed a martial arts studio could start that way. What did I know about it?

I swept my gaze into the corner, where there was a weapons rack waiting. I saw Kendo sticks, bo sticks, rubber knives and bright yellow fake guns. There was other stuff, too; and I recognized pretty much all of it, but I wanted to play it cool, so when Bilson asked if I wanted a tour, I said, "Sure," and let him explain everything to me as though I didn't have a clue what a katana was. I held the blade when he offered it to me and tried to pretend I hadn't once decapitated a couple vampires with one. "Very cool," I said, trying to sound like I was maybe just a little put off by it as well. You know, like a normal woman who hadn't killed more human beings than a small-scale war might be.

"I'm gonna go get the locker rooms ready," he said. "Some of my students are gonna be coming pretty soon. You want to just wait out here?"

"Sure," I said, as he started to head through an alcove hallway at the back of the room. I could see the locker room doors from where I stood.

"By the way," he said, turning back to me. "If it makes you feel any better—Sandra suffers from incontinence." He smiled lamely. "Has to go pee like, every twenty minutes."

I frowned at him. "I'm not sure why that would make me

feel better, but ..."

"Because she pees herself every once in a while, if there's not a bathroom handy," he said, shrugging. "I dunno. I don't have much for you, just figured maybe ..." He shrugged again.

"I'd delight in her misery?" An idea occurred. "That ... does kinda make me feel better, actually."

"Good," Bilson said, smiling, and then he headed back into the locker room.

As soon as he was gone, I was out the door. I needed to follow up on that idea, and if I was lucky, I might just be able to be back before he even noticed I was gone.

27.

They all were piled together in a hangar across the tarmac from the government transport plane, watching on security monitors, with the door cracked open to the blue Denver sky. It was a chilly day, blustery wind sweeping in out of the north, and Scott was sorry he hadn't brought his coat. He could see the Rocky Mountains to the west past the government plane, but he was trying not to get distracted by the view.

"How long do you figure?" This came from Mac the Aussie, who was twirling his knife with lightning dexterity.

"Soon," Scott said.

"What the hell are you gonna do with that thing?" Reed asked, staring at the spinning knife, rolling like a fan on the tip of Mac's finger. "Other than give Sienna another tool with which to perform colonoscopies on you and your team?"

"Har!" Mac grunted. "She can't get my knife away from me." He flipped it and caught it perfectly on the tip of his finger, then moved in a flash, the grip appearing in his hand, blade out.

Reed frowned, studying the motion. "That's ... you're almost like an Artemis, but—"

"I'm not," Mac said, flipping the knife up again. "I've got fast-twitch muscles that are tuned up beyond belief. Watch." He vaulted forward, leaping thirty feet in less than a second.

His arm moved faster than Scott's eye could follow and a pelting fury of forward knife strikes jabbed into the air as though stabbing a live body. Scott shuddered at the display, imagining the tip of that knife perforating the chest, torso and neck of a living human. They wouldn't be living after that.

"That's ... really violent," Augustus said.

"What the hell do you think we're here for?" Mac asked with a nasty grin and darted back over to the rest of them. He stood idle for a second, then asked, loudly, "You ever heard of the twenty-one-foot rule?"

"It's, uh," Scott said, searching his memory. Hadn't Sienna taught this at some point? "It's the distance whereby if you have a knife and your subject has a gun, they can't draw and shoot fast enough to stop you before you—"

"Tear them about eight hundred new holes, yeah," Mac said, still grinning ferally. "For me, it's the hundred-meter rule."

Scott watched the Aussie make the same frightening, repetitive knifing attack. He shivered again, and not from the cold oozing through the crack in the hangar door. "That'll hurt."

"Show them now," Booster said, nodding to Mac. Booster's skin had a light glow to it, and when Mac moved this time, he seemed to go twice as far, and his attacks were blindingly fast; now he was just a blur.

"I seen a speedster move like that," Augustus said.

"I could chop a speedster to shark bait," Mac said with another rough laugh. "Chum the waters, y'know."

Scott looked to Augustus, but Augustus was looking away. It was an impressive display, maybe even enough to catch Sienna off guard. He looked at the security monitors. The airport was visible in the background, planes taxiing, people probably going about their regularly scheduled days as usual. The whole airport was bound to be full of innocent civilians—

No, he thought. *That doesn't matter.*

Does it?

That sick, nagging feeling settled on him again. He hadn't

slept well on the flight, and he'd had to return a phone call when he landed. He blinked. That one had been strange, but he couldn't quite remember what had happened during it, as though he had been having a nightmare in the middle of it. Had it been with Phillips?

"We got motion," Ferko the Medusa said, leaning forward, his hair slithering at his shoulders, itching to escape the barrettes.

Scott stared at the monitor. The transport plane was rocking unnaturally, something going on inside. "That flight crew's going to be serving up a mess," Mac cracked.

"I don't think they're going to make it," Scott whispered, feeling like something had slammed down hard on his forehead. They'd been human beings, innocent, trapped in that plane without knowledge of what was coming.

"Oh, yeah! Here we go," Rudey said, peering intently at the monitor as lightning coursed down the body of the aircraft and a small figure jumped out the side, flinging lightning behind him.

"Aviation fuel is really explo—" Booster started to say, but a deafening boom shook the hangar, rattling the walls as the monitor went white for a moment.

"I have eyes on target," J.J. said, clicking something on the keyboard. "I'm sending tweets from a hundred different accounts, randomized, with some stills I snapped from cameras around the airport. Should help boost this to trending, but ..." He whipped a phone up to his ear. "Yes? Hello?" He used a worried, harried voice. "I'm at Denver airport and there's been an explosion, and there's a—my God, he's—there's a man shooting lightning out of his hands, I think he's a metahuman! OH MY G—" He hung up, then spun around in his chair and smiled. "That ought to get the ball rolling, dontcha think?"

"Yeah," Scott said. "Now we just need to make sure and get a chopper in the air to cover the chaos. If we lose this guy ... it's game over."

"News chopper is already spooling up for takeoff," J.J. said proudly, pointing at one of the camera feeds. Sure enough, there was a news crew jumping in. "Denver PD is also putting a unit in the air. Give it a minute, and this will be all over the news—if it's not already." He flipped one of the monitors, and it switched to a local news station with the words "BREAKING NEWS" splattered all over the screen. "Oh, yeah. Meta attack? It'll go national fast. They'll be hoping she shows up."

Scott stared at the lone figure of the criminal making a break for it down a runway. Airport police cars were already rolling after him, sirens wailing. Lightning man wouldn't make the exterior fence, not nearly in time, and he seemed to realize this, turning around and running back toward the airport. "He's going for the fight," Scott whispered, and somehow, that didn't seem at all good to him.

"Rock and roll," J.J. crowed, pointing to another monitor, where one of the twenty-four-hour cable networks was breaking in with the report from Denver, even without a reporter on scene. "We're in business."

28.

Sienna

I didn't have to go far to execute my plan, just a quick jog down the road, ignoring the chilly wind that was tickling my (why in the hell were they …?) exposed thighs, and making me grimace at the lengths I was going to in order to avoid trouble.

Well, I was about to incur some trouble, but I thought this trouble would be worth it.

I huffed down the street and made it back to the Porta-Potty at the edge of the construction zone, hiding in its shadow. It was on the nearer side of construction site, fortunately, so it was easy to get to. The door was on the opposite side of where I was squatting, which meant I could safely hide here from any of the workers who approached to use the bathroom, and they wouldn't be able to see me unless they were paranoid enough to circle around the toilet first. No one was that paranoid, I figured. Well, no one but me, anyway.

I was there less than five minutes, listening to the background noise of the dirt movers, the bulldozers, and the shouts of a foreman, when I heard a female voice—oh, so familiar—yell, "I'm taking five, John. For the john."

"Dammit, Sandra," Foreman John shouted back. "You just went!"

"And I'm going again," Sandra said with an aura of venom. "You need a doctor's note?"

I heard the foreman grumble something about the halcyon days before women worked on job sites, and it made me raise an eyebrow. Then again, Sandra wasn't exactly a credit to my gender, so I restrained myself from engaging in the bone-splitting revenge I might otherwise if I'd heard someone say what he said under his breath.

Sandra stumped along, whistling a little tune under her breath—Miley Cyrus's *Wrecking Ball*, I thought—and then soon enough she opened the Porta-Potty door, stepped inside, and I could hear her dropping trow and sitting down.

Eve, I said in my head, *can we bind a thread but make it not glow?*

Sure, Eve said, nodding within me in obvious pleasure, *we can make it almost invisible.*

"Excellent," I whispered as Sandra stopped humming inside the Porta-Potty. I did a quick circuit of the toilet, using my net power to thread a heavy strand of nearly invisible light around the center of the door, then twice more at the top and bottom. They wouldn't last more than about an hour, assuming someone big and strong didn't come along and break them, but really, that was plenty enough time for me.

I came around the back again and stopped, leaning my shoulder against the Porta-Potty with a thump that shook the plastic casing. "Hey, Sandra," I said conversationally, loud enough I knew she could hear me inside the toilet.

"What the f—who is that?" Sandra called. I could hear her scuffing her feet. The jangling noise sounded like she was trying to get her pants from around her ankles and belted up so she could come bursting out to confront me.

"It's your new friend Trash, Sandra," I said with undisguised glee. "And I just wanted to tell you if I'm trash ... you're shit, Sandra. Shit." And I pushed the Porta-Potty over on the door side, sealing her in.

She screamed, there was a loud splash, and that frothy, stinking mess of thirty days of construction worker bowel movements and urine came washing out over her. I lifted the Porta-Potty bottom up a few feet, just to make sure she got the full effect of her bath, then lightly set it back down.

"You—you little—"

"Remember, Sandra, you're shit," I said. "To me. To everyone, really. Remember that as you're washing your hair for hours tonight, like I had to do last night." And taking up her whistled rendition of *Wrecking Ball* (it felt right), I sauntered off down the street casually, as though I hadn't just drenched my new enemy in fresh sewage.

I made it back to Bilson's studio just as the first student was coming in, and he held the door for me. He was an older guy, expression serious in contrast to my happy, smiling, whistling demeanor. I could see the Porta-Potty way down the street, still on its side, though it looked like some construction workers were milling around now, contemplating rescuing their erstwhile comrade. None of them seemed all that jazzed about it, for some reason. I suspected it was more than just the way Sandra now smelled. After all, I doubt Bilson had been the only one to learn the hard lesson from her about being careful where he parked his prick.

"Hey," Bilson called out to me as I came in with the other student. "Where did you—"

The guy that came in with me spoke up before I had a chance to answer or he could finish. "Did you hear about what's happening in Denver right now?"

Bilson frowned at him, apparently forgetting my mysterious disappearance. "No. What?"

"There's a metahuman attack going on," he said, pointing at the door as though it were happening out on main street, not hundreds of miles away. "They say the surviving guy from the Vegas thing yesterday escaped while he was being transported and he's fighting it out with the local cops at the airport in Denver."

"Sonofa," I said under my breath. This reeked of Scott like Sandra now reeked of poo. I'd been anticipating a trap, but this was beyond the pale. An airport? A civilian airport, in the middle of the damned day?"

"Jeez," Bilson said in quiet astonishment.

"I gotta go," I said, making for the door. Trap or no, I couldn't just let this happen.

"What?" Bilson asked, frown turning to shock. "You just got here—"

"Incontinence," I said, going with the first stupid story to spring to mind. I cringed inwardly, but went with it, now committed. "I have to go. Literally." And I pushed through the door.

"We have a bathroom he—" Bilson didn't quite get it out before I broke into a run down the street, waiting until the alley before I dodged inside and burst into flight, not caring if I got seen but doubting I would. I needed my hoodie, I needed my wig, and I needed to get to Denver.

29.

Scott

"Wow, this really is a mess," Ferko said, watching, hair still curling and uncurling on its own, flexing as though it were working out.

There were half a dozen police cruisers on fire on the runway as well as at least three airplanes. One of them was a big one that had taxied while awaiting takeoff. Scott hadn't seen any sign of deployed escape chutes before lightning man had lit it up and the thing had exploded with another cracking boom. It was now billowing orange flames and black smoke. Watching it burn turned up that sick feeling that had taken up permanent residence in Scott's belly.

"Bad news about the smoke is we're unlikely to see her come in if she approaches from the directions it's covering," Mac said, his knife still for once.

"I could clear it," Reed said, "but she'd know I was here."

"Lightning dude's not even letting the firefighters put out the planes," Augustus said. He sounded indifferent despite the chaos that confronted them. Fire engines were smoldering, and Scott counted eighteen firefighters down on the tarmac, their distinctive yellow coats standing out against the dull grey.

Holy hell, Scott thought. *What have we done ...?* There was a sweat on his forehead, as though he'd swallowed a dozen jalapeños. He said nothing, though, because Rudey was nodding in satisfaction and not one of the others seemed bothered in the least by the level of havoc on display outside.

The hangar rattled again from a distant explosion, and Augustus said, "There goes another!" Scott scoured the monitors, looking for whichever plane had lit off, but he didn't see one.

"That was a sonic boom," Reed said, jerking his rifle up and flipping the safety off. "She's here."

"Hot damn," Mac said, and again the knife was twirling on his finger, the grin on his face wide. "Showtime."

30.

Sienna

Sometimes, enough was enough, and you simply had to say, "*No mas.*"

With multiple planes filled with people in flames around me, countless cops and firemen and first responders down while trying to help, trying to save people, to stop the chaotic, maniacal threat of Lightning J. (Now definitely standing for Jerkoff, with a capital J) Antipasti, we had reached that point. We should have reached it the day before when he and his dumb buddies tore up half the Strip, but it was fast becoming apparent to me that there was nothing—NOTHING—that these fuckers on the government team wouldn't do to catch me. No stone they'd leave unturned, no slithering monster they wouldn't turn loose to try and kill me.

So when I came out of hyperspeed, I lined up a shot with my finger, and shot a blast of hot gas at Antipasti, FROM DOWNTOWN, as a stupid sports commentator might have said. (Not literal downtown. Figurative, people.)

My shot was good, my aim was true, and this capital-D douchebag burst into flames, screaming and dying right there on the runway like his d-bag bro-friend had the day before, dissolving under my attack like he was the Wicked Witch of the West—but with more flame and no trap door to save his ass. I was a good three hundred meters away from him, too, making the sniper shot that the Denver police probably would have taken in a heartbeat if they could have.

My first task accomplished, I turned my attention to the second. Setting up an ambush for me would mean having a watch post nearby, with a team or multiple teams ready to go. I suspected they'd have air support of some kind or another, if they wanted to cover all the bases, but that wouldn't show up until I was obviously in the kill box.

The smart play for me would have been to exit at top speed, straight up, and then execute a loop once I was above the clouds and haul ass home to Cedar City, then vacate my safe house there in favor of something halfway across the country. That would have kept me from confronting my would-be ambushers, and my main task would have been done.

Unfortunately for me—and my ambushers—they'd probably killed about five hundred civilians today in their zest for drawing me in, and I was madder than Sandra probably was right now (and much less covered in shit).

I wasn't going to let that stand.

I heard them below, in one of the hangars, and zipped down soundlessly, stopping myself a foot above the hangar roof. I stayed there, waiting, listening, as their boots thundered out onto the tarmac. I counted at least ten, some footfalls heavier than others. Friday was obvious, because he sounded like a rhinoceros when he moved. I wondered who the new arrivals were, but I didn't wonder long.

I popped my head over the side of the hangar and started slinging light nets for all I was worth.

Taking out the whole team only took about five seconds. I was fast, they were close, and I got them from behind in ambush, back ranks first. They cried out, of course, and the front ranks turned, but I already had them webbed up before they could raise a gun, a knife or their hands.

I saw Scott in the middle, tied tight with light webs, Reed seething with his rifle bound to his side, Augustus rolled over on his face, and Friday struggling under the burden of extra webs. Because he was extra large. There were also six other guys I didn't know, ranging from one dressed like a South American cowboy to fellows who wore the traditional black tactical gear of SpecOps teams the world over. One of them even had a tactical beard, and was struggling to free a massive knife that was trapped at his side by my light net.

"So ..." I said dryly, my black wig hanging down over my eyes. I blew it out of the way as I hovered there, just above the edge of the hangar roof, peering down at them. "I bet you guys didn't quite see this going how it did."

"Is not over yet!" called one of the new guys. He had a medic patch on his shoulder, and spoke in an Eastern European accent.

"Gothric," said another one sternly. He shook his head (as well as he could under the nets) at the medic, as if to suggest that talking to li'l ol' me was a big no-no.

One of the other black-garbed guys wasn't struggling at all, and then I realized his hair was moving unnaturally. I fired a dozen light webs and secured his whole gourd to the tarmac with a rocking thump, leaving only room for his nose to stick out in order for him to keep breathing. I was tempted to not allow that much, because these guys—these top-shelf assholes—had let a lot of people die to get me here, but I wasn't quite ready to start murdering government employees. "Yeah, don't do that," I said once the Medusa's head was properly secured to the pavement.

"You're not going to stop us," Reed said with steely fury, staring up at me with the most hateful eyes I'd ever seen from him. Seriously. There was a bottomless pit of anger there, a fury that went all the way to the soles of his shoes. "You won't get away with this."

"I'm not getting away just yet," I said cautiously, trying to decide what to do about my brother. For the last month I'd assumed he'd thought I was out of control, but this ... this was something else. "I had to protect my own life in Eden Prairie, Reed," I said, testing my assumption. "McManus turned the reporters into some kind of feral, mind-controlled horde that attacked me." I paused, considering the phrase. "Well, *more* of a feral, mind-controlled horde than they naturally are. I drove 'em off, and none of them got killed, but the others—the prisoners—they had me surrounded. They were going to kill me, Reed."

"You should have let them," my brother said with such guttural fury that it clinched in my mind that this was not my brother speaking. Something had happened to him, something akin to what had happened to those reporters, except he was perhaps slightly more mindful than they'd been. "You should have died!" he said with astonishing vitriol. Even though I knew he wasn't running the show or speaking these words himself, the words still stung.

"She will," said one of the new guys with a wide grin. His skin was slightly glowing. "Right about ... now, in fact—"

As soon as he said it, my hovering seemed to cut out, as though gravity had been switched back on beneath me. My stomach lurched as I dropped, my ass hitting the corner of the triangular hangar roof and sending a wave of pain from my tailbone up. I plummeted to the tarmac below, arms moving at roughly a tenth of my usual Wolfe-enhanced speed, and I slammed into the ground hard.

Something cracked in my leg, in my hip, and I slapped my hands against the ground to ward off the concrete from catching me in the face. It worked, but pain radiated out from my elbow in a screaming way, like a bolt of lightning running up my humerus. My mouth was open in shock, other aches of lesser intensity running through my body.

My ambushers were lying before me, still confined in my nets, until suddenly, Guy Friday jolted out. "Wheeee-haw!" the big man said, swelling as easily he tore through my web.

Reed vaulted up next, struggling as he ripped out of his own. The others broke free one by one, and I struggled to stand on my own two, wobbly feet.

Wolfe? I wondered inside, panic setting in. My hip was in agony, and I could barely stand. My arm was hanging at my side, and I didn't know if I could even move it.

Trying! Wolfe shouted, plainly near panic. *It's—too slow—one of them is—*

He said something in Greek that I didn't quite understand,

but I got the gist.

One of them had stolen my powers, turned them down like a volume adjustment.

And I had feeling that he'd done the exact opposite to the men standing before me, about to attack, which meant I was outnumbered, overpowered … and with no way to escape.

31.

"They're engaging her now," came the voice of one of my Joint Chiefs over the speakerphone, General Forster. I was in the situation room, with a video feed on the monitors from one of three Reaper drones that were orbiting the airport in Denver. That had been Cassidy's contribution to the operation, with some SpecOps teams standing by to insert in case Byerly's meta task force failed.

"What countermeasures do we have in case she tries to leave?" I asked, already fairly certain of the answer.

"We have a full complement of AMRAAM—that's the air-to-air missile—and Hellfires, which are the air-to-surface, ready to launch on your command." There was no equivocation whatsoever from the general. I'd hand-picked him, after all, and he was unlikely to defy my wishes, even if it came to launching missiles in a heavily populated civilian area.

"Excellent," I said. "Stand by, and let's see if they can get her without unleashing hell ... fire." I smiled at my own pun, and settled back in my seat to watch Sienna Nealon's end.

32.

"Fuck." I couldn't think of a better way to describe my situation, which was pretty ugly. I couldn't see any sign of air support for these guys, but really, with my ability to fly struck off my list of options, they didn't necessarily need air support to keep me boxed in their kill zone.

"You're about to be," said the knife guy with the Aussie accent, and he *moved*.

I barely had time to react, and my reaction was inadequate. I popped a fire blast right at him, but instead of it coming out sizzling at five thousand degrees Fahrenheit, it was more like I'd tossed a handful of warm embers at him. He swiveled to miss, executing a dancer-like pirouette, and I shot at him again. I was way too slow, but the only advantage I had was that he was charging at me, so I kept filling the air with my piddly, baby-dragon, soot-and-ashes blasts.

He came around in a spin and caught one full in the face. It was pure luck on my part, because he was moving so fast and I was moving so slowly that I wasn't even consciously reacting, I was just filling the air with my slightly-hotter-than-a-summer-sidewalk bursts. He did scream and spin off like a top, though, so at least there was that. He landed in a pile, and I had a suspicion he'd be popping back up, angrier than ever, in just moments.

Bastian, I said, this is an emergency. *What about going dragon?*

I don't know, Bastian said, sounding uncharacteristically

helpless. *With this sapper doing his thing, you could end up with a partial transformation or in miniaturized form, I have no idea. Might not want to chance it.*

"Shit." I said, trying to not to use the same profanity twice in a row. The guy dressed as a gaucho caught my eye, and I realized he was staring at me with bright green eyes. They were a little too bright, in fact, and I realized about a half second before he shot at me that he was another energy projector, and I dove sideways.

A blast of green energy shot through where I'd been standing a second before, and I sought cover behind some of his compatriots. Well, I actually put Friday and the medic-guy—Gothric—between us, so that Gaucho Green-Eyes couldn't see me, and he'd have to shoot through his pals to hit me. Fortunately, Wolfe had finally managed to get my elbow and leg back to normal, but in about thrice the time it would have normally taken.

Take great care, Wolfe said.

Trust me, I thought very loudly, *it's uppermost on my mind.*

"I've been looking forward to this for a long time," Friday said, almost glowing himself underneath that gimp mask. He raised a fist, and he seemed a lot faster than I'd ever seen him before. It struck me that I was also slower and weaker, which didn't augur good things. I needed to keep him between me and Gaucho Scott Summers, after all, lest I get zapped from the surface of the planet by those green eyebulbs.

"I'mma sing some Rebecca Black at you here in a second," I said, wondering if I had enough strength to counter him fist to fist. Probably not, I figured, but that was okay, because I'd spent the majority of my life training to fight people bigger and stronger than me. Like my mom.

Friday punched at me, and I slapped his blow aside at the last second, keeping it from turning my skull into a bowl of creamed corn. I caught his wrist in the joint of my elbow and brought the heel of my palm down on his elbow. I gave it a little pop, because that was all I had time for, and was rewarded with a grunt of pain as I hyper-extended the joint. He started to use his immense strength to counter, but I scraped a foot down his shin and stomped on the instep of his foot before elbowing him in the ribs and then the belly. I danced outside his reach before he could mount a counter-attack, which would probably have been brutal.

The name of this game was "Don't Get Hit," and fortunately it was one I'd played early and often in life. When you unknowingly train with a meta before your powers manifest, making sure you don't get hit becomes oh-so-important to your continued bone development—right up there with getting enough milk—as well as your dental health. Gothric, the medic, was lingering just to Friday's side in convenient kicking position, so I doubled him over with a twisting kick that probably wouldn't have hurt so much if I hadn't sunk it right into his solar plexus. He'd had his arms perfectly spread in a defensive manner, but just a couple inches too high to keep out that attack.

"Get out of the way!" Reed shouted from behind Friday, and I knew he was trying to get a clear shot at me with that rifle he was toting. The rage in his eyes when I'd talked to him had been killing-level, and I didn't doubt he was going to put me down with whatever means he had at his disposal. It didn't seem likely those means would include a gentle gust when he could bowl me over with a wave of bullets.

I tried to think strategically as well as tactically. They were going to attempt to flank me, surround me, make it a circular firing line. Fortunately the hangar was at my back, but also, unfortunately, the hangar was at my back, limiting my ability to retreat. I threw out a hand and peppered Augustus, who was coming up to my left, with severely-weakened light nets, right in his eyes. He blinked furiously, suggesting I'd bedazzled him and little more, but in a game of seconds, I was just trying to control the crowd so that nobody got close enough to end me while I searched for a solution to the crisis at hand.

You should absorb more souls, Eve pronounced, *at this most opportune of times. May I suggest a lovely, leggy woman with a heart of—*

"No," I said as Friday came back around for another attack. "Why would I want more of you people having sex in my head?"

Friday froze mid-swing. "Whut ... sex?" He sounded almost hopeful.

I threw myself into him with a double foot dropkick, using the remaining vestiges of my flight power as well as my meta strength as a boost. I hit him flush, and all the air went out of him like I'd just popped a balloon. His eyes got big, and he flew backward into Reed, whose "OOF!" I heard as Friday slammed into him, a few rounds of M-16 ammo discharging wildly into the sky as they both came crashing down.

"Damn!" I said, dodging behind Gothric the medic again. I grabbed him by the lapels and held him in front of me as I punched him. I could see Gaucho Marx and his red neck bandana behind him, but I interposed Gothric's head between us, using him as a human shield. Gothric's eyes were wide and glowing. I had him off balance, but I decided that although this temporary stalemate was exactly that— temporary—the team medic was a perfect chance to really test what kind of strength I had left now that they were sapping me.

So I picked up Gothric, taking care to keep his body between us, and heaved him right at Gaucho like a human javelin.

I ran sideways as soon as I released the medic, trying to hedge by grabbing hold of Augustus in hopes he'd also make a good shield, but he fought me off, still half-blind, yanking his arm out of my grasp. It didn't matter; Gaucho had apparently never had a teammate thrown at him before. Even more obviously, Gaucho had not practiced much in the way of physical combat, apparently leaning on his role as team meta-power eye-sniper to the exclusion of all else.

Gothric and Gaucho's skulls met in a beautiful symphony of skull-cracking that I was intimately familiar with by this point in my career. It sounded like a watermelon smacking on pavement, sick and cringeworthy. My strength wasn't enough to burst them both open like overripe fruit, but they both went down with whimpers of pain, Gothric thumping along for another five feet or so in a limp roll. He didn't move, probably just knocked cold, but Gaucho writhed in pain, holding his sensitive little head.

"Medic!" I called, trying to have a little fun in spite of the clearly present danger I was facing. It was just another day, really, and this was the sort of shit I lived for.

"You won't need one in a minute," Medusa said in a low voice, and I realized his hair was curling around me, slithering across the ground like some kind of psychotic plant growth.

"Ewww!" I said, averse to some dude's gross locks snaking over me. I peppered his hair with a burst of ashy flame, and he tensed, neck muscles swelling like he'd tried to pass a boulder. The hair snaked away, retreating back to its mommy, and I dusted him with an ash shot to the face just to be safe. He folded up and screeched, raking his own eyes to try and clear them. "You might need a few drops of Clear Eyes for that," I said. "Some of the locals probably have some, it's Colorado, after all—"

The pavement exploded in a burst of gravel around me, and I knew Augustus had lashed out with his weapon of last resort. He'd reached into the very material that made up the tarmac and ripped the earth-based components out of it, spattering me—and himself—with debris like pellets from a shotgun barrel. A thousand little fires sprang up in my back and legs, and I dropped, landing hard on my elbows again as they broke my fall. Blood trickled down me, like sweat running down my back sides.

Wolfe, I thought, desperately.

I am hurrying, he said, with more than a little desperation of his own. But I knew it was too late as I writhed there next to Augustus, my remaining foes closing in on me, only shadows in my squinted, teary eyes, as they drew closer and closer, ready to end me.

33.

Scott

Scott had hung back during the battle, watching it unfold as though it were something on a movie screen playing out in front of him, unreal, unrealized, blinking his eyes to try and spur himself into some kind of action.

They're going to kill her, some small part of his brain screamed, his fingers stroking the pistol grip of his HK MP5 submachine gun. He let it hang on its sling, his fingers tracing down to the Sig Sauer P226 pistol on his belt, then brought up both hands, wet with perspiration despite the dry, Colorado air. He had so many options at his fingertips—

Good, came the other voice in his mind, *let's help kill her,* but that same faint scream worked in the background over the sound of the flames cooking those loaded airplanes, burning like infernos on the horizon.

People are dying.

Let them die. Kill her.

He blinked. *This isn't worth it.*

Yes, it is.

"She's down," Rudey pronounced, stepping forward, his gun at the ready. He was ready to fire, Scott could see it as his finger tightened on the trigger and he lifted his Eastern Bloc rifle. *Sienna would know what it's called,* Scott thought dully, and this spurred another lancing pain through his skull, as though someone had reached giant hands inside and started to play with his brain—

Scott darted out in front of Rudey, in front of Booster, both of whom were stalking forward slowly, weapons ready. "Hey!" Rudey shouted, as nasty as ever, as Scott interposed his body between them and Sienna, cutting off their clean shot.

"I've been waiting a long time for this," Scott said, his body jerking spasmodically as he walked toward Sienna's fallen form. One of his legs was dragging in a limp, as though fighting him. Rudey started to move to the side and Scott increased his pace, trying to keep himself between the team leader and Sienna's prostrate form. She wasn't making any noise, but she was rocking slightly, and he could see hints of gravel slowly dropping against the pavement as her wounds healed themselves. His leg almost buckled beneath him, but he soldiered on, drawing closer and closer—

Need to be close, that soft voice said. *Danger close.*

KILL HER! the other voice screamed.

"I've wanted ... to ... hurt you ..." He was laboring to get the words out, both sides of him at war with each other, fighting to speak truth and pretense at the same time. "... To ... make you ... pay ..." He reached her and leaned over, cutting off Rudey's shot from the side as he grasped her at the shoulder, making ready to lift her up. He lowered his voice, meta-low, knowing only she could hear it, and said, "The ... smiling ... guy ..."

Sienna's head snapped around and she did exactly what he would have predicted she'd do—exactly what she had trained to do, trained him to do—

She drew Scott's pistol as she flew to her feet, yanking him around to use as a human shield. She fired twice, and Booster went down first. Scott ignored the whiplash effect; she'd heard him, got what he was trying to say. More shots followed, quicker, four of them this time, and Rudey's face dissolved into a mask of blood and bone as her accuracy and speed returned, along with her powers—

She kneed Scott in the back and sent him to the pavement, hard. He landed on a shoulder and heard it crack in dislocation or fracture, casting a look behind him to see Sienna pointing the weapon right at him, barrel wavering as she turned the idea over in her mind—

She apparently decided and launched into the air without firing the shot, disappearing over the hangar and out of sight. *Lucky me,* Scott thought, collapsing from the pain and from the wrestling of two sides of his mind that had battled for control, their conflict still unresolved as he passed into unconsciousness.

34.

Harmon

I stared in near-disbelief at the real-time imagery from one of the Reaper drones on the far wall of the Situation Room. She'd defeated the entire team, killing at least one of the Revelen Spec-Ops people. I didn't care to do names, but I was fairly certain he was the team leader. "I'm going to catch some hell for that later," I muttered. No one heard me.

"Sir," General Forster said from the speakerphone, "she's—"

"Engage and destroy, general," I said with a stab of impatience. I mean, really. Did I have to do all the thinking myself?

Of course I did. That's why I was in charge.

"Aye, sir."

35.

Sienna

I'd caught that something was wrong with Scott. He'd just saved my life, but in doing so he'd acted so very weird that alarms were wailing in my head. As much as they could be given I was already under attack by ten metas who'd somehow—through that smiling weirdo—stripped me of the most of my powers. I hadn't killed him, mainly because I'd been too panicked to do anything but flee once I had the shot. Well, that and point a gun at Scott as my brain leapt to some conclusions that had not been in evidence for a year.

Someone had monkeyed with his mind just the same as they'd done to Reed and Augustus. Bazinga.

That little factoid opened up some other questions, though, too, such as: where the hell were Veronika, Colin and Phinneus, who I'd paid to protect my friends? Where was Kat? And where was Ariadne?

I might have agonized over these questions if I hadn't suddenly become aware of an AIM-120 AMRAAM (Advanced Medium-Range Air-to-Air Missile, in case you were wondering) about thirty yards behind me. "HOLY SHIT!" I screamed, and fired eighteen small-scale light nets along with a few bursts of fire that I tried to direct at the missile behind me as I dove out of the sky like a dead bird. Except I went at more than Mach One.

The explosion was a real eye-opener, as the missile collided with one of my fireballs and lit off. I'd trained for this, strangely enough, after listening to the agency's drone operator, Harper, get drunk in a bar one night and explain exactly what happens to a target being pursued by a drone or a fighter jet. AMRAAMS sought out radar signature, not heat, so they were going to come after me, not any flaming blasts I sent out to try and distract them.

Which meant I wasn't out of the woods yet.

I cranked up the speed, catching a glimpse of another AMRAAM coming in hot behind me. Given slightly more time to react, I launched countermeasures again, but more carefully aimed. This time I caught the missile in a hard light net, and it glowed brightly as I splashed the AMRAAM, the explosion somewhat buffered by my net.

I might—maybe—have been able to outrun the drones (and I was pretty sure it was drones rather than active combat jets) that were firing at me, but I wasn't confident enough to stake my life on it. So I swung around and poured on the speed, flying right back into the teeth of the tiger. Another AMRAAM came zipping by and I tossed a fire behind me as we passed. The explosion warned me I'd hit my target.

I was past Denver proper, about ten thousand feet up. The drones had followed me far enough out of town that I felt comfortable engaging them, knowing that whatever debris I sent raining down was going to end up in mostly unpopulated areas. Apparently that wasn't much of a concern for my enemies, which sent another charge of anger through me as I realized that Scott, in his capacity as task force leader, couldn't have ordered a military drone strike over the United States.

"Harmon," I growled as I picked out a flying dot in the distance and came at it head-on, screamingly fast.

As I drew closer, I realized I'd only slightly miscalculated. I'd expected them to be using the old Predator drones, but no, this one, at least, was one of the new Reapers. Fortunately, they hadn't built them for close-in dogfighting, and while this one had another missile tucked under its wing, it was one of the Air-to-Surface (a.k.a., can only fire at ground targets) Hellfire missiles.

148

I blasted the drone to smithereens, turned north toward another shape on the horizon. I reduced another $17 million dollars of the US Air Force's budget to scrap, and then closed on a third, smoking it out of the sky. "Nice plan, *el presidente*," I said to myself as I made the turn back to the west and hit my afterburners, blasting into supersonic speed. "Too bad you forgot to send out the sheepdogs to mind the flock." I doubted they'd make that mistake again.

36.

I stared at the screens, which were throwing off static along with the simple words "Signal Lost."

Sienna Nealon had destroyed all three of our drones, and most likely escaped.

"We have eyes on target," a voice announced over the conference call, and another image sprung up on the monitor. It was a satellite image, looking down from space, and it zoomed in to give me a slightly blurry view of a human figure jetting across the sky, heading west.

"Loss of visual approaching," that same voice said again. It wasn't the general. It was probably one of his inferiors, watching with him in the Pentagon's situation room. Sienna flew out of the frame, out of the range of our satellite, and that same voice announced, "Loss of visual contact with target."

"I don't suppose we have another satellite up there, just looking down at ..." I lifted my hands up. "What is that? Utah?"

"Yes, sir," the general broke back into the line. "We have another satellite in place over western Nevada and will be able to re-establish contact should she ... come out the other side."

"Wonderful," I said. "So long as she's not planning to stay anywhere in the Mountain Time Zone, we should have her, then." I felt my sarcasm was warranted.

150

"Ahh, well ... yes, sir."

I hung up on the general and his staff and got out of my chair. "If only everyone thought like I did ..." I mused, not for the first time. "It's so hard to find competent people." I stared at one of the wall-hung television screens and reached out to polish a smudge on it. It was a minor thing, but I needed it to be perfect. "There," I said to the empty room, and then headed for the door. I needed to find Cassidy, to impress upon her the importance of correcting this miscalculation immediately.

Either that ... or finding a solution to the other damned problem I had her wrestling with. Because if she'd just get one or the other done, Sienna Nealon would no longer be a problem.

37.

Scott

"What the hell were you thinking?" Reed asked, his teeth bared as if he'd turned into an animal-type meta.

The tarmac of Denver International Airport was still a burning hellscape, though police cars and fire engines were now dealing with some of the chaos that had been unleashed during their operation.

"I was thinking I was going to shoot her," Scott lied, his face flushed, shoulder still aching from where she'd hurled him to the ground. "It's this dream I've had in my heart for, oh, I dunno, a year or so while you were off kissing her ass—" He jabbed that hot poker into Reed, figuring he'd see what sort of reaction he could stir up.

It worked. Reed flushed scarlet and took a step toward him but was held back by Augustus, who was bloodied from his play with the gravel explosion. "Easy, big guy," Augustus said, flatter and with less care than usual. "You'd want to shoot her in the head if you had a chance, too."

"I *would have* shot her if I'd had a chance," Reed said, the hostility burning out of him like waves of fire. "I wouldn't have thrown away my shot!"

"Yeah, you proved that yesterday," Scott said, but it provoked no response.

"Rudi is dead," Ferko said, his hair restored to its place over his shoulders, secured by the barrettes. Scott looked at him for barely a second, unable to much stomach the weird, snakelike movements. "Because you walked in front of us—"

"This is my hunt," Scott said, not putting too much argument into it. "Maybe if your boss hadn't been so busy asserting his dominance by trying to lead the field, he might still have a face."

"Are we gearing up for another fight?" Mac asked, still sporting red, blotchy skin around his eyes where Sienna had burned him. "This time among ourselves?"

"She wasn't as easy as we'd thought she was going to be." This came from Joaquín the Gaucho, who was sporting two black eyes and a bloody nose. Scott couldn't remember if he'd spoken before or not; he didn't think so, based on the way the others of his team halted and listened to him. An aura of palpable discomfort passed between the five who remained, and Scott tried to keep his mildly exuberant glow buried deep within. It wasn't hard, as he was both hurting and still experiencing some sort of split personality feeling.

"I had her turned down to minimum," Booster said, his grin gone. Scott had wondered what it would take to wipe the smile off his face. "She still took out—what, all but three of us?"

"I would have killed her if this lunkhead hadn't gotten distracted by his baby boner and thrown at me," Reed seethed, looking at Friday. "Does your brain lose bloodflow when you're bulking up or were you just thinking with the wrong head?"

Friday stood very still, head swiveling between Reed and Scott. "I was—she just—she said—"

"We all heard what she said," Augustus said, "but none of the rest of us froze in place when she said it. You did that." He adopted a pained look as he picked at a wound, using his powers to extract a tiny piece of stone. "And unfortunately, you didn't even take much of a hit before you went down like Glass Joe in Round One."

"Settle down," Gothric said, putting a hand on Augustus's head.

Augustus stiffened at the touch, and then his eyes rolled skyward in rapture. "Ohhh, damn. You know, this is better than the last massage I paid for." His wounds started to close up before Scott's eyes, and he finally realized the purpose of the medic patch on Gothric's sleeve: *Persephone.*

"Well, boys," J.J. announced as he came out of the hangar, "that was an ass-kicking of the sort I have seldom seen." He didn't seem gleeful about it, Scott realized as he pulled his neck left and right experimentally. It hurt in both directions.

"You've worked with Sienna for years," Scott said. "You've seen her deal out all manner of ass-kickings."

"Yeah, but usually not twenty yards from where I'm sitting," J.J. said. "I mean, I was right over there, peering around the corner, seeing you get whooped on in real time. Very different experience." He shrugged. "Anyway, while I'm sure we're all stinging from this seeming loss—" He seemed surprisingly buoyant now, eyes sparkling, "—it's not all bad news."

"She got away," Reed said simply.

"True," J.J. said, and Scott started to tingle with the faintest hint of worry, "but we had a satellite overhead, watching her vector on approach and exit." He didn't smile, but he looked at them with satisfaction. "We know which way she fled, and we know how long it took her to get here after the news broke, which means ..." now he did smile, but coldly, "...we have a follow-up move." He held up his fist, closed tight. "Next time, we just need to take what we learned, and make sure she doesn't get out alive."

38.

"She got away again, didn't she?" Cassidy asked as I walked into the Oval Office. I hadn't expected to find her here, but there she was, a small laptop sitting on my desk, typing away delicately as I came up behind her.

"To the shock and surprise of all but you, apparently," I said, with more humor than I felt. I stared out for a moment through the bulletproof glass. "Burned through our drones like paper lanterns, tore through the Revelen mercs like they were pre-schoolers."

"Ouch." Cassidy stopped typing. She held her hands gingerly poised over the keys, and I stared down at her. Something was off, and not just Cassidy's usual skittishness. I sniffed; the air held the aroma of something ... burned, mixed with antiseptic.

I reached down over her shoulder and seized hold of one of her wrists—gently, and turned it over. A black burn had already started to heal over on her palm. I could smell it, unbandaged, the wound exposed to the world. I frowned down at her as she looked up at me, and she felt ... blank. There was a tremor of fear that ran through her, as though I would lash out and hurt her. I could feel her pain and worry. "Cassidy," I said softly, "what happened to your hand?"

"I don't know," she said, and seemed to be answering honestly. "I touched a frayed power cord, I think."

I stared at the wound. "I'll call my doctor and have her

155

take a look at—"

"No," she said, trying to tug the hand away from me, but with little force. "I'm a meta, it'll heal. Accidents happen sometimes, even to us."

"You need to be careful," I said, letting her hand go. She truly didn't know what happened, I could tell. She was right, accidents did happen, and an accident such as this would tend to cause some short term memory loss. "You're a vital part of my plan, I can't have you getting hurt."

"Okay," she said, and returned her fingers to the keys, and back to business. "If Nealon went straight through the drones, I don't think you can hold back—"

"Yes, I'm realizing that," I said. "I had hoped to avoid mobilizing the entire US Air Force to engage her over the Homeland. Something about seeing fighter jets shooting missiles above major cities tends to fail to instill confidence that everything's running right."

"I understand the need to balance—"

"I doubt it."

"—But do you really care about short-term polling numbers?" Cassidy finished, a bit lamely for her.

"I care what people think, yes," I said, answering her honestly. It always bothered me when the national mood turned against me. Of course, forty percent of the population would have voted for me even if I started holding executions on the White House lawn, so long as they were of the right people. Another forty percent wouldn't vote for me no matter what I did, and twenty percent tended to decide all the elections. I didn't worry about that forty that hated me—at least not now—but the twenty in the middle? Them, I agonized over.

"That's ... surprising to me," Cassidy said.

"Is there any more human desire than the one that drives us to connect with others?" I asked, sitting down in the chair next to her. "Than the one to love, and be loved in return? I have love for humanity, see, the entire cross-section of it. I loved my wife, though she's been gone so long now that I doubt anyone notices if I don't mention her in a campaign speech. Underneath it all ... I do love people. Even the ones that oppose me with everything they have, though I strongly disagree with them." I chuckled. "My supporters hate them ... don't understand them ... and they don't really understand my supporters, either. There's this gulf of misunderstanding, and even if I tried to bridge it through speeches or outreach, there's a lot of bad blood. Too much, really, to ever reconcile the difference. Two people can have a discussion, but when three hundred and fifty million are doing it, it becomes a very bitter argument." I stared at her, but past her. "I mean to settle this argument once and for all."

Cassidy cleared her throat. "Which do you want me to focus on ... the research or the plan to kill Sienna Nealon?"

"I'll focus on Nealon," I said, taking a breath. "I've got the education bill taken care of, my Deputy Chief of Staff is working on some of the other crises that are popping ... the Middle East again, of course ... I'll put the entire damned military on this, if need be. It's akin to using a nuclear bomb to swat a fly, but I have a nuclear arsenal at my disposal." I sighed. "I will run the plan by you once it's done, though, just to make sure you don't see any obvious holes."

"I keep missing the obvious holes," Cassidy said, sounding slightly contrite. "That's why she's still alive."

"Oh, I think we both know that's not true," I said, standing up. "Sienna Nealon keeps punching new holes in these plans, that's why she's still alive. I only wish she was still on our side. Perhaps pushing her to the margins was a poor choice. I thought I had the measure of her when we met, but her tenacity is ... quite astonishing. Most people would run and hide, not daring to show their face when the entire government was after them. When they write the history books of my presidency, I expect this will be the low point."

"Yes, sir," Cassidy said. I sensed she had other, more sarcastic, responses in mind, but she knew enough to keep them to herself. "I'll probably move back to my tank to work for a while, if that's all right with you."

"Oval Office not quiet enough for you?" I asked with a teasing smile.

"It's ... it's fine," she said, paling visibly, turning her a brighter shade of white. And I would have thought such a thing impossible.

"You don't have to like it," I said, standing up straight and looking out the window again. Darkness was starting to fall out on the lawn. "It's a product of a time before ours. The White House was last heavily renovated—practically turned into a shell and rebuilt from the outside in—during the Truman presidency. That was seventy years ago. The shell is from ... after the War of 1812, I think? When the British burned Washington? Sometimes the things we build stay with us for reasons of tradition long after something better might have come along." I wished the White House photographer had been here; I felt like I was striking a perfect pose for him to capture. "We can do better." I pointed at her, then at me. "*We* will do better. Go work in your tank, if that's better for you. Tradition be damned." I gave her a smile as I left, on my way to the next thing that needed to be done.

39.

Sienna

I made it back to my apartment complex in Cedar City close to the end of the afternoon, when the shadows were getting long across the ground. I was a bloody mess again and I ditched the hoodie and wig in the desert with the staple gun (ow, ow and more ow), mopped my brow with the sweat that was on it, and hobbled back toward my building on a leg that was still aching, if now healed.

That was unnecessary, Zack said.

"I dunno," I said, pretty well over discussing it now that this water had gone under the bridge, "I wiped Antipasti off the planet, which feels like a victory worth doing a touchdown dance for. He did kill an awful lot of people."

And you showed your pursuers you are not to be trifled with, Wolfe said.

"I killed some dude I didn't even know," I said. "A good question would be, 'Who was that guy?' cuz he and his bros didn't sound like Americans, and a better one might be, 'Why is some group of metas who isn't from the US government helping in a manhunt for me'?" I stalked along toward the apartment building, which was coming up pretty fast now. I wasn't moving at meta speed, but in spite of my leg's desire to limp, I wasn't sparing the horses, either. Or hamstrings, maybe?

They've called in outside help, Bastian said.

"Who's called in outside help?" I asked, chewing it over.

"Harmon, right?" I was asking mainly as a survey question to back up my own suspicions.

Seems likely, Eve said.

Their accents, Gavrikov said. *Some were Eastern European. From around Revelen, I think?*

"Revelen again," I muttered. "What the hell is their problem?"

A sky-high poverty rate and lack of access to a warm-water port? Zack asked. *Oh, wait, they just took over Canta Morgana. I guess they sorted that warm-water port issue.*

"It's on the Baltic Sea, so I don't know about that," I said. "I wouldn't want to swim there in January." I frowned. "So Harmon pulls diplomatic strings to bring in outside metas to help wreck my ass. It's starting to feel like he has a vendetta, which is a funny thing considering I'm responsible for re-electing that douche."

Maybe it's not him, Bjorn said. *Perhaps there is a power behind the throne.*

"The governmental version of Cyrano de Bergerac?" I asked. "Whispering in his ear, helping set his priorities?" I shrugged. "Bjorn, that's as good a theory as any I've considered. Cassidy tweaking his strings is a real possibility, especially given that her intelligence allows for first-rate access to blackmail material of the sort even a sitting president might not want released—"

Wait, we are talking about Cassidy? Bjorn asked. *That tiny slip of a thing that you nearly dropped in the cornfields of Iowa?* He laughed, heartily. *Impossible.*

"She's smarter than you, not that it would take much," I said. "Smarter than me, smarter than anyone. At least when it comes to pure intelligence. I wouldn't lay money on her in a fistfight or anything, but she's done enough damage to my life that I'm not going to go dismissing her just because she's puny-looking. She could probably still break a normal human in half."

What are you going to do about her? Zack asked as my shoes hit the parking lot of my complex.

"I've got a plan," I said. "Wait and see." I looked at the building and sighed. "We're gonna have to move out tonight."

That's the safest bet, Bastian agreed.

Yes, you've shown your ass to them twice, which is enough to give them a good starting point when it comes to searching for you, Eve said.

"I didn't show them my ass," I said, looking at my jeans, which were shredded. "I changed out of my ass-displaying shorty shorts before I flew to Denver, thank you very much."

The world thanks you for that, Eve said.

"Oh come on," I said, "don't give me that. I'm at least better than Bjorn."

Eve hesitated before giving me a patronizing, *Sure you are.*

A car horn honked behind me, and I turned as Bilson's El Camino rattled into the parking lot and parked right in front of me. He jumped out like someone had attached a massive spring to his ass and shut the door behind him. "Hey!" He sounded almost relieved. "You missed class."

"Do I need a doctor's note?" I asked.

"Not … with the amount of blood you got on you," he said, looking me up and down again in astonishment. "Your jeans—did they start out shredded like that?"

I looked down again. "Totally. This is the style now, don't you know? It's all over NYC."

"Okay …" He didn't seem convinced. "I thought I was going to teach you some things. Self-defense and whatnot."

I shrugged. "I think I'm good." I started to walk off.

"Wait," he said, and I could tell he was perplexed. I was already disengaging, looking to evacuate my nascent relationship with him before it even started. I was leaving town, after all, so what was the point of leading this guy on? And as hard up as I might have been, the idea of going rock-em, sock-em with this guy between the sheets given how much trouble I'd had with his most recent conquest … well, he'd lost his most of his appeal. I was kinda put off by Sandra's … everything. "Is … is that it, then?" he asked.

"I think so," I nodded. "You seem like a nice guy, but … yeah. Your taste in women—and I'm including myself here—scary, dude. Do better."

I wasn't trying to offend him, but I could see my intention counted for little. "Thanks," he said snottily.

"Sorry," I said with a shrug, and turned away. "Truth is a real bitch. And so is your ex."

"Classy."

"Not one of the top adjectives used to describe me. Did you not see the shorts earlier?"

I bopped out of sight, into the darkened tunnel leading to the interior of the complex. Something jumped out at me, bringing with it the smell of feces and urine slightly—but only slightly—tempered by chemicals. It didn't take a Cassidy IQ to realize it was Sandra, the stupid clown. I reacted without thinking, and popped her in the nose, pulling my punch at the last second. It still created a bloody mess, like I'd smashed a strawberry. She dropped, clutching at her face. "What the—?" she asked, rolling around on the ground.

"He's all yours, if you can convince him you're not a brain-damaged lunatic," I said, dodging around the corner, and heading up the stairs without looking back. "Good luck with that." Cuz she'd sure as shit need it.

40.

I'd spent last the day zipping between Cedar City and Denver, fighting some of the nastiest opponents I could recall being squared off against, the night before flying a multi-ton vault across half the country after committing the most destructive burglary I'd ever heard of, and that following a day of nasty battle in Las Vegas.

I'd also spent the time I should have been sleeping last night washing the smell of garbage out of my hair, which left me pretty well exhausted. I looked around my small apartment, mentally coming up with a list of things I was going to need to do to clear out. I didn't technically have to do any of them; I could destroy a few things and be gone, or even probably just leave them as they were. They were unlikely to tie me to any of my other hidey-holes, but I would have preferred to be a hundred percent sure and just do the thing right.

Also, I wanted to bring my clothes with me, because shopping? Not a favorite activity for Sienna Nealon or any of the army of new identities I could assume.

I was going to have to change my look, though. Maybe start wearing my mohawk up instead of down and ponytailed. It reminded me vaguely of a girl not unlike myself named Adelaide, except she was a lot thinner and cooler looking in her eighties style than I was with my throwback millennial hipster look. Maybe I should go more punk, I thought. It might change the look enough to trip up the video search algorithms that J.J. would be deploying on

Cedar City's video surveillance camera footage once they tracked me back here. They'd get updated pictures for sure, even as much as I tried to be aware of and avoid security cameras. There was simply no avoiding them all, but the good news was that if they didn't find Cedar City for a few weeks, most of the footage would be erased over with new footage by the time they started trying to capture it.

All this ran through my mind, but at a vastly slowed rate. I was wearing down. I'd been tired before I went into the fight in Denver, and the hurt I'd suffered in that battle had coupled with the revelations about my crew being mind-controlled to leave me with even more questions. Who was doing this to them? Where was the rest of my team?

What the hell was going on?

Why was I being fall-guy'd?

For the last month I'd considered—often, depressingly often—that maybe what was happening right now, from my team's betrayal to Scott's hatred of me to the media and nation turning against me was all just an unfortunately timed harvest of all my previous bad actions. I hadn't been a good girl, after all. I'd done *some* good, but some bad, too, and though I'd steadily outrun the shit wave up until now, there was every possibility that I was just finally entering what Churchill called, "a period of consequences."

But that was before I knew Reed, Augustus, J.J. and Scott were all being puppeteered. It was one thing for me to think that Cassidy Ellis was just out there, trying to wreck me because she still hated me. It was another to think there was an active conspiracy in place fomented by the US government to wipe me off the planet with drone strikes and multi-national meta spec-ops teams.

And how did that damned vault at Palleton Labs figure into this? *Did* it figure into it? Or was that some other problem that Timothy Logan was tearing around the corners of?

"The plan," I muttered, picking up my stash of mobile phones and trying to decide whether I should check the internet before I left. I was feeling paranoid, and worried that I might throw up flags like, say, internet searches that could point J.J. in my direction, so I scorched them into nothingness one by one and washed the ashes down the drain in the shower.

I threw every article of clothing into a duffel and put it by the door, grabbed every ID I had and eliminated them as well. I had fresh ones in my other hidey-holes, along with fresh cell phones, too, unconnected to the burners I'd just destroyed.

I checked and rechecked everything. There was no way to eliminate the accumulated DNA around the apartment, so they were going to get that, and it'd confirm for them I'd been here. Same with fingerprints, not that I cared, because that truth was going to get out. Sandra would probably tattle, too, once they knew I'd been here, and that would feed the media flame—if the FBI task force released it to the press.

Or maybe she wouldn't. Maybe Sandra's pride would keep her from admitting I'd rolled her in shit and trapped her there for a while. Heh.

My thoughts chugged to a halt, and I considered the duffel by the door. I couldn't leave right now, it'd be obvious. I needed to leave in the middle of the night, when no one could see me and I could just take off. That put me in a sticky position, worrying that perhaps I was giving Scott and Co. a chance to track me down to this very location, but there wasn't a lot to be done about it. I was exhausted, I needed sleep, and in sleep, I could actually advance the plan.

Yeah. I needed to sleep. My eyelids were embracing gravity like someone had fastened those two big metal Clarys to them and thrown the dumbasses over a cliff.

"All right, then," I said, making my way to my bed. I wished I'd still had the gun I'd taken off of Scott, but I'd left it in the desert for lack of a place to carry it safely on my person. At my next hidey-hole, I was resolved to dress loosely enough to carry a pistol at all times, because if I was going to face this power-sapper again, I'd need other means at my disposal than just my powers.

"Clear your mind," I said, lying back in the soft bedding that I hadn't embraced in almost forty-eight hours. "Focus … focus …" I tried to think of nothing but one person, the one person I wanted to talk to in all the world right now. I pictured her dark hair, her skeletal frame, her little nose, and when the darkness of sleep took hold of me, I seemed to open my eyes somewhere else.

She was there.

"Hello, Cassidy," I said, staring at her across the black background that surrounded us. I smiled. "I've been wanting to talk to you."

41.

She didn't look as scared as she had the time I'd caught her outside Omaha, but Cassidy Ellis didn't look entirely pleased to see me, either. She looked around the dark space surrounding us, an arena of blackness and shadow, and then back at me, keeping her head down. This was a dreamwalk, one of my succubus powers to connect with sleeping people in a shared dream. I seldom used it, and it wasn't a widely known ability, or else the news media would probably be shitting themselves at the thought I could visit them all in their dreams anytime I wished. Cassidy was a quick thinker, and I suspected there was more going through her head right now than I could have even guessed at, especially since she didn't seem altogether surprised to find me in her dreams. "What do you want?" she mumbled.

"Peace on earth, good will toward men and women," I said.

She cocked her head at me, but only for a second. "Because Christmas is coming up in a few weeks. Clever."

"You kindasorta get me, Cassidy. The quips, at least. The far-reaching analogies and references that no one else picks up."

"Uh huh," Cassidy murmured, shuffling uneasily on those stick-like legs. "What do you really want?"

"Questions answered."

"Have you tried Google?" She didn't put much mustard into her reply, and her response landed kind of flat, like she was trying to act defiant without actually being defiant.

Token defense. I wondered why she would do that. Was it just a product of her mad intelligence combined with an utter lack of self-awareness?

Or was it intentional?

"Google can't answer the questions I've got," I said, deciding to plunge right ahead. "Like, for example—where are you, right now?"

She flushed, bright pink. "I—I don't want to tell—"

Whether it was the product of her mind being wildly undisciplined or her unconscious shaping the dreamwalk, the darkness around us receded and was replaced by a stately-looking room with furniture that looked very old. "Huh," I said, glancing around. It could have been a lot of places, I supposed, but one came immediately to mind. "So you're staying at the White House?" I didn't ask it as a question, because I suspected making it a statement was more likely to draw confirmation.

She blushed, but did not answer. It could have been a screen, but I somehow doubted it. "No, I'm in California." Flimsy answer, unworthy of the most brilliant intelligence on the planet.

What the hell was she playing at?

"Interesting," I said, contemplating my next question while Cassidy just stood there, staring at me. She didn't avoid my eyes, but she wasn't communicating much through her own. It was a dull stare, one that drifted, as though she considered herself a temporary prisoner in this place.

"Aren't you going to torture me?" she asked. "I hear you can do that."

She almost sounded like she wanted me to. "I try not to anymore," I said carefully, my brain racing as I tried to tease out what the hell was going on here.

"Sure you don't." That was laced with ... disappointment? She looked away.

"Where's Simmons?" I asked, for want of a better question.

Her face went hard. "Don't know." I believed her and considered jabbing at her to unearth the circumstances of their parting, but passed because ...

Well, because she was just acting weird.

"You might want to hurry," she said, almost triumphantly, but it was hollow.

"We've got all night," I said, frowning at her. "Don't you know how these things work—"

The world shook around me, as though a giant had stepped on the earth next to me. A deep, familiar voice rumbled through my dream, *"GET OUT!"*

I blinked as the rumble subsided, and my mouth popped open in surprise. "I've felt this before …"

Cassidy's eyes gleamed, just for a second, triumphant, but she said nothing.

I *had* felt this before, when Cassidy had me rendered comatose with a poison and Dr. Zollers had tried to dislodge me from my unconscious state before I nuked the entirety of Minneapolis.

"Zollers …?" I murmured, then, more firmly. "Dr. Zollers."

Quinton Zollers appeared in an instant, wearing pajamas, looking slightly sleepy, but awake enough to stare me right in the eye. "Something I can do for you, Sienna?"

The world shook around us again, and Cassidy stumbled to her knees. "GET OUT!" The voice shouted again, louder, as though it were trying to break through into my dreamwalk.

"Ooh," Zollers cringed, blinking his eyes as though someone had shone a spotlight into them.

"Is that—?" I asked.

"Yes," he answered without waiting for me to finish.

The world shook around me again, splinters of light breaking in through the darkness receding. Cassidy just stood there, mute, terrified, and I locked eyes with her for only a second. I knew what was happening now, and I couldn't speak to her, couldn't chance it.

I looked to Dr. Zollers. "Find me," I said, and he nodded.

The darkness broke open, that malicious force that had been clawing at my dream breaking through, and I snapped awake just before it got in. I didn't need to see it, didn't need to face it, not now. I already knew what it was, the last "GET

OUT!" shouted in that familiar voice driving home the identity of the speaker, and giving me the answers to so many questions in the process.

It was President Gerry Harmon.

That son of a bitch was a telepath.

42.

Harmon

"Dammit," I said, feeling the anger burn inside. I'd broken into the dream just a second too late, catching but a glimpse of Sienna Nealon and her pet telepath before they both disappeared like smoke on a clear day.

Cassidy, however, was still there, still waiting, my mind bridging the connection between the two of us, giving me access to speak directly into her head. It was something I didn't choose to do very often; I much preferred to nose around peoples' thoughts without their knowledge. Speaking into their ear, well, that was just a little too much like ... God, I suppose. And perhaps a hair too subtle for me.

I didn't bother to ask what Cassidy had told Sienna; it was obvious, laid bare in her mind. She hadn't told her anything, not really—just the obvious question of where Cassidy was had slipped out. I could forgive that, chalk it up to a weak mind. And Cassidy had a weak mind. For all her power of cognition—and it was considerable—she lacked discipline and emotional control, which caused her to bleed her pain and anguish out everywhere, resulting in stupid choices unfiltered by a wiser mind.

Until I came along.

"I didn't tell her—"

"I know," I said, soothing, patting her mind down in all the right places to suppress the alarm she was feeling. My art wasn't nearly as subtle when it came to emotional control as

171

an empath—like, say, that bastard Robb Foreman—but by messing with thoughts I could provoke certain emotions, play them up. I could even plant false notions in peoples' minds, like I had with Sienna Nealon's idiot brother, or twist motivations already in place, as I had with her ex-boyfriend Scott. He had been a willing pawn, already laboring under memory loss when I'd met him in passing at a party in LA. It had given me a chance to touch his feeble mind, play, take out some of the secrets lurking beneath the surface.

And once they were exposed, I could slither through the open door of his mind as easily as if I'd had a key made. I owned him now, though I had my fingers in so many minds these days my efficacy was reaching its limits. It was something I'd long known; people tended to do my bidding for only so long without a renewal of my influence. It wasn't linked to time, either, it was completely tied to how many others I'd had to dabble in bringing to my way of thinking in the intervening time.

Ultimately, that was why my wife outlived her usefulness. I still loved her, but controlling her had become quite the task.

"She knows I'm here," Cassidy said, eyes flitting nervously about.

"That doesn't matter," I said. "If she comes looking for a fight, I'll tear her mind apart the way I should have when last we met." That produced a slight cringe from me; I hadn't altered her because I knew that Dr. Zollers was waiting in the wings, tied to her mind, and that he'd feel it if I did something.

So I'd let her go. More was the pity. Now I wished I'd taken her for my own and had him killed. That is not as easy for either a president or a telepath to do as you might think. Zollers was canny. I'd read his file. He'd see me coming miles away, as well as any servant I sent to take him off the field of play.

Now Sienna Nealon was my worst enemy when she could have been my most faithful servant.

"If she comes with Zollers at her side, they might overwhelm you—" Cassidy said.

"Sienna's not going to rip through US Secret Service," I

said, confident in this much. "She has too much respect for these enforcers of the law to do that. She views herself as a hero. If she and Zollers come for me it'll be him versus me and her versus the entire Secret Service ... plus a few other tricks I have up my sleeve." I held back on sharing because Cassidy ... well, she was enough of a liability as it was. "No, she'll flail in the wilderness a while longer, and hopefully we won't have to wait too long before the damned military—"

A ringing outside my little connection with Cassidy jolted me, and I grabbed the phone by my bed. Cassidy was still there, though she couldn't hear what I was saying. "This is Harmon," I said.

"Sir," came the voice of General Forster, "we've got her."

43.

Salt Lake City at night didn't provide much of a view of the actual Great Salt Lake, though Scott had felt it as they'd flown over it in the dark, a sparkling, still series of waters that were followed by a nasty swamp on the approach to the airport. "J.J.," he said, trying to keep the tension that had ratcheted up inside him well hidden, "what's the word?"

"The word is that the Air Force has her on satellite," J.J. said. "And she's coming this way."

Scott leaned over the geek's shoulder, the Revelen soldiers and his own team watching closely behind. It was an overhead view, like a GPS map, but something small was moving right there, across it in a hurry. "Damn, she's fast," Booster said.

"Not as fast an AMRAAM missile," J.J. said, a little less cheery than usual. He pointed at three streams following in her wake. "And here they come ..."

44.

I cleared out of Cedar City as soon as I woke up. I'd pushed it too long enough already, taking that nap, and I knew after waking to the knowledge that there was a telepath in the Oval Office bent on destroying me that it was unlikely I was going to be getting any more sleep tonight, if ever.

It all made sense now. Harmon had been wrecked in the first debate by Senator Foreman, who was an empath. Care to guess which type of meta telepaths were weak against?

Yeah. Empaths. Telepaths couldn't pick them up at all. Which explained how Foreman had single-handedly wiped the floor with the fiercest, most seasoned debater in politics. It also explained why Harmon was so damned good at debating—he could read his opponents' thoughts and cut them off before they made their attack, leaving them a spluttering mess. He'd done it enough times that his debate performances were all over YouTube with captions like, "President Harmon DESTROYS ..." Thousands of them. And now I knew why.

Because the bastard cheated.

This was how I'd lost my team, my friends. He'd probably been there, in San Francisco, figured out where they were hiding and dropped by. Who's not going to open the door for the president of the United States? Even Reed, rebellious animal though he was, would have answered that knock.

And lost his mind a few seconds later. Now he was one of

the pod people that were all lined up against me.

"Shit, shit, shit," I said, blasting along at ten thousand feet and heading for the bright lights of Salt Lake City in the distance. Without a phone or GPS, I had to steer from city to city, bright spot to bright spot on the horizon. It wasn't the quickest method of travel, and I frequently ended up going out of the way since I was operating from a map that was in my head, but I knew I was generally heading in the right direction. My destination tonight was Spearfish, South Dakota, another town just small enough to avoid major league attention. I had a safe house waiting there, hopefully one that hadn't been found. I doubted it had, but I had certain traps in place so that I could tell if anyone had gotten into it.

I didn't have any warning when the first AMRAAM missile slammed into me.

The explosion rocked me, shards and pieces designed to destroy a multi-ton airplane perforating my chest, torso and even my limbs. I managed to get my head down in time to avoid serious impact, but the rest shredded the hell out of me even so, the shockwave sending me tumbling. I heard a popping in my chest and I couldn't breathe, my breaths coming quickly and desperately, warm blood flooding out of my lips in a spray with every exhalation.

I spun as I dropped, limp, pain shooting through me, g-forces twisting my body this way and that as I fell out of the sky, heading toward a moonlight-streaked body of water below—the Great Salt Lake? I wondered idly—spiraling hard toward certain death.

45.

Harmon

"We have eight F-22 Raptors in the area," General Forster said over the conference line as I watched the overhead satellite imagery from the Situation Room. "Also an AC-130 Gunship for close support, a few A-10 Warthogs—"

"Spare me the granular detail," I said, waving him off. Even my most loyal generals were constantly trying to get me to sign off on a bigger budget. More toys for them to play with. That was a losing battle.

"Your FBI task force is lifting off from Salt Lake City airport in a Black Hawk—"

"Just say helicopter, for crying out loud!" I said, losing patience. "Do you think I really care whether they're arriving in a specialty helicopter or a paddle boat? Just get them there, dammit. Kill her." Because that was all I really cared about.

46.

Sienna

I couldn't breathe anymore, couldn't get a breath, and panic was setting in. I was choking on my own blood, my chest filled with the pain of my perforated lungs venting air into my chest cavity, like a balloon was swelling painfully within me. I was so high up, so desperately high, the world spinning around, shadowy blue horizon clearly differentiated from the glowing lights of Salt Lake City in the distance.

Gavrikov! I called in my head as time seemed to slow.

Your body is failing! Gavrikov returned.

Wolfe!

I am working on it, give me a moment.

Something burst in front of me and another spattering of pain slapping my chest and torso, fingers of agony digging into my guts, cracking my ribs, peppering my cheeks and peeling them open. I couldn't see out of one of my eyes, I realized as I spun, head feeling as though the blood were pooling around the edges of my skull, threatening to burst out with centrifugal force, and I wondered how things could get any worse.

Then the next missile blew up behind me, and the world went utterly dark.

47.

"Splash one. Bogey is falling," a pilot's staticky voice reported over the speakerphone in the Situation Room.

"Roger that," Ground control replied. "Bogey is down—"

"Keep shooting her," I said.

"Sir," General Forster began, "she's falling out of the sky after multiple missile hits—"

"Hit her with multiple more," I said.

There was only a moment's hesitation, which was more than I was willing to tolerate. "Aye, sir. Wolfhound Six, continue to engage."

"Understood," said the pilot over a crackling radio channel. "Fox Three!"

48.

Scott

It wasn't easy to pick her out of the darkness, a tiny figure falling on a barely lit sky. It was after dark, but the moon was out, and that shadow looked to Scott a little like a bird dropping. If he hadn't had metahuman vision, he might not even have seen her, but see her he did, plummeting as another explosion—smaller and less violent than they looked in the movies—lit off next to her.

"She is getting peppered," J.J. reported with faint glee, laptop sitting across his knees in the back of the helo. The Great Salt Lake was right out there, and they were hovering in place, waiting to see which way she went. Scott just stared, watching her fall, because it was starting to look an awful lot like this hunt and kill mission was about to simplify into a corpse recovery operation.

"And a-salted," Friday guffawed.

You can't let her die, a small voice sounded in Scott's head. *That's our job. Kill her.*

He ignored the second voice, peering at the falling shadow in the distance. She was coming down hard, not even trying to fly, and it wasn't because Booster was draining her. She'd been blasted by the missiles, he was pretty sure.

Scott grimaced, looking out of the corner of his eye. Reed's face was lit by the cargo lights, a rough ecstasy etched on his expression as he watched her drop. *That's not normal,* Scott thought, and it only seemed to reinforce his mutinous musings.

There was only one thing for it.

He didn't bother to raise his hand, because that was just for show, really. He'd gotten beyond that now, simplified things. He concentrated hard on her, on her place in the air as she dropped out of the sky. There was moisture out there—thin, but present.

And it was his to control.

Scott reached out with his thoughts, bringing that moisture together. He could make it maintain position or move as he desired, and he desired to do both. He pulled it out of the air, small amounts, too subtle for anyone back here to see. It wasn't much, but when he packed it solidly enough—

She slowed, almost imperceptibly. He had hands of solid water tugging at her, altering her speed, producing a little drag. He introduced a little more, then a little more, and though she fell, she was no longer gathering momentum. She'd slowed, was drifting—

"She's awake, clearly," Reed said. He lurched out of the helicopter, clutching his rifle, with no sign of hesitation. He lit off a three-shot burst the moment he was clear, even though he was nearly a mile away from where Sienna was falling.

"Dammit," Scott said, jumping out of the copter after him. The lake was beneath him, so he didn't fear the jump or the landing, only that it might steal some of his concentration away from the task at hand. He continued to slow her, trusting that Reed's hastiness wouldn't help him. M-16s weren't accurate at this distance, were they?

His feet landed on a solid pillar of water that rose up to greet him and he slid along automatically, twenty feet up, as though riding a moving walkway. Salty spray tickled his face as he sped up, outpacing Reed quickly. He kept his mind half on the forward motion, half on slowing Sienna. She was probably at less than two thousand feet now, still coming down fairly hard, not exactly drifting like a delicate leaf.

This is going to be tight, Scott thought, trying to decide how best to even handle this. He looked back; Reed was almost keeping up with him, the winds at his command flinging him forward. He'd gotten better, that was for sure. Now he was flying, genuinely flying.

Sienna came tumbling closer, spiraling toward the surface, and for the first time, Scott saw the shadow catching up to her. "Oh, damn," he muttered, and pushed the hands of water to drag her faster.

It was another missile.

He closed his eyes and concentrated on yet another thing, trying to pack water together solidly, tightly enough, ripping it out of the dry desert air and hoping there was enough to—

Another explosion rippled over him, and Scott saw the missile blow up behind her. It was probably thirty feet up, having crashed into the wall of water he'd thrown to protect her—

Something else crashed hard into his shield and Scott felt it ripple as another blast echoed over the Great Salt Lake. Pieces of shrapnel pelted through, and he tried to rob them of their momentum, steal it from them before they stole Sienna's life.

"Come on, come on," Scott muttered. He was slowed in his own forward movement, trying to keep from distracting himself too much. He caught another glimpse of Reed overhead, who was speeding toward his sister—

He'll kill her.

LET HIM!

Scott thrust a spear of water out and smashed it into Reed like a solid wall. It turned him over in midair, knocked him asunder, and down he fell, the wind taken right out of him, unconscious. Scott caught him but let the M-16 fall into the lake.

Sienna was close now, and he reached out a hand—not because he needed to, but because it felt right, as though he could somehow add an extra effort, reach out and control the events playing out before him even though he couldn't, not really. He sped her up as another missile blew off on his last shield, and she hit the water, disappearing beneath the surface without even a splash—

49.

Harmon

"Tango down."

I stared at the screen, at the motion on the water. I couldn't see it very clearly, but I knew that both Reed and Scott were there, using their powers to influence the outcome. I needed to see, so I reached out—first to Reed, because he was the one I'd most recently "acquired," but his mind was hazy, unconscious.

I recoiled, his dreams light and his pain showing through. He'd been hit somehow, I could sense that much, and I didn't care to feel it. I withdrew my consciousness from him and moved on, to Scott ...

He was there, plainly, but something was wrong. Pushing into his mind was like trying to squeeze your foot into a child's shoe, and I strained at the imposition. I could see only hazily through his eyes, as he concentrated on something, and so I forced myself in—

50.

It was not the easiest thing, keeping a living person alive underwater, but Scott was trying. It wasn't the hardest thing for him, either, given that he could breathe water like he had gills. Most couldn't, though, and he knew if he brought Sienna to the surface, those missiles would probably keep coming.

He had to play possum with her, at least for a while. At least until they were sure she was—

The wash of the chopper coming in behind him brought with it something else, a pressure in his head like it was splitting wide. He felt as though he'd been struck with an axe, the blade catching him squarely in the middle of the skull like a piece of wood meant to be chopped.

Scott staggered on his platform of water, and his control faltered. He'd created a web of invisible tubes that stretched down to where Sienna was cradled in the water's depths, the tubes feeding her fresh oxygen from the surface as—

WHAT THE HELL ARE YOU DOING? the voice thundered, that quiet one that he'd been ignoring, defying, fighting—

But it was here now, and louder than before, and suddenly ... the tubes he'd used to feed Sienna oxygen were gone, just gone.

And then ... his powers kicked in, his hand clenching wildly into a fist, and Scott knew he needed to kill the thing that was in those depths, hiding in those waters. It was a monster, something to be annihilated without mercy or remorse. He seized control of the water and started to press the molecules tight, ready to crush the threat lurking beneath the surface ...

51.

Sienna

I woke up underwater, with a mouth full of salty cold liquid, and felt like I was about to be crushed to death by the pressure.

As far as scary wake-ups go, it was probably in my top two.

I gasped for breath but stopped short of inhaling water, which was probably a good thing. The salinity was off the charts, so salty that even in my near-panicked state I knew I was in the Great Salt Lake.

You're healed, Wolfe said, calmer by a hundred degrees than I was, given I was submerged in a lake at night, with the water pressing in on me like I'd reached crush depth. *Move?*

Nice suggestion, I shot back, his calm bringing my panic down a couple notches. *Gavrikov?*

Trying, Gavrikov said, and I strained against the press of the water. It squeezed me, and I could feel the direction gravity should have been pulling me by the resistance of the water as it held me down. I realized squarely in the midst of my fight exactly what was happening.

Scott had hold of me, and apparently he'd gotten Harmon in his head again.

I didn't have a hope of beating him while trapped in the depths of the lake, and my oxygen was bound to run out soon. I thrashed to no effect, the water pushing in tighter and putting my arms to my sides as my ribs started to crack under the weight.

DRAGON! Bastian shouted. *NOW!*

What the hell, why not? I figured and started to transform.

My clothing shredded in a hot second, and my legs elongated like lengths of rope drifting down. My neck stretched like I'd been hanged, twisting through the powerful water pressure bearing down on me. It fought me, tried to push me into the depths of the lake, but it was like the water couldn't quite get a grip as I slithered my way through.

I broke the surface headfirst, sucking in lungfuls of oxygen as I continued to grow, my neck stretching. My wings cleared the surface next, even as tendrils of water tried to snake me back down, and I twisted, ripping my tail free and clearing the surface by fifty feet, picking out the dark shoreline ahead and rushing toward it with full Gavrikov speed. I was exhausted, my body threatening to crash at any moment. Being ripped apart by AMRAAM missiles and dropped into the lake and nearly crushed by my ex, who was under psychic control by the president—

You know, I lead a weird life.

I crashed on a beach, salty flavor on my tongue and night air conspiring to freeze me and make me want a margarita to go along with all the troubles I was presently having. I was definitely on the rocks.

A helicopter's blades came sweeping around, the chop like an announcement that death was coming for me. I staggered up, resuming my human form, tail contracting and splitting into two legs as I sparked up Gavrikov's fire to avoid the feds adding a public nudity charge to my already considerable list of offenses. Sand between my toes squished as Scott came up onto the shore with a splash, a little wall of water at his feet and Reed washed up in his wake. I breathed a sigh of relief to see that my brother, though unconscious, was still alive.

"You won't ... get away ..." Scott said, but his voice was husky and angry, like it had been for months.

"Starting to get that feeling, yeah," I said, my shoulders slumped, my fire leotard lighting up the night with its torch glow. Scott stared at me, his hatred burning like my makeshift clothing. I looked up, wondering how many planes they'd stacked up above me. Judging by the number of missiles they'd pelted me with, it was a lot. Maybe an entire fighter wing.

"You should have joined me," Scott said, but his voice was different, smoother—he sounded like Harmon.

"You should have asked," I said, taking a weak, staggering step back.

"I—" Scott's voice made a return as he grunted in pain, "This is not—I'm not—"

"It's not you, Scott," I said as the chopper edged closer and closer. It'd be landing soon, and I suspected that Team Revelen would come pouring out, along with their sapper, and if I had to fight all these guys off right now, I was going to die on this beach, possibly from exhaustion before any of them even laid a hand on me. "Harmon's in your head, telling you what to do."

"You're—a monster," Scott said, his face manic, eyes wild in the light.

"He's just telling you that," I said, staggering back again. "Planting thoughts in your head ..."

"I know—what you are," he said, and a silken, shadowy wave rose behind him in the darkness. He could crush me with it, drag me back into the surface of the water, drown me easily. "You're a—you're a—" He struggled with it, like Harmon was inside, fighting him, cramming more thoughts in his head that didn't belong there.

I swallowed heavily and dropped to a knee. I couldn't fly. I couldn't run. I'd bled out so much I wondered if I'd lost my entire body's worth of blood volume. I'd been drowned, shot at, and now the hounds that were ready to chase me to the gates of hell were swooping in for the kill.

I had nothing left.

"What am I?" I asked, thumping down on my butt. His wave swept in around me on three sides, ready to crash, ready to drown me, ready to end it all.

"You're a—" His face twitched. "—a—

"Hero."

The words were soft, quiet, and sounded like the real

Scott, the one I'd known before this year had destroyed him, ground him up and fed him to President Harmon. I looked up and saw his face, frozen for one brief moment in placid calm—

And then the anger broke back through and the waves came crashing down around me—

52.

His fury like a cloak around him, Scott drove his waters forward, furious, drowning power at his fingertips. He raged against the space where they'd swallowed up the monster before him, solidifying the water in such a way as to create spear-tips. He drove them in, again and again, attacking with anger and certainty.

Whatever was in there, it needed to be destroyed. It was an implacable foe, it was—

A BEAST.

—and death would surely follow for all those around him should he let off his attack. He had to be sure, had to destroy it utterly, the salt brine splashing around, the night air torn asunder as the strike team approached behind him.

"Leave us a little, huh?" Mac asked, knife flashing in the moonlight. "I had aims to carve her heart and lungs out."

"I don't think you're going to find much of those left," Ferko said in that accent of his, hair twitching wildly. "The water is strong with this one."

"How's Reed?" Augustus asked, and Scott looked back to see Gothric leaning over him, fingers touching the Aeolus on the face. "What happened to him?"

"I don't know," Scott said and faltered, his control over the waves lost. Water rushed out and splashed past, like tide rolling back to join the Great Salt Lake. The waters cleared, slowly, running past him, his feet, past the others, and last of the roiling storm of them dying away before him.

And when it passed … there was nothing there of the monster he'd aimed to kill. No blood, no bones, no tissue …

Nothing.

53.

"Target lost," the general said over the commlink, and I quieted a silent scream in my mind. Scott's waters had receded, disappeared, rejoined the collective of H2O that waited within the Great Salt Lake, and I was left to watch from the satellite view—because I'd grown quickly sick of watching from within Scott's head, once I'd tinkered to make his thinking right once more—as our little vista of the battlefield revealed that the battle was over.

Apparently we'd lost, because somehow we'd lost Sienna Nealon.

I kept a steely control on my voice. "She was right *there*. How did you ... lose her?"

"I don't know, sir," General Forster answered, baffled. "We're reviewing the tape—"

"I doubt it's a tape," I said. "Join the twenty-first century."

"Just a figure of speech, sir," the general said, clearly miffed by my passive-aggressive swipe at him. It was nothing like what I wanted to do. "She—we didn't see her fly out—"

"Yes, I was watching that, too," I said, seething and barely keeping a lid on it. These people around me were worse than useless, they were incompetent. One little thing I wanted done, and it couldn't even be finished. She'd been broken on that beach, I'd seen to it before I had to recuse myself from Scott Byerly's entirely-too-small brain. Technology had failed, but worse than that, men had failed. Men always failed, though, that was the hallmark of humanity—a series of continuous failures.

I reached out and touched the general's mind. It wasn't difficult; we'd met many times before, and I'd seen in his thoughts, twisted them a little to make him more loyal. Loyalty was one thing, but competence was another, and it was something I couldn't instill with my powers. Not at this point, anyway.

I ventured deeper into his mind, could see the room in the Pentagon where he was watching a similar screen to mine, could smell the cold, stale coffee in the mug in front of him. A half-dozen junior officers were all around him, rushing, working, trying to figure out how they'd screwed this up.

There wasn't an ounce of deception within him. It wasn't a failure of integrity; it was the failure of him being a moron. I could abide a lot of things, but my temper had reached its end with stupidity.

So I reached into the part of his mind that governed control of his tongue, had him shift the floppy, muscular instrument in question so as to block his airway, and then numbed that part of his brain so he couldn't fix what I'd done. Then I left his mind—such as it was—because I had no desire to take a front row seat for what was going to happen next.

The gurgling noise over the open line heralded my return to my own skull. It wasn't a pretty sound, but then, it never was. "General?" I asked politely. "General?" I said again, when he didn't answer.

The gurgling turned into a choking, and then I heard a clatter on the other side. "General!" someone shouted, and a great thud suggested to me that the general had fallen out of his chair.

"What's going on?" I asked, sounding greatly concerned, I hope.

"The general is choking, sir!" one of the lesser officers shouted.

"My goodness," I said. "Someone give him the Heimlich maneuver." I wasn't helping with this suggestion; a Heimlich would no more save him than it would someone with cancer.

He needed an ambulance or a corpsman or something of the sort, and even those were unlikely to help. Perhaps a tracheotomy might save him, but I suspected it was too late.

More thudding, more choking, the sound of a chair being overturned. I listened all the while, disinterested, keeping my eyes on the monitors in front of me. Fortunately, not everyone had taken their eye off the ball due to the general's unfortunate circumstances. The satellite view was slowly running back, then forward, the time-stamp indicating that it was around when I'd left Scott's mind after pushing him to act again. There wasn't much to see, just a quick flash of a line around the area in question. I peered at it, wondering what I was looking at.

"He's dying!" someone shouted on the other end of the line, briefly stirring me back to remember what was going on.

"Someone call an ambulance," I said, knowing it was too late for that. "This is terrible timing for a choking incident. What did he eat? A whole ribeye?"

"He hasn't eaten anything, sir!" that same fellow shouted on the other side of the call.

"Well, this is ill-timed in any case. I need analysis, we're trying to capture a fugitive. He'll probably be fine—"

"Sir, he's turning purple."

I considered removing the block I'd put in his mind and just as quickly dismissed it. He'd earned this fate, and whatever had happened, Sienna Nealon was gone. "Deal with him, and someone get a new officer on the watch. We have a situation to deal with."

The answer came a moment later, deflated and chastened. "Yes, sir."

I sat back in my chair and listened to the general finish his last moments on this earth, the satellite view spooling backward, then forward again, that line moving around the area in question ...

What the hell was it?

54.

"She's gone," Augustus said, shaking his head as the chopper set down behind them, whipping the already saturated air around them so that droplets of salt water tickled Scott's face.

"I can't believe she bushwhacked me like that," Reed said, looking bedraggled.

Scott couldn't understand exactly how Sienna had pulled off the escape, but he knew she had. She was a monster, a holy terror that couldn't be fully explained. However she'd done it, she'd handed them a loss, less bloody this time but no less humiliating. He just counted himself lucky he hadn't heard from Phillips or the president yet. They were probably boiling.

He'd had her. She'd been right beneath the fury of his waves, and she'd escaped.

How the hell had she managed that, with satellites overhead and F-22s stacked up for miles?

"Have we got eyes on the ground?" Scott asked, heaving himself into the chopper, where J.J. was working on his laptop.

"We've got eyes everywhere," J.J. said, "from the banks of the lake all the way out to the bounds of the city. Facial recognition is running as we speak on every camera we can access. If she puts her head outside, we'll see, and our satellites are running thermal now. I've got a room full of

195

Pentagon analysts trying to back-trace where she went, but … it's like she vanished." He shrugged.

"You think she has a new power?" Reed asked. His brow was creased, and he looked as furious as Scott had ever seen him, like a Cro-Magnon seeking someone to club, his ponytail sopping wet over his shoulder. Scott drew the water out without thinking.

"Maybe," Scott said as the helo lifted off. His team was in, and they were moving, trying to get positioned in case they caught a glimpse of her. How could she have escaped this dragnet they had on her? She'd been there, on the beach, just below the waves, ready to die. If she'd gone up, the F-22s would have caught her, if she'd run away, the satellite would have tracked her movement …

What the hell had just happened?

55.

Sienna

I woke up in a room filled with pre-dawn light, newspapers taped to the windows, faint sky giving them a backlight. My head leaned against a thin pillow, and I was covered in a threadbare sheet, which was fortunate, because the room was chilly. My hair was still slightly wet and my throat ached a little, reminding me of when I was a kid and would regularly catch colds that my mom brought home from the hospital but never experienced herself thanks to her meta powers.

"Uhhh," I moaned, sitting up. The room around me was white, painted wood paneling, weathered and aged. The light fixture above me was an empty socket, no hint that it had had a bulb in it for years. One of the walls was cracked, the paneling revealing splinters where someone had crashed into it and never bothered to repair it. The place stank, too, stale air around me in place of brewing coffee, which is what I really wanted.

I heard a soft voice say something outside the door, and then a whipcrack noise, as though Indiana Jones were fighting a lion just outside my room. I gathered my wits about me, my body aching slightly from what I suspected had been a horrendous beating. I vaguely recalled what had happened—being shot down by AMRAAM missiles, nearly crushed by Scott's powers when Harmon reasserted his mind-control over him, then nearly passing out from the constant whippings on the shores of the Great Salt Lake as Scott was poised to take me out of the world at Harmon's command.

Then someone had grabbed me and after that ...

Well, hell. I didn't remember squat.

I stood up and my back cracked. "Anyone remember what happened?" I asked quietly, staring at the door, which was, like the rest of the room, painted white and faded from the passage of years.

I thought we were dead from waterboy until we didn't die, Eve said, unsurprisingly droll.

It took us a while to figure that out, Bjorn said. *We just assumed the darkness of being in your head was actually hell.*

"Doubt you'd get laid in hell," I mumbled, staring transfixed at the door. Someone was out there, and I was marshaling all my faculties so I could come out swinging if need be.

Someone saved you, Zack said. *Someone strong, someone good if they managed to get away from everything the government was throwing your way. That was a damned near inescapable trap they sprang on you. Maybe you oughta be grateful for a quarter second before you start throwing down with whoever this is?*

"I'll think about it," I said, still staring at the door. They weren't coming in; maybe they didn't know I was awake.

"You can come out, you know," came a voice from the other side, putting the lie to that thought. It was a man's voice, muffled. He was speaking in a near whisper so I couldn't tell much about him. "Just standing there leering at the door isn't going to answer any of your questions."

He proffers an invitation, Wolfe said, plainly intrigued.

"Saddle up, peeps," I said and went for the doorknob. "Time to get answers—or at least one." I turned the knob, which squeaked as I slowly pulled the door wide.

"Oh, oh! Hold on!" the man said as I opened the door. "Shit!"

The door swung wide and I stood back, bracing myself. I saw his movement, but he was a shadow, no lights obvious in that room, either. He was moving swiftly, waving his hands to the left, as though trying to signal someone I couldn't see outside the door frame.

I stood there, waiting in case this heralded an attack, my hands up and my feet in a loose defensive stance. I was ready for the fight if it came, rested enough after passing out to continue the battle. If the someone who had grabbed me intended to use me for ill purpose, they were about to get a snootful of pain in response to that notion.

The shadow in the door shouted, "Wait! Wait!" still waving his hands to the side of the frame. I recognized his voice as familiar, and then I tumbled to who it was just as that whipcrack I'd heard through the door sounded again, and a cloud of dust blew out of the carpeting in the main room and swept in on me like a wave of sand, stinging my cheeks and palms as I held up my hand to block it from my eyes.

When it cleared I was left looking at the two shadows now waiting for me in the main room. I couldn't see them, but I didn't need to, because I knew who they were now. The one who'd just arrived was carrying a cup of coffee—the one I'd "requested" when I'd wakened—well, I'd thought about requesting, anyway, and would have as soon as I realized who I was dealing with. That request might as well have been real, voiced out loud and in person to one of my rescuers, who was standing in front of me now, waiting, taking up my cup of coffee from my other—newly arrived—rescuer: Colin Fannon, the speedster.

"Colin," I said, stepping out of the room. I shouldn't have been totally surprised to see him. Technically, I was his most recent employer, after all. I started to voice this thought, but the other man cut me off.

"You shouldn't have been surprised to see me, either," he said in that world-weary, smartass, knowing way that he had. "I go looking for trouble and hard cases, after all, and yours—right now—is about the hardest case of all. It's been a real headache trying to find you, I'll have you know, and since I can read the future—that's saying something, Sienna." He smiled, and it was filled with a kind of boyish charm that belied his—I presumed—hundreds of years of experience and life.

"Whatever the case may be," I said, giving him a smile right back, "it's nice to see you, Harry Graves. Cuz heaven knows, I could use all the help I can get right now."

56.

Harmon

"That was a speedster," I said, tracing the line with my finger on the screen. "A metahuman with the ability to run and move at extremely high speeds." I was settled in my seat in the empty situation room, talking on the speaker to the colonel who had been assigned to take over for General Forster. So far he had not annoyed me enough to plot his death, but then, the day was young and my rage still not settled.

"Like the Flash," some young lieutenant said in the background.

"Or Quicksilver," said another.

"Yes, like those," I said impatiently. "He—or she—came running in and snatched up Ms. Nealon, whisking her away before our man's attack could fall. He was too low for radar to detect him, so he skipped under the F-22s, and he struck at exactly the moment when Agent Byerly's attack fell … it was perfectly timed. Expertly, really." I leaned back in my chair. "Have we followed the line to its origin, yet?"

"Working on it, sir," came another voice on the phone. "It's heading back to Salt Lake City, so we should have a clear view thanks to the satellite still being in geosync orbit."

"If this speedster outruns our satellite, I'm going to be very upset," I announced. I didn't make it sound ominous—or at least no more ominous than the president of the United

201

States telling his subordinates he was going to be mad if they failed him.

"We're trying, sir," this new colonel said. "This isn't our usual sort of tactical exercise."

"Trace the line back to the origin," I said. "And let's get our team in there."

"How is a team going to fight a guy who can move so fast you can't even see him?" One of the lieutenants muttered, so low I shouldn't have been able to hear him. I did, though, of course.

"Don't ask, don't ask," his compatriot answered. "The president sounds like he's gonna lose it on the next person who says anything."

It was not a bad question, and I wouldn't have lost it on them. I needed a contingency to deal with the speedster, and I needed it quickly. The sapper that Revelen had sent over was probably the key, though he'd need to know in order to be ready for what he'd be facing. I muted myself on the military conference call and picked up another phone sitting just down the table. "Get me FBI Agent Byerly," I said to the secretary on the other end, "he'll be on a transport helicopter involved in the current operation in Salt Lake City." I hung up.

Two minutes later, the phone rang. "Byerly here."

"Agent Byerly," I said. "You're going to be facing a speedster in addition to Ms. Nealon. It's how she escaped your dragnet. Tell your Booster to be ready to slow him down."

"A speedster?" Byerly seemed to be speaking to his crew. There was a pause, and then his voice came back strong and affirmative. "Yes, sir. We'll be ready."

"We're tracing them now. Get airborne and we'll send you along the moment we have a vector on them."

"Understood, sir. We won't—" I hung up before he had a chance to reassure me in a way I wouldn't believe.

I stared at the map as the technicians at the Pentagon continued to trace back the line of the moving speedster in slow motion through the streets of Salt Lake City. It ran back through neighborhoods, quickly, even in the slow-motion. I should have known Sienna Nealon wouldn't be alone forever. That was the problem with her; it seemed like she never ran out of surprises.

57.

Sienna

I stared at Harry Graves and Colin Fannon, my rescuers, in something just short of amazement. "What the hell are you doing here, Harry?"

Harry stared back at me, eyes twinkling in amusement. He'd been that way when I'd met him in Chicago earlier this year, too, just the sort of irascible, old-man-in-a-young-man's-body that you occasionally got with a long-lived meta. He could be crabby in a "Get off my lawn!" kind of way. Other times, he was just hunkered down trying to find booze and ... skirts, I guess? That was probably what he called them. He was handsome enough that he probably got more than a few.

"Veronika called me," Harry said, looking as placid as if he were sitting somewhere other than in a shithole abandoned house in Salt Lake City.

"What?" I asked, gaze flicking to Colin, who nodded.

"Yeah, she was worried about you," Harry said.

"We barely got out of the house in San Francisco when the president showed up," Colin said. "I was on recon, and when I saw him coming ... well, the girls were mostly out back, in the yard, talking and drinking some wine and whatnot ... the boys were in the front of the house—"

"Sounds like a very sexist party," Harry commented, flashing me a grin.

"Veronika got most of them out, but Harmon was already

204

in by that time," Colin said. "Phinneus didn't take a shot at him, because ... well ..."

"Because it'd be assassinating the president," I said, nodding along. "So he sweeps in and—"

"We didn't know what was happening," Colin said, his eyes searching around the bare room. "I was carrying the others out two and three at a time, getting them off-site as fast as I could. I saw Harmon do ... something ... to Reed, saw his whole personality change, through a window, and he turned and pointed to us. I ran off right then with Veronika and Kat. We were the last ones to get out."

"Who came with you?" I asked, swallowing heavily.

"That angry Italian doctor, Perugini," Colin said, ticking them off. "Phinneus. Veronika, Kat, Abby—she's a fireball, too." His eyebrows rose.

"What about Ariadne?" I asked.

"No," Colin shook his head. "She was inside sleeping at the time. I assume ... Harmon got her."

I gritted my teeth. "This whole time I've been thinking—"

"That everyone betrayed you, the world was against you," Harry said, kind of bored. "That's why Veronika called me. She figured you might have that reaction." He looked right at me. "And you wouldn't have had to go through all that if you'd just picked up your phone a few days ago. Or set up your voicemail."

I stared back at him. "Huh?"

"I've been calling you, fool," Harry said impatiently.

I thought back to a few days earlier, when my phone had rung with an unknown number. "Wait ... what? How?"

"Oh, well," Harry said with relish, obviously enjoying the opportunity to tell me how hard he'd worked for me, "it goes like this—once we knew you were within a certain distance of Vegas, I started mentally dialing all the phone numbers in the area, asking for you. Do you know how long I had to sit there, dialing every Utah, Nevada, Arizona, New Mexico, California—all those numbers—in my head. Days." His eyebrow crept up as he threw that one at me. "Even as fast as my mind works, it took days until I tumbled on your Utah numbers. I even had the probability come up, finally—

1 in 99 you'd answer, but at least then I knew your number. Hours, I spent, working the scenarios. Boring hours, let me tell you—"

"You have my gratitude," I said with only a little sarcasm, and Harry nodded with self-satisfaction. "Now how do we—"

Harry picked up a beer can and popped it open, draining its contents in mere seconds. Then he squeezed it, crushing the can between his fingers. He let it drop to the floor, at which point Colin zoomed down and swiped it up, looking quite put out. "Recycle," Colin said.

"You see a bin in here anywhere?" Harry let out a short belch. "Besides, that thing is gonna be in the FBI headquarters evidence vault until the end of time, it ain't ending up in a landfill."

That took a second to sink in on me. "What?" I asked, rising alarm.

"Oh, yeah," Harry said, "they're coming. Two minutes out."

"And you just tell me this now?" I asked, looking around at the newspaper-covered windows as though they might come crashing in any second.

"Nothing you can do about it until they get here," Harry shrugged. He closed one eye, thinking. "Oh, wait. Colin, two doors down—there's a gun in the bedside table. Be a dear and get it, will you?"

Colin scowled at him, and I got a hint of their working relationship. "I don't like guns."

Harry looked at him like he was a dullard. "It's not for you. It's for her." He pointed at me. "They're deep sleepers, so ... go, will you?"

Colin looked mutinous, but dutifully shot out the door. He returned a moment later with a Glock 17 clutched between his thumb and index finger like it was a dirty diaper. He extended it to me and I took it. "Thanks," I said.

The sound of a helicopter in the distance permeated the building, and that burgeoning panic I felt got a little bit higher in my throat. "Shouldn't we—"

Harry waved me off. "They've got a satellite overhead, I

think."

"You *think*?!"

He closed his eyes. "Yeah. Satellite overhead." He opened them again to find me staring at him. "What? I imagined Colin taking me to the Pentagon and running from room to room until we found the one where they're watching us. Question answered, eh? Too bad you die in that scenario …" He shrugged. "I'm not all knowing."

"That's not very comforting, Harry."

"You'd need to stuff me with feathers in order to call me a comforter," he said.

I just stared back at him. "You probably had … what … fifty scenarios pop through your head, and that's the best joke you could come up with for the occasion? Stuff you with feathers? How about I stuff my hand up your—"

He chortled. "I really just wanted to have the conversation go down that path, honestly, so I could hear you threaten me with amateur proctology."

"What?!"

"Here they come," he said, sidling up to a wall and motioning for me to get over to a sliding glass door. "I'm about to lose power … or some, anyway." He made an annoyed noise deep in his throat, as though he'd never been this inconvenienced. "Sapper, what a bastard …"

I leaned against the wall by the sliding glass door, papered over so that I couldn't see out and my enemies couldn't see in. The helicopter rotors grew closer and closer, the sound closing in on us as our options narrowed, and I shut my mouth, suppressing the questions that were rising like my panic, hoping that Harry knew what the hell he was doing.

58.

I watched the helicopter hover over the house, the ziplines rolling out the sides and back. I couldn't actually see that part, except watching through Scott's eyes at a distance as he and the boys zipped down, surrounding the house on all sides. It was loud in his head, though, and I recused myself, feeling a little exhausted from the day's mental labors. As much as I might have wanted to watch from within, it was going to be a safer bet to watch from the monitor, hoping that this time—finally—they might get the drop on Sienna Nealon.

Dammit.

"Have the F-22s stand by to level the house if this goes wrong," I said.

There was a moment's pause, disbelief sinking in. "Uh, sir ..." the colonel said. "This is a US city. We can't do that."

I prepared to press against his mind. I needed to be careful; pushing him would mean someone else was likely to slip my grasp. Probably McSorley, McCluskey or Shane, whom I'd had to badger into voting for my education bill. Weak-willed little tree slugs. "Pray tell, why not?" I asked.

"Uh, well," the colonel said, "the F-22s are loaded with AMRAAM missiles—those are air-to-air only—"

I sighed, loud enough to encourage him to shut up. "Do you have any drones standing by?"

"Yes, sir," the colonel said. "With Hellfire missiles which

will—"

"Great," I said with false enthusiasm. "Do move them in so we can execute if need be." I tried to sound reassuring, but I didn't care as long as he followed my orders.

"Aye, sir," the colonel said. I had to push him a little because he wasn't eager to blast a suburban area in the US with drone fire for some reason. "I feel compelled to warn you, sir, that a Hellfire missile explosion is not a contained thing." He was pressing against my will, and his was stronger than the general's had been, probably because his sympathies had not been naturally with me. I'd need a new military liaison soon, someone more malleable. "There will be collateral damage—"

"That's a shame," I said, twisting a few of his thoughts while I feigned interest, "but Sienna Nealon has caused enough death that to let her flee again would be to sign the death warrants of enough innocent Americans to justify this action." I spoke as coldly as I could. I didn't relish the thought of killing innocent people, but by the same token, I'd reached my limit with Sienna Nealon. She was the only one now who could stop me. Well, her and this unknown speedster.

"Aye, sir," Forster said, appropriately chastened. "Drones moving in, and the team is standing by for your order."

I frowned. Why did they need to wait for me? "Execute," I said, hoping they would take that literally and spare me from unleashing bombs in a civilian neighborhood. After all, if that got out, it wouldn't reflect very well on me.

59.

The Black Hawk's rotor wash was hammering at Scott, pushing him against the side of the house. He made a motion to Booster, who nodded; his skills were in play, which meant hopefully that Speedster was slowed down, and Sienna was brought to a crawl. They'd been pursuing her doggedly for days now, from Denver to the shores of the Great Salt Lake to here, in the sprawling reaches of Salt Lake City itself. She hadn't really had much time to rest, so hopefully that meant she was dogged out. She'd certainly been about ready to fall on the shoreline, though that had been a few hours ago. Surely she hadn't rested up, not with them after her?

Well, if she had, hopefully she was still resting now, and they'd just take her quietly, like they had that woman in Cheyenne, the one with the—

Baby?

Scott drew a sharp breath, like cold water had scrambled over him again, washing down his head, his hair, his face, his chest. He drew a frigid breath of early morning air, the purple dawn in the distance feeling as though it was jolting him awake.

What the hell am I doing? he asked himself, feeling the weight of the submachine gun slung against his chest. He stared at the black length of the weapon, like someone had shoved an unexpected puzzle piece in his hand and he was looking at what he had so far, trying to figure out where it went. It was as though he'd thought he was putting together a scene of a mountain meadow in full, flowery bloom, but with the adding of this piece, realized it was a bloody murder scene instead.

Augustus signaled to him from across the door, trying to catch his attention. Scott took a breath and stared up at his teammate with wide, panicked eyes. "What the hell are we doing?" Scott asked, taking gasping breaths.

Augustus just stared at him, blankly for a moment, and said. "Oh. Right." And he reached out a hand, ripping up the yard behind him quietly, cloaking himself in earth and rock, growing three feet in the process, like a golem, only a slit for his eye and his hand exposed enough to keep a finger on his weapon's trigger.

"That wasn't what I m—" Scott cut himself off. He remembered the voice that had invaded his mind, ripping through his thoughts—no, snaking through them—as easily as if it had the keys to his brain. "Harmon," he whispered to himself, trying to recall what he'd said on the shores of the lake …

"We need to go," Reed hissed in the night, almost lost under the chopper's wash. "Now."

"Yeah, man," Augustus said, clad in his earthen battle armor, only his eyes showing through the crust of soil. "Let's kick this off."

And without waiting for confirmation from Scott, he stepped back and blasted a dirt-covered foot through the sliding glass door before wading into the house.

60.

Sienna

I knew it was Augustus leading the charge the minute I saw a swollen, dirt-clad foot come crashing through the newspaper-covered sliding glass door. He didn't stop with the foot, either, using earthen shoulder pads to shield his face as he stepped through, sending the glass fragments shattering to the floor.

I was limited in what I could deploy against him and remain non-lethal. It would have been easy to shoot him in the eye hole, probably—with my strength and dexterity turned down by the booster, it might not have been as easy—but I didn't want to kill him. He was armored, too, which was bad news for me, especially since my strength wasn't what it should have been. He was carrying an M-16, and I didn't want that to come in play, so the obvious answer came immediately to mind—

I reached out and flicked the pin out of the rear assembly of his gun. It shot out and bounced ineffectually off his dirt-armored chest, and he swung his weapon around to fill me full of lead. I slapped the bottom of his magazine, though, and the M-16 broke apart at the rear where I'd knocked the pin out, rendering it completely useless as anything other than a club until he repinned it.

"What the—" He stared for a second at the M-16, now a right angle in the middle of the weapon where it should have all been neatly mated together in a long rifle. I didn't stand there and wait for him to figure it out, though; I flicked the front pin, too, and the M-16 broke cleanly in two.

"Tee hee," I said, and launched myself backward as he swiped at me with the barrel and upper receiver. It missed my nose by an inch, and I cursed my newfound slowness even as I heard the crash of a door getting kicked in behind me.

I hit my back, staring at the door for a brief second. I knew Augustus would recover, but I didn't know how long it would take him. "That guy!" Harry shouted from across the room, and I glanced to see him pointing with one hand and smacking Reed in the nose with the other. My brother didn't look like he was taking the beating gracefully, but I followed Harry's point to the door that had just crashed in.

There were two guys standing backlit by the chopper's searchlight. One of them was the Medusa, and the other was probably the Booster, hidden just behind the Medusa.

I snapped off three quick shots, but Mr. Medusa's hair got in my way, the bullets caught harmlessly on his locks as I cursed and rolled. Augustus brought a foot down where I'd been lying just a second earlier and crashed through the floor into the crawlspace beneath the house. I cringed as I kept rolling; that blow would have disemboweled me easily.

"Here, let me," Harry said, and I saw him drop Reed, whose nose was pure red, like it had been smashed properly. Harry produced a gun in one hand while warding off attacks from Gothric the Medic with his other. I boggled; where in the hell had he gotten it? I blinked and saw Reed had an empty holster on his belt. Harry blind-fired three times over his own shoulder, the sound deafening in the close confines of the house, muzzle flash illuminating the battle.

I didn't see any way he would have been able to hit anything, let alone somehow dodge Mr. Medusa's wavy hair, which had blocked all three of my shots, but as I turned to look at the door, I saw Booster's skull was much more open to the air than it had been a second ago—as in the entire top of his head was missing and Mr. Medusa was staring back at him in horror.

Power surged through me, lightning speed, and I felt it,

like I was coming out of the water and taking a deep breath for the first time in ages. "Wheeeeee," I said, shooting to my feet. Mr. Medusa was bringing his head around, weapon at the ready—

I fired twice with my purloined Glock and twice with Gavrikov's flames compressed into a bullet-sized shot. Medusa caught both bullets with his hair, but when he tried to catch the flame bursts, the first passed right through and hit him in the chest, and the second caught him in the face. His skull broke open like his compatriot's as things melted that weren't supposed to melt, and he dropped in an instant.

"This is why we had to do this," Harry shouted over the fray at me. "Because if we don't take them out, they'll follow us when we try and make our esca—" He froze as he tossed Gothric into a nearby wall. It wasn't a fatal move, and Harry's eyes had glazed over. "Uh oh," he said, and I only had a second to wonder what would make him fearful before I found out.

61.

Harmon

It was obvious from the overhead thermal imagery that the battle wasn't going well. The helicopter had moved off, and the thermal satellite scan showed three very clearly hostile "tangos," as the military called them—Sienna Nealon, her speedster friend, and one other—cutting through my FBI task force and the Revelen spec-ops team with ease.

"Disappointing," I said.

Someone was still lurking outside, pinned against the wall and failing to enter the fight. I had a feeling I knew who it was, and it was another unfortunate mark against the fellow. Scott Byerly was quickly turning into the worst personnel staffing decision I'd made since I'd sent Sienna Nealon packing.

"Weakness," I sighed. To hell with the colonel, to hell with McSorley, McCluskey and Shane. I needed this finished, and I could see that there was only one way I could manage it.

I closed my eyes and plunged into the all-too-small mind of Scott Byerly, ripping him off the wall outside the house and jerking him, unwilling, into the battle within.

62.

Scott

It came in the form of pain, all the nerve endings in his skull afire. He resisted, of course, because now he knew what the voice was, in clearest terms—Gerry Harmon.

Yes, the voice said, *you're such a clever fellow, figuring out after almost a year that I've been playing with your mind. Good on you. But unfortunately, that doesn't mean I can't still play, it just means I have to devote more of my attention to doing so, which is ... annoying. So annoying. Now ...*

Let's move.

Scott's back left the wall and his body twisted as his legs worked without his command. He stepped around and into the confines of the abandoned house, boots crushing the shattered glass shards that lined the doorway. Augustus was rising just inside, his hulking earth armor a dark shadow in a poorly lit room, about to step forward and fight again.

That slithering feeling ran through Scott's mind. *Belay that,* the voice sounded, and suddenly Scott could see Augustus through the armor, as though he were here, too, in his mind. *And you, as well.* Reed was there, too, and dazed, his nose bleeding profusely, the three of them present in Scott's mind, Harmon speaking directly to them.

What do you want from me? Scott asked, Harmon's face like a swollen statue that obstructed his view. Harmon was all there was, from here all the way to the ends of the universe. Scott's eyes were blinded by the man, by his enormity.

"I want you to stand there and shut up while I do the job you were supposed to do," Harmon said in a clipped voice.

Scott, with no other choice but to obey, felt as though he were being smashed, suffocated ... he didn't want to give in, but what else was there ...?

Resist.

Like her.

He chafed at the bounds around him, but the pressure was too great, like the water he'd buried Sienna in when he'd thought she was a monster. She wasn't, though, was she? She was a ... a ...

Hero?

"*A MONSTER,*" Harmon's voice insisted, blotting out everything else.

Okay, Scott thought, choosing his fight. He looked around, around the edges of the face that filled his consciousness, looking for an out, even as Harmon began to speak through him to someone else.

63.

Sienna

"You're a nearly interminable pain in my ass," Gerry Harmon's voice sounded from Scott's mouth. It was a creepy effect, and I could tell it had that same impact on others because Colin shuddered visibly. "Most people I fire have the good grace to go the hell away, but not you."

"I'm so very special," I said, swallowing hard. Augustus was just standing there, looming, covered in dirt. I could kick his ass out the door and across the lawn, but I was waiting to see what was so damned important that Harmon had decided to pause and address me directly.

"You really are, I'll give you that," Harmon said, Scott's lips moving in the most bizarre sort of puppetry I could imagine. "Far from normal, far from what everyone else is—"

"Well, what is normal these days?" I threw out the first stupid comeback that came to mind.

"Oh, you know," he said. "It's what you wish you were on the days when everything is just too much and you feel like you're overwhelmed." Scott smiled, a twisted sort of smile that would perhaps have looked more at home on Gerry Harmon's face. "I'm not a psychopath, you know."

"That's reassuring," Colin Fannon muttered.

"I can feel the pain I cause," Harmon went on, apparently too caught up in his monologue to care about the peanut gallery. "But it's necessary. Change seldom results from anything less than pain. Think about it—in the wake of World War One, there was a worldwide movement toward peace. They outlawed war, swore they'd never fight another one—"

"All well and good," I said. "At least until a guy came along and took full advantage of everyone else deciding not to go to war."

"Exactly," Harmon said with a nod of Scott's head. "Unity only works when everyone buys in. As long as there's a rogue element, someone operating for their own wretched purposes ... it will fail every time. So many different agendas, but they all have one thing in common—they're out for themselves, to carve out their bit of happiness, without care for what happens to everyone else." Scott cocked his head, a gesture that wasn't his. "Do you know what Sovereign's problem was?"

I felt like I'd been hit in the face. "Uhh ... that he needed a Fleshlight, desperately, instead of convincing himself that I was the only one for him while simultaneously embarking on a scheme designed to piss me off?"

Scott made a *tsk*-ing sound, and I felt a swell of irritation that Harmon was lecturing me while hiding behind my friends to do so. Harry wasn't saying anything, and he was still there, which suggested to me I was supposed to keep talking. "I like how you take world domination schemes and make them personal, make them all about you. As if you're the only one they affect. Has your psychiatrist friend ever told you you're self-involved?"

"You're the one who was just telling me what a unique pain in your ass I am," I snarked back. "Clearly you're feeding my ego."

Harmon chuckled, and again it was so strange to hear his laughter channeled through Scott. "I met him, you know. Sovereign. A man thousands of years old, desperate for love, someone who wanted his mommy to hold him." He sneered. "I harbor no such weakness."

"Why are we talking about Sovereign?" I asked, glancing at

Harry, whose eyes suddenly widened.

"Oh, I'm just stalling you," Harmon said, grinning with Scott's mouth. "Only another second and—"

The first missile came crashing through the roof, and the house exploded around me.

64.

Harmon

"What a terrible conversationalist she is," I said, shaking my head. "'Me, me, me, me, me.'" I made a faux gagging noise.

The house on the screen was blossoming as the drone-shot Hellfire missiles came raining down on that quaint Salt Lake neighborhood. The view was such that I could see they were tearing into the houses next door, half of each them hauled down into dust and wreckage. It was a regrettable tragedy, but necessary, in the scheme of things. Just as Mr. Byerly, Mr. Coleman, and Mr. Treston's unfortunate demises would be—

I blinked. Something was wrong. I could still feel Coleman, Treston and Byerly, which meant—

"DAMN YOU," I said, rising out of my chair in a fury I seldom felt. I forced my way back into Byerly's mind, determined to end this one way or another—

65.

Sienna

"Put 'em down over there," Harry ordered Colin, and Colin obliged, picking up Augustus and Reed and dragging them both around the corner at warp speed. The house was at least two blocks away now, explosions still echoing through the dawn. We were spread out over a lawn, cars moving past on the streets. People were sticking their heads out their doors all up and down the road, and we were exposed, like a butt with no pants to cover it. Colin zoomed back, picking up Scott, who was staring straight ahead like automaton, ready to carry him off away from us—

Scott smacked Colin sideways with a blind, writhing throw of the hand, and fell to his knees. When he raised his head, Scott was wearing Harmon's maniacal, utterly-out-of-place grin. When the house had blown up, Harmon had ditched out of Scott's mind and he'd keeled over, making it easier for Colin to zoom us all out of there in an eyeblink. Colin had even saved the surviving members of the Revelen squad, though he'd had the decency not to bring them anywhere near us when he set them down. I couldn't decide whether I approved or not, but he'd moved too fast for me to really make a choice. It was done, and I hoped wouldn't have to kill them later, because I was pretty tired of those guys already.

"I can see that I'm going to have to take the kid gloves off," Scott said in Harmon's voice. "I've been too nice about this—"

"Oh, that was nice, droning neighborhoods filled with innocent people?" I asked, staring right at him.

"It's as nice as I get," Harmon said, and Scott lurched upright. "Did you ever realize what happened to Edward Cavanagh?" Scott leered, and suddenly his eyes pitched up, as though someone had grabbed him and wrenched his head back.

"No!" I lunged forward, throwing out a hand. I needed to get to Scott, though I had no idea what I'd do when I was there. I didn't have the power to kill a telepath, not from this distance, and I couldn't just—

Not kill, Bjorn said in my head, *but perhaps distract for a moment—*

"Yesss," I whispered, and unleashed the Norseman.

Bjorn's power was the war-mind, and he loosed the mental attack on Scott, who was already making a choking sound from what Harmon was doing to him. On his knees, Scott was jerking, insensate, but the moment the war-mind hit, his entire mien changed.

Scott screamed sharply, clearly in pain, but no longer mute with it. It was something almost physical, and it started as Harmon's voice, just briefly, then died as Scott's own took over. He clawed at the asphalt pavement, his fingers coming up bloody and then tracing across his scalp and cheeks, leaving trails of crimson that glistened in the dawn's light. His eyes rolled up, and then caught mine.

"Help me," Scott moaned, and then his eyes rolled up again as Harmon seized control once more.

"That was annoying," Harmon's voice overpowered Scott's, and I knew my gambit had failed. "Now watch me—"

"Nope!" Harry shouted, and I looked back in time to see him riding on Colin's shoulders as the speedster zoomed over to me, scooped me up in his arms, and before I could protest—wail, scream, fight back, anything—he shot off down the street, leaving Scott in the clutches of President Gerry Harmon ...

To die.

66.

Scott

The pain was exquisite, head-bursting. The ravens had come and brought a spell of relief in the form of their own agony—Scott had an aunt, Judy, who had visited that particular torment on him once or twice when she'd lost her temper—and then Harmon had reasserted himself, shoving his way back into Scott's brain like he'd rammed a hand in through the ear canal.

Death was now sure, death was now certain, and it would come as a sweet relief after all that had happened. Harmon's voice coming through his throat, his lips had been like scourging fire sweeping through his brain and out his voicebox and mouth. He could feel the president's grip on his brain tightening as he squeezed, blood vessels reacting to the pressure. It would build and build, feeling like it would be eternal, but he knew it would not last forever.

Sooner or later, the blood vessel walls would fail, would rupture, and his head would experience a glorious explosion within. He'd stroke out and drop, his muscles losing all control, his body forgetting to breathe in the catastrophe of the damage. He almost couldn't remember to breathe now, the pain was so great—

Sienna's face was there, and he could see it—like an angel in the light, like a monster when his view changed and she seemed to fall in shade. She was the crux of the problem, the solution to it, and she was reaching out for him. He feared and longed for her touch, knowing it brought death and perhaps, somehow, salvation.

But it didn't last. She disappeared in a blur, just a flash and she was gone, monster and hero disappeared from his view. Scott fell, face down, President Harmon still clawing at the back of his head, ready to release the pressure in his brain in one glorious blast that would surely—thank heavens—lead him into death.

67.

Harmon

I almost killed him right there. Byerly, I mean. I certainly wanted to, even after she was gone. She probably assumed I did. Now that she was aware of my control over his mind, I'd essentially inflicted almost maximum damage. Killing him in front of her was the last thing I could do to torture her, and unfortunately, her compatriots—the Speedster and that other man—knew it. Quick thinking on their parts, getting her out of there.

I let him go. Well, I let the killing pressure go, anyway. I held onto Byerly's brain, because he was still the head of my FBI task force, even in his somewhat reduced condition.

I sagged back in my chair in the Situation Room. "What am I going to do about you?" I asked, peering loosely into Byerly's thoughts. Until recently his mind had been a well-organized place; if you pictured it as a long hall covered on both sides by filing cabinets, it had once been all in order. Every file in its place, and I knew where they all were. It had been easy to manage him then, when he didn't know I was inside, peeking around, adding a few files here and there as needed to give him motivation in the appropriate directions.

Now he was aware of my presence. Aware and aggravated, as though I was the one who'd fiddled with the files to begin with. Now the cabinets were upended, some fallen over into the aisle, others with their contents simply strewn over the floors. It was unfortunate, but it was also a product of me reaching my limits.

I was so very sick of my limits.

I pushed the button on my phone, holding tightly to Byerly's mind. "Ms. Krall, would you be so kind as to tell the girl in my office to join me in the situation room?"

There was a short pause. "I—there's no girl in your office, sir—"

"Yes, there is," I reached out and brushed her mind, telling her that there was nothing unusual about this. Keeping Cassidy in the White House without anyone noticing or commenting had been a fairly easy thing to do for me. I anticipated that if I had to maintain an iron grip on Mr. Byerly, it would perhaps not be so easy in the near future.

"Ah, uh … yes … sir …" Ms. Krall went off to do the job I'd asked of her. I didn't have to push her like this, usually. I must have been slipping.

I sighed. Jana would surely waiting outside the Situation Room as well, on call in case I needed her. I probably would soon. I stared at the screen, and spoke to the speakerphone after taking myself off mute. "Are you tracing the movement of that speedster?"

"Yes, sir," the nameless colonel said. "We've got him. He's in downtown Salt Lake City, and we've got him—uh … uh …"

I closed my eyes. "Your report, colonel?"

"They've … entered a local Starbucks, sir," he said.

"Good," I said and readied myself to dive back into Byerly's mind so I could get this done properly. "Let's finish this."

68.

Sienna

At Harry's orders, Colin stopped at a Starbucks and we all went inside, casually smoothing our air-ruffled clothes. I smelled smoky but not burnt, which was a plus, but it had still felt weird being carried like a bride by a guy, especially one traveling at several hundred miles per hour on foot.

Colin must have done a lot of cardio, because he wasn't even breathing hard when we bopped into the Starbucks. I was dressed in scuffed-up jeans and a worn-out hoodie that Harry had apparently dressed me in, my mohawk on plain display now that I'd pulled my hoodie back. He'd even brought a pair of crappy boots that were pretty much my style. Harmon and company knew about my new look now, but odds were the general public didn't, which was the only advantage in our favor. "Here," Harry said, and offered me a pair of glasses that weren't too far off from the ones I'd been wearing for the last month.

I put on the glasses and found one of the lenses cracked. I flicked it out into one of those dome-topped trash cans, scoring a nice two-pointer by swishing it straight through the top. "Nothing but net," I pronounced as I navigated overcrowded tables with young professionals typing away, mostly on Apple products, their coffees and Chai teas steaming in front of them.

"Should we order something?" Colin asked, a little nervously. He was wearing running pants—no surprise—

along with a matching wick-away top, and his hair was long enough to get in his eyes. He would have looked just as normal in a beanie cap and a vest, or whatever hipsters in Seattle wore nowadays.

"What?" Harry shook out of a daze to look at him. Our resident Cassandra was dressed in a slightly more classic style—a rumpled dress shirt that looked like he'd slept in for a week, khaki trousers with as many wrinkles as Harry probably would have had if he'd aged like a normal person, and scuffed-up dress shoes that looked like they'd been bought at a low-end department store. He wore a belt that was one of those woven leather ones worn by men in the seventies or possibly before. I wasn't alive then, so I couldn't be sure. "No, we're not ordering anything."

"I'm hungry," Colin said plaintively. "It takes a lot of calories to do what I do, you know?"

"Steal something, then, but make it quick," Harry said, mostly ignoring him as he answered. "We're heading out the back in two minutes." He swiped a coffee cup off an abandoned table and handed it to me.

"I'm not drinking that—" I started to say.

"Hold it as a prop, and ditch the hoodie," he said. "Leave it in the garbage in the ladies' room." He rattled the cup at me. "Go. Now."

"Fine," I flounced away, taking the cup and heading for the women's room. I rolled my eyes as I disappeared inside. I quickly crammed my hoodie into the trash can, which left me sporting a sleeveless tee that exposed a little cleavage. I stared at myself in the mirror for a second, appalled, and not for the first time since I'd done this changeup. I had it in mind to go with something frumpier next time. Maybe a nice full-length frock. Or one of those Mormon girl dresses. Those would cover me nicely, though they'd probably look slightly out of place wherever I landed next.

I came out of the bathroom to find Harry and Colin waiting for me, lingering like perverts just outside. Harry had a coffee cup of his own now, and a newspaper. "All right, here's what we do—"

"Did he get food?" I asked, pointing to Colin.

229

"Yeah, I got a few cold things out of the case out front," Colin said uneasily. "Not proud of it, though. Shoplifting is beneath me."

"Yeah, no, you should totally leave fingerprints and a credit card trail for the government to find," Harry said. "Wouldn't want Sienna here to suffer the only consequences of these crimes."

Colin stared straight ahead. "I left fingerprints at the house—"

"It got blown up, remember?" Harry waved him off.

"Yeah, but you didn't know that was gonna happen," Colin said, frowning. "And you didn't make me wear gloves at any point—"

"I see short term, not long," Harry said, sounding like he was annoyed with this line of inquiry. "Get out that door in the next ten seconds, or start planning how you're going to fight your way out of a full encirclement. You walk with Nealon, I follow along two blocks behind you and a street over." He leaned in close to both of us, peering past just to make sure no one was listening. I checked too; they weren't. "Follow my instructions, walk arm in arm, and you'll make it to the rendezvous point, ninety percent certain."

"Wait, what—what's the ten percent uncertainty?" Colin asked.

"You get handsy with her, it gets bad," Harry said, causing me to shoot a laser look at Colin, who blushed. "Oh, the odds just improved nine and a half percent, as if by magic," Harry deadpanned. "Go. I'll be behind shortly. Arm in arm, but ... you know, politely. For your health." And he gave us a shove out the door.

"Were you really thinking about getting handsy with me?" I asked as we walked along, Colin's sleeved arm locked in my bare one. It was chilly, wind whipping through the streets of Salt Lake City, which was waking up.

"To add to the cover!" Colin said, a little too quickly. "I think it would have, uh, given depth to the role that we're, uh, playing—"

"Just hang on to my arm, Cassanova," I said, and walked up the block as Harry had suggested.

This part of town looked as though it was torn between antiquity and modernity. Next to old brick buildings stood sleek, modern ones with glass-and-sandstone facades. I suspected a lot of renovation was going on, but I didn't have time to indulge my curiosity by stopping and studying the architecture. Not that I would have even if I hadn't been walking down the street arm-in-arm with an apparently handsy speedster while the government was pursuing me.

The block passed quickly, buildings giving way to a park as we strolled, arm in arm, Colin slightly twitchy at the low speed, along the street. I saw Harry pop out on the corner ahead, casually waiting for the crosswalk symbol to go green, which it did almost as soon as we arrived.

"Fancy meeting you two here," he said as we caught up to him. He kept his head down and cleared his throat. "Stay back at least ten feet from me. We're going into this parking garage up ahead."

"What then?" I asked, looking around to make sure no one was around to hear us. A couple people were across the street, but no one was in earshot.

"We're going to steal a car and get the hell out of town," he said, and disappeared suddenly as he changed direction and entered a glass-fronted door to the garage.

The garage was expansive and looked like it served both a residential building as well as public parking. I thought that was odd, but admittedly I didn't know squat about municipal parking. I was used to the suburbs, where there was abundant land and you parked in any lot you wanted for free. In cities, where space was at such a premium, I'd seen the signs proclaiming hour parking, extortionate rates, and all that fun stuff. I avoided the hassle whenever possible by flying.

I sighed. I didn't think I'd be doing much flying for a while, not with AMRAAM missiles greeting me every time I went aloft lately.

Harry led us up to the second floor, where he walked down the line of vehicles, looking at each in turn and muttering so low that only meta ears could hear him. "No," he said, shaking his head at a Chevy Volt.

"But it's so eco-efficient," Colin said mournfully.

"Fancy being pulled over in Provo?" He glanced back. "No? We're going with something less likely to cause the owner to immediately file a stolen vehicle report. Something like …" He walked down the line five more cars. "… This," he pronounced, stopping before a Chrysler 300C.

Colin's face fell. "Oh, man."

"In we get," Harry said, walking over to the door and opening it. I blinked; man, people must have been honest in Utah, because that was the kind of stupid you couldn't get away with in most cities. I let Colin take shotgun cuz he was taller than I was, and I squeezed into the back seat as Harry fumbled under the dashboard. "You know, this used to be easier," he said, staring hard at a bundle of wiring. "Alas." He ripped three wires apart and started crossing them until the car honked the alarm once and then started without further protest. "This will get us as far as Idaho Falls." He brought the long, silvery beast into motion and headed for the exit. "We can get the plane to meet us there, I think."

I blinked at him. "What plane?"

Harry grinned broadly. "Don't get me wrong, I do enjoy getting into a spot of bother every now and again while trying to help you, young lady, but … I'm getting paid for this. We all are. Veronika's in contact with your employer's agent, and we've got full license to do whatever we have to—how'd Veronika put it? 'Aid Sienna Nealon however necessary.'"

I stared at him. My employer's new agent had authorized payouts to people to help me. I felt taken aback, not quite sure how to respond. "That would have been good to know thirty days ago," I finally decided, trying to be judicious in my reply.

"Better late than never," Harry said, turning us north, toward the freeway, and taking us out of the federal dragnet that was encompassing Salt Lake City.

69.

Harmon

"The Starbucks is clear," Reed Treston's staticky voice sounded over the piped-in speaker in the Situation Room. I had my eyes closed, basking in semi-darkness, a little light penetrating through my eyelids. I had my focus on Scott Byerly, holding him without crushing his mind utterly, while Reed and Augustus and the surviving members of the Revelen crew checked the last known location of our fugitives.

"I have no sign of the speedster leaving the building," the commsat operator spoke through to me.

"He probably left at regular speed," I said, closing my eyes. "Watch the building for three people departing." That would be too easy, though, wouldn't it? "Watch for two people departing as well. You have a new description on Sienna Nealon." I kept my eyes tightly shut. "Check the security camera footage in the Starbucks, Treston."

"On it," Reed said tightly. He wasn't wavering yet, but that was because my imprinting was fresh. "It'll be a few minutes."

"By all means, take your time," I said with all sarcasm, "I'm sure they're not getting farther and farther away by the second." I hit the mute button on the speakerphone as Cassidy entered, her laptop clutched under her arm. She wasn't wearing that wetsuit she so frequently wore, thankfully. I was at my limit of being able to cover for her,

233

after all, and manipulating the thoughts of the Secret Service agents outside as well as Jana so that a woman without a security clearance or any sort of ID could enter the White House Situation Room was one more drain on my abilities.

"You sent for me?" Cassidy asked, holding her laptop in front of her chest like some sort of shield.

"Sienna Nealon continues to fail at dying," I said, closing my eyes once more. I didn't need to look at her face to know Cassidy was displaying a subtle interplay of emotions— mostly relief at the fact that I was failing in my attempts to end this little bitch as spectacularly as she had. "For such a blunt instrument, for such an unknowing ... uncouth ... *barbarian*, she certainly is good at causing problems."

"She's not what you expected," Cassidy said, as though I were looking for catharsis instead of aid.

"I don't care what she *is*," I said, "so long as she will *be* a corpse, and soon." I opened my eyes. "In that vein, what do you have?"

"I don't, but—" Cassidy rushed to say more before I could give her an angry earful, "... I do have a new formula that's being manufactured as we speak."

I stared at her. "And your simulations ...?"

"Eighty-five percent." She shrugged to absolve herself in case of failure. "I thought it might be worth a test run."

"Indeed it is," I said, leaning back in my chair. "You have a subject in mind?"

"You have a few we could try it out on," she said without guile. "But if need be—"

"No," I said, the idea lodging in my brain. There was merit there. "I like that. But ... we'll need to study long-term side effects."

"Provided it's used on existing metahumans, I can't conceive of a lasting side effect," Cassidy said. "Because our DNA regenerates damage at such a rapid pace, even something truly toxic could be metabolized out—"

"Remember, I know people, not chemistry," I said.

"High-level metas will heal from whatever it does," she said with another shrug. "The worst you'd experience is a regression of effect, which could conceivably be offset by regular dosing … but that might introduce toxicity—you know what, never mind," she finally caught on. "We'll see what happens on the trial."

"So you want me to use Sienna Nealon's friends as test subjects," I said, chuckling softly to myself. "Cruel."

Cassidy stood there, still using her laptop as a shield. It wouldn't protect her from anything I would attack her with, but the protective instinct was simply that; instinct. "They would heal," she said again. "Cancer, tumors, paralysis … all them have enough power that they'd—"

"I approve," I said. "Assuming we've really lost her again, I'll have them brought back here, and you can proceed with clinical trials." I paused in thought. "Where is this drug being manufactured?"

Cassidy blushed. "One of Cavanagh's old outfits in Frederick, Maryland. They don't know they're doing it for us, it just … appeared in their system. It was the closest R and D facility I could subvert."

"That'll work," I said, and then, remembering how she'd started the conversation, I felt a curious desire for commiseration. "How many times did she dodge your attempts to kill her?"

Cassidy swallowed visibly. "I … don't know."

"Don't know?" I almost laughed. "I have a hard time believing you didn't keep count."

"Do *you* enjoy wallowing in your failures?" she asked, with an air of snottiness that was tied to her youth and how much I'd just wounded her with my incisive critique.

"Enjoy them? No," I said, "but I do find them instructive. I'll take stock of what's happened today and yesterday, for instance, and see if I can apply it in the future. It seems to me I suffered from a perfect storm, a confluence of events that fell entirely in her favor." How else could one describe an escape from a highly-trained metahuman task force, the entire US Air Force, and real-time satellite tracking with hundreds of eyes on its feed?

"Do you know what you'll come up with?" Cassidy asked, starting to lower the laptop. "Variables you can't explain. Maneuvers that seem impossible for anyone, even a meta, to pull off. Ingenuity that breaks every box you try and put her in—"

I laughed. "How appropriate, that analogy."

Cassidy flushed. "Because of her upbringing."

"I've never believed in the undefeatable foe," I said. "You watch these TV show nowadays, and they've always got their master criminal—Moriarty, Hannibal Lecter, Khan ... what's the name of that fellow on *The Blacklist?* Spader plays him wonderfully. Whatever the case, they're always the smartest man in the room. They're ten steps ahead of the entire government and even when they get imprisoned—in a glass cage, as inevitably happens—and they come face to face with the good guy who dogs them ... they're already planning their escape, because imprisonment was their idea." I leaned back in my chair and shut my eyes. "You're the smartest person in the world, Cassidy, when it comes to sheer intelligence. I'm the smartest when it comes to moving people. I know their minds. I know how they work. I've controlled influencers throughout the world to get the results I want. I am not just the smartest person in the room, I *control* the smartest people in any room." I looked up to find her quavering slightly. "Through thought, through other ... methods of compulsion you're familiar with." I closed my eyes once more, enjoying the darkness.

"Sienna Nealon is a philistine," I said. "She never even finished high school, never set foot in a college. She's never been the smartest person in any room, even when she's alone in one. She has all the social skills of a wild ferret, and that's where her strength is. She's crafty. She possesses power and animal cunning, with a gut instinct for human nature. That's not intelligence. That's not brilliance in any measurable sense of the word. She knows cruelty and force, and she knows when they're aimed her way, that's all. She's been on the swinging side of the stick enough to know how to avoid hard end. But she can't dodge forever. Not what I'm bringing to bear on her. This will ultimately come down to a show of force—as it did on the shores of Salt Lake just a few hours ago—and she won't always have other people darting in to save her at the last minute. She's an idiot, a rube, a troglodyte, and these are her last days on this earth. Mark my words. She can't stand against the might of Washington, and she damned sure cannot stand against the two of us united against her. We will outthink her."

Cassidy did not speak, but I could feel her nod of acquiescence. She excused herself from the room, and the fatigue claimed me. I dozed off in the chair, passing into the realm of sleep, enjoying silence in my mind for the first time in days, knowing that what I had just said was most certainly true.

70.

Scott waited in the car for the others to return, a vehicle borrowed from the local FBI field office. The pressure of Harmon in his mind had been intense, suffocating, and left him feeling desperately confused—well, not even confused, anymore, just sure that Sienna Nealon was not the villain she was being painted as and just as sure that if she crossed in front of the barrel of his gun, his finger would be compelled to pull the trigger.

It was painful, knowing his mind was not his own, but Scott wasn't railing against it. Not now. He'd already lost that battle and had no interest in a painful replay, especially not when he felt the slithering serpent tendrils clutching at his mind fading into the recesses as Harmon slackened his grip. What was that? He almost felt ... sleepy? Except he wasn't terribly sleepy, surprisingly. Perhaps it was Harmon on the other end, all tapped out after a hard day of mind-controlling others.

Reed opened the car door and got in the driver's seat. Augustus followed, getting in the passenger side. The three Revelen survivors were in the vehicle behind them—Gothric the Medic, Joaquín the Gaucho with the green eye beams, and Mac the Knifer, as Scott had taken to thinking of the Aussie. "Halfway home," he muttered, rebellious enough to sneak that thought out while Harmon was napping.

"What?" Reed looked back at him, dead serious. "What

did you say?"

"I said I want to head home if we don't have any leads," Scott said, and Reed seemed to let it go. He was still nominally in charge of this op, after all—it wasn't as though Harmon had told anyone that he had to directly mind control Scott at this point. That would probably be embarrassing and bring up questions that even someone as brainwashed as Reed couldn't fully ignore. "*Do* we have any leads?"

"She's got a new look on the security cam footage," Reed said dutifully.

"You didn't notice that in the house fight?" Scott asked. *How mind-numbed is he, not to see that?*

"Yeah," Augustus said, rubbing his hands together from the chill, "li'l sister got herself a tank top going on, with a dyed mohawk and hipster glasses." He didn't laugh, which he would have if he hadn't had a telepath suck the life out of his brain. "Wouldn't have pictured that for her."

"Sienna will do anything to avoid the cold clasp of justice," Reed said sternly.

What the hell did Harmon do to your brain to bring out this vengeful side of you, Reed? Scott wondered. It had to have something to do with inflating his sense of self-righteousness and decreasing his ability to see anything in shades of grey. Then again, Scott had felt the sudden, inexplicable urge to kill Sienna, and it seemed to have manifested in the form of seeing her as some sort of subhuman monster anytime she was in his sight and thinking about her in the most loathsome, reviling terms when she wasn't.

"We're gonna fit it on her, though," Augustus said, and they did a little fist-bump in the front seat. "She's gonna get clapped up—in a coffin."

"She went out the back exit," Reed went on. "Satellite techs at the Pentagon are following her movements now that they have an updated description. We just have to wait for them to find her."

"Hrm," Scott said and started to fumble for his phone. He didn't have it; it had probably been lost in one of the battles. "Augustus, I need your phone," he said, trying to keep his idea on the down low so that Harmon couldn't hone in on it later. He'd felt the killing fury rise through their connection and figured he had one major rebellion left before the president decided it wasn't worth it and snuffed him from two thousand miles away.

"Yeah, sure," Augustus handed him the phone. Scott selected J.J.'s name out of the short list of contacts and dialed. It only rang once before it got picked up. "It's Scott. I need you to run analysis for me."

"Uh, okay," J.J. said, calmer than he would have been if he wasn't also being mentally manipulated. "I'm on this satellite thing now—"

"The Pentagon's working on that, right?" Scott asked, knowing damned well that J.J. would do the job faster.

"Well, sure, but—"

"I know where she's going," Scott said, turning both Reed and Augustus's heads immediately. "Or at least where she'll end up."

"Go on," J.J., Augustus and Reed chorused in perfect, nerve-rending harmony.

"She knows the president is her enemy now," Scott said, speaking to all of them, knowing he'd get roughly the same response. "How long do you figure it is before she does what she does and comes right at him?"

"That's not going to solve her problem," Reed said.

"Oh, she'd do it, too," Augustus said.

"Oh, shit," J.J. said. The responses slightly surprised Scott; he was expecting a uniform reply. Perhaps Harmon hadn't completely scrubbed their brains out, then.

"J.J.," Scott said, "I need you to do an analysis of the most likely avenues Sienna would use to assassinate President Harmon." He swallowed heavily, fearing a stir in his mind that did not come, fortunately. "We need to know how prepared the Secret Service is for this contingency." He blinked at Reed and Augustus, who were nodding along in tandem, back to their new programming.

"Aye, sir," J.J. said, and Scott heard him tapping away at the keys a moment later. "I'll get right on it, priority one."

"Good," Scott said, and hung up. Reed and Augustus both

turned back around, staring wordlessly out the front windshield. Scott didn't break the silence, but he didn't expect there was much going on in either of their heads. That was all right, though, because he was doing enough for all of them, though it was along a line neither of them would have approved: *Once J.J. finishes with that study … how the hell do I get it to Sienna?*

71.

Sienna

I slept through every leg of the trip, secure in the knowledge that Harry Graves, one of only a few people I'd ever met who could see the future, was watching over me. I slept on the car ride to Idaho Falls, where I boarded a chartered plane paid for by my employer. I slept on the jet, which took me to Los Angeles, to one of the smaller airports where I passed no TSA checkpoint and no baggage claim before getting into the back of a black limo like some movie star. And I slept in the limo as it delivered me to the beachfront house of Steven Clayton, Hollywood hottie.

Okay, I made that name for him up. Or *People Magazine* did. One of us.

By the time I ended up on his doorstep, I felt almost human again in terms of rest, though I suspected that the makeup I'd applied before I fled Cedar City had long ago been washed off, probably in the briny depths of the Great Salt Lake. My hair was similarly a wreck, what little of it there was left, but I also didn't fuss too much about this, because … well, there was nothing I could do. Also, the government was trying to kill me, so a bad hair day just didn't feel that apocalyptic.

"Hey," Steven Clayton said when he opened the door. He was a tall drink of handsome, and he wrapped me up in his arms as I let him. I let out a long sigh, because I felt like a cat sleeping in a warm beam of sunshine.

Then I realized his forearms were in skin to skin contact with my underarms and hurriedly had him set me back down before the touch of my powers got too intense and I ate his handsome soul.

He brushed his light arm hair as though he expected flakes of ash to come dropping out. "That really does burn."

"I should come with a warning, like a pack of cigarettes," I said sadly. "'May be hazardous to your health.'" I looked him over again—he still looked like the sexiest man of the year or whatever title he was vying for now—and sighed. "Good to see you."

"Good to see you, too," he said, ushering us in. He shook Colin's hand, then Harry's, like a real man. Colin gave him a limp fish, and I could practically feel the disapproval radiating from Steven, but Harry gave him a squeeze, enough to make Steven hide a cringe.

I wondered what was sparking their little grapple back and forth, but I didn't have time to delve into it, because a blond streak came shooting at me, screaming, "SIENNA!"

Kat crashed into me as I got an arm up. She slid in and squeezed me a lot like Steven had, only maybe a touch harder because she was a meta. "Urk," I said, "Kat."

She let go in plenty of time to avoid feeling the burn, leaving her delicate hands on my side but safely on the fabric of my tank top. "I was so worried about you until we saw you in Vegas!"

"I would have called, but … I didn't have a phone with your number programmed into it," I said, turning perhaps a little scarlet in the cheeks. "Also, I figured you had, ahem …"

"Betrayed you?" she fished with a big smile, poking at me with her words. Like she did. Kat was not a huge brain, but she knew enough to occasionally score a point. If I hadn't known her for as long as I did, I would have ascribed it to luck, but I think it had something to do with her empathy, which—despite my occasional complaints to the contrary— did exist, and was quite powerful when applied. She could heart to heart like no one.

"What's going on, girlfriend?" Veronika said, sassing me as

she came up the two short steps from the living room to break my hug with Kat. She extended a hand. I assumed we were shaking like dudes, but just as I reached to grasp hers, her skin turned blue and burst into plasma flames, searing my palm and causing me to jerk back my hand to avoid losing it entirely to the intense heat.

"Ow! Asshole!" I said, flapping my hand as though that would speed up Wolfe's healing of the burn.

Veronika cackled like an old lady, which she might have been for all I knew. "Haha, I'm just messing with you." She got serious. "I'd ask how your trip was, but the part I saw on the news involved getting shot down by fighter jets, so … I'm guessing it was still better than crossing a TSA checkpoint?"

"Less groping of my private parts, anyway."

"Always a downside," Veronika said, making a sound of disappointment.

"Is she here?" A voice sounded from behind the sunlit view. Steven's house looked out on the Pacific, and it was midday, and sunny, and even I couldn't complain about that. Mostly because I was inside and not getting sunburned.

Abigail—Abby—peered out at me from behind a wall, then slowly crept out further. She was wearing something not unlike my top. I'd sorta cribbed my new style from her, down to the hair color. "Oh, wow," she said, giving me the once over. "You look a lot cooler as a fugitive."

"Thanks," I said. "I borrowed your fashion sense for this cover identity's look."

She shrugged, blushing with the perceived compliment. "You wanna raid my closet later? You're looking a little ragged."

I glanced at the clothing I was wearing, which indeed had seen better days. There were a lot of holes, none of them in places that would get me cited for public exposure, except maybe in Utah. "I might take you up on that, unless I decide to go a different direction with my look."

"Where is she?" Dr. Isabella Perugini emerged from behind Abigail, pausing in Abby's shadow as she took me all in. I didn't know quite what to expect from her, so I braced, figuring the most likely response was going to be a fusillade of angry recriminations punctuated by florid Italian curses (were there any other kind of Italian curses, really?).

What I got instead was another hug, a charging-nearly-knock-me-over hug from a woman who'd called me many, many nasty names over the course of our relationship. She squeezed me tight, pressing her cheek against mine and then kissing me on both as she broke away, a tear glittering in the corner of her eye before it traced a line down her olive cheek. "It is so good to see you, Sienna."

"Thanks," I said, lost for words. "I ... saw Reed this morning."

She stiffened, bristled. "I trust he is still ... a puppet with the President's hand up his ass?"

"I don't think that's how he's actually controlling them," I said, brushing past her and into a huge living room/kitchen combo that fully embraced the Malibu view. "Harmon's a telepath—"

"Tell us something we don't know," Veronika said as she slouched down the steps again behind me. Everyone else—Abigail, Steven, Veronika, Colin, Harry, Kat, even Perugini, followed slowly, as if afraid that sudden movement would break the web of conversation as it was beginning.

"Okay," I said, taking that as a challenge. "Scott's been under some form of his control probably since our visit to LA last November," I nodded at Kat and Steven, "and Cassidy Ellis is working with him, in the White House, but under duress—"

"What do you mean, 'under duress'?" This came from Perugini. "She tried to kill you before. She nearly did kill Reed."

"I know," I said, turning to look at the beach view, "but I had a talk with her, and she gave away a lot more than she would have if she'd been happy with her current working conditions." I chewed my lip. "She as much as admitted she was in the White House, she called in Harmon to break into the dreamwalk, which totally exposed him for what he was—"

"We could have told you what he was," Kat said.

"I didn't know you were on my side, okay?" I threw up my hands. "I spent the last month hiding and wallowing, figuring everyone turned on me. I'm sorry for doubting you, all right?" I didn't look anyone in the eyes. "I have abandonment issues for some unknown reason, and I jumped to the wrong conclusion—"

"Damned right you did," Kat said. "We were here all along, trying to figure out any way we could to get word to you. Poor Harry sat and thought about dialing a phone for days. It was so sad. Also, I haven't been shopping in a month."

I couldn't contain my sarcasm, not even when presented with so obvious a display of Kat's loyalty. "Truly, no one has suffered as you have suffered."

Veronika snickered. "So Harmon's your big bad, huh?"

"Well, he's bad," I said. "Badder than I ever realized, anyway."

"How bad is he?" Abigail asked, tentatively. "That's … that's not a joke setup, I sincerely want to know. I mean, I voted for him. I feel pangs of guilt. Also, fear, because unlike the rest of you, I have never been a fugitive. Or in a fight."

"It's an open question," I said, "but I'll tell you what I suspect—Edward Cavanagh was one of his biggest donors, right?" I looked around. Realizing that neither Augustus nor J.J. was there to back me up, my gaze settled on Abigail.

"So I've heard …" Abigail said awkwardly, obviously feeling singled out.

"Think about everything we've tied Cavanagh to this last couple of years," I said, and then realized that, really, no one in the room knew what the hell we'd tied Cavanagh to. "Uh, okay, well—he was responsible for funding Dr. Doomsday in Chicago—"

"Ohhh," Harry Graves said, throwing up a finger, "yeah—!"

"Okay, yeah, that," Colin said with a nod.

"Right," Veronika said, "that asshole that used the DNA we volunteered—"

"For money," I pushed in acerbically.

"—to create an anti-metahuman plague," Veronika

finished, giving me a daggered look of her own. "Why did he do that again? Because a meta girl rejected him or something?"

"I think his wife left him for a meta?" Kat asked, looking up at the ceiling as if trying to recall.

"Who gives a shit?" I asked. "Point is, he was funded by Cavanagh. And Cavanagh also had his fingers in something else—manufacturing a serum that gave normal humans meta powers. Like, it unlocked it in their DNA. That was how I met Augustus—"

"Wait, so is Augustus not a real meta, then?" Abigail asked. She seemed to ponder this. "Could I get some of that serum? Because I'm wondering, you know, now that I'm a fugitive and at risk of getting in a fight, like—maybe that could help me not die. Very important to me. Crucial, really."

"We don't have any of the serum," I said, "but Cavanagh was also linked to another solution that suppresses meta powers—"

"That douche came up with suppressant?" Veronika let out a sigh of disgust. "If he wasn't already dead, I'd kill him myself—"

"And that's another thing," I said. "When I was talking to Harmon today—"

"Talking to him how?" Steven asked, handsome face creased with concern. "Did he show up to—"

"He channeled himself through Scott, like a demon," I said. "But he as much as admitted to killing Cavanagh just before he tried to blow a pressure valve in Scott's head. He killed Cavanagh, either to protect himself from the blowback with the election coming up, or maybe from something even worse coming out if Cavanagh talked to the cops." My thoughts thundered along. Cavanagh *was* going to talk, too. Senator Robb Foreman had seen to that.

"Wow, there's a lot going on here," Veronika said softly, with a look on her face that said she wanted to back away from this mess like she'd never seen any of it.

"So Cavanagh funded this other thing out in Oregon called Palleton Labs—" I started.

"This guy is starting to sound like the corporate version of that sperm donor who knocked up like a thousand women," Abigail said. "You know, the one Vince Vaughan played in that movie—"

"I remember Palleton Labs," Kat said, looking suddenly lively. "That was where Augustus got ragdolled through all those walls and floors—"

"There was a vault on the top floor." I bypassed whatever meandering road Kat was going to go down in favor of pursuing my own to the end. "Timothy Logan, this ... worthless turd that I paroled from the Cube, back before parole from the Cube became the cool thing to do—"

"It wasn't that cool," Steven deadpanned. "I think it ended up being pretty hot for most of those releases, in fact ..."

"Because she burned them to death," Kat giggled.

"*Anyway*, Timothy and his cronies broke in, tried to get into the vault, but they couldn't, even with Gavrikov powers," I said. "So I stole the vault—"

"Whoaaaaa," Steven said, frowning, "I thought you were innocent of all the stuff they accused you of—"

"Well, I was," I said. "I mean, I burned those bad guys up in Eden Prairie because they were beating me to death. But the vault thing, I mean it was a Cavanagh-funded installation. I just assumed the seeds of evil were, you know, fair game for the taking—"

"What did you find inside?" Dr. Perugini asked, managing to stay on track.

"I couldn't open it," I said, pacing in front of the bright windows. "Turns out, they treated the metal with this—well, it's a meta power that grants additional strength through this imbuement process. It's how Mjolnir became this invulnerable, badass, mythical weapon—"

"Wait, so Mjolnir was a real thing?" Steven asked, brow furrowed.

"This is just the most educational day ever," Abigail said.

"Is that the hammer wielded by Chris Hemsworth?" Kat asked.

Idiot, Bjorn opined.

I will hurt you in your imaginary genitals, Gavrikov said. That settled things down quickly, which was surprising given how much of a douchebag Bjorn was.

"Yeah," I said, "that one. Anyway, the vault has been treated by a meta who's given it the same sort of impregnability factor. I tried to burn through—nothing. Punches don't do squat. I ripped it out of a building and flew across multiple states and there wasn't a ding to show for it."

"Maybe you didn't burn it hard enough," Veronika said with a smirk, lifting her plasma hand. It glowed blue, and I could practically feel the heat wafting off it, like a mirage in the desert. "Wanna try with something a little stronger than fire?"

72.

Scott

They caught a flight back to DC once it was obvious the trail was cold. They'd lost it somewhere north of Salt Lake City. A team of military analysts was trying to trace it even now, but a complex pattern of evasions and a car switch somewhere along the way under cover of a garage left them guessing, trying to narrow down probabilities that were increasingly improbable. That was fine with Scott, who was still enjoying the absence of President Harmon's mental touch. Any sudden alert might just wake the president, after all, and that would be nothing but bad for him.

"You let her get away," Mac the Knifer said from his seat across from Scott in the government plane. He was playing with that blade of his, and the thing was gleaming in the afternoon sunshine leaking in through the open shade.

"Yeah, I totally summoned a speedster to come pick her up," Scott said. He could feel the gaze of Augustus and Reed on him, watching, listening. Probably J.J., too, though that was a little more fifty-fifty since the geek was still working on the White House threat assessment in the back of the plane. At least he wasn't working on tracking Sienna. "That's on me."

"You didn't breach and clear," Mac said, leaning forward, knife still on his fingertips. "You could have washed her right out of the house if you'd been of a mind to. Instead you started speaking in tongues—tongues that don't belong to you." He stared at Scott with a fierce look. "When did you start speaking other peoples' minds?"

"I've got more thoughts than fit in my own head," Scott said carefully. "I doubt you'd understand."

Mac's eyes narrowed, reflected in the glare of the knife as he brought it up to rest, dull edge against his nose. "I *don't* understand. But I know weirdness when I see it, and a Poseidon that suddenly starts talking in another man's voice … that's weird. The sort of weird that killed Rudi, Ferko and Ambrus—"

"Ambrus?" Scott asked, raising an eyebrow. "Oh. Booster."

"Damned right," Mac said. "Now I'm bound by orders to go along with this increasingly improbable mission. But I don't have to like it. And don't count on me following your lead anymore. The next time I get a chance to cut out Sienna Nealon's lungs, I'm taking it. Stand back or I'll carve out your voicebox. All your voiceboxes, if I find more than one." And with his mind apparently spoken, Mac leaned back in his seat and was snoring within minutes.

"He doesn't even consider you threat enough to worry you might kill him in his sleep."

Scott turned to see Gaucho Joaquín chortling, his sparkly vest catching the sunlight like the knife had.

"You don't consider me much of a threat, either," he observed, though Joaquín's eyes stayed firmly on him.

"*Sí,* but I always keep watch," Joaquín said. His eyes widened and briefly glowed. "Sleep with your eyes open, yes? This is a lesson I learned early."

"Sound advice," Scott said.

"Sounds like advice you should heed," Gothric the Medic said in his heavily accented English. "Maybe someone blames you for the death of our compatriots."

"Were you close?" Scott asked warily. He looked at Reed and Augustus, but suspected he wouldn't get much backing from either of them if the Revelen team turned on him.

"We'd been through more than you can imagine," Gothric said. Joaquín just nodded.

"I can imagine quite a lot," Scott said.

"Imagine this," Gothric said, dark eyes on Scott just the way Joaquín's had been. "Sovereign's old group Century is coming to your nation, intent on destroying every single meta."

"Not hard to imagine, oddly enough," Scott said.

"Oh, but in America he did not even come close to finishing the job," Gothric said. "In Europe, they killed ninety percent of us, easy. Only the truly cunning outrun Century. Either the ones who go to ground," he mimed lowering his head, "or those who fight back so hard that Century decides—'You know, it's not worth it for these. We go around them, come back later with more strength.'" Gothric made a sour face. "Revelen was one of the only places that Century just … left alone after two attempts at extermination. Rudi always said they would come back later, once Sovereign had the world, and just … nuke us. What could we do? Small country, small population." He shrugged. "We banded together there. We stood there, together." He made a hateful face. "Together. The six of us. Some others. We all made it out alive because we—" He bit his fist, then pulled it out of his mouth and shook it, "—we made them pay for coming to us. We stood against them. All they sent mercenary and meta alike. All of us. Together." His brow became a dark line. "Until today."

"You did watch her kill Sovereign and Century, right?" Scott asked, a little more casually than he might have if he hadn't been facing death in the form of presidential mind-control. "The world did. I assume you have TVs in Revelen … internet, maybe?" He watched his barbs provoke a slight stiffening from Joaquín. "She whipped all of their asses. *She* did. Not her plus all her friends, whatever the media might have said. We fought some, but she did the killing. She wiped them out. I'm guessing whatever Century sent at you, they were corpses when you were done with them over in Revelen." His face tightened to match those he was speaking to. "They were ash and bone and blood and pieces when she killed the rest of them and their king shit leader over here. You wanna be mad at me? Go ahead." He settled back in his own chair, and closed his eyes. "Kill me in my sleep if you think it'll help your shot the next time you go fist to fist with her. You shoot your little eye beams," he made a vague gesture at Joaquín, "you see if you can choke her with a plant or something," he waved his hand at Gothric the Persephone, "and maybe, who knows, Mac the Knifer will get lucky and cut her lungs out. Then she'll grow a new set and he'll spend the rest of his short life being fed his own entrails." Scott really was feeling a little drowsy. "Because those other two zombies," he waved at Reed and Augustus, knowing they wouldn't have a clue what he was talking about, "they're going to be about as much help to you as the cold corpses of your newly-departed friends." He smiled, feeling the swirl of sweet sleep twisting around in his brain, ready to draw him in, and he could practically hear the shuffling discomfort he'd awoken in Joaquín and Gothric. They wouldn't be sleeping on this flight, that much was sure. "'Nighty-night."

73.

Sienna

"This isn't as much fun as I thought it would be," Veronika complained as I carried her over Montana. We'd taken the chartered plane up to a nearby airfield, hopefully minimizing our risk of getting caught by a careful watcher of satellite footage. Also, carrying Veronika from LA to Montana at a thousand miles an hour? Probably not healthy for her. Or me, come to think of it. She gets cold, she lights off, we both fall out of the sky screaming and burning.

"Because I'm carrying you or because it's effing freezing?" I asked.

"It's freezing," she said, lips blue and chattering, the moon barely visible as it cast its silvery light over the cloudy sky. At least we had that working for us, too, probably interfering with the satellites. "How do you stand this?"

"Because I'm not a giant whiner," I said with a straight face, and she got serious quick.

"Oh, no you din't," she said, destroying the word "didn't" in the process of drawing my attention to it.

"Oh, yes I—hey, we're here." I brought us down in a low sweep toward the hidden place where I'd stashed the vault. I came in low for a landing, dropping Veronika in a thatch of bushes. She screamed at me as she landed, but I figured it was fair game for her nearly burning my hand off earlier.

"That was reciprocity, I guess," Veronika said. She was quick. "You owed me that for the hand." She brushed a twig out of her hair. "And at least this isn't the desert, where I'd get a cactus up my ass."

"Note to self: detour to Arizona on the way home," I said, "though I must say, after a month in Utah—"

"Why would you go and do a thing like that to yourself?" She shook her head sadly. "Was it some sort of self-flagellation?"

"It was nice there," I said, "with mostly nice people. Except for that one bitch that dumpstered me—"

"You let someone put you in a dumpster?"

"I needed to be incognito. Plus, I tipped a portable outhouse over on her as a reply in kind." I frowned, thinking about it. "I wonder if Sandra has figured out she got effed up by Sienna Nealon yet?"

"She'll figure it out eventually," Veronika said, brushing a stray leaf out of the crack of her too-tight pants. They weren't too tight for her, but she was clearly way more confident in her body than I was mine, even with the Abigail-ification of my wardrobe. She walked up to the vault and just stared at it for a second. "You carried this thing all the way out here from Portland?"

"Yep."

She raised her eyebrows, impressed. "Nice job, Nealon. You're like, my hero, or something." She raised a fist and crackled the knuckles one by one. "That said, you should never send a girl to do a woman's job."

"And you should never send a woman in a girl's pants," I quipped back, drawing an amused look from Veronika.

"Girl, you know my ass looks good in this leather. You weren't just checking out the branches you tried to violate me with."

"I wouldn't violate you, even with a branch, but you just keep thinking I would."

"God, you're such a stick in the mud, Nealon. Why can't you be a stick up my ass instead?"

I was never quite sure how to take Veronika's borderline flirtation with me, but fortunately, she got to business before I had to give it much more thought. Her hand lit up like a lantern, and she plunged it into the specially imbued metal that comprised the vault. Her fingers pressed against it lightly, like mine had, making it look a little like she was casting a magical spell or something.

"This is really hard material," Veronika said. "Like … really hard."

"You're searching for a way to make that dirty and failing to come up with a guy's name to drag into it, aren't you?"

"Oh, I could go down that dirty road if I wanted." She flashed me a grin. "But I like to keep you guessing." She turned back to the vault, a look of concentration visible on her face. She pushed her hand against it and the vault squeaked, moving slightly against her pressure.

And her fingers melted a few centimeters into the surface.

"Yeah, baby," Veronika whispered, "I would have burned Thor's hand off and violated him with his own hammer. Who's harder than that?"

"I'd doubt he'd be, after having a big honking hammer placed where the sun don't shine."

"You don't know, he might have been waiting all his long life for a girl like me."

"Then he died waiting, cuz he ate it in Norway back in the 1600s." I tried to recall Bjorn's memory of him, which was somewhat dim, like Bjorn himself. "Also, Chris Hemsworth—way better than the original casting."

"That's disappointing," Veronika said, pushing her fingers deeper into the vault as they sunk in up to her fingertips. "This is really taking a while. Good thing I've got you to banter with or I would have given up out of boredom already."

"Suddenly you're sounding a little like my psycho aunt Charlie."

Veronika almost choked, spinning around to face me, hand still buried in the vault up to the wrist. "Oh God! Charlie Nealon's your aunt?"

"Oh, gah—tell me you didn't—with her—"

"What?" Veronika stared at me, frown on her face. "With Charlie? Hell no! I just—she's a psycho, is all. It wouldn't take meeting her for more than five minutes for anyone to figure that out." She set her feet, steadying herself to get back to work. Beads of sweat glistened like diamonds on her forehead in the bright blue glow.

"Really?" I mused. "It took me about six months to figure it out." Veronika stumbled slightly but tried to cover herself. "But she was probably putting on a good show for me because I was her niece and all ..."

"Whatever happened to psycho Charlie?" Veronika asked. "She make it out of the war?"

"Unfortunately—or maybe fortunately?—no. The Wolfe brothers got her in Vegas right before it ended."

"Ouch," Veronika said, not turning back to look. "Sorry-not-sorry to hear it."

"Yeah, well, I'm sorry-not-sorry to tell you."

"Ooooh," Veronika said as her fingers slid through the slag metal of the vault. "Hot! Hot!" She paused, bringing her hand down slowly. Now that she'd cut through, she slowly slid her hand along and carved the vault open like she was slicing a thick wheel of cheese. It took her a few minutes of applied pressure and colorful swearing, but she opened up a hole big enough that she could fit through it with ease and I could—well, sorta squeeze through if need be.

"Watch the edges," she said.

"Yeah, I get it, the plate's hot," I said, drawing the heat from the edges into my hand and dissipating it. It left a little steamed feeling because it was hotter than what I was used to dealing with by a lot. "Yeouch."

"You always knew I was hot, baby," Veronika said, slipping through the hole in the vault and lighting her hand up once she was inside.

"You know they make a feature on your cell phone that can work as a flashlight," I quipped, ducking into the metal confines of the vault, my pants catching on one of the edges. I rolled my eyes and shimmied my hips until it dislodged. "Clearly you have something against curves."

Veronika gave me a cursory glance back. "I was pretty sick of cutting that hole by the time I got done, so just consider yourself lucky I made it big enough for you to squeeze through at all, darlin'."

"You really are a master of the compliment sandwich," I

said, "if calling me 'darlin' was a compliment at all."

"What the hell is this, darlin'?" Veronika asked, being snide and informative all at once.

I stepped up next to her, not daring to light up my own hand for fear of combusting something. The walls of the vault were lined with shelves that had apparently been carefully built into the sides of the structure. On the shelves were rows of test tubes filled with liquid. They all looked blue in the glow of Veronika's white light, and they all had labels with various dates and bar codes printed on them. "Huh," I said. "Well, Palleton was a lab, I guess."

"These test tube trays are bolted to the shelves," Veronika said, bending over to look at the underside of the shelves. "You flew this thing a quarter of the way across the country after breaking it out of a building and ..." she looked around, "... I don't see one fallen test tube."

"I think they have the occasional earthquake in Oregon," I said. "Ring of Fire and all that."

"Still," she said, peering at one of the test tubes, "they spent some time on this. And they locked it up in a vault that, like, no one could access without permission." She picked up the test tube she was looking at. "The problem is ... how do we figure out what the hell this even is?"

I scanned the vault. In addition to the thousands of test tubes, there was a shadowy place in the corner, against the back wall. "I dunno," I said, walking past her, looking into the darkness, "but maybe ... yeah, here." The shadowy place in the corner was a cabinet that had been secured to the floor like the rest of the shelving, but it wasn't locked with any additional security, just a simple handle. Probably figured that if you were in the vault, you were supposed to be.

I opened the handle and the cabinet swung wide. It smelled like musty paper, and I did find a couple blank note pads on the second shelf, along with a portable hard drive and a list of instructions for its use. "Jackpot," I muttered as I held the little square of plastic aloft.

"Cool find, bro," Veronika said, "but we don't have a computer, and if we need to decode it or something, I'm guessing the crew you've got isn't going to be much help."

She paused in thought. "Maybe that Abigail chick? I dunno."

"Doesn't matter," I said, staring at the little piece of tech in my hands, hoping that finally, finally, I might be close to solving at least one mystery. "I know someone who can open this. I just need to get ahold of him …"

74.

Harmon

"Sir?" Jana's voice stirred me out of my sleep, and I blinked to wakefulness to find her staring down at me, very formally. The Situation Room was quiet, and my back had a kink in it that would disappear as soon as I got up and walked around. Meta healing powers were quite the boon.

"How long was I out?" I asked, standing up and stretching. I didn't really need to stretch, but it looked appropriate for my supposed age.

"Most of the day," Jana said stiffly. "I had Ms. Krall cancel some of your appointments, but we're reaching a congressional meeting that can't be put off."

"Oh, I don't want to meet with Congress," I said, rubbing my forehead. "This is about their problems with the EPA regulation issuance, isn't it?" I reached out and touched Scott Byerly's mind, and found him not very far away at all, and heading toward me. That was convenient. At least he hadn't had a chance to defy me or cause problems while I was sleeping. "When is the FBI task force arriving?"

"In the next few minutes," Jana said.

"Them I'll meet with. Tell the congressional delegation to screw right off." I frowned, not quite satisfied. "Also, I need a cup of coffee and a sandwich."

"Yes, sir."

"Jana," I said as she started to leave. "Make sure you use the words 'screw right off' when you tell the congressional delegation what I said, all right? I don't want them rescheduling. I don't have time for this."

She blinked. "You don't have time for democracy, Mr. President?"

I blinked right back at her, caught off guard by her candidness. "This isn't democracy," I said, defaulting to a certain style I had of going professorial when challenged. "It's a republic with democratic ideals. I'm the executive branch and they're the legislature, and while I enforce the laws I'm under no obligation to meet with them because they're having a tantrum—"

Jana must've figured if she was in for a penny, she was in for a pound. "Sir, their complaint is that your branch is writing the laws, not enforcing them."

That took me aback. Most people didn't argue with the president. "I'd like my coffee and sandwich, now, please," I said, turning away from her.

"Yes, Mr. President."

I covered my face and rubbed my eyes. I was too close now to worry about these trifling complaints. I wouldn't have wanted to hear them even if I hadn't been approaching the fruition of what I'd been working toward for so long, and since I was ... I really had no time for them at all.

"I bet FDR didn't have deal with this bullshit," I muttered, conveniently ignoring any number of times when he had, in fact, dealt with being told no. But I wasn't going to have to deal with it for much longer, I reflected, as I headed toward the Oval Office.

Hopefully not much longer at all.

75.

Sienna

I hadn't wasted time going back to LA; Veronika had called the others and had them charter another plane to Montana. They arrived a few hours later, and by then we had a rental house and were set up. I'd finally gotten hold of a burner phone and figured out a way to get the number I'd been searching for.

As it turned out, directory assistance was my Huckleberry in this case. Next thing you knew, I'd be using one of those old phone books. I dialed the number, starting with the Atlanta area code, and waited.

The phone rang as I stood there, hoping for an answer. "Pick up," I whispered. "Pick up—"

"Hello?" An older lady's voice answered in a tone that suggested if I were a telemarketer, I might do well to start praying for my immortal soul. If such a thing existed.

"Hi Mrs. Coleman," I said to Augustus's mom, "It's Sienna Nealon. Uh, Augustus's old boss—"

"I know who you are," she snapped, clearly not happy with me for assuming she was an idiot. "Maybe you can explain to me why Augustus hasn't called me in a month?"

"Uhh ... I don't know ... I haven't talked to him in probably just as long—"

"Who is that?" a soft voice asked in the background.

"It's Augustus's old boss," Mrs. Coleman said, clearly prioritizing her company over me.

"Edward Cavanagh?" The voice was female, and clearly not happy at the thought. "Cuz I was sure he was dead."

"No, Sienna Nealon," Mrs. Coleman said.

"Can I just —" There was a scuffling sound, and the other voice became clear, a woman's. "Hello? Sienna?"

"You took my phone, girl!" Mrs. Coleman sounded pretty put out. "Ungrateful!" There was a pause. "Also, you got a scrappy grip there for such a little thing—"

"Hi, Taneshia," I said.

"What's going on with Augustus?" she asked, so very serious. "We haven't heard from him in weeks."

"About that …" I said. "Have you heard from Jamal?"

"Sure, he's staying here now," Taneshia said, sounding a little taken aback.

"Get him, please?"

"Not until I get an answer to my question." She was pretty firm about it.

"All right, well," I said, "he's being mind-controlled by the president of the United States into hunting me down."

There was a long silence at the other end of the phone. "Let me get Jamal," Taneshia finally said. "JAMAL!"

"Damn, girl, you don't shout in my house!" Mrs. Coleman yelled, kinda breaking her own rule.

No one said anything for a few tense moments, and then soft footsteps made their way through the phone and I heard someone pick it up. "Hello?" Jamal asked quietly.

"It's Sienna," I said. "I have problems."

"Other than felony warrants?" he asked dryly. "What's wrong with my brother?"

"Mind control," I said. "By President Harmon."

A pause. "No shit?"

"LANGUAGE, boy!" Mrs. Coleman said. "You ain't talking like that in my house!"

"I'mma need to step outside for a minute," Jamal said, and I heard him walking.

"I better not hearing you swearing out in my yard either, making a damn fool of yourself in front of the neighbors and God and everybody!"

There was a click of a door shutting, and Jamal said, "So

what are you doing to fix matters?"

"Well, I'm cracking the case of Harmon's master plan at the moment," I said. "Figure if I can defeat him, he'll, you know, let loose of your brother's brain."

"You're going to go up against the whole government?" Jamal asked.

"What's she doing?" Taneshia asked in the background. I guess she'd followed him.

"Starting shit with the government, sounds like," Jamal said.

"Damn," Taneshia said.

"I have a hard drive from a project Harmon seems to be heavily invested in," I said. "It was something I think he had Cavanagh on before he died."

"That's an interesting tie," Jamal said. "He wasn't just a donor, they were pals, huh?"

"Long suspected, more or less confirmed in my mind, now," I said. "I got a whole mess of test tubes and hard drive that, uh … well, I tried just plugging it into the laptop on hand, but it didn't do anything."

"I got you," he said. "Give me a few minutes and let's get some things set up, see what we're dealing with."

"Thanks, Jamal," I said.

"Don't thank me yet," he said, the door squeaking as he went back into his house. "I've got no idea what you're going to find with this, but if it's anything like the stuff we've dug up on Cavanagh so far …" I could hear him shudder through the phone. "… You might not be that glad we dug into this by the time it's through."

76.

Harmon

It was beginning to feel like progress when Cassidy walked in with the little box, her hands shaking. "Is that it?" I asked, and she nodded, not even close to a smile. "Good, because the test subjects will be here in a moment."

"You're going to test it on ... Sienna Nealon's friends?" Cassidy asked, looking particularly nervous.

"I am," I said. "Unless you'd also like to volunteer." She looked at the box, pondered it for less than a half second, and then shook her head, almost sadly. "I guess we're stuck with them, then. I'd like to make sure there's no fatal side effects before I try it on myself."

"I understand," she said and looked at the box once more, caught somewhere between fear and envy. She knew what it contained, but also the risks. Truthfully, I wouldn't have wanted her to take it, for more than one reason.

"Sir," Ms. Krall buzzed in, "your next appointment is entering the building now."

"Excellent," I said, "send them in, without any ado, once they get here." I leaned against the Resolute desk, taking a deep breath.

"Are you planning on using it yourself as long as it doesn't kill them?" Cassidy asked.

I looked at her, questioning her intelligence before I realized that, once again, this was a human nature question. "Not immediately, no," I said, adding an aura of patience I didn't really feel. "I want slightly longer-term results before I inject myself. You mentioned long-term toxicity effects, and it doesn't do me any good if it wears off in hours or causes eventual cell damage or something of that sort. It needs to be permanent, without any nasty side effects, like death. The purpose is to make things better, and that would only cause chaos in the long run."

Cassidy nodded, the box shaking in her hands. I stared at it; it was such a little thing, to hold the fate of the world in its plastic sides. I couldn't keep from smiling as we waited for our test subjects to arrive.

77.

"You guys left me!" Guy Friday shouted, coming out of a black sedan parked under the White House portico as Scott got out of the SUV. A cold wind whipped through, and Scott shuddered, the Revelen team piling out behind him, Augustus and Reed getting out on the other side. "You just ditched me back in Salt Lake City, didn't even check to see if I was all right after that house exploded!"

Scott stared blankly at him. *Another victim of the president's lack of concern for civilian casualties, I guess.* "I forgot about you, sorry." He didn't feel that sorry.

"How could you forget me?" Friday swelled, hulking out in front of him. Scott cast a look at Reed, who was coming around the hood, watching the big man uneasily. "I'm not small! And I'm witty! I'm tons of fun, okay?"

"You're like one of those sea monkeys," Augustus said. "We add water and you get all swole."

"Yeah, like—" Friday's head snapped around. "*I am not a sea monkey!*"

"You left one of your people behind," Director Phillips said, emerging from behind the Sedan that Friday had been waiting in. "That's disgraceful, Agent Byerly. Cause for severe reprimand and … consequences."

Worse than having the president of the United States sitting in your brain on the regular? Scott thought, but kept the idea icily trapped in his head. "Sorry," was all he said, and he went for the door.

"I don't know what's wrong with you lately, Byerly," Phillips said, falling in behind him. Scott could hear the rest of the team following behind, Mac breathing a little too eagerly. He must have been relishing the coming dressing-down. "This operation has been a disaster from the start."

"I don't know what's wrong with me either, sir," Scott said, keeping himself from saying, *Maybe you should take me off the case.* "I just don't feel entirely like I'm myself lately."

"If you think you're going to have a future in this agency, you better get yourself in line," Phillips went on, voice rising as Scott continued to walk with his back to the Director. *How much has the president messed with his brain, to make him such an ass?* Scott wondered. "Otherwise, you're going to be out."

"That'd be a terrible shame, sir," Scott muttered under his breath.

"What?"

"I'll try harder," Scott said as they passed into the secretary's office just outside the Oval one.

"The president is waiting for you," the older lady behind the secretary's desk said, and the Secret Service agents opened the door for Scott and the others to pass.

Scott barely kept from drawing his gun as he entered the Oval office; the president wasn't the only one inside, and the other—

Well, he knew her.

"I see you recall Ms. Ellis," President Harmon said to him as Scott twitched; his gun hand had been halted from drawing the new Sig he'd picked up, his fingers trapped in what felt like concrete but was really just empty air.

"Hard to forget. The last time I went to meet her, I got shot," Scott said, his neck suddenly aching as though he were wounded again.

Cassidy Ellis, for her part, looked away from him. She was holding a little plastic box as though it held cigars and she was ready to distribute them for a party.

"Never thought I'd meet the president," Mac said, sauntering into the Oval Office like he owned the whole damned country. Scott could see him out of the corner of his eye, and it irritated him even more than not being able to draw his gun.

"Life's just full of surprises, isn't it?" Harmon said amiably. "You must be Mac, Joaquín, and Gothric. So kind of you to come help us."

"We go where we're ordered," Gothric said stiffly.

"I'm sorry about your comrades," Harmon said, not sounding too torn up. "It's always terrible to lose people in these situations."

"We might not have lost anyone if your boys had all been in the game," Mac said with a harsh rumble.

"Tell me about it," Friday said, sounding like a bitter whiner. "I got stuck in Salt Lake City and had to fly commercial home. I was sitting next to a lady as big as a fridge. I had to shrink down to my smallest size and she still stole my armrest!"

Harmon ignored him. "I understand my team could have performed better—" He paused and looked at Director Phillips, who was standing by the door. "Andrew ... would you mind waiting outside? I need to talk to these gentlemen about the mission, and some new possibilities, but ... frankly, it's above your classification level."

Phillips blinked. "I'm ... I'm the Director of the FBI, sir. My classification level is—"

"It's SAP/SAR," Harmon said, as though that explained anything. "Special project. You understand. You're not cleared for it. Please wait outside."

"Yes ... sir ..." Phillips looked like he'd been jacked in the junk, but he made his way out the door without another word of protest.

"Good, now that he's gone, let's talk meta business," Harmon said, scanning the crowd. "I have something that will help you catch Sienna Nealon." He clapped his hands. Cassidy jerked slightly in surprise, then stepped up and opened her little box to reveal several hypodermic needles filled with a green-tinged fluid. "All you need to do is take a dose of this and suddenly you'll find yourself ... a lot more prepared to deal with Ms. Nealon and her shenanigans." He smiled.

"'Shenanigans'?" Mac asked, reddening. "She killed three of our people."

"You think the term sounds too light considering what she's done?" Harmon asked, looking at Mac without much care. "I understand. This will allow you to equalize things. To aid you in your vendetta against her." He peered at Mac, and Scott could almost feel the Aussie pause, the mental assault going on beneath his facade. "You should take a dose."

"I ... I'm going to," Mac said, and thrust out a hand. Cassidy pushed out the box and Mac grabbed a syringe, stabbing it into his arm and injecting it. He blinked his eyes a few times after the plunger had been pushed. "Ooof ... I feel a little ... ughhh ..."

"Mild nausea as a side effect," Harmon said, sounding like he was noting it for reference. "Helpful." He turned his gaze to Joaquín, who was watching Mac with something bordering on alarm. "You should try it, too."

"I don't want t—" Joaquín blinked, the energy that had been building in his eyes dissipating. "Okay," he said robotically, and grabbed a needle, jabbing himself in the arm with meta speed. He dropped to his knees a second later, doubling over, collapsing onto the cream-colored pizza-slice rug that held the seal of the United States at its center, moaning. "Augh ... ."

"More nausea. Possible balance issues. Okay." Harmon looked to Gothric. "And you?"

Gothric's alarm vanished, and he grabbed a needle, jabbing himself without comment. He swayed, but stayed on his feet.

"Sir?" Reed asked, still fiercely determined. "Do you want me to—"

"Let's just make sure this doesn't kill them, first," Harmon said pleasantly. "No point throwing away your lives for no reason." He paused, seemed to think about it, then looked at Scott. "You—try it out."

"I don't think s—" Scott felt himself jerk, that presence swelling in his mind once again, blooming like a storm cloud that suddenly appeared on a clear day. "Okay," he said, and was suddenly next to Cassidy. He could see her wide eyes as

270

Harmon's presence receded somewhat in his mind. The command was still firm, still there.

"I'll help you," Cassidy said, picking up the needle herself and setting the box down on the desk. She tapped it gently, making sure a small dot of liquid spurted from the tip of the needle, then slid it into the presented vein on his forearm.

Scott grunted, not from pain but from the violation. He held himself still, though, fear of Harmon pushing himself back into his mind enough to keep him steady.

"Shhh," Cassidy whispered, meta low, low enough that Harmon could not hear—surely not, right? "Keep fighting," she said, so *sotto voce* he wasn't even sure he'd heard her. Then she turned away, taking the spent needle with her, and Scott was left with a feeling like something was squeezing his guts.

He looked around the Oval Office and found the others staring at Mac, who was on his side, on the floor, shuddering. "This doesn't look as promising as it should," Harmon said, shaking his head, fingers on his chin, contemplation clear on his face.

"It's—I don't—" Cassidy said, her hands, now empty, shaking visibly. Or was that his own body, Scott wondered, doing some shuddering of his own. The pain was intense, was like a giant had hold of him and was somehow plowing fingers into his skin, massaging every single cell—

"AIIIEEEEEEEEEE!" Mac let out an earsplitting scream, and began to shake, foam dripping out of the corner of his mouth.

"Aren't you glad I waited on you now?" Harmon asked Reed, who didn't answer. "We might need more test subjects."

"Wait, you tested something on these guys?" Friday asked. It took Scott a moment to realize that of all the people in the room, Friday was perhaps the only one now unafflicted in any way by Harmon's control. "Like a flu vaccine?"

"Better than that," Harmon said, as the pain came crushing in on Scott and he added his own voice to the chorus of screams now filling the Oval Office. There was nothing but pain—no walls, no ceiling, no floor. Scott was in an ocean of pain, drowning in it, being stripped of his flesh one square inch at a time by giant fingers, his head being ripped open and great scoops of his brain being pulled out—

"They kinda seem like they're dying," Friday said from between Scott's screams. How could it hurt this much? How could it be this painful to—

"Well," Harmon said as the world started to go dark around Scott, "you can't make omelet without, you know ..." He met Scott's eyes as they started to slide shut. "And let's be honest, Byerly ... you were never that good of an egg anyway."

78.

Sienna

"Oh, wow," Jamal said over the phone, a crackle in the background as I waited for him to finish unlocking the damned drive. He'd been at it for a while, sending his little electrical pulses over the internet to try and open it up. I'd long ago passed boredom and was now into the realm of "pondering suicide just to end it," but this was the first sound of hope I'd caught from him in a long time. The sun was almost coming up over Montana at this point, which meant—hopefully—more than one of these long nights I'd been experiencing was about to be over.

"Please tell me that's a result and not amazement at another wall of astounding encryption," I said, giving voice to the tedium as I stared out the living room window; we'd exchanged mountains and trees for beach and sun, and I wasn't loving the change so far. I wanted the beaches and sun back.

"Yeah, no, this thing is giving it up," Jamal said. "I'm just—boggling at what I found."

"Care to share?" I growled. I hadn't heard Taneshia in hours, which I assumed meant she was passed out somewhere on the other end of the line.

"I'm not sure you want to hear this," Jamal said, and he actually sounded uncertain, like my homicidal menace wasn't motivating to him or something.

"I haven't stayed on the phone with you all night because

you give good chat, okay? It's been mostly long silences, and I could do that all by myself—"

"Yeah, all right," Jamal said, "I'm just trying to make sure I'm reading this right. It's a little outside my field, okay? This is biochem, not tech. And it's … damn."

"Jamal … please. As English as you can."

"So …" Jamal said, winding up for the pitch, "… it looks to this philistine like Harmon and Cavanagh were working on a serum to enhance a meta's powers by opening up … I don't know how to say this in a way you're going to understand … other skill trees."

"You're right, I didn't understand that. What's a skill tree?"

"Other powers," he said. "Like … as I read this, genetic research determined that whatever power you've got, there are other, unrealized ones locked in your genetic code. Like … similar genes. Also, boosted ability. So there's parallel powers available, and also just a flat-out boost of what you've already got. Cavanagh was trying to figure out how to make that happen, a serum to unlock all that."

I covered my face. "Wait. So they already had a suppressant to eliminate powers for a period of time … and a serum to unlock powers in non-metas … and now they were working on—"

"A way to expand powers," Jamal said. "Along two different pathways—boosting what you got, and expanding to other, nearby powers on the … tree, for lack of a better word."

"I still don't quite get this tree thing," I said.

"They have an example here, maybe it'll help—flight powers," he said. "They're a skill tree. For a boost, you'd be able to fly faster—like twice as fast. Three times, four times. For unlocking a parallel power … flying is just control of an aspect of gravity, so for the parallel tree, you'd suddenly be able to affect other objects—"

"Like Jamie Barton—Gravity—up in New York," I said, feeling like I might have gotten it.

"Exactly," Jamal said. "So maybe she'd suddenly be able to—I dunno, fly, which maybe would be next to controlling wind … it's a little complex, and I don't see how it all relates.

Anyway, it's a broadening of your powers to … other stuff in the neighborhood. Augustus, for example, if he had his powers broadened, he might suddenly be able to go all Magneto and control metal in addition to earth-based rock and sand and whatnot."

"Eep," I said. "That'd just about give him mastery over the physical world, because he can already control glass, too."

"Yeah, it's got real potential to open things up," Jamal said. "I wonder what the parallel powers to lightning are …?"

"Did this serum work?" I asked. "Or was it all just—"

"Looks like Palleton Labs figured out the parallel part, just not the boost," Jamal said. "They figured out how to do it temporarily at first, then more definite long-term … but they never finished confirming it because their test subjects … well, looks like they might have escaped."

"Wise choice on their part," I muttered. Suddenly Timothy Logan's interest made sense. Those metas he'd broken into Palleton with … they were probably either some of the test subjects in question, or they knew those people. It was all starting to make sense.

"Seems like," Jamal said. "So … anyway. That give you an idea what Harmon was after?"

I thought about it a second. "What do you think would be more interesting to a telepath, the parallel powers or—" I froze, a chilling thought occurring to me. "Ummm … Jamal?"

"Yeah. I'm with you. The boost, right?"

"What would a boost do to a telepath?" I asked, shivering in the middle of the living room of the rental house. The others were sleeping, wisely, long ago sick of staring at me with a phone up to my ear.

"It'd give him strength, right?" Jamal asked, sounding like he wasn't entirely sure himself. He paused, and I could hear him reading. "I mean, these boosts they're talking about on this doc … they're not small. We're talking about going from being able to control lightning to … I dunno, generate all the electricity in the world. One hundred billion gigawatts or something."

"So if it was a telepath, they'd go from being able to control a few minds to …" I swallowed heavily, not wanting to say it out loud.

"If I had to make a guess?" Jamal did a loud *GULP!* of his own. "Telepathy is reading minds. But this … you wouldn't just read a mind or five minds or ten minds … you could read … all of them. They have a word for it in the old comic books I used to read …

"They called it an omnipath, because they could read—and I guess, control—every single mind … every single person … in the world."

79.

Harmon

"How are you feeling?" I asked. I didn't care about their well-being, of course, but if I was going to use this serum myself, I wanted to make sure it wasn't going to leave me dead. It would be hard to save the world from itself if I were dead.

"Ughhhhh," the Australian said, holding his head. He looked up at me, his eyes were glazed. At least he had managed to pull himself into a chair. "Feel like I'm about to chunder."

"Use the bucket if you feel the need," I said, sliding a small wastepaper basket toward him. I looked at the gaucho-themed fellow. What was it with these people and their gimmicks? The Australian had a knife, this guy was dressed like a South American cowboy, and Friday wore a gimp mask. Well, he had other problems, obviously, stories in his head that I wish I hadn't discovered, but ... I still didn't know why all these people needed gimmicks. I never had a gimmick. Being president was enough gimmick for me, I supposed.

"And you?" I asked the gaucho.

"I feel ... sick," he answered. "But ... better?"

"Just hang on until that statement no longer ends with a question mark." I eased over to Cassidy. "It doesn't seem to have killed them." She watched them warily. "That's a good sign, right?"

277

"It's unlocking components of their DNA right now," she said. "I suppose it's not a painless process."

"Judging by the amount of pain they seem to have experienced, I should say not." I looked at Augustus, Reed and Friday, who had yet to take any of my new miracle serum. "Well, the others are pulling through. Might as well get started on you gentlemen."

"Yes, sir," Reed and Augustus chorused, as they should have.

"Uhhh ... I'd rather not," Friday said, eyes moving around quickly through the slits in his mask.

"Please, I insist," I said, brushing against his mind. He was fearful, of course, his thoughts whirling.

I caught a whiff of what he was going to do a moment before he did it. "PASS!" he yelled, swelling to the size of a truck and smashing through the wall of the Oval Office so quickly I barely had time to cover my eyes, let alone grab control of his spinning, whirling mind. I could feel him, his thoughts tightly packed like a slippery ball. He was surprisingly disciplined in his thinking. He broke into a run across the White House lawn and then leapt into the air, sailing over the fence and out of sight.

I was left staring out across the south lawn, Friday's mind retreating from my easy grasp, a massive hole in the wall of the White House. Dust from the demolition work just performed in the office filled the air with a white tinge. Cassidy rose to her feet next to me, staring out the hole after him, her mouth hanging open. "Close that before you attract flies," I said, catching her gently under the chin and shutting her trap. It would keep her from saying something stupid, as well.

"Isn't the Secret Service going to freak out about this?" she asked.

I was already shutting them down, though, and it was once again straining the hell out of me to do so. I sighed as I tweaked about twenty minds in a row. Fortunately it was only a mildly blustery day in Washington, nothing I couldn't handle, or I might have felt compelled to leave the West Wing immediately. "Hopefully no one got cell phone footage of that," I said. "At least it's not tourist season."

"You think they missed a giant meta bursting out of the wall of the West Wing and leaping over the White House fence into DC?" Cassidy had clearly lost any objectivity; she looked like she was ready to cry.

"It's entirely possible someone saw it," I said, "but we're not visible from behind the fence here, which means ... no one can see the hole in the wall and the Secret Service is quieted for the moment. I'll deal with this later." I eyed the box in her hands, with its remaining needles. "Give them the serum," I nodded to Reed and Augustus. That would leave two hypodermic needles of the serum remaining. I saw her glance at them as well, and it didn't take someone of Cassidy's intelligence to deduce what she was thinking. I mentally slapped the thought out of her head, and she jerked slightly. This serum might have only been the boost power, but I didn't need her getting any smarter. Besides, it wasn't exactly tested, and the results had been skewed. Unlocking powers and boosts seemed indelibly tied together, which meant that once the dust settled on our test subjects, it was entirely possible they could experience both a boost of existing powers as well as the unlocking of new ones tangential to their current abilities.

The last thing I needed was Cassidy Ellis—the foremost mind on the planet—accidentally developing telepathy or omnipathy as a secondary power while her intellect was enhanced by the boost.

"Okay," Cassidy said, a little unevenly. I had avoided reading or interfering in her mind as much as possible, preferring to leave her intact to do her work with only occasional spot-checks to make certain of her loyalty. This slap I needed to do, though, because the idea of her developing powers was not a threat I wanted to deal with at the moment.

I watched her inject Reed and Augustus one by one, and swept my gaze over the suddenly windy, dust-filled room. Scott Byerly was still curled up in a ball in the middle of the room, apparently so out of it that he hadn't even noticed the giant bastard smash his way through the wall. I could feel his mind, but it was near unconscious, and folded in on itself. I prodded it slightly, and he stirred, a stray thought floating to the top of his mind.

"Interesting," I murmured, for it was.

"What's that?" Cassidy asked, shutting the box with the needles in it. I caught sight of the two remaining ones before she did so. Augustus and Reed were both standing tall, owing more to my control of them than a lack of effect on their bodies. If Scott hadn't been such a mess mentally, he would have still been on his feet as well.

"Mr. Byerly took some initiative and commissioned a look at White House security from a metahuman threat such as Sienna Nealon," I said, prodding through the idea. "Not a bad thought, though I doubt his motives were pure." I looked at Cassidy and smiled. "I don't think he much cares for me interfering in his thoughts."

Cassidy swallowed heavily, and I sensed the rebuttal before she made it. She almost didn't, but she had to know I read it by the narrowing of my eyes, so she put it out there. "Most people won't … when the time comes."

"That's why it has to be permanent, you see," I said. Of course she knew, but I needed to reaffirm the reasoning. Cassidy had a powerful mind; it was only natural she would consider all the possibilities. She'd seen that this was the ultimate, best scenario for the world. "Finally, everyone will think the way I think and see things the way I see them. No more war, no more internecine squabbles." I clutched my fingers into a fist. "This world has been divided, angry, one part in conflict with another, confused, drifting in seven billion individual directions … Lincoln said that a house divided against itself could not stand, and he was right. We've been divided against ourselves by nature for our entire existence. How can we possibly expect to conquer the challenges facing mankind—poverty, war, environmental calamity—when we don't even all acknowledge the same problems?" I took a breath of cool, autumnal air. "I can see it all, you know. Just like you do. And the solutions, they're out there … but not everyone sees the problems. If they saw it as I do—as we do," I remembered to include her, "we could finally put aside these squabbles and grievances and unite ... and make real progress. All the ills of humanity could be eliminated in a year. We would finally have ... unity."

Her mind was the only one really moving in the room other than mine, and it was whirling swiftly, as it always did, so swiftly that I could almost not keep up. I did catch a stray thought, like a child thrown off the merry-go-round by its momentum, and Cassidy knew I'd caught it, for she gave it voice a moment later.

"Are you sure you should ..." She coughed quietly. "People ... they want to do things themselves—"

"Come on, Cassidy," I said, spinning on her, my exasperation showing. She knew better. "Do people—the majority of people—do things that are healthy for them, if given the option? They still smoke even though they know it causes cancer. They use fossil fuels at a rate that will render our world uninhabitable. The sick go untreated, the poor go hungry. People make terrible choices every day, ones that make them more miserable, they even put themselves at the mercy of drugs that control their thoughts. Even the ones who are supposedly clear-headed high achievers—they pursue money and victory, often in the absence of compassion and care. People are foolish and short-sighted, selfish and self-deluded. They cut off their noses, vainly thinking it will make their face more attractive, or simply not caring about the long-term repercussions. People are fools, unable to manage their own lives. And I will fix it—all of it—for them." I swelled at the thought.

"Yes, sir," she wilted, as she should have.

The superiority of my argument was as obvious as the paleness of her face. I looked over at Byerly, who had yet to stir. "And then there's him," I muttered. I would have to assume full control of him once more in order to insure that he did what was necessary—once he woke up, of course.

"How long do you want to wait before you ... try this yourself?" she asked. Her voice was still, quiet—she'd gotten hold of herself, finally.

"Not long," I said, straightening up. I could scarcely

contain myself. It was finally here, after all—the solution to all the world's problems.

I just needed to make sure it wouldn't kill me and leave the world in an even worse state.

The phone on my desk beeped. "Sir, Director Phillips wishes to speak with you. He's received an emergency—"

"Sir," Phillips cut in, "I just got FLASH traffic from Agent Rocha at the NSA." I rolled my eyes, but he kept speaking, unaware that he was stepping all over my moment in here. "He's picked up an intercept, a call that's now gone encrypted but started out in the open—voice recognition identified one of the speakers as Sienna Nealon, sir."

I raised an eyebrow. "You have her?"

"We do, sir," Phillips said. "She's in Montana."

80.

Sienna

Meet me in DC, I thought hard, hoping that my message would get through to its intended target. My eyes were closed, the fireplace in the corner of the rented lodge crackling where someone had flipped the switch to light it up. I'd called for everyone to assemble, figuring it was time to get this show underway, because the way I figured it—given what I thought Harmon was up to—there wasn't a moment to waste.

"So he's going to … take over the world with his brain?" Abigail asked, distilling the craziness down into the most concise explanation.

"That's my best guess," I said, opening my eyes and looking at the girl with the black and pink hair. She looked about as uncertain as I felt, maybe a little sick, too, because the thought of someone taking over our brains? Not a happy one.

"Wow," Colin said, leaning against the fridge, twitching slightly, so quickly I couldn't see his fingers move when he did so. "That's some serious fascist stuff right there, mind control."

"That is not even fascism," Dr. Perugini said. "It goes beyond."

"She's right," I said. "It's past being even an authoritarian who wants to rule the world with their own iron fist. An authoritarian will leave you alone if you stay within their lines—"

"Small consolation, that," Steven Clayton muttered.

"—Harmon's a totalitarian," I said. "He wants total control of our every thought and action, to be the god of the mind who rules the world from on high. Every action, every motion, every single person will be under his thumb if I'm right about this. There will be no dissent because no one will be strong enough to dissent." I had a sudden, vague idea, and wondered if empaths might be immune to omnipathic control as they were from telepaths.

"Being controlled by a god-king is not my idea of a cool time," Veronika said, looking at her immaculate nails.

"Nope," Harry said, peering straight ahead. "Huh."

"Huh what?" Phinneus Chalke asked, his wrinkled lips pursed as he stared at Harry.

"Well, I see a bit of zombie-ism in our futures now that I'm looking ahead," Harry said, head bobbing as he thought it over. "Plus or minus three days, it's happening. People'll just stop talking and start moving, like one of those, uh—well, like an old movie. Probabilities are climbing as we stand here."

"And you didn't notice this before?" Kat asked, her eyes wide with fear. Personally, I thought Kat had the least to lose from being mind-controlled.

Be nice to my sister, who has believed in you through everything, Gavrikov warned me.

Yeah, yeah. Except for that time she let me spill my guts then betrayed me to the press.

"I don't walk around with my head in the far future," Harry said, shrugging.

"So it's actually happening," I said, dragging my gaze away from Harry.

"Do you think he'll implement like, a full, nationwide recycling and composting program?" Colin asked, like he was actually considering this as some kind of good thing. "Because, I mean, trying to see the bright side here—"

"The bright side here is that you'll no longer have a mind of your own," I said, "not that you ever did." I covered my eyes. "We need to get on the jet and head for Washington."

"Whoa," Abigail said, standing up abruptly. "And do what?"

"Overthrow the lawfully elected government of the United States, obviously," Dr. Perugini snarked. She leaned her head back on the couch in a way that would have given even me a crick in the neck.

"Oh, wow," Colin said, his mouth hanging open.

"Sienna …" Kat had paled noticeably, "… this is really it, isn't it? She's not wrong about what we have to do."

I looked at Harry once more for confirmation, and he nodded. "She's not wrong," I agreed, and the meeting descended into about five different kinds of groans.

"Man, I didn't know when I came along on this that I was signing up to be some kind of revolutionary nutbag—" Colin said.

"'The tree of liberty needs to be refreshed from time to time with the blood of patriots and tyrants,'" Steven said, almost whispering.

"Okay, well, I'm in," Kat said quietly but firmly.

"Insurrection," Veronika said, looking at the ceiling. "I'm not sure I can be paid enough for this."

"I quite fond of my mind, so … I reckon I'm in," Harry said.

"You're all out of your minds," Phinneus said, and he clacked his rifle butt against the ground, silencing us. He was looking at me with quiet intensity. "You're going head-on with the government of the United States?"

"It's what I've been doing the last few days," I said.

"No, you haven't," Phinneus said. "You've been running, and that's a smart move. You're not ready for the head-on. I saw the *Civil War*, sweetheart—"

"We've all seen Civil War," Abigail muttered, "that's why it made a billion dollars at the box office."

"The actual one," Phinneus said, "North versus South."

"Oh," Abigail said.

"Phinneus," Veronika said, shaking her head, eyes closed. "You're being patronizing with the 'sweetheart' thing. Don't be a fossil."

"I saw the full fury of the government of the United States

come crashing down," Phinneus went on, undeterred by Veronika's chiding. "I saw two armies fight each other, and I picked the side I was on—the one that said we were going to free men and women and children from bondage. I saw everything we brought to bear against the men in grey, and let me tell you something—it's only going to be worse, now. They lost a generation and so did we—"

"Yeah, this fight's not going to be that big," Veronika said.

"It's going to be bigger, don't you see?" Phinneus asked. "They've got missiles and planes and nuclear bombs now—"

"They've turned several of those loose against me the last few days," I said. "Trust, I'm aware of what they're going to throw at us."

"I don't think you are," Phinneus said, giving me a hot look. "I ain't impugning the rightness of your cause, but they're coming down on you with everything now, if Harmon's what you say he is. Everything. Because war has changed—"

"War never changes," Abigail said, stock serious, then looked around, as if for approval. "*Fallout 4*." She looked questioningly. "Anyone? Seriously?"

"We have got to get you your boyfriend back," I muttered, and turned my attention back to Phinneus.

"I got it," Colin said, and Abigail put out a fist for him to bump, which he did so speedily that Abigail cringed and pulled back, her hand shaking.

"Phinneus," I said, "I've been shot out of the sky by F-22s, blasted by drone strikes, and had the FBI's meta task force plus a foreign spec-ops group turned loose on me. You think I don't know that war has changed, or that Harmon is going to throw everything at us to keep us off him long enough to—well, to take over the world?" I frowned. "God, that sounds cheesy. But he's going to do it. He has the means."

"Who even wants to dive that deep into the heads of everyone in the world?" Perugini wondered. "What kind of a sick mind would delight in the idea of controlling everyone like—like puppets?"

"Isn't that kind of the idea of laws in the first place?" Abigail asked. "Government, I mean? To, y'know, put the kibosh on the bad things people do so we can get on with the good?"

"If we're all going full zombie, I don't see us getting on with the good," I said, getting a nod from Harry. "We all get put to whatever glorious purpose our fearless leader decides is best for us." That chafed more than a little, honestly.

"I know what help I'd be in this situation," Phinneus said, shaking his head. "None."

"Phinneus, you're a crack shot," I said. "You could—"

"Blow the president's brains out at a distance of a thousand yards?" He caught my look, and I saw the disgust in his own. "I've been an assassin for a lot of years. I've killed a lot of people that way." *And almost me,* I was thinking. "I don't think you want the optics of me doing that to the president." He shook his head, looking at the ground. "I know I don't."

"I'd like it better than being mind-controlled and having my will stripped away," I said. "Loads better."

"I ain't doing it," Phinneus shook his head. I got the feeling he had a personal objection to this. "You kids will do fine without me."

"Odds don't change whether he's with us or not," Harry said with a shrug. "Too negligible."

"Best of luck, folks," Phinneus said, and he hefted his rifle, his six shooter on his hip. "I'm sure you'll get it done." He glanced at Harry, who shrugged again. "And if not, I guess we'll all be on the same team again soon enough anyway." He headed out the front door, not bothering to close it behind him.

"Do I need to come along?" Veronika asked, looking at Harry. "Do the odds change measurably if I don't go? Just curious, because I don't like pointless fights. I've got other things I could be doing."

"Like sewing," I said.

Veronika shot me a frown. "How did you know I like to sew?"

"That was ... such a wild guess," I said. "I was totally joking."

"Odds are tough to gauge on this," Harry said, peering

into the empty air in front of him in total concentration.

"Why is that?" Kat asked. She glanced at me. "I mean, I'm in no matter what, I'm just … curious."

Harry blinked a few times, like he was coming back to himself. "Well, you know, when you get into the tenths of percents, it's hard to—" He froze then cringed, like he'd looked so far into the future he hadn't realized what he was doing in the now. "Ahhh … I mean …"

"Shit," Colin said, his head tilting back. "So basically … what we're doing here is so unlikely to see success … that we might as well not even go at all?"

Harry looked stricken, but the cat was out of the bag now. "It's … really tough odds," he said, and I could feel the mood in the room fall as it settled on everyone that we basically had no chance at all of winning this fight, no matter what we did.

81.

"… I hope you get this message in time," I said into the phone. "I know it's asking a lot of you, but … there's a lot on the line, so …" I didn't know what else to say, so I just said, "Thanks. Bye," and hung up.

"Man, the hopelessness in this place is so thick I could cut it with a plastic spoon," Steven Clayton said, leaning against the door to the back deck. Frost was on the grass down below, shining in the morning sun where it hadn't melted yet.

"Well, that's what happens when the guy who can read the future tells you that you're pretty likely to be mind-controlled by the president no matter what you do," I said, slipping my phone back in my pocket. "It's not exactly inspiring."

"I could probably still do the St. Crispin's Day speech if you feel like the troops need motivating," Steven said with a wry smile.

"Dunno how much that'd help, honestly, given that three of the troops don't really hold manhood at all, to say nothing of cheap," I said, showing off my Shakespeare. "Points for being classically trained, though."

"I actually like theater," Steven said. "A lot of my generation of actors don't, but … I like going up on stage, finding the character and getting in there night after night. Sometimes you find something different depending on the performance." He put both elbows on the deck railing and leaned over next to me. "I imagine Harmon's not going to spend a lot of time digging deep into our skulls to discover the individual nuance and character unique to all of us."

"With seven billion heads to command," I said, "I'd imagine he's not. He seems like a real top-down, big-picture kind of guy. A damn the torpedoes, on to the next problem kind of fellow."

"That's the problem with politics nowadays," Steven said, musing as he stared out into the backyard, the tall pines clustered behind the rental house. He must have caught my mildly curious stare. "It's all grand proclamations and policy prescriptions from on high. He's never talked about the trade-offs inherent in his solutions."

"You mean like the downsides to mind-controlling the entire world?"

"Yeah, that's kind of a big trade-off for world peace," Steven said with a fair helping of irony. "Feels like that ought to be discussed in committee or debated in Congress before it gets implemented, you know?"

"Pretty sure taking over peoples' minds is a violation of due process," I said. "Not that it matters, I suppose, since I've violated all manner of constitutional rights in my day, but …"

"But you're not the president," he said. "And, generally speaking, you did it to people who were violating the rights of others anyway—taking away their life, liberty or property. Not saying fair's fair, but … there were considerations. If Harmon's really going to do it to the whole world …" He made a kind of hissing noise. "Ugh. We're not even people anymore if he does this. We're one massive organism with its will subverted to whatever he wants." He snorted mirthlessly. "It's like that joke about if you're not the lead dog, the scenery never really changes."

"Yeah, it's gonna be all dog ass from here on."

Steven chuckled, then the laughter died. "Seriously … what do you think he's going to do once he has this power?"

"I don't know," I sighed. "I met him once, and my read was that he's a massive dick. Maybe he believes he really can rule better, which would not be unusual for people seeking his office. Maybe he wants to work through his control issues with the world as his canvas. Or maybe he's just sick of not being able to unilaterally ram whatever hare-brained solution he's got churning in his head this week through a divided Congress. I'm not a mind reader, so I don't couldn't tell you."

"I think he's a true believer," Steven said. "Or a really great actor, I don't rule that out. But I think he believes he's got the answers—"

"And the rest of us are too stupid to steer our own lives?"

Steven's head wobbled. "I would concede that point in at least a few cases."

"Yeah, I'm sure his central-planning concept for solving all our problems is gonna work out super swell," I said, doing a little leaning over myself. Harry had warned me that we needed to leave in a certain window in order to maintain even the small chance of success we currently enjoyed, but we had a little time yet, and within that window there was no appreciable change to the odds. Which meant I had no particular hurry moving me forward right this second. "Because Gerry Harmon surely knows what a herdsman in Mongolia needs, and what a farmer in a Mississippi needs, and what a shopkeeper in Abu Dhabi needs—"

"He *could*," Steven conceded. "If he's really able to read all those minds—"

"That's the ultimate arrogance," I said. "It's the reason we're all going to become zombies if this plan goes through, you get that, right? It's because in order to solve all the world's problems, we have to sublimate ourselves to the greater good." I murmured it, chantlike, straight out of *Hot Fuzz*, "The greater good, the greater good."

"Hey, I'm not signing up for his convenient, one-thought-fits-all plan," Steven said. "Just trying to work through the motivation here."

"The motivation is the same as it's been for every other petty tyrant that's risen up in pursuit of power while telling himself he's an altruist," I said, my hackles fully raised. I was ready to kick Gerry Harmon's presidential ass right now, if it presented itself. "Because he knows better than us plebes how to run our lives, clearly, and he's going to prove that point. We're dumb, he's smart. We're unsophisticated, know-nothing idiots, and he's got all the answers to what ails us.

He's going to fix the world, and all we have to do is stand back and let him rope us into the solution. No more dissonance," I said, "no more disagreement, no more argument. We will march in lockstep, like a hive-mind, with no rejection of thought tolerated. He won't even allow us to have our own minds to rebel, don't you see? No chance of thoughtcrime when he controls your thoughts."

"That's a grim picture," Steven said.

"It's the death of self," I said, "in pursuit of forced selflessness. Except it's not selfless when you're forced to do it any more than it's charity if I steal from you and give to the poor."

"Damn you, Robin Hood."

"I'm serious," I said. "The end is the same, but how we get there means a hell of a lot."

"Clearly not to Harmon," Steven said.

"Why would it matter to him?" I mused. "He's not the one utterly losing himself to pull this off. He doesn't have to deal with the consequences of having his own desires erased in order to accommodate the hive-mind. He still sits at the top of the food chain, dictating down to the rest of us. He could kill ten million people—starve them to death, whatever—in order to meet the greater good need, and he'd probably consider it an acceptable losses. He's not dealing with us as people. We're just cogs in his machine."

"What are you going to do about it?" Steven asked. "I mean … you do have a plan, right?" He eased a little closer to me, and I remembered how he'd made overtures when last we'd met.

"A few," I said. "I don't leave home without a plan or at least some ideas to improvise with." I shot him a look. "You're staying behind, by the way. Perugini and Abigail need someone to watch after them."

"I don't think Abigail is going to need my supervision," he said, "but I'll take them home with me, hunker down until this thing … goes whichever way it goes."

"Thanks for not pushing back on this," I said, not really wanting to look at him.

"Oh, I don't know how much good I'd do in a flat-out

meta fight—or whatever you're waltzing into," he said, and lowered his voice. "I'm just … glad I got a chance to see you again."

"Oh," I said lamely. "Well … you're seeing me now."

"I am." His arm was brushing mine. "Did I tell you I really like the punk look you've adopted?"

"She stole that from me!" Abigail shouted from inside. I didn't even know she was listening, but I turned and saw her just inside the door, pacing back and forth with a bag slung over her shoulder. "And, uh … I'm totally fine with going back to Cali, because I do not want to get squashed in a meta battle before I get my mind jacked."

"Way to keep your priorities straight," I shouted back.

"Hey, at least if I get mind-jacked I can come back out of it later," Abigail said, turning to head for the front door, bag over her shoulder. "Kind of tough for a human to recover from squashing."

"The lady makes a point," Steven said. "Still … if you needed extra help …"

"I've called in some favors," I said. "Taneshia and Jamal are already on a plane to DC, they'll meet us there. And I … did some other stuff, too." I kept this vague in case somehow Steven got captured. It wasn't likely, but Operational Security was pretty paramount when you were dealing with tenths of a percentage for success margins.

"I hope so," he said, and I caught Harry waving me in. "Looks like you're out of time."

"Not yet," I said, and looked up into his eyes. "I, uh …"

"You're going to do it," he said, without a trace of hesitation. "You'll win. I know you will."

I raised an eyebrow. "Oh, really? Why is that?"

"You're Sienna Nealon," he said in a very offhand manner. "The bad guys haven't beaten you yet."

"But … that could mean I'm due," I said, fumbling for words.

"Nah," he said.

"You sure about that?" I didn't see how he could be; maybe just good acting.

"I'm sure," he answered, lightning fast, and with a depth

293

of conviction that raised my eyebrows almost to my hairline. Or what was left of it after shaving the sides of my head.

"Harmon's a pretty smart guy," I said, "and he's got Cassidy Ellis on his side. They're like ... miles smarter than me. And I'm not just saying that because that's a crappy metaphor. Cassidy's the smartest person on the planet, and Harmon ..." I shuddered slightly. "Every newscaster and interviewer swears he's the most brilliant mind on the planet, which I guess means I'm doubly screwed in terms of the brains arrayed against me."

"Maybe he's not that smart," Steven said with a shrug. "He knows what people want to hear, after all, and he knows ... everything about them if he's talking to them. I mean, you're right, maybe he is blindingly intelligent and you really are just totally screwed, but ... so far, he seems to me like the rest of us: he does some smart things and some dumb things, because it's really hard to tell which is which when you're in the heat of the moment sometimes. You're still standing here, after all." He smiled.

That was not an unreasonable point. "What if he beats me?" I asked, letting that little fear squeak out.

"Well, then we're all pretty well cooked, so ... it's all upside from where I'm sitting," Steven chuckled. "The worst that can happen is what the odds makers say is going to happen, so ... working back from that, if you snatch victory from the jaws of defeat ... kudos to you."

"I don't like to lose," I said sourly.

"Then don't," Steven said.

"It's not quite that easy."

"I don't know how meta fights go," he said, "but it seems to me you've really only got one advantage here, since ... the whole world is almost against you."

"Oh, I have an advantage? Do tell."

"It's you, silly," he said, smiling. "You keep kicking the ass of everyone that comes at you. Yeah, this is a new thing, I'll admit, someone taking over all the minds in the world, but ... you haven't quit yet. You haven't lost yet. And he's just ... waiting there to get his ass kicked. Killed," Steven amended. "Because you're probably going to have to kill him. I hate to be an ass, but ... this is kinda your wheelhouse, all the way."

"You're not wrong," I said. Harry appeared at the massive window, gesturing with a finger across his neck. I frowned at him, and he jerked a thumb over his shoulder in the universal sign for "Let's GTFO!"

"You're going to get clear of this, you know," Steven said, startling me away from looking at Harry, who was now doing some sort of mime involving an invisible noose around his neck. "You'll save the world, clear your name. Everything will be back to normal before you know it."

"You sure about that?" I asked, as Harry did a full body shudder that was either him faking getting electrocuted or getting his prostate checked. It wasn't clear.

"Of course I am," Steven said. "You're a hero. It's what you do. I just hope ..." Here he went sort of shy. "... I just hope I get to see you again afterwards—" He turned around and finally caught sight of Harry. "What ... the hell is that?"

"His impression of a man getting beaten up by a bunch of invisible assailants, I think." Harry was gyrating. "I better go before he launches into his impression of being trapped in an invisible box."

Steven chuckled. "You can do this, Sienna."

"I'll try," I said, as I turned to leave.

"Then you'll win," he said, another vote of confidence in an ocean of them.

I didn't turn around for that one, though, because what else was there to say?

82.

I stared out the window of the chartered Gulfstream at the dusty plains of South Dakota. I really didn't care much for South Dakota, at least not in the middle. The west end, with the Black Hills, was beautiful. The east end ... less so, but still geographically somewhat distinct. The middle, though ...

The middle of the Dakotas was a giant stretch of dusty prairie that didn't look that different from a desert to me. Sunrise could be beautiful there, and sunset could be gorgeous, but the middle of the day was a one-star shitshow of the sort that even the Iowa State Fair wouldn't have invited into its grounds. (I hate Iowa, so this says a lot.)

"Yay," Veronika said without enthusiasm. "We're flying off to fight the president of the United States, who is an incredibly powerful telepath who could probably make us all into his personal sex monkeys." She paused, thinking that over, then gave it a shrug that I didn't want to interpret.

"Eww," Kat said so I didn't have to.

"Maybe he's going to do good things with the power," Colin said hopefully, twitching in his seat. I could tell he was wishing he'd run to Washington. Or maybe that he was wishing he'd run to the other Washington, the one he called home. "Maybe he's going to save the world."

"I'm sure he thinks so," I said. These lunatics always thought they were doing something good for the world—unless they were so locked into selfishness that they were certain the world was their enemy. That was pretty rare, though. Once you got to a certain level of grandiosity, they almost always thought they were doing the world a favor as they racked it up.

"Yeah," Harry said like he was some kind of authority, "there is a certain scale of plan that requires a mind that thinks they're doing a world of good." He shot me a sly grin, telling me he'd once again stolen the words that were about to come right out of my mouth. "Asshole," he mimicked, stealing my most probable reply.

"I was going to say—"

"Ooh, salty," he said, pursing his lips at me. Well, I couldn't say it now; he'd both stolen my thunder and seemed to enjoy it.

"So, we've gotta fight Reed, Scott, and Augustus, too, right?" Kat asked.

"And Friday, presumably," I said. "Plus the surviving members of that merc team or whatever that joined them."

"Tell me they're a B team," Veronika said.

"Harry, Colin and I beat their asses pretty good, so ... yeah," I said. "They're probably not going to be too bad. We just need to make sure we don't kill Augustus, Reed, Scott ..."

"Everyone else is fair game for killing, though, right?" Veronika asked, looking mildly concerned. "Because these hands?" She held up her perfectly manicured hands. "They don't do nonlethal."

"If you're gonna rip the flaming heart out of someone, just make sure it's not one of ours," I said. "You can kill Friday or the mercs ... guys ... whatever."

"Friday is the guy with the gimp mask," Kat said helpfully.

"Why does it always get kinky with you people?" Veronika asked.

"You live for kinky," I said. She just shrugged. "We're going to have help, so watch out for them, too."

"You mean other than Taneshia and Jamal?" Kat got their names right, which impressed me. I guess she'd met Taneshia at least once, though.

"Yeah," I said. "Hopefully. I tried to get a message to Zollers, so ... hopefully I'll have his help." I took a deep breath and held it. "And ... maybe some others."

"How long to Washington?" Colin asked, twitching again.

"A few hours," I said, leaning my head back in my seat. "Best to sleep, if you can."

"As if," Colin said, waving for the cabin attendant. "Can I get a cup of coffee?"

"I don't think you need that, twitchy," Harry said.

I tuned them out, staring down at the dusty, endless plains of South Dakota. I was riding off into trouble again, for the millionth time. I should have been used to it, but somehow ...

I blinked my eyes; sleep was coming for me, I could feel it. I guess I was used to it if I was going to be able to sleep before launching into what was probably one of the most dangerous battles I'd ever gone into. Definitely one of the ones I was least likely to win.

"I have all the strength in the world," I whispered to myself, so low no one could hear me, "but no power."

And it was true. The US government was against me. I was on the run. And the man who sat atop that structure of power ... he was about to do something that would completely destroy the free will of every human on the planet. I imagined his mind spreading out across the globe like black tendrils, slipping into peoples' ears and turning their joyful, hateful, loving, desperate expressions into the same blank mien. We would feel nothing but what he wanted us to feel, think nothing that he didn't want us to think. There would be no more joy, no more falling in love, no more sitting around on a Saturday doing whatever the hell you wanted as the leaves fell outside. Total control.

It was my mother's dream for me as a child come true, but on a global scale.

"I'm gonna stop you, Harmon," I whispered again as I started to nod off, my eyes slipping down. I fell asleep in the sun, thinking of my enemy.

83.

Harmon

I hadn't meant to fall asleep sitting in the wreckage of the Oval Office, but I had. The chair was just too comfortable, which you might not expect for something that was bulletproof, but it was. It wasn't like I could feel the Kevlar panels in the back, after all. Just the padding up front, in all the right places.

The world around me took on a particularly bright sheen, as though the fading autumn sun was more potent now than it had been when I'd slipped off to sleep in my empty, exposed to the elements office. It brought to mind the idea of a nap in a winter garden and someone pouring poison into my ear, for some reason. Except I didn't have a brother to inherit the kingdom, nor a son to lose his mind avenging me.

"Why are you thinking of Hamlet?" A quiet voice asked, and I turned to see her standing there.

My enemy.

Sienna Nealon.

Her hair was that dyed mohawk that I'd seen on the latest surveillance photos, the ones that were being distributed to every law enforcement agency in the country even now. She was looking around the bright, sunlit office, taking it all in. Motes of dust drifted across a sun beam, and I wondered why I felt so warm given my environ's sudden exposure to the elements. I certainly hadn't covered myself in a blanket.

I realized what was going on after a moment of staring at

her. "This a dreamwalk, then?"

"They said you were smart," Sienna said cautiously, eyeing me as though I might explode without warning.

"I think you've seen the power of my mind now," I said confidently.

"They never mention you being humble, though, for some reason."

"Humility is not a highly prized asset in our modern world," I said. "Have you ever seen anyone make money or get elected to high office by being reticent to talk about their achievements—even the marginal ones?"

"You'd know more about that than I would," she said, shoving her hands in her pockets. She eyed the hole in the wall. "I'm just gonna say it, because it's like the elephant in the room—or maybe like the elephant just left the room—there is a massive hole in your wall." She pointed at it, as though it might have escaped my notice. "What's up with that? Did you try and bring your ego inside and find it didn't fit through the doors or what?"

I chuckled lightly. "That was your friend Friday, I'm afraid."

"Ugh," she said, in the manner of a teenage girl. "He's not my friend."

"I don't think he has any friends," I said. "It's just a figure of speech." I looked around. "So … are you still hiding?"

"Maybe," she said, and the vision around me shook slightly, as though turbulence were hitting the White House grounds. I knew it wasn't on my end of the dream … "You've got a pretty evil scheme cooking, you know."

I paused and stared at her, and I knew. "You opened the vault."

"Wasn't easy," she said. "But … yeah. Booster serum? Expanding meta power? You and Cavanagh were experimenting on an awful lot of human beings to do all that."

"I didn't have anything to do with it, I'm afraid." I said.

"You had everything to do with it," she said quietly. "Do you know who he was experimenting on in Atlanta? Homeless people. And do you know what the guy he funded in Chicago did with his research? He damned near wiped us all out—"

"I told you," I said calmly, "I didn't have anything to do with it. Cavanagh was a science guy. I brainstormed with him, came up with a concept. He ran with it—"

"He ran with it, all right," she said, turning her head. "He ran with it in every direction, handed the idea off to—I don't even know how many ancillary labs. Palleton, though, they might have come the closest to what you were looking for, mightn't they?" She looked right at me.

"And what did they come up with, exactly?" I asked. "I don't have any connection to them, after all—"

"Not a direct one, I'd imagine," she said. "They came up with a parallel—I would call it lateral—powers serum."

"Did they?" I asked mildly. "Interesting. Something to ... pull out the residual powers on the DNA chain that might not have been activated? Probably a fascinating bit of research."

"Probably a whole lot more dead homeless people," she said, clearly intending it as a rebuke. "Is that your governing philosophy? Kill whoever you have to in order to make progress happen?"

"The world is not a gentle place, Miss Nealon," I said. "People die every day. You can't make an omelet—"

"I'm not getting a fucking omelet," she said, "and you're not breaking eggs. You're going to break peoples' lives."

"I'm going to fix peoples' lives," I said.

"At the cost of what?" she asked. "For the low, low price of ... what? Our free will?"

"You really do know about the boost, then," I murmured.

"Omnipath," she said. It sent a little chill down my spine that she even knew the word. How had she gotten this close? Everything I'd done had been an effort to keep her blinded, keep her away from what I was doing, either by killing her or simply holding her off until things were done. "The man who knows all, sees all, controls all." She said it like an accusation.

"The man who knows all *should* control all," I said. "Does it not make sense that the wisest of us—the one who *sees*—

301

should be in charge of fixing—saving—"

"You've confused omnipathy with omniscience," she said. "You may know what's in peoples' minds, but people are flawed—"

"I will help make them less so."

"—And if you're viewing the world through that flawed lens, then your actions are going to bend toward whatever *you* think is right—"

"I'll know what's right. I already do."

She stared at me, almost forlornly. "Did you ever take Ethics 101?"

I almost snorted. "Did you? Because as I recall, you didn't even go to school."

"That must make me dumb, then," she said. "But since you're smart, you must know about the 'Trolley Problem.'"

I sighed. "Naturally." It taxed my patience, being lectured by an idiot. "A trolley rolls along a track, with five people tied to the track ahead. An observer waits nearby, next to a switch. All they need to do to save the lives of those five people is to flip that switch, and the trolley will divert, crashing into one person and costing them their life. Five lives for one, a simple trade-off on the face of it?"

"On the face of it," she agreed.

"But you've probably heard of the more complex permutations," I said, ripping her little illustrative example out of her hands. "What if you had to push a corpulent human being onto the track to stop the trolley—commit murder yourself in order to save those five people? Or what if there were no guarantees that you would save any of them? Then, of course, there's the ethical dilemma of sacrificing the one in the first place—who was not even in any peril until you flipped that switch—"

"I like that you automatically put me in the role of the decision maker," she said.

"In your heart of hearts, you saw Sovereign's point," I said, and she flinched slightly. "With your power, come the occasional thoughts of what good you could do with them if you didn't limit yourself to swooping down out of the sky and pushing the baby carriage out of the path of a speeding bus." Dust drifted across the sunbeams between us. "You see a problem and you act to solve it, but all the problems you see are of the emergency variety—like Vegas. Trouble rears its ugly head and you come to save the day, ignoring the root causes of the problem. You work on the micro level, turning your small mind toward small action. You do your part, but it's a small part," I said a little nastily, my impatience with her attempt to draw me into an ethical debate for which she was incredibly unprepared manifesting itself in the pettiness of my reply. "The larger problems, though, you can't touch. But I can. And I will."

"Better living through chemistry."

"Better living through consensus," I said. "I see the problems that others don't, that others ignore, that others— like you—won't address because your brain doesn't function sufficiently to even grasp them. I see them, and I will drive us toward the solution." I spoke with passion of a sort I seldom displayed anymore, even on the campaign trail. "You think you're the hero?"

"I think I'm smart enough not to assume I know the answer to everything," she said.

"Congratulations," I said, "that just makes you smart enough to know you're dumb—no mean feat, in your case. You try to be the hero, but your successes are so minuscule as to almost not matter at all." I looked at her with the disdain I felt. "Look at you—master of the physical world— flame and light nets and dragon power and flight and strength all at your command. They call you the most powerful person in the world because of your ability to move the physical. But they miss the point. The body is nothing without the will, and humanity is nothing without the will to fix what ails the body of us. You're their hero because you're the one who operates at their level—"

"A low level, in your estimation."

"—a low level in *fact*," I said angrily. She was taxing my patience. "People seek a savior because they can't see a way to save themselves. They pour all their hopes into these vessels that they elevate, making them into the modern equivalent of gods, ignoring their deities' feet of clay—John

Fitzgerald Kennedy, Franklin Delano Roosevelt, Martin Luther King, Jr. They were men with ideals, ideas, but flawed and human." I said the words with disgust. "Now they live as revered legends in the modern mind, not because they were paragons of virtue but because we desired them to be more than simple agents of worthy change. We build myths around them, make them more ..." I chortled, "... beyond human."

"They moved the dial of change," she said, clearly blind to both my anger and my reasoning. "Isn't that what heroes do? More than others."

"That's what they've done," I said with disdain. "Until now." I looked her over with disgust; she really was nothing impressive. "But then a new hero came, and it was you ... but you showed your flaws. And people are willing to look—eager to look for flaws, so now they've got nothing left to believe in—a big, empty center in the middle of their lives." I smiled, watching her for signs of a reaction. My anger was almost spent, and she'd retreated behind a still mask. "Until I come along."

"And take away the will that they have to hope and believe in others," she said. "Until you take away self-determination, and democracy and all the other achievements of humanity up to n—"

I snorted again. "Most of humanity for most of history has not had any say in their governance. Few people experience democracy even today. You know what people really care about? The illusion of control while things are being taken care of to their advantage. I will right the wrongs, and they won't know any better. Isn't that good enough?"

"Until you run a trolley into them for the greater good, sure," she said, jarring me.

"I—what?" What she'd said hadn't made any sense.

"It's the trolley problem, like I said." She stared at me. I didn't see any signs that what I'd told her had made an impression. Clearly she had a thick head, wasn't listening, didn't care— "You'll be standing up on the bridge and see the imminent chaos, which means when it comes time to throw a switch ... you'll be the guy to do it. I bet millions die in the first year." She said it mildly, but with confidence.

"Millions will die this year whether I rule the world or not," I said, shaking my head. She truly was a moron. *She's airborne,* I thought very hard, sending the message to one of the minions I had out there. I knew he'd intuitively realize who I was talking about. She was his obsession, after all.

I know, the answer came back. *We almost have her.*

"But only I am willing to take the responsibility," I went on, not missing a beat, "willing to accept death as the price for the great days yet to come. I'm willing to do what's necessary, whether it's push a Supreme Court Justice to let your enemies out," I smiled at her, catching a flicker of interest at my admission that I'd screwed up her life entirely, "or cause an old boyfriend's stolen memories to surface, giving him a reason to be angry with you—an anger which was easily enflamed, by the way. You're isolated, cut off— and you always will be, because once people see your flaws, they can't stop looking at them."

"You turned my family against me," she said in quiet accusation.

"Why do these people who say, 'We're family,' about their friends always seem to be the ones with the most obvious mommy and daddy issues?" I wondered aloud, striking her again with my wit. She didn't react. Again. It was infuriating. Didn't she know these were aimed perfectly at her? Or was she too idiotic to notice?

"Why does the guy with the glaring personality disorder, massive ego, and utter inability to handle a personal life of his own think that he's the one who should manage the lives of the rest of us?" she asked, hitting me dead center and causing me to sputter slightly. I hadn't expected that; I couldn't read her mind here for some reason. Not that I wanted to.

The Oval Office shook around me, but faintly, as though it were happening on the other end of this dream. "I think that's your cue," I said, nodding at her. "I don't expect we're going to meet again after this, Miss Nealon." I called her that mostly to irritate her. "So—"

"You're the smart one, so I guess you'd know," she

305

snarked at me.

"—so this is farewell," I said as the world shook around us again and she looked around uncertainly. The Oval Office began to fade, and my eyes snapped open to find her gone, dust still fluttering across the fleeting beams of sunlight that made their way in through the hole. I was in my chair, comfortable despite of the autumn chill—warm because I had a feeling that halfway across the country, Sienna Nealon's plane was coming crashing to the ground.

84.

Sienna

I woke up to the sound of the plane breaking up around me. It was disturbing, I'll admit, somewhere between waking up that first time with two unknown guys in my house and waking up underwater in the Great Salt Lake. This was, perhaps, slightly less unnerving than that once I remembered that I could fly.

It got more unnerving again when I remembered that none of my companions could.

"AIEEEEEEEE!" Kat shrieked, as one might expect when suddenly belted into a seat that was attached to no plane, no wings, and no engines. It was a just a chunk of the fuselage with a seat bolted to it, falling out of the afternoon sky toward the dusty plains below.

"Crap," Veronika said mildly, clothing rippling around her as she fell like a skydiver, no seat on her. She caught my eye. "Ummm ... help?"

I turned my head as Colin leapt from one piece of the plane to another, snatching up the pilot, co-pilot and cabin steward, grabbing them and stowing them, one under each arm and the last hanging around his neck. "Little help here?" he called to me, feet planted on a piece of the tail fin.

I had a breath of panic, realizing I was still fastened into my own seat. Dark clouds filled the sky around us, tornadoes spinning and churning the air. I had a sudden realization about what had happened to our plane, and it wasn't a happy thought. There was no way I could save all these people. I had only two arms, two legs and a back ... where the hell were they going to hang onto me where I could save them?

I turned my head and Harry was there, just sitting in midair, flipping through a magazine, calm as could be. He turned his head to look at me, lips even, as though he were not falling out of the sky at hundreds of miles per hour, his magazine pages practically ripping out from wind shear.

"How are our odds looking now, Harry?" I asked.

"Nary a change," he said, as calm as if he were sitting in an airport somewhere waiting for a flight that was about to be called for boarding. He looked at me, unblinking, and then nodded. "Dragon."

"Huh?" I blinked, and the answer came slamming in like a hammer to the head. "Oh! Right."

I needed more square footage to save these people, that was the hang up. If only there were some way to create more places for them to hang onto me ... like turning into a massive, multi-story dragon. *Bastian,* I said, and got the nod.

My clothes shredded like they always did, my legs joining together in my massive tail as I turned into a snakelike creature of the sort that would have been worshipped and feared in ancient times. The screaming around me subsided as Kat and Harry both collided with my back and grabbed onto my scales as my sensation died, the nerves disappearing beneath the hardened scales. I felt the weight of Colin and the airplane crew land on me, turning my head to be sure, and then Veronika caught me around the neck, signaling that I was good to go.

"Hang on," I said, my voice changed now that I'd gone into Quetzlcoatl mode. I dove for the earth, slowing slightly over the natural pull of gravity, resisting it a little bit at a time so as not to jerk my passengers to a sudden, violent stop in mid-air. Because that would kill them, and I was trying to save them.

The wind whipped over the ridges that stuck out of the back of my head in lieu of hair, and I did a quick loop to slow myself under the suddenly blackening skies. It almost looked like night now, darkness shrouding us. I still had that foreboding feeling, and I knew what I was about to be up against. I could have tried to run, but the likelihood was I'd have been struck from the sky by a massive tornado. I would probably survive it, but it might send my passengers plummeting to the earth, which would have ruined my efforts to save them.

"Colin!" I called over my shoulder, "The minute we land, get the crew to a distance of at least ten miles. Preferably twenty."

"Got it," he called back. We were only a couple hundred feet from the earth now, and I could see the tornados coming, sweeping down out of the sky. There was one in particular, one that looked miles wide, coming at us from the east, and I suspected that was the one to watch.

I came to a landing, or within a couple of feet of one, my belly nearly touching the earth. I felt my passengers hop off, and Colin streaked south in a blast of wind, off to carry out my command. Veronika walked up beside my neck and stroked it gently. "Nice lizard," she said, smirking. "You know, I gotta be honest. Do you realize how phallic you look right now?"

"Oh, shut up," I said as the wide tornado in front of us came whipping closer and closer. "Harry?"

"They're coming, yeah," he said, stepping up beside Veronika and still paging through his magazine. I blinked as I stared at it; it was a girly mag, with a naked woman on the cover.

Veronika paused and tilted her head, doing a double take. "Really, Harry?"

He extended it to her. "You want to borrow it? Only a five percent chance it survives this fracas, so get your looks in now."

"It's grossly exploitative," Veronika said, still cocking her head sideway to look at the cover model. "And ... kinda sexy." She brought her head up straight. "But mostly exploitative."

"You're such a puritan, Veronika," Harry said with a cackle, eliciting an exasperated huff from her.

"Um, Sienna," Kat said from my other side, looking pretty

bedraggled, "I don't have much in the way of living plant life to work with here."

"Play medic, Kat," I said, "unless you see an opening."

The tornado in front of us dipped closer to the ground, vortex subsiding as it touched, and six figures came strolling out casually, as though they had just stepped off a plane's stairs rather than being dropped out of the sky by a force of nature. The tornado withdrew only a dozen feet, hanging above them, under control—

Under my brother's control.

"Nice to see you showing your true face to the world," Reed called, his own still twisted with that vicious fury that had marred him every time I'd seen him lately.

"Oh, this old thing?" I flapped one of my wings around like I was brushing my cheek. It wasn't an easy thing to do because my wing instinctively wanted to flap even though I didn't need it to fly. "I just threw it on in a hurry."

They came strutting across the plain like the cast of a Western doing their power walk into danger. Gothric the medic, Gaucho Marx, his eyes already aglow, and the Aussie with the knife, which was spinning in his hand so fast I could barely see it.

Then there were the three I cared about—Scott, Augustus, and Reed.

"This ain't gonna go well for you, Sienna," Augustus shouted. He should have known better than to talk.

"Jamal, Taneshia, and your momma are wondering why you don't call anymore," I said, and watched him blink like a robot shorting out. "I told them it was because you were too busy being President Harmon's assclown."

Augustus's eyes flickered, looking back and forth, like he was trying to think of something—a reply, a memory, something—but failing.

"Don't let her get in your head," Reed said, voice like steel.

"Harmon's already done that," I said. "He's a telepath, you know. He's controlling your minds, putting in thoughts."

"Like a puppeteer sticks his hand up a puppet's ass," Kat said, making things awkward. "The puppet in this case would be you," she clarified, in case it wasn't obvious what she'd meant.

"Ain't nobody does that to me," Augustus said, riled. "Except Tanesh—" His eyes went blank, like his programming had skipped the track again.

"I'm gonna slip inside you and carve you up," the Aussie said, brandishing his blade. I swept off the ground a few feet, just out of easy reach, and his expression turned furious. "Where do you think you're going?"

"42 Wallaby Way, Sydney, Australia," I quipped. I had an idea for how to deal with him, but it wasn't one I was looking forward to executing.

"What?" He frowned at me, deep crease lines cutting into his brow as the knife flashed. "I'm going to cut your heart out."

"You'll need to find it first," I said. I didn't really know where it was in my dragon form, and I hoped it wasn't in an obvious place. *Bastian?*

I've never gotten an MRI in this form before, sorry, he snarked at me. *They don't make machines big enough.*

"Let's get this show on the road," the Gaucho said, and his eyes started glow. I dove to the side, hoping to draw his fire, and the plains beneath me erupted in battle.

85.

Scott

The main objective obvious, her dragon form hovering over those three other people that were standing in opposition. He knew Kat, of course, but the other two ... he didn't have a clue. One was a guy, dressed kind of shabbily, and the other was a woman who looked to be in her late thirties/early forties, dressed so crisply she might have been US Secret Service except for her flair for style.

Get in there, Harmon's voice compelled him. He should have known the man was there, right behind his ear, ready to push him into action. *Kill her—*

Scott drew moisture out of the air with efficiency he'd never had before. He wielded a blast of water and channeled it at the shabbily dressed man, who stepped easily out of the way of Scott's new and improved beam. It was only an inch in diameter, but it could carve through a human being easily, tearing them in half if he chose to. The man ran oddly, jerking left and right in perfect time, dodging every blast Scott sent his way.

A precognitive, Harmon's voice sounded in his head. *Now it's starting to make sense how she's been one step ahead.* A pause. *Kill him.*

Scott brought up his other hand, channeled water in a blast through his mouth, and let loose with all three streams. He triangulated and brought them together in a convergence of death, one which would surely carve the precognitive to

312

pieces—

The man did a flip sideways, snaking between two blasts, and then charged, sliding to the left when Scott brought the beams around to decapitate him.

You're useless, Harmon pronounced, and there was a surge of pain in Scott's head. *I'd kill you right now, but I doubt she'd notice given what she's dealing with.*

Scott turned his attention to look, just for a second, to see what Harmon was talking about. Tornadoes were snaking down out of the sky, scrub brush was growing like tentacles, and together they were working in concert to drag Sienna's dragon form back to the earth. She was fighting, but failing.

Now you watch her die, Harmon said.

"I'll carve your heart out, bitch!" Mac shouted, and he was moving in a flash, at her side in less than an eye's blink, ripping into her and stepping between the ribs, knife flashing as he carved between the dragon scales—

He was going to kill her, Scott knew, a scream in his head like distant thunder … because how could she defend herself from him now that he had carved his way past her defenses … now that he was inside her?

86.

Sienna

"This was not my bestest plan ever," I muttered as the Aussie ripped through my side and started carving internal organs. Fortunately, my innards were not as easy to cut through as he'd probably hoped, and I was ready for this particular—and somewhat stupid on his part—gambit.

I started to return to human form, something which looked considerably less grand than my sweeping expansion into a graceful, reptilian dragon. Coming back to human after that was a little like a—well, like a—like a —

You know what, there's really no appropriate analogy for it. Not one you could tell to the kids, anyway, because it involved me going from what looked a long, narrow snake into a short, tiny human. Fill in the blanks, gutter mind.

Unfortunately for the Crocodile Dundee impersonator shredding his way through my belly, the transformation back could be done in about two seconds. I didn't usually like to rush it; I liked to take my time, let my joints settle as my bones and internal organs snapped back to filling a tiny cavity in torso rather than a fifty foot long snake body.

This time, I rushed. It usually didn't hurt. This time it did, for obvious reasons.

"GACK!" I heard him say as I contracted to human—and much smaller than Aussie knifeman—size. He barely got the shout out in time, before my internal organs—set to heal rapidly thanks to Wolfe's present intervention—fought back

314

against the resistance they found in my guts. My ribs broke against him and reformed, broke and reformed, shoving against his skull and face and chest and legs and—it was a lot of smashing. Like my body was trying to chew him up, experiencing breakage for its efforts, but healing and trying again.

His body? Not so much able to heal rapidly.

It felt like something ruptured inside me, something that wasn't supposed to be there, and fortunately my body expelled the mass as it healed. It hurt like hell, like I was passing a stone out of my stomach, but fortunately I expelled the foreign body right at the exact moment I had Gavrikov light up my one-piece unitard and my full mane of flaming hair (for effect). The crush of organic matter that shot out of my stomach just happened to catch fire as I dumped it unceremoniously out of me and staggered back, watching the mashed piece of mushed bone and shredded flesh try and draw its last breath as fire seared it black.

"Whoops," I said mildly as the remains of the Aussie shuddered once and then lay there, looking like nothing so much as the victim of a tragic cattle mutilation that involved turning the poor thing inside out. Well, it was better than trying to birth him out of my hoo-ha, anyway.

"Mac!" Gaucho shouted, his eyes lighting up as he looked at me. They burst into a glow, and I just happened to quickdraw first, lifting my hand as I stood upright, now unencumbered by the world's biggest artificial turd trying to squeeze out of my belly. I fired a flaming burst of gas and it passed Gaucho's blast in the air—

87.

Scott

That was ... revolting, Harmon said mildly, looking at the remains of Mac the Knifer as Sienna set him aflame after expelling him from under her ribcage like she'd dropped off an artificial pregnant belly. The knife itself came clattering to the ground, though no one noticed as Sienna took aim and shot at Joaquín just as Joaquín fired back at her.

His blast caught her in the side and vaporized half her chest, spinning her around and dropping her to the earth. Her tiny bullet of flaming gas caught him in the head, though, and Joaquín dropped as well, much more limply, and much more definitely dead.

"Joaquín!" Gothric screamed, charging up as he let loose of his grip on the native plant life to hurry to the last member of his team.

"Yeah, no," the dark-haired woman said, rushing up to him and planting a hand on the back of Gothric's neck. "Not so quick, sweetheart—you, I can kill." Her hand blazed a bright blue, and Gothric's neck disintegrated, his head and body tumbling free of her grasp—and each other.

The ground shook in fury, earth turning up in a quake of mighty proportions, and the sky blackened as those same massive tornados threatened to come down on them. Scott stood there, watching as Sienna struggled back to her feet, her side covered in flame in lieu of clothing, wound already healed, her eyes burning as she stared at Scott, hovering a few inches off the ground to dodge the effects of Augustus's earthquake.

"You in there?" Sienna asked, looking right at him.

"I'm here—" Scott said, but was cut off by the blinding pain once more.

"I'm here," Harmon said, speaking through him. "And you're—"

88.

"—Not nearly as amusing as you think you are," I said, staring through the waterboy's eyes at Sienna Nealon, who was giving good glare considering all the miles between us. I might have been shaking in my boots if I'd ever worn them in my life. "So congratulations, you killed some feebleminded loaner troops from Revelen." I swept around, looking for the box that Cassidy should have left behind. I didn't have a choice in the matter now, I needed it.

I slammed a palm down on the phone. "Ms. Krall, find me Cassidy Ellis."

"Who?"

"The girl who was in here earlier," I shouted through the receiver, trying to keep track of Scott Byerly's mind as I ordered her to remember. "Find her! She should be in the Lincoln Bedroom. Also, have the new woman from finance brought in immediately." I hit the button to disconnect us before Ms. Krall could simper at me.

I refocused, turning to Augustus and Reed. Tornadoes set down on the plains, which shook with a fury unlike anything that had been unleashed since the times of primitive metas, as her friends let loose around her—

318

89.

Sienna

I blasted Reed in the face with a net of light and the tornados receded as his control momentarily loosened. I did the same to Augustus, but the earth didn't stop shaking. Not that it mattered to me; I was hovering above it.

"Well, the rest of us could use a lift," Harry complained, keeping his balance so well that I could scarcely tell he was standing in the middle of a 10.0-magnitude earthquake.

"Yeah, this ain't fun, Sienna," Veronika said, wobbling on uneven legs.

Colin zipped out of top speed, and I made a motion quickly toward Kat, Veronika, and Harry. "DC," I said. Colin shot over the rattling earth and grabbed the three of them in a blur, carrying them off … I dunno how, honestly. Two on his back, one like a bride? It was kind of funny to imagine him with Harry riding along in his arms, probably still flipping through his dirty magazine while Veronika tut-tutted him from Colin's back and Kat squeaked, hanging on for dear life to Veronika's shoulders.

"You think removing your friends from this battle will save them?" Scott asked in President Harmon's voice.

"It'll save them for now," I said. "That's what I do, remember? I operate at too low a level to really fix things, so … I just stall death, really. Hold it back for a little while."

"Pathetic," Harmon pronounced.

"Well, we can't all be super-genius elites who are the only

319

ones with the wisdom to rule from on high," I said. "Some of us have to do the day-to-day saving. Some of us have to put out the fires, stop the criminals, build things, fix things … heaven knows you wouldn't want to get your hands dirty doing any of that."

Scott's eye twitched as I threw Harmon's elitism in—well, not *his* face, strictly speaking. I wondered if it would have any effect. "You know why I take this mantle on myself?" Harmon asked.

"Because no one else is arrogant enough to believe they can micromanage the entire human race?"

"Don't be an idiot," he laughed. "Lots of people think they can do that. Laws are about that the more granular they get. It's a philosophy, the idea of using law and government to perfect man. I'm the only one who has the power to do it, though. I'm the hero—"

90.

Harmon

"—That you've always thought you were," I said. The door to the Oval Office opened and Cassidy slipped in, box in her hands. Another woman followed, staring blankly at me, having been dragged out of the budget department. "I can be the one to solve the world's problems, make you irrelevant. What need will there be for you when crime is over? When fires are eliminated by everyone working in perfect unity? When war is finished, when no one has to worry any more about—"

"Blah blah," she said. "Little man wants to be a god, wants to rule over it all—I bet you were bullied as a child."

"That has nothing to do with—" I snapped, then composed myself as I waved for Cassidy to bring the box to me. "You're cunning, I'll give you that. You might have been useful once."

"I wouldn't have joined you anyway," she said, nodding her head at me—well, at Scott. "You complain about me being dumb, but you take away the brains of anyone whose lines of thought disagree with yours."

"Because they don't know," I said. "They don't *see*."

"You're a freaking telepath, dumbass," she said. "If you can't make them see with simple visuals and persuasive explanations … have you considered maybe your argument for how the world should be run is just a giant sour lemon that appeals to nobody but you?"

"There's no point in arguing with you," I said, as Cassidy opened the box to reveal the hypodermic needles.

"By your standards, there's no point arguing with anyone," she shot back, causing my temperature to rise. "You're in the highest office in the land. You're supposedly brilliant. You're a freaking mind reader. You could try and persuade people, but you don't care about winning them over because it's easier to run them over and just do what you want to do. Because they're stupid, you say. So clearly, you're the better man, the better—their better, I guess, which means you have the right to rule."

"Exactly," I murmured, taking the syringe and searching for a vein. Finding one, I plunged the needle in, pushing the plunger in all the way. "I am better. I am smarter. I know more than any of you—"

91.

Sienna

"—And it's time for me to take a page from your book and show everyone what real power is," Harmon said through Scott's mouth, that creepy ventriloquism echoing over the plains of South Dakota as Augustus's quakes settled down and Reed's tornadoes dissipated in anticipation of what was about to happen. "Not the force of strength you show, the paltry physical sort that manifests through violence, but true power. The power of the mind."

I felt a cold, clutching sensation of fear. I had a feeling I knew what was coming too, and the outcome was a big, fat gamble—

"No more walls between us all," Harmon said in a mocking tone. "No more barriers between humanity."

"No more privacy, no more secrets, no more thoughts of our own," I singsonged. "No more lust, no more love, no more happiness—"

Scott's eyes were transfixed on me in a very annoyed, very un-Scott way. "What—no—*stop that!*"

"Make me," I said, knowing that if he'd just stuck a needle in his arm like I thought he had, I was too far from Washington to do anything about it if I was wrong about what would happen next.

His eyes flared. "I will. In just a—" He paused, cold realization of his own hammering home. "Why am I not ... the others ... they collapsed and felt—" He bristled, straightening up as my suspicion turned out true, confirmed by him. "Cassidy."

"Turns out that the girl standing next to you, your right hand person," I said, trying to distract him, "maybe wasn't so keen about letting you run her head, either. She's supposed to be pretty smart, though, so if she doesn't buy into your bullshit about a better world being better for her—"

92.

Harmon

"—I don't hold out a lot of hope for anyone else being persuaded to your way of thinking," she said across the distance between us as I saw red. Blood red.

I broke out of the South Dakota vision and looked up at Cassidy, who was quivering before me. "That's not the real solution." I nodded at the box. "Not the solution you gave the others."

Cassidy stuck her chin out in defiance. "No."

Suddenly, the electrical burns on her palm made sense. "You've been hiding things from me, Cassidy," I said, taking a step toward her as she jerked back. "You've been hiding things from yourself, too … shocking yourself to kill the brain cells holding your memories … what have you been up to?" I reached out and seized her mind in a way I'd never done before, desperation turning me to want to throttle the answer out of her with near-physical violence.

I always hated physical violence. But I was starting to see the appeal now.

"I … don't know …" Cassidy said, and I could tell it was the truth. Cassidy was too clever by half; she'd fried the parts of her brain that had worked against me, covering her tracks so that she only dimly suspected what she'd done, the truth coming out until she'd have to shock it out of herself again. She had a mind without peer; performing micro brain surgery with a torn electrical cord was well within her

325

capacity. She held up scorched palms, fresh wounds there to underscore what she'd done, and recently. "I ... don't know where the ... solution is, either ..."

"Of course you don't," I whispered. "But the problem is, Cassidy ... this makes you rather useless."

"Hey, dumbass." Sienna Nealon's voice broke through my blinding rage, and suddenly I felt a shock of pain as she punched Scott Byerly in the jaw, knocking me to the ground. I stared up at her, on the South Dakota plain, blinking away the surprise. "I'm over—"

93.

Sienna

"—here," I said, staring down at Scott, who had a stunned expression that didn't quite belong to him. I wondered how long it had been since Gerry Harmon had felt a punch to the face, and knew that however long it was, it was too long. His was a face that deserved to be punched, and often.

"Yes," Harmon said, propelling Scott back to his feet, water churning at his fingertips. "There you are, indeed." I hoped Cassidy was using the opportunity to run. "And here I am, apparently stuck at your level."

"You won't like my level," I said and punched Scott in the face again. I took it easy on him; I was mostly aiming to piss Harmon off so he'd forget about Cassidy. "Because I'm about to drag you down to it and beat you with experience."

Scott staggered, lip bleeding, and he turned back around. His voice broke through for a second. "Do—do what you have to—Sienna—"

"That's enough out of you," Harmon said, reasserting control.

"Is there anyone on planet earth who agrees with you enough to go along with what you want?" I asked, putting my dukes up. It was for show; I could throw a punch faster than Reed, Augustus and Scott combined.

Scott blinked at me, and I knew it was Harmon showing through as the anger broke across his face. Someone sucker-punched me in the side of the head, the only sound of

327

warning a crunch of earth, and I realized that apparently these boys of mine had gotten a speed upgrade along with their serum boost.

A tornado swept out of the sky at me and I threw up a hand, blasting it away with a quick burst of fire, and found Scott coming at me with his fists, water covering them. He punched at me and I punched back, my fists on fire and dissipating his shield of water with each blow, steam hissing as we met each other in battle.

A wall of rock came at me and I launched into the sky, barely evading Augustus's attack. It looked like a fist of stone the size of a pickup truck reaching out of the plains, and another tornado swept down at me, this one with Reed clutched in its depths. I was buffeted about before righting myself, gritting my teeth as Scott soared up on jets of water to strike at me.

"Son of—" I muttered, punching him in the belly as he went past. He tried to slap me down, but he lacked the skill if not the speed.

"I think I've figured out why everyone else failed to kill you," Augustus said, in Harmon's voice. He shot at me on a wave of rock, and then it changed into a bullet-stream of gravel that I barely dodged. It winged past, drawing blood from my arm as I yanked it away. He was playing for keeps; that would have disintegrated me if I'd been directly in its path.

"You just don't quit," Reed said, hitting me with a blast of air that caused physical pain, as though it had been hardened into ice. He, too, spoke in Harmon's voice, and I reached out and cranked him with a backhand, snapping him in the jaw and sending him spinning out of the way.

"That's generally considered a virtue," I said, turning to anticipate Scott's incoming attack. It was a triple beam of water of such intensity that I had to launch two hundred more feet in the air to avoid it carving off anything more than my left hand—which hurt, by the way. *Wolfe,* I said, cringing at the pain.

"Getting pummeled and rising again is not a virtue," Harmon Augustus said, climbing on a pillar of rock to come at me, still spitting a stream of stones out of his improvised chariot. This was not going to be an easy fight. "A smarter person would figure out how to stop getting hit."

"Oh, yeah?" I turned and blasted Augustus in the eyes with a net of light, then rocketed at him, knocking him into unconsciousness with a right hook that set his head to wobbling. He dropped, his pillar of earth disintegrating into a storm of falling rocks as I caught him and dropped him gently—well, gently for me—on the plains below. "Let's see if you can figure it out," I muttered and whipped back around to come at Reed at the speed of sound.

I caught my brother in the jaw, heard the crack, and watched his eyes roll. He went ragdoll, too, and started to fall out of the air, but I grabbed his arm and got him to the earth before I absorbed his soul. I set him down with relative ease, too, and then came in for a landing as Scott drifted back to the earth, his jets of water lowering him for his own landing.

"'A smarter person would figure out how to stop getting hit,'" I said mockingly.

"I'm not the one getting hit," he said as he cut the jets, but his eyes were burning from the insult and—I suspected—the secondhand pain I'd inflicted through his surrogates.

"We're not done just yet," I said with a smile, my hair and torso blazing with fire.

"Oh, I think we're done," Harmon said, and Scott rattled off a scream of pain, clenching his eyes shut.

It took my breath away, seeing him waver like that. I had a bad feeling I knew what was coming next, and it wasn't going to be good. "You chicken—"

94.

Harmon

"—shit," she said, and I could feel her rage across the distance between us. She had that look on her face, all red and intense, as though her fiery hair—an impressive little visual trick, I might add—might light up as a metaphor for her anger.

"You're a master of the physical," I said, shrugging Scott's shoulders for him. "The body is your domain, as I've said. I cede that ground to you. You could certainly pummel me in a round of fisticuffs, as you've proven here." I smiled thinly. "But only a fool would fight you that way."

"You must be a fool, then," she spat back at me, "because that's what you just tried."

"It was an exercise in entertainment more than anything," I said, trying to assuage my wounded pride. I'd thought I could beat her, it was true, but there was no shame in acknowledging her mastery of the physical arena. She was made for this combat, this kind of fight, and she was welcome to it. I'd never had to throw a punch in my life, and it had been foolish of me to start now, no matter how tempting it might have been. "We both know the real fight is in the mind."

I strode around my desk, pausing for a moment to slap the intercom switch. "I need security camera footage from the Secret Service, Ms. Krall. I need to know everywhere the girl who was just in here has been over the last day or so." I

330

waited for Ms. Krall to catch up, jogging her mind with a slight prod. "Have them put that together for me, will you?" I cut her off when I knew she'd gotten it. I needed to find out where Cassidy had been, where she could have hidden the serum, because she'd fled while I was distracted with Sienna Nealon, and now I was left with a woman standing in my office, staring at me. "I'll be with you in a moment, dear," I said to her, and she just blinked back at me.

"I know what you're going to do—" Sienna said, a wind blowing across the Dakota plains, sending dust into the air from where Augustus's earthquake had ripped up the ground.

"I doubt it," I said lightly, speaking through Scott again. "I'm going to give you a chance to be a hero again. One last time, probably, depending on how you answer this challenge." She grimaced, her eyes fluttering closed.

I reached out and seized hold of Augustus Coleman's mind, causing him to shake where he lay on the ground. Then I took hold of Reed Treston's mind and made him convulse where he'd fallen. Finally I threaded my thoughts out and took hold of the mind of the woman standing in front of me, her reddish hair wavering as she shook, her smoky grey eyes evincing a hint of pain. "I'm looking at Ariadne Fraser," I said mildly. "She's a handsome-looking woman, you know. I hear you have some affection for her."

"You bastard," Sienna said, and a tear streamed down her face.

"You wanted to play the hero," I said. "That forces me into the role of the villain. So … now I've got Mr. Byerly, Mr. Coleman, Mr. Treston … and Ms. Fraser. I'm in their heads. And I'm going to do to them what I did to Edward Cavanagh …

"Unless you kill yourself right now."

95.

Sienna

"Unless you kill yourself right now."

Harmon's threat rang in my ears. I closed my eyes, plains dust blowing against me, little grains singeing themselves against my flaming body and hair, sounding like a bugzapper crisping them as they blew through. "You coward," I said, feeling a little wetness on my cheeks; he had almost everyone I cared about in his grip, and he was about to squeeze their brains into mush.

"I'm comfortable playing the villain for you, knowing I'll be the one to save the world in the end," Harmon said through Scott's lips—lips I'd kissed, lips I'd loved. I'd thought over the last few months that there was nothing left of the love I'd had for him.

Until I realized that all this time ... he'd been under the control of someone else.

"You die, and I let them live," Harmon said. He paused, watching me. "Come on. You're the hero, aren't you? Isn't this an easy choice? It's not as though you've got much to live for, is it? You've lost your home, you're a fugitive from justice—I mean, you couldn't go home even if you still had one ... and it'd be hard to do that job that you love so much from jail. I mean, assuming, for some reason, I fail in my endeavor here. Which is unlikely.

"I've turned the world against you, Sienna," he went on, sounding like he was relishing my pain. "I've turned your own 'family' against you." He said "family" with a special sort of skepticism. "Even if you miraculously escape this moment and free them ... do you think their minds are going to be in working order? Your brother has killed an innocent woman and shot an infant. Your pal Augustus has abandoned his own family to chase you. And let's not even discuss what I've made of this man," Scott's hands ran up and down him. "Of course, I had some help from you in that regard before I found this poor fellow. And Ariadne?" He chuckled, and it sounded gross and sinister. "Well ... she's going to be the most difficult of all to put back together. Because she ..." His look was pure venom. "... She doesn't even remember your name. Which is how it will be for everyone in the world soon enough."

"It seems so clear to you, doesn't it?" I asked, my voice delicate as crystal. "So high ... and mighty ... and above us all?"

He blinked. "Well ... yes. Of course."

"Being controlled by you is no kind of life," I said, looking at Augustus, shaking on the ground. "Being a puppet of yours is not living." Reed convulsed, hard, bucking against the upturned earth.

"Having their heads explode due to a massive aneurysm isn't much fun, either," Harmon said, as Scott shook and cried out in his own voice. "You have about ten seconds to decide before the damage becomes too much for their bodies to repair. I know you're not that bright, but ... I'd hurry if I were you."

I closed my eyes and reached out with my thoughts. *If you're there ... if you can hear me ... if you're in DC ... please ... stop him.*

"Remember, you're an idiot, which means thinking it over is not in your best interest," Harmon said. "Your brilliant mind got you into this situation; it seems unlikely to get you out or save your friends."

I saw a warm, familiar, enigmatic smile in the darkness of my mind, a reassuring voice that reached across the miles:

I'm on it.

Doctor Zollers.

"Well, I'm going to take this silence and your stupidity as a 'No,'" Harmon said, and I opened my eyes to see Scott shake, his face turning blood red. "Unless you want to take back your—" He froze, locking eyes with me, "—your—your ... what the—"

96.

Harmon

"—Hell?" I felt my connection with Augustus, Reed and Scott fade into nothingness, as though someone had slapped hard against my mind, knocking me out of theirs. I blinked, staring at the blank face of Ariadne Fraser standing before me. She was as close to a lobotomy patient as I'd ever encountered, but she could still balance a spreadsheet. Scooping Sienna Nealon out of her mind had been hard work, but it had been worth it, I thought. She was my ace card, waiting in the hole in case somehow Nealon got too close to the mark.

"Looks like you're my last hostage," I said, and she stared at me, blank of face. Someone was blocking me from the others, and I had a feeling I knew who that was, but Dr. Quinton Zollers would have a hell of a time keeping me from killing Ariadne Fraser and retrieving the serum before Sienna Nealon got here to "save the day." He wasn't on the premises, after all, and however strong his mind might have been, I could at least keep him out mentally while the Secret Service kept him out physically.

The phone beeped. "Mr. President, the Secret Service has compiled the footage you've asked for if you'd like to step out and—"

"Just a minute, Ms. Krall," I said, coming around the desk, triumphant. I had this. Victory was at hand. All I needed was the serum, a little boost, and Dr. Zollers wouldn't be playing any more games. He'd be just another amoeboid like the rest, in my thrall, working toward the goals of humanity. I stared at the Resolute desk, knowing my success was only moments away, and that Sienna Nealon was still at least minutes from DC, even if she hurried—

Something grabbed me by the back, yanking me out the hole in the wall that Friday had made. "What the—" I yelled, but I was already speeding along, propelled through the air in a straight line. The White House shrunk below me before I even managed to get out another yell, the West Wing shrinking until it looked like a little building block on the ground far beneath. I couldn't even see the Secret Service agents on the roof as dots, and I was high enough up in less than a minute that the air was starting to get thin.

My mind sped along; Sienna Nealon had still been thousands of miles away, unable to snatch me—and I hadn't felt hands on my back in any case. No, this was different, it was as though gravity itself had been turned on its ear, reversing and pulling me away.

I slowed in my ascent, hanging, my mind lashing out and finding nothing to take hold of. That damned Doctor Zollers, he was blocking me even here, so far above the earth.

I came to a halt like an elevator that had reached its floor, and I hung there, suspended above Washington, DC. It was such an ugly sprawl. I looked down at the Capitol building, powerless to move myself, and I felt a shudder of chagrin as I realized that once more, somehow, this mistress of the physical realm had turned my best-laid plans against me.

I saw movement to my right and turned my head. There was a woman there in a black and white costume, quite stylish really, and I rolled my eyes. "Who the hell are you?" I asked out of habit, even though I already knew who she was before she opened her mouth to answer.

97.

Jamie Barton

Her name was Jamie Barton, but everyone knew her now as Gravity, the hero of Staten Island. She hovered there, above Washington, DC, with an anxious feeling in the pit of her stomach, like she was doing something wrong and about to be caught at it. Well, that was no surprise, was it? She'd just kidnapped the President of the United States, after all.

"I'm just going to have to keep you here for a few minutes, sir," Jamie said, a little nervously. This hadn't been her idea, obviously, but when Sienna Nealon had called and laid out the case for what needed to be done ...

... Well, it was hard to ignore her, especially when words like "telepath" and "plot to take over the world," came into play. Outlandish as they may have sounded.

"I don't know what you've been told," Harmon said, straining like he was trying to concentrate on her, "but whatever it is—"

"I hear you're a telepath," she said, becoming more confident—though only marginally—the longer she was in place here, with the president before her. "That you were going to try and take over everyone's minds."

"Isn't that the most ludicrous thing you've ever heard?" Harmon asked, shrugging his shoulders against the gravity channel that was keeping him suspended in the air.

"Close," Jamie said.

"Come on," Harmon said, wheedling. "Let me down. Go

on about your life, and we'll pretend none of this ever happened. I don't know what Sienna Nealon has told you, but it should be obvious to anyone with a brain that she's the villain here—"

Jamie swallowed hard. "No, sir. I'm keenly aware of exactly how it feels when someone else paints you as the villain. And I don't think she is, in this instance."

Harmon cocked an eyebrow at her. "I know you had a rough time when everyone turned against you, but—"

"I very much doubt you do, sir."

Harmon chuckled lightly, though there didn't seem to be much humor in it. He seemed to be straining, as though his mind were elsewhere. "I need to—ah—"

"Just wait here a few minutes, sir," Jamie said, pulling gently on another gravity channel. "Answers are coming."

She started to activate another gravity channel as Harmon stared at her. "What are you doing?" he asked.

"Bringing a friend up," Jamie said, concentrating only a little on that other channel. She'd received the direction on where to put it via a voice in her head, which was a peculiar thing, something that lent a little credence to the story Sienna Nealon had left on that voicemail. She'd been at work when Sienna had called and had only checked her purse later. That had sent her scrambling, first to decide whether she should believe it, and then to decide whether it was something she should act on.

She'd still been undecided until she saw the hole in the West Wing, and the president walking around inside like nothing was wrong. That was weird, right? Wouldn't the Secret Service have evacuated him under normal conditions if there were a hole in the Oval Office? She'd yanked him up, easy as pie, and not a single agent had followed him out, pointing guns at the air, looking for the threat.

Something was rotten in DC, but then, that was hardly surprising.

Jamie slowed the gravity channel as her other guest appeared, balanced and calm in a way that Harmon hadn't managed. The president looked like he was hanging by his armpits; the new arrival looked like he was sitting on a cushion of air.

"Hello, Jamie," said the older man, almost reclining on her channel, "My name is Dr. Quinton Zollers, and I'm friend of Sienna's." He had a gleam in his eye, and his smile was amused, even as he dangled thousands of feet above the city of Washington, DC. "And a telepath, obviously."

"Oh, obviously," Harmon said, squinting in anger at Zollers.

"You seem a little worn out, Mr. President," Zollers said, switching his attention to Harmon, the blue afternoon sky a lovely backdrop for the most bizarre conversation Jamie had ever been a part of. "Have you been overexerting yourself?"

"I run a rough schedule," Harmon said, his features relaxing, concentration seeming to falter. He looked away from Zollers.

"Well, I imagine taking over the world is a full-time job," Zollers said.

"What are you going to do with me?" Harmon asked, staring off into distant white, sunlit clouds.

"That's not my call to make," Zollers said. "Or hers," he inclined his head toward Jamie. "We're just keeping you here until—"

"Until Sienna Nealon arrives to kill me," Harmon said with sudden ferocity. He looked right at Jamie. "Do you condone murder?"

Jamie felt like she'd been hit in the face. "I—no!"

"We're not going to murder you, Mr. President," Zollers said.

"Forgive me if I don't take you at your word as you kidnap me out of the White House and suspend me above the city," Harmon said.

"If we wanted you dead," Zollers said pleasantly, "I could just switch off Ms. Barton's gravity channel right now and let nature take its course."

Jamie felt her stomach drop. If he could really do that … and Harmon could do the same … "Oh my goodness," she whispered.

"You're starting to see the scope of the problem now," Zollers said. "Yes, he has the same powers I do, but he's gone and tired himself trying to control too many people over the last few days. His defenses are weak enough that I could sit on him for quite a while without similarly exhausting myself." He cocked his head, looking right at Harmon. "But that formula you had developed, Mr. President ... that was a dirty trick. Taking away peoples' lives ... their wants, their desires ..."

"The world would have thanked me," Harmon snapped, and Jamie almost gasped; it sounded like an admission to her. "Once it was done. No more problems. No more worries."

"No more self," Zollers said. "No more individuals. No more sense of identity apart from the group." He shuddered, still sitting on air with a calm that was impressive considering how most people Jamie lifted up tended to freak out at ten feet. "Forgive me if, as a psychiatrist, I find that ... unpalatable."

"Well, it would put you out of work, so I understand your reticence to embrace the revolution," Harmon said with surprising cheer. "It would also put all the defense contractors out of business, though, so ..." He shrugged. "What is it the capitalists call it? Creative destruction?"

"Ah, here she comes," Zollers said, and it was so; Sienna Nealon streaked out of the sky and slowed, breathless, her body glowing with a very dim flame.

"That's a good look on you," Jamie said. "Very *Hunger Games.*"

"Yeah," Sienna said, looking down at the flame that wrapped her torso, "I didn't have time to pick up new clothes, so ..." She shrugged and glanced at Harmon. "Any chance I can borrow your coat?"

Harmon glared at her. "I would tell you to go jump off a building, but I think we all know that would be pointless." He remained there, sullen, then finally rolled his eyes and stripped off his jacket, tossing it to her. Sienna caught it and wrapped it around herself, rolling up the sleeves so her arms didn't disappear in them. Harmon wasn't a large man, but he was still considerably bulkier than Sienna. She let the flames die down around her as she buttoned the coat, and was left with a V-shaped strip of her chest between her breasts exposed, as well as her legs. Her hair stopped glowing as well, revealing a bright pink mohawk.

Jamie raised an eyebrow. "That's, uh ... stylish, I guess."

"You'd know better than I would," Sienna said, folding her arms awkwardly in front of her, as though the V-shaped exposure of her chest made her uncomfortable. Her arms blocked most of the view, not that Jamie could see anyone around them who cared. Harmon was staring in the other direction, still plainly sullen. "Thanks for coming," Sienna said.

"Your message got my attention," Jamie said, staring at the president of the United States with mounting unease. "He's really a telepath?"

"Yeah," Sienna said.

"And he was going to take control of all our minds," Jamie said. That was not a question. She was pretty convinced of that.

"He came pretty close, I'd say." Sienna shifted in the air. "If not for you, he would have done it."

"Wow," Jamie said, shifting on her gravity channel in discomfort. "I, uhm ... what are you going to do with him?"

Sienna stared at Harmon, who gave her a glance. "To be determined," she said. "But I gotta get him out of here. Zollers can only hold him off for so long."

"I can last a while longer," Zollers said. "But I wouldn't wish to give the president too large an opening to escape."

"Where are you heading?" Jamie asked nervously. She still felt like she'd gotten involved in something she shouldn't have stuck her nose into.

"Northeast, I think," Sienna said, glancing at Zollers, who shrugged. "Away from people."

"Um, okay," Jamie said, certain she didn't want to know any more than that. There was one nagging question in her mind, though, and she found the courage to ask it. "Any chance you can drop me back in New York?" She felt the ragged edge of exhaustion starting to work on her. "Because I had to take the train on the way up, and after sitting here waiting for you ..." She let out a little sigh. "Yeah, I'm kinda tired."

98.

Sienna

We dropped Jamie back in Staten Island as we flew over and were out of sight before she had even ridden her gravity channel to the ground. I was keeping it just over the speed of sound, Zollers clutching tightly to my back, and my hands grasping President Harmon firmly underneath his armpits.

"This could have been paradise," Harmon said somewhere over Massachusetts.

"I doubt it," I said, quippy once more. "Boston is only paradise for the truly deranged."

After a few minutes, a very important thought occurred to me: "Hey, since I'm carrying the president, does this mean *I'm* Air Force One?"

Harmon twisted his head to look back at me, face written over with disgust. "You're certainly thick enough to be."

"You're awfully saucy for someone who could be dropped unceremoniously at any time."

He reached up and patted me on the shoulder, then dropped his hand down to the side of my neck, where it rested for a few seconds, as though he were trying to reassure me or something. "I'm sorry. What I meant to say was that you're not nearly as fat as the last Air Force One."

"You really, truly are a dick," I said, reaffirming my initial assessment of him.

He patted me on the neck again, probably because it was the only part of me he could easily reach. I dropped him a little lower, and he broke contact, grabbing my arm just below the sleeve until he realized I wasn't going to let him go. "I regret sending you that fruit basket now."

"Ariadne ate it anyway," I said, glaring at him. "Did you really erase her mind of—"

"Anything related to you?" he asked. "At the risk of finding myself in sudden freefall, I cannot tell a lie—yes, I did."

"You lie all the time," I said, seething. "She'd better be all right."

"She's no worse off than your ex-boyfriend, whose memories *you* stole," Harmon sniped back at me.

Zollers patted me on the shoulder, but it was more comforting and less condescending than Harmon's attempt. "Don't let him get to you." I could hear the strain in his voice.

"Yes, don't let me get to you," Harmon agreed, the wind whipping past us. "I'm about to be dead anyway, aren't I?"

"That's to be determined," I said. I really didn't know quite what to do with him yet. I had a vague idea of where I was carrying him, though, as we passed over the Atlantic and went "feet wet," as they call it in the military.

"Oh, goody," Harmon said as we flew toward the darkness of the coming night, and on into the growing uncertainty.

99.

Scott

He woke up in sight of a small town, no sign of the battlefield where he'd faced off with Sienna against his will. The late afternoon sun and chill wind that swept across the plains suggested that it was about to get a lot colder. Plains dust had settled over his ripped and shredded suit and it hurt to open his eyes, but that burning headache had mercifully vanished.

"Where am I?" Reed asked, sitting up next to him.

"Ohhh, man," Augustus moaned, not bothering to get up. He was clutching his head like it had been squeezed in a vice. "Anyone else had a train squeezed through their ear?"

"I'm looking for the tracks right now," Reed said, eyes shut tight against the pain that seemed to be a commonality between the three of them. "I think someone shoved one up my nose, hard."

"She must have ... beat him," Scott said, causing Reed and Augustus to look at him cock-eyed.

"Who?" Reed asked, still squinting hard. He coughed, spitting dust off his tongue.

"Sienna," Scott said, closing his eyes. "She must have taken out Harmon, or stopped him, or something."

"Wait, whut?" Augustus muscled himself up to sitting. "Man, what are you talking about?"

"Harmon," Scott said, clutching his head as though it were still in danger of exploding. "He's been controlling our minds these last few months." They both looked at him blankly. "We've been hunting Sienna all this time ... you remember that, right?"

"I remember ..." Augustus said, slowly, as though thinking it through. "I mean, we were after ... but ..." He stared into space. "She was a dangerous fugitive, though, right?"

Scott shook his head and immediately regretted it because it hurt. He stared at the town in the distance. "She's always dangerous. And she was a fugitive, yeah, but ... I don't think she had anything to do with what they accused her of."

"That can't be right," Reed said quietly. "We ..." He blinked. "I mean ... the things we did ..."

"Oh, shit," Augustus said. "How long has it been since I've called Taneshia?" He fumbled for his phone, rummaging through his rumpled suit's pockets before coming out with it. He let out a gasp of relief. "It still works." He dialed frantically, pushing the phone to his ear. "Taneshia! Yeah, it's me!" He frowned. "Where are you?"

Reed just stared blankly. "I haven't ... called Isabella in weeks." He blinked a few times. "Why ... wouldn't I call her? Why wouldn't I see her?" He shuddered. "What ... did I ... do?" His hand came slowly up to his mouth, covering it as though to suppress something terrible coming out.

"It wasn't you," Scott said hastily, remembering the nightmare of Harmon's mind, forcing him along whatever line he pushed. He could feel something faintly, in the distance, at the reach of his powers ...

The last remnants of the plug in that baby's leg where he'd kept the child from bleeding to death. It wasn't terribly far away, Scott could feel, still and unmoving, blood still racing around that final remnant. It was even clearer to him now that there was more power at his disposal. He remembered the serum that had caused so much pain, and it thundered through his own blood even now, its work already done.

"Reed," Scott said, pushing to his feet. "You should go home."

"I need to find Isabella," Reed said, staring straight ahead across the infinite horizon.

"What are you doing in DC?" Augustus asked, pacing back and forth behind them. "Never mind. I'll come to you. I'm—yeah, I don't know, but it's—I'm sorry I didn't call, baby. I don't know what's wrong with me. I'll be there real soon, though. I love you, too." Augustus hung up and stepped in front of them, his face set and determined. "Man, I gotta go home. I don't even know what's wrong with me. I haven't been going to class, I haven't—" He held up a hand in front of his own mouth. "What the hell happened to us?"

"Something pretty fucking awful," Reed said, still staring straight ahead.

"That's truth," Augustus said, and he caught sight of the town at last. "What do you think? Can we get an Uber from there to the nearest airport? I'll go in with y'all on it." He fished out his phone again, staring at the screen. "Oh, hell yes. We are on. Fifteen minutes and they'll pick us up right over there." He pointed to a dirt road in the distance, only a few hundred yards away.

"I'm in for that," Scott said, and he stooped to grab Reed under the arm, helping him to his feet. Reed accepted the weight slowly, as though unsure he wanted to be standing. "You need to go home, Reed. You need to find Isabella and go home."

"Do I even have a home anymore?" Reed whispered, still staring straight ahead. "Do I have … Isabella anymore?" He shoved off Scott's help and staggered a step before pitching over, landing on one knee, planting both hands palm-first in the dirt. He breathed heavily, so heavily his shoulders shook with the effort. "What … did … we … DO?" He turned his head around and his cheeks were coursing with tears, washing away the thick layer of dirt that covered them.

"I don't know, dude," Augustus said.

"It wasn't us," Scott said, keeping his distance. He felt like stepping closer would just enflame Reed, make him likely to run or freak out again. There was good cause for freaking out; Reed had done terrible things while under Harmon's grip. Scott felt a shiver crawl up his spine. Things Scott even felt guilty about, even though he hadn't done them himself.

"I pulled the trigger on …" Reed whispered, and he turned

his head to the ground and threw up, emptying the contents of his stomach, the smell of bile mixed with coffee hitting Scott's meta-enhanced sense of smell and nearly causing him to gag. "What did I do?" he whispered.

"Reed, you couldn't have—" Scott started, but he didn't finish.

Reed planted both hands in the earth and with a blast of wind that swept the dust into the air around him, he launched off. A tornado reached down out of the sky and swept him up, lifting him into the air and carrying him off. He disappeared into the clouds as they rolled away, off toward the horizon, heading east.

"Yo," Augustus said, pulling his hands back from his face as the dust storm caused by Reed's exodus started to recede, "you're still in on splitting this Uber, though, right?"

100.

Harmon

I felt like I was suspended from a hawk's talons, being taken back to the nest to be stripped to pieces and eaten. It probably wasn't far from the truth, that metaphor. The cold had long since chilled my cheeks to numb, and we were now passing over snowy ground, leaving the endless ocean behind. I was hard-pressed to determine where I was being flown, other than northeast, but I was seriously regretting giving Sienna my jacket, for more than one reason.

I reached a hand up again and caught her wrist, rubbing my fingers and palm along hers. "Just making sure you're still there," I said, lying through my teeth and suspecting that Dr. Zollers couldn't tell. He was doing a magnificent job of fending off any attempts I made on her mind, but fortunately my defenses were not so weak that he was able to access my thoughts.

Very fortunate, actually, because I had a plan, and it would have been terrible if he could have seen it coming.

"If I were to let you go, I think you would notice," Sienna said, brushing my hand off again with a shake. "This is far enough," she announced after another few minutes, and we started to descend as the darkness fell around us. I looked around; there wasn't a light anywhere on the horizon.

She brought us down on a floe of ice a little off the coast. My shoes landed in a patch of snow several inches deep, crunching as she dropped me. Snow came easily over the sides of the loafers and soaked my socks, and I squirmed against the chill.

I folded my arms over my chest and looked around. Little particles of snow were flurrying around me, very occasionally. "What is this? Is this your hometown?"

"It's a giant, floating piece of ice in the ocean," she shot back, the doctor still hanging on her shoulders. He was avoiding her touch, carefully clinging to the coat, though it looked like his teeth were chattering. She dropped him off carefully and came down herself, her bare feet hovering about three inches off the snowy floe and her husky thighs trailing up to hide beneath the tail of my jacket. It covered her fairly well, except at the neck.

"And is this to be my grave?" I looked around, still no sign of civilization or humanity anywhere nearby.

"Hard to say." She just hung there in space as Zollers came around to stand next to her, still shivering against the chill.

My eyes narrowed as I stared at her. "You're here to judge me, then?"

"We are a jury of your peers," Zollers said, doing a little stomping himself as he started walking a path around the floe to try and keep warm. I watched him out of the corner of my eye, trying to time my move for maximum impact.

"I don't think so," I said.

"Oh, right," Sienna said, hovering closer to me, playing into my plan. "I forgot. You're peerless. You're so smart. So much smarter than me ..." She grinned wickedly. "Say, if you're so smart ... why do I keep beating you?"

I started to open my mouth to defend against her allegation. "I don't believe you have."

"You're stuck on a block of ice in the middle of the ocean," she said, extending a hand to indicate the horizon. "I haven't frozen you into the ice like Captain America yet, but it's not out of the question—"

"And here I preferred the elegance of you killing me," I said.

"At what point do you acknowledge," she said, rolling her eyes at me and irritating me further, "that if you keep getting beaten by lowbrow little me ... then maybe you aren't as smart as you think you are?"

"If you're trying to wound my vanity ..." I kept as straight a face as I could, "... you're doing a bad job. Obviously you had assets I didn't count on. People you could rely on that I didn't anticipate. Naturally, I didn't come after you as early or as strong as I should have because ... well ..." I shrugged. "If my plan had worked, you would have been on my side in any case. Besides," I said, figuring I'd throw a little cloud of dust in her direction, "I never wanted you dead nearly as badly as ... others did."

That provoked a frown. "Others? Like ... Cavanagh and ...?"

"Others you haven't had the pleasure of meeting yet." I smiled, and checked Dr. Zollers's position. He was well behind me, and out of easy reach.

"What the hell do you m—" Sienna started to say, drawing closer to me.

I sprung on her and blasted Dr. Zollers with everything I had simultaneously. He staggered from my mental assault, putting him off guard for just a second, which I used to leap and grab Sienna by the wrist with one hand and lodge the other firmly on her neck. I took her in hand and squeezed, holding tight as the wind picked up and snow blew all around us.

101.

Sienna

When Harmon jumped me, I was so surprised that it actually took me a few seconds to respond. It was pretty out of character for him by this point, leaping at me and putting his hands on me. Don't get me wrong, he struck me as the sort of impotent weasel who would respond to a woman with violence whenever all his other grandiose plans and powers had failed; I just wasn't ready for him to leap at me in the snow and grab me around the throat and the wrist.

I staggered back a step from the force of his aggressive maneuver; he stared at me furiously, and I could feel him lashing at my mind, at the barriers that Dr. Zollers had erected between us. The clash was bleeding through, but only a hair, and I squeezed my eyes shut as I took stock of the situation.

And then I started laughing.

I laughed for a good few seconds, then lifted my hand, dragging his along with it. He'd clamped on my wrist pretty good, but it wasn't exactly painful, especially compared to the things that others had done to me in my life. His chokehold was similarly pathetic, too, too high on the neck and grabbing my chin as though he were about to pose me like a model.

"Well," I said, looking him right in the eye, "this is embarrassing."

He was breathless, red in the face, and staring straight at

351

me. "Oh?" He didn't seem to get the clue.

"You called me the master of the physical domain," I said, looking at him evenly, not even bothering to throw off his hands, "but your last ditch plan is to assault me physically?"

"As you said, it's last ditch." He smiled thinly. I had a feeling he'd be moving those hands in a moment.

"You got that right," I said. "You really are bad at this. Your grip is several inches away from doing real harm to me in either direction." I stared at him, waiting for him to get it and try to adjust. His hand was clamped pretty good, and while I could have just ripped it off or burned it off, I figured taking the patient tack was smarter. Controlling my annoyance was good character building.

"You've got it all wrong," Harmon said, his hand holding even tighter to my wrist. He paused, probably for dramatic effect, and then broke into a wide smile. "I'm not trying to hurt you."

"Well, you're succeeding at that," I said as the chill started to burn at my skin, "now let go of me before you—"

I blinked.

He stared at me, still smiling.

And suddenly it was very clear what he was doing.

"Sienna!" Zollers yelled, hurrying through the snow toward us, "He's going to—"

Harmon yanked himself closer to me, pushing his cheek against mine and anchoring an arm around my neck. He kept that grip on my hand and wrapped his other arm around my head, pushing his palm against my face. Our skin was flush, and mine was flushed, the chill I'd mistaken for the frost actually a burning sensation across every point of skin-to-skin contact between us.

I couldn't see his eyes from where I was, my head practically on his shoulder, but I could see his face in my mind's eye. "Shhhhhh ..." he whispered, and I could hear him in my mind as well as in my ear, and not because he had broken through Dr. Zoller's telepathy barrier.

All those little touches on the flight here ... all the times he'd grabbed at my hand ... a few seconds here, a few seconds there ...

He'd been burning through the small window of time before my succubus powers activated.

And now, with his hands on my skin, his face pressed against mine ...

He'd run down the clock.

I could hear him in my head because he was almost there, his soul draining from his body and into mine. The rush of heat was unbearable, unbelievable. I hadn't fully absorbed anyone in years, and I'd forgotten how intense it was, how much of a thrill it was ...

How much I craved to devour souls.

I breathed hard, wanting to rip his hands from me but simultaneously not. I wanted to tear his soul out of his body but I didn't want him in my head. My skin burned with both hatred for him and desire for his soul, and it caused me to hesitate a vital moment.

There was a howling as my powers worked, the screaming of Harmon's body dying as his soul left it. I could have vaporized him with the power of fire, could have thrown him from me, severed his limbs with all my strength turned loose, or simply ripped away and headbutted him into oblivion.

But I did none of those things, because somehow I waited a second too long to do any of them.

His soul tore free from him with one last, rattling scream, and President Gerard Harmon's body went limp against me, his grip failing and his corpse toppling to the snowy ground with a crunch.

"Sienna," Zollers said, grabbing at my arms, touching the sleeves of my purloined jacket. "Are you all right?"

Uh oh, Zack muttered in my head.

Oh, wonderful, Eve said. *More sausage for this party. As though we didn't have enough already.*

New playmate, said Wolfe.

Hmph, Bjorn snorted.

Uh, Commander-in-Chief, Bastian said awkwardly.

Bozshe moi, Gavrikov muttered.

Roommates, Gerry Harmon distastefully, voice echoing in my head. *It's been quite a while since I've cohabitated with anyone.*

This should be ... well, unpleasant, honestly. It felt like he was speaking directly to me. *But not as unpleasant as dying, so at least there's that.*

"Son of a bitch," I muttered as the snows blew around me. I looked Dr. Zollers right in the eye and answered his question. "Hell no, I'm not all right. Now I've get this bastard in my head." I sighed. Where the hell was the justice in this?

Well, you are a criminal, Harmon said, and I sensed he was enjoying my torment. *So this is a little bit of justice in itself, isn't it?*

"Bastard," I muttered, and meant it. I looked down at his lifeless body, shaking my head. This was not how I had planned this going. At all.

The best laid plans of mice and men ... Harmon said.

"He's being sanctimonious in your head right now, isn't he?" Zollers's expression was a perfect cringe of sympathy. Unfortunately, his sympathy didn't do me any good.

"Worst. Day. Ever." I said, torching Harmon's body into oblivion. It didn't make me feel any better. "Let's get the hell out of here before we freeze to death. We need to make another stop anyway." Although, honestly, I wasn't sure freezing to death was a worse fate than the one I was looking at now—eternal imprisonment for the sarcastic, dickish, now-ex president of the United States ...

In my head.

102.

Cassidy Ellis opened the door and closed it in the space of seconds, breathing heavily the whole time. The small DC hotel room smelled of fear, which was something Cassidy reeked of in abundance. I'd had Zollers's help in tracking her to here, and I stayed perfectly still at my place in the corner chair until she flipped the light switch, fiddling with the purse in her hands.

When she saw me, her eyes widened and she dropped her purse with a thump.

"Hi," I said, not bothering with any overtly threatening motions.

"I didn't want to help him," she said before I could even get a running start on any of the things I might have said to her. "He *made* me help him, threatened me—well, threatened Eric—" Anxiety was causing a severe case of verbal diarrhea. "But I didn't want any part of it, and that's why I tried to help you—well, you and Scott—"

"Rein it in there, cowgirl," I said, waving a hand in hopes it might silence her bout of expulsive explaining. "I'm not here to hurt you."

You go everywhere expecting to hurt people, Harmon said in my head, causing me to grind my teeth. *It's your raison d'être.*

"Did you kill him?" Cassidy asked, and because she was so damned breathless, I couldn't tell if she was frightened or thrilled by the idea.

Suicide by succubus is an interesting cause of death, wouldn't you say? Harmon asked.

I rolled my eyes again. "Strictly speaking ... yes and no."

"But ... he's dead, right?" Cassidy seemed very focused on this, and I couldn't decide whether it was because she wanted to be sure he was gone or she wanted leverage on me. It could have been both, for all I knew.

"Well, he's not going to be a problem for you anymore, that's for sure," I said, trying to restrain my annoyance as Harmon hummed a few bars of *For He's a Jolly Good Fellow* in my head.

She stared at me, eyes almost piercing me, then she seemed to relax. "You absorbed him? No ... he tricked you into absorbing him."

"Sadly," I said, wishing I could roll back time an hour or two and vaporize Gerry Harmon or drop his body into the Atlantic Ocean for porpoises to feed on before he'd had a chance to use my brain as an escape pod. Did porpoises feed on dead bodies? I lived in hope, in my dreams. "Listen, about this serum—"

"Yeah ..." Cassidy said, making it a definitive enough statement that I didn't bother to go on. "I don't know where I hid it in the White House—"

"Because you fried your own brain?"

"Yes." She held up burnt palms. "I couldn't take a chance on him reading the location, so ..."

"What are the odds someone finds it?" I asked, thinking specifically of the Secret Service, who would probably be turning the entire White House upside down looking for clues to Harmon's sudden disappearance. I had a feeling I knew who they'd blame, too.

"Hopefully low," Cassidy said. "I'm not stupid, and I was trying to hide them from a pretty smart guy, so ..." She shrugged. "It's not like we can go looking for them, and ... that's not the only place where the formula exists."

"Is it in your head?" I asked, frowning at her.

"Are you going to blow my brains out if I say yes?" she asked in a whisper, almost ghostlike, specter of fear casting a long shadow over her.

"No! Everybody always assumes I'm going to kill them." I blew out a harsh breath. "I'm not planning to kill you,

Cassidy." I clenched my jaw. "Though I will come after you again if your dumb ass starts getting into trouble. How can a girl as smart as you keep getting into stupid trouble? I mean, really, robbing the Federal Reserve? Could you have picked a higher-visibility crime?"

"That was something Eric wanted to do," Cassidy said quietly, lapsing into silent contemplation for a moment before going on. "So … you're not mad about all the things I—"

"I don't think we're going to be friends anytime soon," I said, causing Cassidy to seem to retreat within herself, "but … look at me." I laughed. "I'm a criminal and you're not, now. Keep it that way, don't cross me, and … you'll be fine."

"I … hope I don't ever see you again," Cassidy said. I could tell she meant it.

"That makes two of us," I said, slipping out the window. "The serum, though …"

"I had to give him the formula," she said, following me to the window. "I had to make it for him. But … I don't think he was the only one after it."

I felt a little chill, remembering Harmon's crack about other people trying to kill me. Ones I hadn't met yet. "You think he had a backer?"

"Maybe." Cassidy's face got a little pinched. "But it doesn't make much sense, does it? Anyone who was backing him … they'd get their brain taken over by him the moment he got that boost, wouldn't they?"

"Unless they were an empath, I guess," I said, floating just out the window. "Or a boosted telepath themselves?"

"Who'd want to subject themselves to that?" Cassidy asked, peering out at me. "I mean … that's as close to hell as I can imagine, personally."

"You're not the only one," I grunted. "But Harmon did seem to suggest … there was somebody else who had his back. Somebody else helping him."

"He did manage to call in a hit squad from Revelen," Cassidy said. "They're a country in Eastern Europe—" she started to say, as though I were a moron.

"I know where Revelen is," I snapped. "And it's not the

first time I've had trouble come from that direction lately."
Not even close. "Unfortunately, I'm not welcome in Europe
right now, and I'm not welcome here in the US—"

"It's a cold and lonely world," Cassidy said, with a strange
amount of sincerity.

"So long, Cassidy. Remember—"

"I'll stay out of trouble," she promised, never taking her
eyes off me as she shut the window. For some reason ... I
believed her.

103.

Scott

He barely realized his phone was ringing until he picked it up. He was staring through the window at a baby in the ICU, still healing from the gunshot wound the child had suffered. Scott blinked, the sounds of beeping around him like a dull lullaby, nurses moving to and fro speaking in hushed whispers.

"Hello?" he answered the phone.

"Dude," J.J. said, sounding a little rough on the other end, "where are you?"

"Cheyenne, Wyoming," Scott answered without conscious thought. He felt … exhausted. Not just from the fight and Harmon using him like a sock puppet, but from … whatever that serum had unleashed in him. He could feel the power throbbing through him, straining to be used. Every single fixture in the hospital that thrummed with water, every sink, every water fountain … Scott could feel it. The pipes were like veins in the walls that he could almost see, and that was something he'd never experienced before. "I'm at the hospital."

"You okay?" J.J. asked.

"I'm …" Scott's voice trailed off. "I don't know."

"Are you wounded?"

"Not as such, no," Scott said, staring at the baby beneath the thick screen of plastic. He reached out and touched the window between them.

"Good, cuz … shit is hitting the fan here, man," J.J. said. "What happened with Sienna?"

"We fought," Scott said. "She won. Harmon lost."

"Whaaaaat? What the hell did the president have to do with it?"

"He was … never mind," Scott said. "What do you want?"

"Director Phillips asked me to call you," J.J. said. "Which … can anyone explain why I'm working for this douche again?"

"Mind control," Scott said.

"That … would explain it, if true," J.J. said, somewhere between skepticism and amusement. "Anyway, the president is missing, dude. Gone. Huge hole in the wall of the Oval Office, and he's just—kaput. I mean, we suspect Sienna, but … there's not anything tying her to the scene. Friday's missing, too, and we've got video footage of him fleeing the scene sometime—probably—before Harmon disappeared."

"Yes," Scott said quietly, "well … good riddance."

"Ummm, that's our boss."

"Your boss," Scott said. "I'm done."

"I don't think Director Phillips is going to want to hear that …"

"I don't care what he wants to hear," Scott said, a bracing amount of give-a-shit flying loose of him.

"I won't be passing that along to him," J.J. said. "So … any idea where Sienna is?"

"No clue."

"Hmm," J.J. said. "Maybe she's in Wakanda."

"Where?"

"Never mind," J.J. said. "Reed would have gotten it. Speaking of … I can't seem to reach him. Or Augustus. Are they …?"

"They're fine … ish," Scott corrected. "I suspect you're going to get their resignations, though."

"I don't blame them," J.J. said. "I'm thinking about quitting again myself."

"You should."

"Maybe I will."

"Maybe you will—what?" The voice of Andrew Phillips

broke in on the other side of the line, blaring in Scott's ear.

"I quit," J.J. said. "Peace, Scotty." And then there was the sound of a phone being fumbled.

"Byerly?" Phillips asked. The sound of J.J. shouting something profane in the background almost overpowered the sound of his voice.

"I'm here."

"You need to get back to Washington now," Phillips said. "This place is coming apart."

"Well, I'll cry some salty tears over that," Scott said reflexively.

"What?"

"Nothing," Scott said.

"Get back to headquarters," Phillips said. "We have an investigation to mount, and none of your team is responding."

Scott almost told him where to stick his investigation, and the team. They were all gone, and all the better for it, really. He imagined it'd be a while before anyone saw Reed again, anyway. He was going to be spending some time climbing out of the hole he was in. Scott felt more than a little bad about it, but … He stared through the window. *I have guilt of my own to work through.*

"Byerly," Phillips said with more urgency. "Did you hear me? We have work to do. Nealon's off the radar again, and the president's missing. These events are probably connected. We need to get to work on this."

He almost said it—what he was thinking. Something stopped him, though.

She stole my memories.

"Are you there?"

But they're hunting her because of a bullshit investigation the president put in place. They think she's a villain …

I thought she was a villain.

"Byerly?"

But she's not.

"I'm here," Scott said, and somehow … the decision was made. He stared through the glass. *I've got guilt to work through. And it's not going to get excised by just standing here …* "I'll catch the next flight," he said, and hung up.

I didn't ask for this job …

The baby stirred, making a whining noise, and Scott had to turn away quickly lest he be tempted to shatter the glass, reach in, try and give the child some comfort. A nurse was making her way over anyway. *That's not my job, either …*

My job is to catch Sienna Nealon.

He smiled thinly, the only one in on a private joke.

I'm going to be the absolute worst at this job … and just maybe … somewhere, somehow …

… I'll find a way to clear her name.

Taking a deep breath, Scott turned from the ICU window and headed for the elevator. He had a lot of work to do. Badly, but work, nonetheless.

104.

Sienna

I picked up Zollers from the roof of the hotel and carried him off down the street, grounding us both in Fairfax, Virginia, out of sight in a park. "You hear all that?" I asked, once we were safely down and nestled in a copse of trees where no prying eyes or ears could hear or see us.

"Through you, yes," he said, looking as serious as he ever did. "Sounds like you've got more enemies out there."

"What else is new?" A beat. "My team is out there, somewhere ..." I waved my hand. "Harry, Veronika, Colin, Kat ... Taneshia, Jamal ..."

"Augustus is coming, too," Zollers said. "He's snapped out of Harmon's spell."

I made a sound of disgust deep in my throat at the thought of Harmon's effects on my friends. "Where's Reed?"

Zollers frowned. "I ... don't know. Out there somewhere. He's ..." His expression shifted to concern. "He's in distress. In pain."

"Dammit." I cursed the new presence in my head. Somehow, I'd gotten the less raw end of this deal than Reed had. "What about Scott?"

"He's a little more ... settled," Zollers said. "Augustus is racing to meet up with your group." He didn't suggest the obvious, which meant he already knew what I was thinking. Instead he took the long way around. "They're just across the Potomac, you know. Waiting for you. Wondering what to do."

"You should go tell them what to do," I said. "Go home."

"Sienna—"

"This fight is over," I said, keeping up my stern facade, even though he knew—he knew—I was dying inside. "Even if they manage to overlook Harmon's death, I'm still wanted for that incident in Eden Prairie. The public is still against me because of my past getting revealed by the president ..." I shrugged. "However I might have hoped this fight went, I basically got out of it with the least good solution—which is to say I didn't lose, because I saved the day, but I'm still kinda screwed."

Zollers took a moment to compose a reply. "You saved the world."

"Again," I said, singsongy once more. It kept me from crying. "But no one will know, and no one cares. I'm a criminal, Doc."

"You have friends. Friends who would help you—"

"Aiding and abetting a known fugitive is a felony," I said, smiling faintly. "Trust me. It's a thing. I should know, I used to enforce it. Speaking of which ... you should probably go."

"Any one of them would help you," Zollers said, "and so would I. All you need do is ask."

"I can't think of anything I need help with right now," I said, smiling sadly. "And they've done enough already. So have you."

I could see the resignation sprout up as he looked at me. "Be careful, Sienna. Being alone ... it's not good for you. It's not good for anyone," he amended, "but especially not for you."

"It's how it has to be," I said, lifting off into the air. I'd need to go high, high up, maybe head south ...

And also? Find some clothes, I realized as Zollers politely averted his eyes to avoid staring straight into my bare crotch, which Harmon's jacket did not quite cover at this angle.

It's not how it has to be, Zollers sent me, *it's how you're choosing to play it.*

"It's better this way," I said, hoping he could hear me. And really … it was better. Easier.

For everyone but me.

Epilogue

President Gerry Harmon appeared to be dead. That was not an immense surprise to the Watcher. He'd been an arrogant man, thinking he ruled the whole world. He did not, though, and his death at the hands of such an enemy—her, of course—was to be expected. Harmon had been getting out of hand in any case, his plans bleeding out and threatening other endeavors.

That was the problem with creating a coalition of powerful people the world over. Ambitions clashed. The Watcher kept an eye on these things from a distance, perhaps not as closely as he might have liked, but that was just as well. Wherever the Watcher went, good tidings did not follow.

The Watcher sat in the darkness, contemplating the United States. Losing the head of the country was a minor setback, at worst. There were other avenues they could take if, for some reason, something was required from that nation. Other events were more pressing, in any case. The situation in Scotland, for instance, was beginning to reach a boil ...

But it was still comfortably within expectations. Sienna Nealon, though ... she was a pestilence, the Watcher thought. Even more dangerous now that she was on the run. She had little to lose, and that meant when cornered she might be capable of increasingly desperate maneuvers.

No, that wouldn't do. Someone would have to deal with her. Someone would deal with her, he was sure. And if not ...

Well, it would come to the Watcher killing her, sooner or later. The thought did not bother him. He had killed worse, after all.

He took a breath of the stale air, taking in the silence around him, and turned his eyes to the place where the Sleeper waited. "Rest easy," he said, though he knew the Sleeper could not hear him. "All is ... as it should be."

This was true. The world was in its proper shape. Soon enough, the interval would pass, and the Sleeper would waken.

And if she were not already dead by then ... Sienna Nealon would surely die after the awakening.

Sienna Nealon Will Return in

HOLLOW

Out of the Box
Book 12

Coming January 17, 2017!

Author's Note

For the last couple years, the two biggest requests I've gotten as relates to Sienna were, 1) Give her a boyfriend, and 2) Put more souls in her head. This year, I answered both requests! BWAHAHAHAHA! (That's my maniacal laugh. I'm still working on it.) The moral of the story is that you want to be very careful what you ask me for, because I'm never going to give it to you in the way you expect, for that would be boring.

A few pages after this modest note you'll find an updated list of upcoming Out of the Box books coming out in 2017. Just titles and approximate release months, if you're into that sort of thing. If you want to know immediately when future books become available, take sixty seconds and sign up for my NEW RELEASE EMAIL ALERTS by CLICKING HERE. I don't sell your information and I only send out emails when I have a new book out. The reason you should sign up for this is because I don't always set release dates, and even if you're following me on Facebook (robertJcrane (Author)) or Twitter (@robertJcrane), it's easy to miss my book announcements because...well, because social media is an imprecise thing.

Come join the discussion on my website:
http://www.robertjcrane.com!

Cheers,
Robert J. Crane

ACKNOWLEDGMENTS

Editorial/Literary Janitorial duties performed by Sarah Barbour and Jeffrey Bryan. Final proofing was handled by Jo Evans. Any errors you see in the text, however, are the result of me rejecting changes. I owe a special apology to Jo for boobtacularly forgetting her incredible acknowledgments to the Sanctuary Series as I was thanking everybody in volume eight. Mea culpa, mea maxima culpa on that one, Jo.

The cover was once more designed masterfully by Karri Klawiter of Artbykarri.com.

The formatting was provided by nickbowmanediting.com. Well, by Nick, anyway.

Once more, thanks to my parents, my in-laws, my kids and my wife, for helping me keep things together.

Other Works by Robert J. Crane

World of Sanctuary
Epic Fantasy

Defender: The Sanctuary Series, Volume One
Avenger: The Sanctuary Series, Volume Two
Champion: The Sanctuary Series, Volume Three
Crusader: The Sanctuary Series, Volume Four
Sanctuary Tales, Volume One - A Short Story Collection
Thy Father's Shadow: The Sanctuary Series, Volume 4.5
Master: The Sanctuary Series, Volume Five
Fated in Darkness: The Sanctuary Series, Volume 5.5
Warlord: The Sanctuary Series, Volume Six
Heretic: The Sanctuary Series, Volume Seven
Legend: The Sanctuary Series, Volume Eight

A Haven in Ash: Ashes of Luukessia Trilogy, Volume One*
(Coming Late 2016/Early 2017!)

Ghosts of Sanctuary: The Revenants Series, Volume One*
(Coming 2018, at earliest.)

The Girl in the Box
and
Out of the Box
Contemporary Urban Fantasy

Alone: The Girl in the Box, Book 1
Untouched: The Girl in the Box, Book 2
Soulless: The Girl in the Box, Book 3
Family: The Girl in the Box, Book 4
Omega: The Girl in the Box, Book 5

Southern Watch

Contemporary Urban Fantasy

*Forthcoming

Made in the USA
Columbia, SC
06 September 2020

19720671R00207